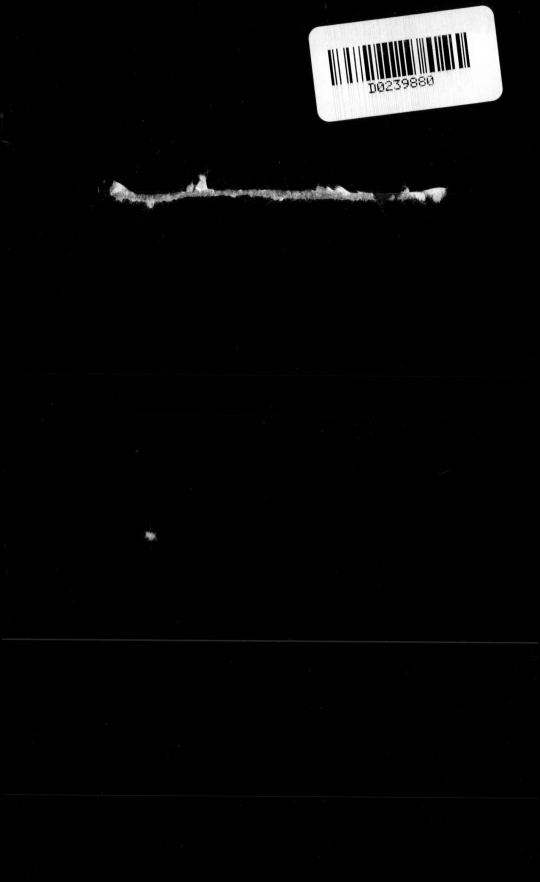

CRIMINAL

KARIN SLAUGHTER

CRIMINAL

Century · London

Published by Century 2012

2 4 6 8 10 9 7 5 3 1

First published in Great Britain in 2012 by
Century
Random House, 20 Vauxhall Bridge Road,
London SW1V 2SA

www.randomhouse.co.uk

Addresses for companies within The Random House Group Limited can be found at:
www.randomhouse.co.uk/offices.htm

The Random House Group Limited Reg. No. 954009

A CIP catalogue record for this book
is available from the British Library

ISBN 9781846057960 (HB)
ISBN 9781846057977 (TPB)

The Random House Group Limited supports The Forest Stewardship Council
(FSC®), the leading international forest certification organisation. Our books
carrying the FSC label are printed on FSC® certified paper. FSC is the only forest
certification scheme endorsed by the leading environmental organisations,
including Greenpeace. Our paper procurement policy can be found at:
www.randomhouse.co.uk/environment

MIX
Paper from
responsible sources
FSC® C016897

ound by Clays Ltd, St Ives Plc

to Kate—
editor, friend.

CRIMINAL

one

August 15, 1974

LUCY BENNETT

A cinnamon brown Oldsmobile Cutlass crawled up Edgewood Avenue, the windows lowered, the driver hunched down in his seat. The lights from the console showed narrow, beady eyes tracing along the line of girls standing under the street sign. Jane. Mary. Lydia. The car stopped. Predictably, the man tilted up his chin toward Kitty. She trotted over, adjusting her miniskirt as she navigated her spiked heels across the uneven asphalt. Two weeks ago, when Juice had first brought Kitty onto the corner, she'd told the other girls she was sixteen, which probably meant fifteen, though she looked no older than twelve.

They had all hated her on sight.

Kitty leaned down into the open window of the car. Her stiff vinyl skirt tipped up like the bottom of a bell. She always got picked first, which was becoming a problem that everyone but Juice could see. Kitty got special favors. She could talk men into doing anything. The girl was fresh, childlike, though like all of them, she carried a kitchen knife in her purse and knew how to use it. Nobody wanted to do what they were doing, but to have another girl—a newer girl— picked over them hurt just as much as if they were all standing on the sidelines at the debutante ball.

Inside the Oldsmobile, the transaction was quickly negotiated, no haggling because what was on offer was still worth the price. Kitty made the signal to Juice, waited for his nod, then got into the car. The muffler chugged exhaust as the Olds made a wide turn onto a narrow side street. The car shook once as the gear was shoved into park. The driver's hand flew up, clamped around the back of Kitty's head, and she disappeared.

Lucy Bennett turned away, looking up the dark, soulless avenue. No headlights coming. No traffic. No business. Atlanta wasn't a nighttime town. The last person to leave the Equitable building usually turned off the lights, but Lucy could see the bulbs from the Flatiron glowing clear across Central City Park. If she squinted hard enough, she could find the familiar green of the C&S sign that anchored the business district. The New South. Progress through commerce. The City Too Busy to Hate.

If there were men out walking these streets tonight, it was with no amount of good on their minds.

Jane lit a smoke, then tucked the pack back into her purse. She wasn't the kind to share, but she was certainly the kind to take. Her eyes met Lucy's. The dead in them was hard to look at. Jane must've felt the same. She quickly glanced away.

Lucy shivered, even though it was the middle of August, heat wafting off the pavement like smoke from a fire. Her feet were sore. Her back ached. Her head was pounding like a metronome. Her gut felt like she'd swallowed a truckload of concrete. Cotton filled her mouth. Her hands felt the constant prick of pins and needles. A clump of her blonde hair had come out in the sink this morning. She had turned nineteen two days ago and already she was an old woman.

In the side street, the brown Olds shook again. Kitty's head came up. She wiped her mouth as she got out of the car. No dawdling. No giving the john time to reconsider his purchase. The car drove away before she could shut the door, and Kitty teetered for a moment on the high heels, looking lost, afraid, and then angry. They were all angry. Fury was their refuge, their comfort, the only thing that they could truly call their own.

Lucy watched Kitty pick her way back toward the corner. She gave Juice the cash, trying to keep her forward momentum, but he caught her arm to make her stop. Kitty spat on the sidewalk, trying to look like she wasn't terrified as Juice unfolded the wad of cash, counted off each bill. Kitty stood there, waiting. They all waited.

Finally, Juice lifted his chin. The money was good. Kitty took her place back in the line. She didn't look at any of the other girls. She just stared blankly into the street, waiting for the next car to roll up, waiting for the next man who would either give her a nod or pass her by. It'd taken two days, tops, for her eyes to develop the same dead look as the rest of the girls. What was going through her mind? Probably the same as Lucy, that familiar chant that rocked her to sleep every night: *When-will-this-be-over? When-will-this-be-over? When-will-this-be-over?*

Lucy had been fifteen once. From this distance, she could barely remember that girl. Passing notes in class. Giggling about boys. Rushing home from school every day to watch her soap. Dancing in her room to the Jackson Five with her best friend, Jill Henderson. Lucy was fifteen years old, and then life had opened up like a chasm, and little Lucy had plummeted down, down into the unrelenting darkness.

She had started taking speed to lose weight. Just pills at first. Benzedrine, which her friend Jill had found in her mother's medicine cabinet. They took them sparingly, cautiously, until the feds had gone crazy and banned the pills. The medicine cabinet was empty one day, and the next—or so it seemed—Lucy's weight ballooned back up to well over one hundred fifty pounds. She was the only overweight kid in school save for Fat George, the boy who picked his nose and sat by himself at the lunch table. Lucy hated him the same way he hated her, the same way she hated her own reflection in the mirror.

It was Jill's mother who taught Lucy how to shoot up. Mrs. Henderson wasn't stupid; she had noticed the missing pills, been pleased to see Lucy finally doing something to get rid of her baby fat. The woman availed herself of the drug for the same reason. She was a nurse at Clayton General Hospital. She walked out of the emergency room with glass vials of Methedrine chattering like teeth in the pocket of her white uniform. Injectable amphetamine, she told Lucy. The same as the pills, only faster.

Lucy was fifteen years old the first time the needle pierced her skin.

"Just a little bit at a time," Mrs. Henderson coached, drawing a red tinge of blood into the syringe, then slowly pressing home the plunger. "You control it. Don't let it control you."

There was no real high, just a lightheadedness, and then of course the welcome loss of appetite. Mrs. Henderson was right. The liquid was faster than the pills, easier. Five pounds. Ten pounds. Fifteen. Then—nothing. So Lucy had redefined her "just a little bit at a time" until she was drawing back not five cc's, but ten, then ten turned to fifteen, then her head exploded and she was on fire.

What did she care about after that?

Nothing.

Boys? Too stupid. Jill Henderson? What a drag. Her weight? Never again.

By the age of sixteen, Lucy was just under a hundred pounds. Her ribs, her hips, her elbows, jutted out like polished marble. For the first time in her life, she had cheekbones. She wore dark Cleopatra eyeliner and blue eye shadow and ironed her long blonde hair so that it slapped stiffly against her impossibly thin ass. The little girl her fifth-grade PE coach had, much to the delight of the rest of the class, nicknamed "Steam Roller" was model-thin, carefree, and—suddenly—popular.

Not popular with her old friends, the ones she had known since kindergarten. They all spurned her as a waste, a dropout, a loser. For once in her life, Lucy didn't care. Who needed people who looked down on you for having a little fun? Lucy had only ever been a token anyway—the fat girl to pal around with so the other girl could be the pretty one, the charming one, the one all the boys flirted with.

Her new friends thought Lucy was perfect. They loved it when she made a sarcastic quip about someone from her old life. They embraced her weirdness. The girls invited her to their parties. The boys asked her out. They treated her as an equal. She finally fit in with a group. She finally didn't stick out as *too* anything. She was just one of many. She was just Lucy.

And what of her old life? Lucy felt nothing but disdain for everyone who had inhabited it, especially Mrs. Henderson, who abruptly cut her off and said Lucy needed to get her shit together. Lucy's shit was more together than it had ever been. She had no intention whatsoever of giving up her new life.

All of her old friends were squares, obsessed with college prep, which mostly consisted of debating which sorority they would rush. The finer points of these sororities, whose Victorian and Greek Revival–style mansions dotted Milledge Avenue and South Lumpkin Street at the University of Georgia, had been part of Lucy's vernacular since the age of ten, but the lure of amphetamine reduced her Greek to a forgotten language. She didn't need the disapproving glances from her old friends. She didn't even need Mrs. Henderson anymore. There were plenty of new friends who could hook her up, and Lucy's parents were generous with her allowance. On the weeks she was short, her mother never noticed money missing from her purse.

It was so easy to see now, but at the time, the spiraling down of her life seemed to happen in seconds, not the actual two full years it had taken for Lucy to fall. At home, she was sullen and sulky. She started sneaking out at night and lying to her parents about stupid things. Mundane things. Things that could be easily disproven. At school, Lucy failed class after class, finally ending up in rudimentary English with Fat George sitting in the front and Lucy and her new friends in the back row, mostly sleeping off the lows, biding their time until they could get back to their real love.

The needle.

That finely honed piece of surgical steel, that seemingly innocuous device of delivery that ruled every moment of Lucy's life. She dreamed about shooting up. That first prick of flesh. That pinch as the tip pierced vein. That slow burn as the liquid was injected. That immediate euphoria of the drug entering her system. It was worth everything. Worth every sacrifice. Worth every loss. Worth the things she had to do to get it. Worth the things she all but forgot about the second the drug entered her bloodstream.

Then, suddenly, came the crest of the last hill, the biggest hill, on her roller coaster ride down.

Bobby Fields. Almost twenty years older than Lucy. Wiser. Stronger. He was a mechanic at one of her father's gas stations. Bobby had never noticed her before. Lucy was invisible to him, a pudgy little girl with lank pigtails. But that changed after the needle entered Lucy's life. She walked into the garage one day, her jeans hanging low on her newly lean hips, bell-bottoms frayed from dragging the floor, and Bobby told her to stop and talk awhile.

He listened to her, too, and Lucy only then realized that no one had really listened to her before. And then, Bobby had reached up with his grease-stained fingers and stroked back a piece of hair that was hanging in her face. And then, somehow, they were in the back of the building and his hand was on her breast, and she felt alive under the bright glare of his undivided attention.

Lucy had never been with a man before. Even high as a kite, she knew she should say no. She knew that she had to save herself, that no one wanted spoiled goods. Because as improbable as it now seemed, back then there was still a part of her who assumed that despite the slight detour, one day she'd end up at UGA, pledge herself to whichever house she chose, and get married to an earnest young man whose bright future met with her father's approval.

Lucy would have babies. She would join the PTA. She would bake cookies and drive her kids to school in a station wagon and sit in her kitchen smoking with the other mothers while they complained about their boring lives. And, maybe while the other women discussed marital discord or colicky babies, Lucy would smile pleasantly, remembering her reckless youth, her crazy, hedonistic affair with the needle.

Or, maybe one day she would be on a street corner in the middle of Atlanta and feel her stomach drop at the thought of losing that homey kitchen, those close friends.

Because, while sixteen-year-old Lucy had never been with a man before, Bobby Fields had been with plenty of women. Plenty of young women. He knew how to talk to them. He knew how to make them feel special. And, most important, he knew how to move his hand from breast to thigh, from thigh to crotch, and from there to other places that made Lucy gasp so loudly that her father called from the office to see if she was okay.

"I'm all right, Daddy," she had said, because Bobby's hand had felt so good that Lucy would've lied to God Himself.

At first, their relationship was a secret, which of course made it more exciting. They had a bond. They had a forbidden thing between them. For nearly a full year, they carried on their clandestine affair. Lucy would avoid Bobby's gaze when she made her weekly trek to the garage to count quarters with her daddy. She would pretend Bobby didn't exist until she couldn't take it anymore. She would go to the dirty bathroom behind the building. He would grip his greasy hands so hard around her ass that she would feel the pain when she sat back down beside her father.

The hunger for Bobby was almost as intense as her hunger for the needle. She skipped school. She fabricated a part-time job and fake sleepovers that her parents never bothered to verify. Bobby had his own place. He drove a Mustang Fastback like Steve McQueen. He drank beer and he smoked dope and he scored speed for Lucy and she learned how to go down on him without gagging.

It was all perfect until she realized that she couldn't keep up her fake life anymore. Or maybe she just didn't want to. She dropped out of high school two months before graduation. The final straw came the weekend her parents took a trip to visit her brother in college. Lucy spent the entire time at Bobby's. She cooked for him. She cleaned for him. She made love to him all night, and during the day she stared at the clock, counting down the minutes until she could tell him that she loved him. And Lucy *did* love him, especially when he got home at night with a big grin on his face and a little vial of magic in his pocket.

Bobby was generous with the needle. Maybe too generous. He got Lucy so high that her teeth started chattering. She was still high when she stumbled home the next morning.

Sunday.

Her parents were supposed to go to church with her brother before driving back, but there they were, sitting at the kitchen table, still in their traveling clothes. Her mother hadn't even taken off her hat. They had been waiting up all night. They had called her friend, her alibi, who was supposed to say that Lucy had spent the night. The girl had lied at first but after only the slightest bit of pressure told Lucy's parents exactly where their daughter was and exactly what she'd been up to for the last several months.

Lucy was seventeen by then, still considered a child. Her parents tried to have her committed. They tried to have Bobby arrested. They tried to prevent other garages from hiring him, but he just moved to Atlanta, where no one cared who fixed their car so long as it was cheap.

Two months of hell passed, and then, suddenly, Lucy was eighteen. Just like that, her life was different. Or different in a different way. Old enough to quit school. Old enough to drink. Old enough to leave her family without the pigs dragging her back home. She went from being her daddy's girl to Bobby's girl, living in an apartment off Stewart Avenue, sleeping all day, waiting for Bobby to come home at night so he could shoot her up, screw her, then let her sleep some more.

The only regret Lucy felt at the time was toward her brother, Henry. He was in law school at UGA. He was six years older, more like a friend than a sibling. In person, they generally shared long moments of silence, but since he'd gone away to school, they had written each other letters two or three times a month.

Lucy had loved writing letters to Henry. She was the old Lucy in all of her correspondences: silly about boys, anxious for graduation, eager to learn how to drive. No talk of the needle. No talk of her new friends who were so far outside the margins of society that Lucy was afraid to bring them home lest they steal her mother's good silver. That is, if her mother even let them through the door.

Henry's responses were always brief, but even when he was covered up in exams, he managed to send Lucy a line or two to let her know what was going on. He was excited about her joining him on campus. He was excited about showing around his baby girl to his friends. He was excited about everything, until he wasn't, because her parents told him that his darling sister had moved to Atlanta as the whore of a thirty-eight-year-old hippie, drug-dealing gearhead.

After that, Lucy's letters came back unopened. Henry's scrawl informed her, "Return to sender." Just like that, he dropped Lucy like trash in the street.

Maybe she *was* trash. Maybe she deserved to be abandoned. Because once the rush wore off, once the highs turned less intense and the lows became almost unbearable, what was there left to Lucy Bennett but a life on the street?

Two months after Bobby moved her to Atlanta, he kicked her out. Who could blame him? His hot young fox had turned into a junkie who met him at the door every night begging for the needle. And when Bobby stopped supplying her, she found another man in the complex who was willing to give her anything she wanted. So what if she had to spread her legs for it? He was giving her what Bobby wouldn't. He was supplying her demand.

His name was Fred. He cleaned planes at the airport. He liked to do things to Lucy that made her cry, and then he'd give her the needle and everything would be okay again. Fred thought he was special, better than Bobby. When Fred figured out the gleam in Lucy's eye was for the drug and not for him, he started beating her. He didn't stop beating her until she landed in the hospital. And then when she got a taxi back to the apartment complex, the manager told her that Fred had moved out, no forwarding address. And then the manager told Lucy that she was welcome to stay with him.

Much of what came next was a blur, or maybe it was so clear that she couldn't see it, the way putting on someone else's glasses makes your eyes cross. For almost a year, Lucy went from man to man, supplier to supplier. She did things—horrible things—to get the needle. If there was a totem pole in the world of speed, she had started at the top and quickly hit bottom. Day after day, she felt the dizzying spin of her life circling the drain. Yet, she felt helpless to stop it. The pain would kick in. The need. The yearning. The longing that burned like hot acid in her gut.

And then finally, the very bottom. Lucy was terrified of the bikers who sold speed, but eventually, inevitably, her love of the speed won out. They tossed her around like a baseball, everyone taking a hit. All of them had fought in Vietnam and were furious at the world, the system. Furious at Lucy, too. She had never overdosed before, at least not bad enough to end up in the hospital. Once, twice, a third time, she was dropped off the back of a Harley in front of the Grady emergency room. The bikers didn't like that. Hospitals brought the cops and the cops were expensive to buy off. One night, Lucy got too high and one of them brought her down with heroin, a trick he'd picked up fighting Charlie.

Heroin, the final nail in Lucy's coffin. As with the speed, she was a quick convert. That deadening sensation. That indescribable bliss. The loss of time. Space. Consciousness.

Lucy had never taken money for sex. Her transactions until this point had always had an air of bartering. Sex for speed. Sex for heroin. Never sex for money.

But now, Lucy found herself in desperate need of money.

The bikers sold speed, not heroin. Heroin belonged to the coloreds. Even the Mafia was hands-off. H was a ghetto drug. It was too potent, too addictive, too dangerous for white people. Especially white women.

Which is how Lucy ended up being tricked out by a black man with a tattoo of Jesus on his chest.

The spoon. The flame. The smell of burning rubber. The tourniquet. The filter from a broken cigarette. There was a romantic pageantry to the whole thing, a drawn-out process that made her former affair with the needle seem woefully unsophisticated. Even now, Lucy could feel herself getting excited at the thought of the spoon. She closed her eyes, imagining the bent piece of silver, the way the neck resembled a broken swan. Black swan. Black sheep. Black man's whore.

Suddenly, Juice was at her side. The other girls cautiously moved away. Juice had a way of sensing weakness. It was how he got them in the first place. "What it is, Sexy?"

"Nothing," she mumbled. "Everything's dyn-o-mite."

He took the toothpick out of his mouth. "Don't play me, gal."

Lucy looked down at the ground. She could see his white patent leather shoes, the way the bell-bottom of his custom-made green pants draped across the wingtips. How many strangers had she screwed to put the shine on those shoes? How many back seats had she lain down in so he could go to the tailor in Five Points to have his inseam measured?

"Sorry." She chanced a look at his face, trying to gauge his temper.

Juice took out his handkerchief and rubbed the sweat off his forehead. He had long sideburns that connected to his mustache and goatee. There was a birthmark on his cheek that Lucy stared at sometimes when she needed to concentrate on other things.

He said, "Come on, gal. You don't tell me what's on your mind, I cain't fix it." He pushed her shoulder. When she didn't start talking, he pushed her harder to get the point across. He wasn't going away. Juice hated when they kept secrets from him.

"I was thinking about my mother," Lucy told him, which was the first time she'd told a man the truth in a long while.

Juice laughed, used the toothpick to address the other girls. "Ain't that sweet? She been thinkin' about her mammy." He raised his voice. "How many'a y'all's mama's here for ya now?"

There was a titter of nervous laughter. Kitty, ever the suck-up, said, "We just need you, Juice. Only you."

"Lucy," Mary whispered. The word nearly got trapped in her throat. If Juice got pissed off, none of them would get what they wanted, and all that they wanted right now, all that they needed, was the spoon and the H that Juice had in his pocket.

"Nah, it's all right." Juice waved off Mary. "Let her talk. Come on, girl. Speak."

Maybe it was because he said the same thing that you'd say to a dog—"speak," like Lucy would get a treat if she barked on command—or maybe it was because she was so used to doing exactly what Juice told her to do, that Lucy's mouth started moving of its own volition.

"I was thinkin' about this time my mama took me into town." Lucy closed her eyes. She could feel herself back in the car. See the metal dashboard of her mother's Chrysler gleaming in the bright sunlight. It was hot, steamy, the sort of August that made you wish you had air-conditioning in your car. "She was gonna drop me off at the library while she did her chores."

Juice chuckled at her memory. "Aw, that's sweet, girl. Your mama takin' you to the liberry sose you can read."

"She couldn't get there." Lucy opened her eyes, looked directly at Juice in a way she'd never before dared. "The Klan was having a rally."

Juice cleared his throat. He cut his eyes to the other girls, then zeroed back in on Lucy. "Keep going." His deep tone wedged a splinter of cold into her spine.

"The streets were blocked. They were stopping traffic, checking cars."

"Hush now," Mary whispered, begging for Lucy to stop. But Lucy couldn't stop. Her master had told her to speak.

"It was a Saturday. Mama always took me to the library on Saturdays."

"That right?" Juice asked.

"Yes." Even with her eyes open, Lucy could still see the scene playing out in her head. She was in her mother's car. Safe. Carefree. Before the pills. Before the needle. Before the heroin. Before Juice. Before she lost that little Lucy who sat so patiently in her mother's car, worried that she wasn't going to get to the library in time for her reading group.

Little Lucy was a voracious reader. She gripped the stack of books in her lap as she stared at the men blocking the streets. They were all dressed in their white robes. Most of them had their hoods pulled back because of the heat. She recognized some from church, a couple from school. She waved at Mr. Sheffield, who owned the hardware store. He winked at her and waved back.

Lucy told Juice, "We were on a hill near the courthouse, and there was a black guy in front of us, stopped at the stop sign. He was in one of those little foreign cars. Mr. Peterson walked right up to him, and Mr. Laramie was on the other side."

"That right?" Juice repeated.

"Yes, that's right. The guy was terrified. His car kept rolling back. He must've had a clutch. His foot was slipping because he was so panicked. And I remember my mama watching him like we were watching *Wild Kingdom* or something, and she just laughed and laughed, and said, 'Lookit how scared that coon is.'"

"Jesus," Mary hissed.

Lucy smiled at Juice, repeated, "Lookit how scared that coon is."

Juice took the toothpick out of his mouth. "You best watch yourself, gal."

"Lookit how scared that coon is," Lucy mumbled. "Lookit how scared . . ." She let her voice trail off, but it was only like an engine idling before it was gunned. For no reason, the story struck her as hilariously funny. Her voice went up, the sound echoing off the buildings. "Lookit how scared that coon is! Lookit how scared that coon is!"

Juice slapped her, open palm, but hard enough to spin her around. Lucy felt blood slide down her throat.

Not the first time she'd been hit. Not the last. It wouldn't stop her. Nothing could stop her. "Lookit how scared that coon is! Lookit how scared that coon is!"

"Shut up!" Juice punched his fist into her face.

Lucy felt the crack of a tooth breaking. Her jaw twisted like a Hula Hoop, but she still said, "Lookit how scared—"

He kicked her in the stomach, his tight pants keeping his foot low so that she felt the toe of his shoe scrape her pelvic bone. Lucy gasped from the pain, which was excruciating, but somehow liberating. How many years had it been since she'd felt something other than numb? How many years had it been since she'd raised her voice, told a man no?

Her throat felt tight. She could barely stand. "Lookit how scared that—"

Juice punched her in the face again. She felt the bridge of her nose splinter. Lucy staggered back, arms open. She saw stars. Literal stars. Her purse dropped. The heel of her shoe snapped off.

"Get out my face!" Juice waved his fist in the air. "Get outta here 'fore I kill you, bitch!"

Lucy stumbled into Jane, who pushed her away like a diseased dog.

"Just go!" Mary begged. "Please."

Lucy swallowed a mouthful of blood and coughed it back out. Pieces of white speckled the ground. Teeth.

"Get on, bitch!" Juice warned her. "Get on outta my sight."

Lucy managed to turn. She looked up the dark street. There were no lights showing the way. Either the pimps shot them out or the city didn't bother to turn them on. Lucy stumbled again, but kept herself upright. The broken heel was a problem. She kicked off both shoes. The soles of her feet felt the intense heat of the asphalt, a burning sensation that shot straight up to her scalp. It was like walking on hot coals. She'd seen that on TV once—the trick was to walk fast enough to deprive the heat of oxygen so your skin didn't burn.

Lucy picked up her pace. She straightened herself as she walked. She kept her head held high despite the breathtaking pain in her ribs. It didn't matter. The darkness didn't matter. The heat in her soles didn't matter. Nothing mattered.

She turned, screaming, "Look at how scared that coon is!"

Juice made to run after her, and Lucy bolted down the street. Her bare feet slapped against the pavement. Her arms pumped. Her lungs shook as she rounded the corner. Adrenaline raced through her body. Lucy thought of all those PE classes in school, when her bad attitude had earned her five, ten, twenty laps around the track. She had been so fast then, so young and free. Not anymore. Her legs started to cramp. Her knees wanted to buckle. Lucy chanced a look behind her, but Juice was not there. No one was there. She stumbled to a stop.

He didn't even care enough to chase her.

Lucy bent over, bracing her hand against a phone booth, blood dripping from her mouth. She used her tongue to find the source. Two teeth were broken, though thank God they were in the back.

She went inside the booth. The light was too bright when she closed the door. She let it hang open and leaned against the glass. Her breath was still labored. Her body felt as if she'd run ten miles, not a handful of blocks.

She looked at the phone, the black receiver on the hook, the slot for the dime. Lucy traced her fingers along the bell symbol engraved in the metal plate, then let her hand move down to find the four, the seven, the eight. Her parents' phone number. She still knew it by heart, just like she knew the street number where they lived, her grandmother's birthday, her brother's upcoming graduation date. That earlier Lucy was not completely lost. There still existed her life in numbers.

She could call, but even if they answered, no one would have anything to say.

Lucy pushed herself out of the phone booth. She walked slowly

up the street, in no particular direction but away. Her stomach
clenched as the first wave of withdrawal made itself known. She
should go to the hospital to get patched up and beg the nurse for
some methadone before it got really bad. Grady was twelve blocks
down and three over. Her legs weren't cramping yet. She could make
the walk. Those laps around the high school track hadn't always felt
like a punishment. Lucy used to love to run. She loved jogging on
weekends with her brother Henry. He always gave up before she did.
Lucy had a letter from him in her purse. She'd gotten it last month
from the man at the Union Mission, where the girls took their down-
time when Juice was mad at them.

Lucy had kept the letter for three whole days before opening it,
afraid it would be bad news. Her father dead. Her mother run off
with the Charles Chips man. Everyone was getting divorced now,
weren't they? Broken homes. Broken children. Though Lucy had
been broken for a long time, so it was nothing to open and read a
simple letter, right?

Henry's cramped script was so familiar that it felt like a soft hand
on her cheek. Tears had filled her eyes. She read the letter through
once, then again, then again. One page. No gossip or family news,
because Henry was not that way. He was precise, logical, never dramatic. Henry was in his last year of law school. He was looking for a
job now because he'd heard the market was tough. He would miss
being a student. He would miss being around his friends. And he
really missed Lucy.

He missed Lucy.

This was the part she had read four times, then five, then so many
more that she had lost count. Henry missed Lucy. Her brother missed
his sister.

Lucy missed herself, too.

But Lucy had dropped her purse back on the street corner. Juice
probably had it now. He'd probably shaken it out onto the sidewalk
and combed through everything like it belonged to him. Which
meant he had Henry's letter and Lucy's kitchen knife that was sharp

enough to cut the skin on her leg, which she knew because she had done it last week just to make sure she could still bleed.

Lucy took a left at the next corner. She turned around to look at the moon. It punctured the black sky with the curved edge of its fingernail. The skeleton of the unfinished Peachtree Plaza hotel loomed in the distance—the tallest hotel in the world. The whole city was under construction. In a year or two, there would be thousands of new hotel rooms opening downtown. Business would be booming, especially in the streets.

She doubted she'd live to see it.

Lucy tripped again. Pain shot up her spine. The damage to her body was making itself known. Her rib must be fractured. She knew that her nose was broken. The clenching in her stomach was getting worse. She would need a fix soon or she'd go into the DTs.

She made herself put one foot in front of the other. "Please," she prayed to the God of Grady Hospital. "Let them give me methadone. Let them give me a bed. Let them be kind. Let them be—"

Lucy stopped. What the hell was wrong with her? Why was she leaving her fate to some bitch nurse who would take one look at her and know exactly what she was? Lucy should go back to her strip. She should make up with Juice. She should get down on her hands and knees and beg him for forgiveness. For mercy. For a hit. For salvation.

"Good evening, sister."

Lucy spun around, half expecting to see Henry, though he had never greeted her that way. There was a man standing a few feet behind her. White. Tall. Covered in shadow. Lucy's hand flew to her chest. Her heart pounded underneath her palm. She knew better than to let some john sneak up on her like that. She reached for her purse, the knife she kept inside, but too late remembered that she'd lost everything.

"Are you all right?" the man asked. He was clean-cut, something Lucy hadn't seen in a long while, except on a pig. His light brown hair was shaved into a buzz cut. Sideburns short. No shadow of a beard even this late at night. Military, she guessed. Lots of guys were coming home from Nam. In six months, this asshole would be just like all the other vets Lucy knew, wearing his dirty hair in a braid, beating down some woman and talking shit about the Man.

Lucy tried to make her voice strong. "Sorry, handsome. I'm done for the night." Her words echoed in the cavern formed by the tall buildings. She was aware that she was slurring, and straightened her shoulders so he wouldn't think she was an easy target. "Closed for business."

"I'm not looking for business." He took a step forward. He had a book in his hands. The Bible.

"Shit," she mumbled. These guys were everywhere. Mormons, Jehovah's Witnesses, even some of the freaks from the local Catholic church. "Lookit, I don't need saving."

"I hate to argue, sister, but you look like you do."

"I'm not your sister. I have a brother, and you're not him." Lucy turned around and started walking. She couldn't go back to Juice right now. Lucy didn't think she could stand another beating. She would go to the hospital and make such a stink that they'd have to sedate her. That, at least, would get her through the night.

"I bet he's worried about you."

Lucy kept walking.

"Your brother?" the man asked. "I bet he's worried about you. I know I'd be."

She clutched her hands together, but didn't turn around. Footsteps followed her. Lucy didn't quicken her pace. Couldn't quicken her pace. The pain in her stomach was strong, a knife cutting through her viscera. The hospital was fine for one night, but there was tomorrow, and the next day, and the next. Lucy would have to find a way back into Juice's good graces. Tonight had been slow. Even Kitty wasn't bringing in much. Juice was all about cold, hard cash, and Lucy was betting this Jesus freak had at least ten bucks on him. Sure, Juice would still beat her, but the money would soften his blows.

"I want to call him." Lucy kept a careful pace. She could hear the man following, keeping his distance. "My brother. He'll come get me. He said he would." She was lying, but her voice was strong. "I don't have any money. To call him, that is."

"If it's money you want, I can give you that."

Lucy stopped. Slowly, she turned around. The man was standing in a sliver of light that came from the lobby of a nearby office building. Lucy was too tall, five-ten with her shoes off. She was used to looking down at most people. This guy was well over six feet. The hands that held the Bible were huge. His shoulders were broad. Long legs, but not lean. Lucy was fast, especially when she was scared. The minute he took out his wallet, she would grab it and dash away.

She asked, "You a marine or what?"

"4-F." He took a step toward her. "Medical disability."

He looked capable enough to Lucy. He probably had a daddy who bought him out of the draft, same as Lucy's dad had with Henry. "Give me some money so I can call my brother." She remembered, "Please."

"Where is he?"

"Athens."

"Greece?"

She sputtered a laugh. "Georgia. He's in college. Law school. He's about to get married. I wanna call him. Congratulate him." She added, "Get him to pick me up and take me home. To my family. Where I belong."

The man took another step forward. The light picked out the features of his face, which were normal, even average. Blue eyes. Nice mouth. Sharp nose. Square jaw. "Why aren't you in college?"

Lucy felt a tingle at the back of her neck. She wasn't sure how to describe it. Part of her was afraid of the man. Part of her was thinking she hadn't talked to a guy like this in more years than she could remember. He wasn't looking at her like she was a whore. He wasn't proposing a transaction. There was nothing in his eyes that told her he was a threat. And yet, it was two in the morning and he was standing in the empty street of a city that pretty much closed its doors at six o'clock after all the white people went back to the suburbs.

The truth was, neither one of them belonged here.

"Sister." He took another step closer. Lucy was shocked to see the concern in his eyes. "I don't want you to be afraid of me. I let the Lord guide my hand."

Lucy had trouble answering. Years had passed since anyone had looked at her with anything close to compassion. "What makes you think I'm afraid?"

"I think you've lived with fear for a long time, Lucy."

"You don't know what I've—" She stopped. "How do you know my name?"

He seemed confused. "You told me."

"No, I didn't."

"You told me your name was Lucy. Just a few minutes ago." He held up the Bible for emphasis. "I swear."

All the saliva in her mouth was gone. Her name was her secret. She never gave it away to strangers. "No, I didn't."

"Lucy . . ." He was less than five feet away from her now. There was that same concerned look in his eyes, though he could easily take one more step and wrap both hands around her neck before she knew what was happening.

But he didn't. He just stood there holding his Bible to his chest. "Please, don't be scared of me. You have no reason to be afraid."

"Why are you here?"

"I want to help you. To save you."

"I don't need saving. I need money."

"I told you I'd give you all the money you need." He tucked the Bible under his arm and took out his wallet. She could see bills stacked neatly in the fold. Hundreds. He fanned them out in his hand. "I want to take care of you. That's all I've ever wanted."

Her chest shook. She eyed the money. There was at least five hundred there, possibly more. "I don't know you."

"No, not yet."

Lucy's foot stepped back, but she needed to go forward, needed to grab the cash and run. If the man sensed her plans, he didn't show it. He stood there with the hundreds looking like postage stamps in his large hands, not moving, not speaking. All that cash. Five hundred dollars. She could rent a hotel room, keep herself off the street for months, maybe a year.

Lucy felt her heart banging against her shattered rib. She was torn between snatching the dough and running for her life and just plain running *from* her life. The hair on the back of her neck stood at attention. Her hands were shaking. She felt heat radiating somewhere behind her. For a moment, Lucy assumed the sun was coming up over Peachtree Plaza, streaking down the street, warming her neck and shoulders. Was this some sign from above? Was this finally her moment of salvation?

No. No salvation. Just money.

She forced herself to take a step forward. Then another. "I want to know you," she told the man, fear making the words slur on her tongue.

He smiled. "That's good, sister."

Lucy made herself return the smile. Made her shoulders curve so she looked younger, sweeter, innocent. And then she grabbed the wad of cash. She turned to run, but her body jerked back like a sling-shot.

"Don't fight me." His fingers were clamped around her wrist. Half her arm disappeared inside his grip. "You can't escape."

Lucy stopped fighting. She didn't have a choice. Pain was shooting up her neck. Her head was throbbing. Her shoulder crunched in the socket. Still, she kept her fist wrapped around the money. She could feel the stiff bills scraping against her palm.

He said, "Sister, why do you crave a life of sin?"

"I don't know." Lucy shook her head. She looked down at the ground. She sniffed back the blood that dripped from her nose. And then she felt his grip start to loosen.

"Sister—"

Lucy wrenched away her arm, her skin feeling torn, like a glove ripping off. She ran as fast and as hard as she could, feet slapping pavement, arms pumping. One block. Two. She opened her mouth, taking deep gulps of air that sent stabbing pains into her chest. Broken ribs. Busted nose. Shattered teeth. Money in her hand. Five hundred dollars. A hotel room. A bus ticket. Safety. All the H that she could handle. She was free. Goddamn it, she was finally free.

Until her head flew back. Her scalp felt like the teeth of a zipper being wrenched apart as chunks of hair were snatched out at the root. Lucy's forward momentum didn't stop. She saw her legs shoot out in front of her, feet level to her chin, and then her back slammed down flat to the ground.

"Don't fight," the man repeated, straddling her, his hands wrapping around her neck.

Lucy clawed at his fingers. His grip was relentless. Blood poured from her torn scalp. It went into her eyes, her nose, her mouth.

She couldn't scream. She blindly reached out, trying to dig her fingernails into his eye sockets. She felt the side of his face, his rough skin, then her hands dropped because she couldn't hold up her arms anymore. His breath quickened as her body spasmed. Warm urine ran down her leg. She could feel his excitement even as a sense of hopelessness took over. Who was Lucy fighting for? Who cared if Lucy Bennett lived or died? Maybe Henry would be sad when he heard the news, but her parents, her old friends, even Mrs. Henderson, would probably feel nothing but relief.

Finally, the inevitable.

Lucy's tongue swelled in her mouth. Her vision blurred. It was useless. There was no air left for her lungs. No oxygen going to her brain. She felt herself start to give, her muscles releasing. The back of her head hit pavement. She stared up. The sky was impossibly black, pinholes of stars barely visible. The man stared down at her, the same concerned look in his eyes.

Only this time, he was smiling.

two

Present Day

MONDAY

Will Trent had never been alone in someone else's home before unless that person was dead. As with many things in his life, he was aware that this was a trait he shared with a lot of serial killers. Fortunately, Will was an agent with the Georgia Bureau of Investigation, so the empty bathrooms he searched and the deserted bedrooms he tossed all fell under the category of intrusions for the greater good.

This revelation didn't help ease his mind as he walked through Sara Linton's apartment. Will had to keep telling himself he had a legitimate reason to be here. Sara had asked him to feed and walk the dogs while she worked an extra shift at the hospital. Barring that, they were hardly strangers. They'd known each other for almost a full year before they'd finally gotten together two weeks ago. Will had spent every night here since. Even before that, he'd met Sara's parents. He'd dined at her family's table. Given all of this familiarity, his feelings of trespass didn't really add up.

Which still didn't stop him from feeling like a stalker.

Maybe this came from the way Will felt being alone here. He was pretty sure that he was obsessed with Sara Linton. He wanted to know everything about her. And while he wasn't seized by the urge to take off his clothes and roll around naked on her bed—at least, not without Sara there with him—he felt the compulsion to look at all the things on her shelves and in her drawers. He wanted to flip through the photo albums she kept in a box in her bedroom closet. He wanted to peruse her books and scroll through her iTunes collection.

Not that he would act on these impulses. Unlike most serial killers, Will was aware that any one of these things crossed the line into creepy. But the desire left him feeling unsettled all the same.

He looped the dogs' leashes around the hook inside the hall closet. Sara's two greyhounds were piled onto the living room couch. A ray of sun bleached their fawn-colored fur. The loft was a penthouse corner unit, which was one of the perks of being a pediatrician instead of a lowly civil servant. The L-shaped wall of windows gave a stellar view of downtown Atlanta. The Bank of America Plaza that looked like the builders had forgotten to remove the scaffolding up top. The steplike Georgia Pacific tower that was built over the movie theater where *Gone with the Wind* premiered. The tiny Equitable building sitting like a black granite paperweight beside the pencil cup of the Westin Peachtree Plaza.

Atlanta was a small town in the scheme of things—the population inside the city limits was slightly north of five hundred thousand. Bump that out to the metro area and it was closer to six million. The city was a Mecca on the Piedmont, the center of business in the Southeast. Over sixty languages were spoken here. There were more hotel rooms than residents, more office spaces than people. Three hundred murders a year. Eleven hundred reported rapes. Nearly thirteen thousand aggravated assault charges.

More like a small town with a chip on its shoulder.

Will made his way to the kitchen and picked up the water bowls from the floor. The thought of going home to his small house made him feel lonely, which was strange considering Will had grown up wanting to be nothing but alone. There was more to his life than Sara Linton. He was a grown man. He had a job. He had his own dog to look after. He had a home. He'd even been married before. Technically, he was still married, though that hadn't mattered much until recently.

Will was eight years old when the cops dropped off Angie Polaski at the Atlanta Children's Home. She was eleven, and a girl, which meant she stood a good chance of being adopted, but Angie was mouthy and wild and no one wanted her. No one wanted Will, either. He'd spent most of his early life being checked in and out of the children's home like a dog-eared library book. Somehow, Angie made all of it more bearable. Except for the times when she was making it unbearable.

Their marriage had taken place two years ago. It had been perpetrated on a double dog dare, which might explain why neither of them took it very seriously. Angie had lasted less than a week. Two days after the civil ceremony, Will woke up to find her clothes gone, the house empty. He wasn't surprised. He wasn't hurt. Actually, he was enormously relieved that it had happened sooner rather than later. Angie disappeared on him all the time. Will knew that she would be back. She always came back.

Only, this time, for the first time, something had happened while Angie was away. There was Sara. There was the way she breathed in Will's ear. There was the way she traced her fingers down his spine. There was her taste. Her smell. There were all these things Will had never even noticed with Angie.

He clicked his tongue as he put down the water bowls. The dogs stayed on the couch, unimpressed.

Will's Glock was on the counter beside his suit jacket. He clipped the holster onto his belt. He checked the time on the stove as he pulled on his jacket. Sara's shift ended in five minutes, which meant it was at least ten minutes past time for Will to leave. She would probably call him when she got home. He would tell her he was doing paperwork or about to get on the treadmill or some other lie that made it clear he hadn't been sitting around waiting for her to call, and then he would run back over here like Julie Andrews prancing up that hill in *The Sound of Music.*

He was heading to the front door when his cell phone vibrated in his pocket. Will recognized his boss's number. For a split second, he considered sending the call to voicemail, but he knew from experience that Amanda would not be easily deterred.

He answered, "Trent."

"Where are you?"

For some reason, he found the question intrusive. "Why?"

Amanda gave a weary sigh. He could hear noises on her end—the low murmur of a crowd, a repetitive clicking sound. "Just answer me, Will."

"I'm at Sara's." She didn't respond, so he asked, "Do you need me?"

"No, I most certainly do not. You're still on airport duty until further notice. Do you understand me? Nothing else."

He stared at the phone for a moment, then put it back to his ear. "All right."

Abruptly, she ended the call. Will had the distinct feeling she would've slammed down the receiver if such a thing were possible on a cell phone.

Instead of leaving, he stood in the foyer, trying to figure out what had just happened. Will replayed the conversation in his head. No obvious explanation jumped out. Will was used to his boss being obtuse. Anger was hardly a new emotion. But while Amanda had certainly hung up on him before, Will couldn't fathom why she cared where he was at the moment. Actually, he was surprised that she was even talking to him. He hadn't heard her voice in two weeks.

Deputy Director Amanda Wagner was an old-timer, from that

group of cops who easily bent the rules to make a case but stuck to the manual when it came to the dress code. The GBI required all non-undercover agents to keep their hair half an inch off their collar. Two weeks ago, Amanda had actually slapped a ruler to the back of Will's neck, and when he hadn't taken the hint, she'd transferred him to airport duty, which required Will to hang out in various men's toilets, waiting for someone to sexually proposition him.

Will's mistake was mentioning the ruler to Sara. He'd told her the story as a sort of joke as well as an explanation for why he needed to run up the street to the barbershop before they went to dinner. Sara hadn't told Will *not* to get his hair cut. She was so much smarter than that. She'd told him she liked his hair the length that it was. She'd told him that it looked good on him. She'd stroked the back of his neck while she said this. And then she had suggested that instead of going to the barber, they go into the bedroom and do something so filthy that Will had experienced a few seconds of hysterical blindness.

Which was why he was looking at spending the rest of his career doing a Mr. Bojangles under the bathroom stall of every men's toilet in the busiest passenger airport in the world.

But it didn't explain why Amanda had felt the need to locate Will on this particular day at this particular time.

Or the sound of people gathered in the background. Or the familiar clicking noise.

Will went back into the living room. The dogs shifted on the couch, but Will didn't sit down. He picked up the remote and turned on the television. A basketball game was on. He flipped to the local station. Monica Pearson, the Channel 2 anchor, was sitting behind her news desk. She was doing a story on the Beltline, the new transportation system that was hated by everyone in Atlanta except for the politicians. Will's finger was on the power button when the story changed. Breaking news. The image of a young woman appeared over Pearson's shoulder. Will turned up the volume as the story was tossed to a live news conference.

What he saw made him sit down.

Amanda Wagner stood at a wooden podium. A handful of microphones were in front of her. She was waiting for silence. Will heard the familiar sounds: cameras clicking over the low murmur of the crowd.

He'd seen his boss do hundreds of news conferences. Usually, Will was in the back of the room, trying to stay off camera, while Amanda basked in the glow of undivided attention. She loved being in charge. She lived to control the slow trickle of information that fed the media. Except for now. Will studied her face as the camera closed in. She looked tired. More than that—she looked worried.

She said, "The Georgia Bureau of Investigation has released an Alert Bulletin on Ashleigh Renee Snyder. The nineteen-year-old female was reported missing at approximately three-fifteen this afternoon." Amanda paused, giving the newspaper journalists time to scribble down the description. "Ashleigh lives in the Techwood area and is a sophomore at the Georgia Institute of Technology."

Amanda said more, but Will tuned out the words. He watched her mouth move. He saw her point to different reporters. Their questions were long. Her answers were brief. She didn't put up with much. There was none of her usual bantering back and forth. Finally, Amanda left the podium. Monica Pearson returned. The photo of the missing girl was back over her shoulder. Blonde, pretty, thin.

Familiar.

Will took his phone out of his pocket. He touched his thumb to the speed dial for Amanda, but didn't press the number.

By state law, the GBI had to be asked by the local police before they could take over a case. One of the rare exceptions was with kidnappings, where timing was critical and abductors could quickly cross county and state lines. An Alert Bulletin would mobilize all of the GBI field offices. Agents would be called back in. Any collected evidence would be given top priority at the labs. All the agency's resources would be directed toward this one case.

Every resource but Will.

He probably shouldn't read anything into this. It was just another way Amanda had found to punish him. She was still mad about Will's hair. She was petty enough to make a point of keeping him off a case. That was all it was. Will had worked kidnappings before. They were awful cases. They seldom ended well. Still, every cop wanted to work one. The ticking clock. The tension. The chase. The adrenaline jolt was part of the reason they joined in the first place.

And Amanda was punishing Will by keeping him off the case.

Techwood.

A student.

Will turned off the TV. He felt a drop of sweat slide down his back. His mind couldn't settle on any one particular thought. Finally, he shook his head to clear it. That was when he noticed the time on the cable box. Sara's shift had ended twelve minutes ago.

"Crap." Will had to move the dogs before he could stand up. He headed to the front door. Abel Conford, Sara's neighbor, was in the hallway waiting for the elevator.

"Good after—"

Will ducked into the stairwell. He took the steps two at a time, eager to leave so Sara wouldn't think he'd been mooning over her. She lived a few blocks from the hospital. She would be here any minute.

She was actually already here.

Will saw her sitting in her BMW as soon as he opened the lobby door. For a foolish split second, he considered darting into the trees. Then he realized that Sara had already seen his car. His '79 Porsche was parked nose-out beside her brand-new SUV. Will couldn't open his door without hitting Sara's.

He muttered under his breath as he plastered a smile onto his face. Sara didn't return it. She was just sitting there gripping the steering wheel, staring straight ahead. He walked toward the car. The sun was bright enough to turn her windshield into a mirror, so he didn't notice until he was right up on her that she had tears in her eyes.

Instantly, his issue with Amanda ceased to matter. Will pulled the handle on the door. Sara unlocked it from the inside.

He asked, "You okay?"

"Yep." She turned around to face him, propping her feet on the running board. "Bad day at work."

"Want to talk about it?"

"Not really, but thank you." She traced her fingers along the side of his face, tucked his hair behind his ear.

Will leaned in closer. All he could do was look at her. Sara's auburn hair was pulled back into a ponytail. The sunlight brought out the intense green of her eyes. She was wearing her hospital scrubs. There were a few drops of dried blood on the sleeve. She had a series of numbers scribbled on the back of her hand. Blue ink on milky white skin. All the patient charts at Grady were on digital tablets. Sara used the back of her hand to calculate dosages for patients. Knowing this last week would've saved Will two sleepless nights of insane jealousy, but he wasn't one to quibble.

She asked, "Were the dogs okay?"

"They did all the things dogs are supposed to do."

"Thank you for taking care of them." Sara rested her hands on his shoulders. Will felt a familiar stirring. It was like there was an invisible string between them. The slightest tug and he was incapacitated.

She stroked the back of his neck. "Tell me about your day."

"Boring and sad," he answered, which was mostly true. "Some old guy told me I have a nice package."

She gave a sly smile. "Can't arrest him for being honest."

"He was pleasuring himself when he said it."

"That sounds like something fun to try."

Will felt the string go taut. He kissed her. Sara's lips were soft. They tasted like peppermint from the lip balm she used. Her fingernails scratched into his hair. He leaned in closer. And then everything stopped when the front door to the building banged open. Abel Conford gave them a scowl as he stomped toward his Mercedes.

Will had to clear his throat before he could ask Sara, "Are you sure you don't want some time to yourself?"

She adjusted the knot in his tie. "I want to go for a walk with you, and then I want to eat an entire pizza with you, and then I want to spend the rest of the night with you."

Will looked down at his watch. "I think I can fit that in."

Sara slid out of the car and locked the door. Will tucked the key fob into his pocket. The plastic hit the familiar cold metal of his wedding ring. Will had taken off the ring two weeks ago, but for reasons he couldn't begin to decipher, that was as far as he'd gotten.

Sara took his hand as they walked down the sidewalk. Atlanta was at its most spectacular in late March, and today was no exception. A light breeze cooled the air. Every yard was packed with flowers. The oppressive heat of the summer months seemed like an old wives' tale. The sun cut through the swaying trees, lighting up Sara's face. Her tears had dried, but Will could see that she was still troubled about what had happened at the hospital.

He asked, "Sure you're okay?"

Instead of answering, Sara wrapped his arm around her shoulders. She was a few inches shorter than Will, which meant she fit like a puzzle piece under his arm. He felt her hand slip up under his suit jacket. She hooked her thumb over the top of his belt, just shy of his Glock. They passed the usual foot traffic in the neighborhood—joggers, occasional couples, men pushing baby strollers. Women walking dogs. Most of them were on their cell phones, even the runners.

Sara finally spoke. "I lied to you."

He glanced down at her. "About what?"

"I didn't pull an extra shift at the hospital. I stayed around because . . ." Her voice trailed off. She looked out into the street. "Because no one else was there."

Will didn't know what else to say but, "Okay."

Her shoulders went up as she took a deep breath. "An eight-year-old boy was brought in around lunchtime." Sara was the pediatric attending in Grady's ER. She saw a lot of kids in bad shape. "He OD'd on his grandmother's blood pressure meds. He took half her ninety-day supply. It was hopeless."

Will kept silent, giving her time.

"His heart rate was less than forty when they brought him in. We lavaged him. We ran through the glucagon. Maxed out on dopamine, epinephrine." Her voice got softer with each word. "There was nothing else I could do. I called the cardiologist to put in a pacemaker, but . . ." Sara shook her head again. "We had to let him go. We ended up shipping him to the ICU."

Will saw a black Monte Carlo coasting down the street. The windows were down. Rap music shook the air.

Sara said, "I couldn't leave him alone."

His attention moved away from the car. "Weren't the nurses there?"

"The ward was already packed." Again, she shook her head. "His grandmother wouldn't come to the hospital. Mom's in jail. Dad's unknown. No other relatives. He wasn't conscious. He didn't even know I was there." She paused a moment. "It took him four hours to die. His hands were already cold when we moved him upstairs." She stared down at the sidewalk. "Jacob. His name was Jacob."

Will chewed at the inside of his mouth. He'd been in and out of Grady as a kid. The hospital was the only publicly funded facility left in Atlanta.

He said, "Jacob was lucky to have you."

She tightened her grip around him. Her gaze was still lowered, as if the cracks in the sidewalk needed further study.

They walked on, both silent. Will felt a weight of expectancy. He knew that Sara was thinking about Will's childhood, the fact that his own life could've ended the same way Jacob's had. Will should at least acknowledge this, remind her that the system had done better by him than most. But he couldn't find the words.

"Hey." Sara tugged at the back of Will's shirt. "We should probably turn around."

She was right. The foot traffic had thinned out. They were nearing Boulevard, which wasn't the best place to be this time of day. Will glanced up, blinking at the bright sun. There were no tall buildings or skyscrapers blocking the light. Just rows and rows of government-subsidized housing.

Techwood had been like this neighborhood up until the mid-nineties, when the Olympics had changed everything. The city had razed the slums. The inhabitants had been moved farther south. Students lived in the upscale apartment buildings now.

Students like Ashleigh Snyder.

Will spoke before he could stop himself. "Why don't we go up that way?"

Sara gave him a curious look. He was pointing toward the projects.

He said, "I want to show you something."

"Around here?"

"It's just a few blocks this way." Will pulled at her shoulder to get her going again. They crossed another street, stepping over a pile of litter. Graffiti was everywhere. Will could practically feel the hair standing up on the back of Sara's neck.

She asked, "Are you sure about this?"

"Trust me," he said, though as if on cue, they approached a seedy-looking clump of shirtless teenagers. All of them sported scowls and low-hanging jeans. They were a veritable rainbow coalition of tweakers, representing almost every ethnicity Atlanta had to offer. One of them had a small swastika tattooed on his fish-white belly. Another had a Puerto Rican flag on his chest. Ball caps were turned backward. Teeth were missing or covered in gold. All of them held liquor-shaped brown paper bags in their hands.

Sara leaned closer to Will. He stared back at the kids. Will was six-three on a good day, but pulling back his jacket sent the stronger message. Nothing discouraged conversation more than the fourteen rounds in a government-issued Glock model 23.

Wordlessly, the group turned and headed in the opposite direction. Will let his eyes track them just to make it clear they should keep moving.

"Where are we going?" Sara asked. She obviously hadn't planned on their afternoon stroll turning into a tour of one of the city's most crime-ridden areas. They were in the full glare of the sun now. There was no shade in this part of town. No one planted flowers in their front yards. Unlike the dogwood-lined streets in the more affluent areas, there was nothing here but bright xenon streetlights and clear open spaces so the police helicopters could track stolen cars or fleeing perpetrators.

"Just a little bit more," Will said, rubbing her shoulder in what he hoped was a soothing manner.

They walked silently for a few more blocks. He could feel Sara tense up the farther they got from home.

Will asked, "Do you know what this area is called?"

Sara glanced around at the street signs. "SoNo? Old Fourth Ward?"

"It used to be called Buttermilk Bottom."

She smiled at the name. "Why?"

"It was a slum. No paved streets. No electricity. See how steep the grade is?" She nodded. "The sewage used to back up here. They said it smelled like buttermilk." Will saw she wasn't smiling anymore. He dropped his arm to Sara's waist as they turned onto Carver Street. He pointed to the boarded-up coffee shop on the corner. "That used to be a grocery store."

She looked up at him.

"Mrs. Flannigan sent me there every day after school to buy her a pack of Kool 100s and a bottle of Tab."

"Mrs. Flannigan?"

"She ran the children's home."

Sara's expression didn't change, but she nodded.

Will felt an odd sensation in his belly, like he'd swallowed a handful of hornets. He didn't know why he'd brought Sara here. He wasn't generally impulsive. He'd never been one to volunteer details about his life. Sara knew Will had grown up in care. She knew that his mother had died shortly after he was born. Will assumed she'd figured out the rest on her own. Sara wasn't just a pediatrician. She'd been the medical examiner back in her small town. She knew what abuse looked like. She knew what Will looked like. Given her training, it wasn't hard to put together the clues.

"Record shop," Will said, pointing out another abandoned building. He kept his arm around her waist, guiding her toward their ultimate destination. The hornet sensation got worse. Ashleigh Snyder kept flashing into his mind. The photo they showed on the news must have been from her student ID card. The girl's blonde hair was pulled back. Her lips showed an amused smile, as if the photographer had said something funny.

Sara asked, "Where did you live?"

Will stopped. They had almost passed the children's home. The building was so changed that it was barely recognizable. The Spanish Revival brick architecture had been completely bastardized. Large metal awnings eyebrowed the front windows. The red brick had been painted a rheumy yellow. Chunks of the façade were missing. The huge wooden front door that had been gloss black as long as Will could remember was now a garish red. The glass was caked with dirt. In the yard, Mrs. Flannigan's white painted tires no longer held tulips and pansies. They were no longer white, either. Will was afraid to guess what was inside them now, and he didn't want to get close enough to find out. There was a sign slapped onto the side of the building.

"'Coming soon: Luxury Condos,'" Sara read. "Not too soon, I'm guessing."

Will stared up at the building. "It didn't used to be like this."

Sara's reluctance was palpable, but she still asked, "Do you want to look inside?"

He wanted to run away from here as fast as he could, but Will forced himself to walk up the front steps. As a kid, he'd always felt a certain amount of dread every time he entered the home. There were new boys constantly in and out. Each of them had something to prove, sometimes with their fists. This time, it wasn't physical violence that sent a cold fear through Will. It was Ashleigh Snyder. It

was the unreasonable connection Will was making because the missing girl looked so much like his mother.

He pressed his face close to the window, but couldn't see anything
other than the reflection of his own eyes staring back. The front door
was secured with an expensive-looking padlock. The wood was so
rotted that one yank on the hasp pulled out the screws.

Will hesitated, his palm flat to the door. He felt Sara standing behind him, waiting. He wondered what she would do if he changed
his mind and walked back down the stairs.

As if sensing his thoughts, she said, "We can go." Then, more
pointedly, "Why don't we go?"

Will pushed open the door. There was no expected creaking of
hinges, but the door caught on the warped wooden floor so that he
had to shove it open. Will tested the floorboards as he entered.
Though it was still light out, the house was dark, thanks mostly to
the heavy awnings and dirty windows. A musky smell greeted him,
nothing like the welcoming scent of Pine-Sol and Kool 100s Will
recalled from his childhood. He tried the light switch to no avail.

Sara said, "Maybe we should—"

"Looks like it was turned into a hotel." Will pointed to the caged
front desk. Keys still hung from the cubbyholes along the back wall.
"Or a halfway house."

Will glanced around what he guessed was the lobby. Broken glass
pipes and tinfoil littered the floor. The crack addicts had demolished
the couch and chairs. There were several used condoms melted into
the carpet.

"My God," Sara whispered.

Will felt oddly defensive. "Picture it with the walls painted white,
and the sofa this big, yellow, kind of corduroy sectional." He looked
down at the floor. "Same carpet. It was a lot cleaner, though."

Sara nodded, and he walked toward the back of the building before she could run out the front. The large open spaces from Will's
childhood had been chopped up into single-room apartments, but he
could still remember what it had looked like in better times.

He told Sara, "This was the dining hall. There were twelve tables.

Kind of like picnic benches, but with tablecloths and nice napkins. Boys on one side, girls on the other. Mrs. Flannigan was careful about letting the girls and boys mingle too much. She said she didn't need more kids than she already had."

Sara didn't laugh at the joke.

"Here." Will stopped in front of an open doorway. The room was a dark hole. He could easily picture how it used to be. Flowery wallpaper. A metal desk and wooden chair. "This was Mrs. Flannigan's office."

"What happened to her?"

"Heart attack. She died before the ambulance got here." He continued down the hallway and pushed open a familiar-looking swinging door. "The kitchen, obviously." This space, at least, hadn't changed. "That's the same stove from when I was a kid." Will opened the pantry door. There was still food stacked on the shelves. Mold had turned a loaf of bread into a black brick. Graffiti marred the back of the door. "Fuck you! Fuck you! Fuck you!" was carved into the soft wood.

Sara said, "Looks like the addicts redecorated."

"That was always there," Will admitted. "This is where you had to go if you acted up."

Sara pressed her lips together as she studied the bolt on the door.

Will said, "Trust me, being locked in a pantry wasn't the worst thing that ever happened to a lot of these kids." He saw the question in her eyes. "I was never locked in there."

She gave a strained smile. "I should hope not."

"It wasn't as bad as you're thinking. We had food. We had a roof over our heads. We had a color TV. You know how much I love watching television."

She nodded, and he led her back into the hallway toward the front stairs. He tapped a closed door along the way. "Basement."

"Did Mrs. Flannigan lock kids down there, too?"

"It was off limits," Will answered, though he happened to know that Angie had spent a lot of time down there with the older boys.

Carefully, Will walked up the stairs, testing each step before letting Sara follow. The scruffy treads were just as he remembered, but he had to duck at the top of the landing to keep from smacking his head on a structural beam.

"Back here." He took purposeful strides down the hallway, acting as if this was exactly what he'd planned to do with his evening. As with downstairs, the space was divided into single rooms that met with the needs of the prostitutes, drug addicts, and alcoholics who'd likely rented space by the hour. Most of the doors were open or hanging off their hinges. The plaster around the baseboards had been nibbled away by rats. The walls were probably crawling with their offspring. Or cockroaches. Or both.

Will stopped at the next-to-last door and pushed it open with his foot. An iron cot and a smashed wooden table were the only contents. The carpet was a fecal brown. The one window in the room was cut in half, the other side shared with the next-door neighbor.

"My bed was here against the wall. Bunk bed. I got the top."

Sara didn't respond. Will turned around to look at her. She was biting her lip in a way that made him think that the pain was the only thing keeping her from crying.

"I know it looks awful," he said. "But it wasn't like this when I was a kid. I promise. It was nice. It was clean."

"It was an orphanage."

The word echoed in his head like she'd shouted it down a well. There was no getting past this difference between them. Sara had grown up with two loving parents, a doting sister, and a stable, solidly middle-class life.

And Will had grown up here.

"Will?" she asked. "What just happened?"

He rubbed his chin. Why was he such an idiot? Why did he keep making mistakes with Sara that he'd never made with anyone else in his life? There was a reason he didn't talk about his childhood. People felt pity when they should've felt relief.

"Will?"

"I'll take you home. I'm sorry."

"Please don't be. This is your home. Was your home. It's where you grew up."

"It's a flophouse in the middle of a slum. We're probably going to get stabbed by a junkie as soon as we leave."

She laughed.

"It's not funny, Sara. It's dangerous here. Half the crime in the city happens—"

"I know where we are." She put her hands on either side of his face. "Thank you."

"For what? Making you need a tetanus shot?"

"For sharing part of your life with me." She gently kissed him on the lips. "Thank you."

Will stared into her eyes, wishing he could read her mind. He didn't understand Sara Linton. She was kind. She was honest. She wasn't storing up information to later use against him. She wasn't jabbing her thumb into open wounds. She wasn't anything like any woman he'd ever met in his life.

Sara kissed him again. She stroked his hair back over his ear. "Sweetheart, I know that look, and it's not going to happen here."

Will opened his mouth to respond, but stopped when he heard the sound of a car door slamming.

Sara jumped at the noise, her fingers digging into his arm.

"It's a busy street," Will told her, but he still went to the front of the house to investigate. Through the broken window at the end of the hallway, he saw a black Suburban parked at the curb. The glass was smoked black. The freshly washed exterior sparkled in the sun. The back end was lower than the front because of the large metal gun cabinet bolted into the rear of the SUV.

Will told Sara, "That's a G-ride." A government-issued vehicle. Amanda drove one exactly like it, so he shouldn't have been surprised to see her get out of the Suburban.

She was talking on her BlackBerry. A hammer was in her other hand. The claw was long and nasty. She swung it at her side as she walked toward the front door.

Sara asked, "What's she doing here?" She tried to look out the window, but Will pulled her back. "Why does she have a hammer?"

Will didn't answer—couldn't answer. There was no reason for Amanda to be here. No reason for her to call and ask Will where he was. No reason to tell him to report to the airport like she was giving a child a time-out in the corner.

Amanda's voice carried through the closed window as she talked on the phone. "That's unacceptable. I want the full team answering to me. No exceptions."

The front door opened. It creaked this time. Will heard footsteps across the floor.

Amanda made a disgusted noise. "This is my case, Mike. I'll work it how I see fit."

Sara whispered, "What is she—"

Will's expression must've stopped her. His jaw felt clamped shut. He was gripped by a sudden, inexplicable fury. He held up his hand, indicating Sara should stay there. Before she could argue, Will headed down the stairs, stepping carefully so the treads wouldn't creak. He was sweating again. The hornets in his gut had worked their way into his chest, trapping his breath.

Amanda tucked her BlackBerry in her back pocket. She gripped the hammer in her hand as she started down the basement stairs.

He said, "Amanda."

She spun around, grabbing the handrail for support. There was no mistaking the look on her face for anything but absolute shock. "What are you doing here?"

"Is the girl still missing?"

She didn't move from the top stair. She was obviously still too shocked to speak.

He repeated his question. "Is the girl still—"

"Yes."

"Then why are you here?"

"Go home, Will." He'd never heard anything like fear in her voice, but he could tell now that she was deathly afraid—not of Will, but of something else. "Just let me handle this."

"Handle what?"

She rested her hand on the doorknob, as if she wanted nothing more than to close him out. "Go home."

"Not until you tell me why you're alone in an abandoned building when there's an active case."

She raised an eyebrow. "I'm not actually alone, am I?"

"Tell me what's going on."

"I'm not—" Her words were cut off by a loud crack. Panic filled her eyes. Another crack came like a shotgun blast. Amanda started to fall. She clutched the doorknob. Will lunged to help, but he was too late. The door slammed closed as the stairs collapsed. The noise rumbled through the building like a charging freight train.

Then—nothing.

Will jerked open the door. The knob rattled at his feet. He stared down into absolute blackness. Uselessly, he flipped the light switch up and down.

"Amanda?" he called. His voice echoed back at him. "Amanda?"

"Will?" Sara was on the landing. She quickly took in what had happened. "Give me your phone."

Will tossed her the phone. He took off his jacket and holster and got down on the floor.

Sara said, "You are *not* going down there."

Will froze, startled by the order, the unfamiliar sharp tone of her voice.

"We're in a crack house, Will. There could be needles down there. Broken glass. It's too dangerous." She held up her finger as the phone was obviously answered on the other end. "This is Dr. Linton from the ER. I need a bus and rescue sent to Carver Street for an officer down."

Will provided, "Street number's 316." He sat on his knees and leaned his head into the basement as Sara rattled off the details. "Amanda?" He waited. No response. "Can you hear me?"

Sara ended the call. "They're on their way. Just stay there until—"

"Amanda?" Will glanced around the hallway, trying to put together a plan. Finally, he turned around and got down on his belly.

Sara pleaded, "Will, don't."

He elbowed back until his feet hung down into the basement.

"You're going to fall."

He edged back farther, expecting any moment for his feet to hit solid ground.

"There are broken pieces of wood down there. You could shatter your ankle. You could land on Amanda."

Will gripped the edge of the doorjambs with his fingers, praying that his arms wouldn't give. Which they eventually did. He dropped straight down like the blade on a guillotine.

"Will?" Sara was in the open doorway. She got down on her knees. "Are you all right?"

Pieces of wood poked into his back like sharp fingers. Sawdust filled the air. Will's nose had banged into his knee so hard that pinpoints of light exploded in front of his eyes. He touched the side of his ankle. A nail had scraped across the bone. His teeth ached at the memory.

"Will?" Sara's tone rose in alarm. "Will?"

"I'm all right." He felt his ankle squick as he moved. Blood pooled into the heel of his shoe. He tried to make light of the situation. "Looks like I was right about needing that tetanus shot."

She mumbled a shocking expletive.

Will tried to stand, but his feet couldn't find purchase. He blindly reached out, thinking Amanda was close by. He got on his knees, leaning out farther, and finally was rewarded with a foot. Her shoe was missing. Her pantyhose were torn.

"Amanda?" Carefully, Will picked his way across the shards of wood and broken nails. He put his hand on her shin, then her thigh. He gently felt along until he found her arm folded over her stomach.

Amanda moaned.

Will's stomach roiled as his fingers followed the unnatural angle of her wrist. "Amanda?" he repeated.

She moaned again. Will knew she'd have a Maglite in the Suburban. He dug his fingers into the front pockets of her jeans, trying to find her keys. He could send Sara out to the car. She would have to search for the flashlight. He would tell her it was in the glove compartment or one of the locked drawers. She would spend several minutes looking for the light, which was exactly what Will needed.

"Amanda?" He checked her back pockets. The tips of his fingers brushed along the broken plastic case on her BlackBerry.

Suddenly, Amanda's good hand clamped around his wrist. She asked, "Where's My-kel?"

Will stopped searching for the keys. "Amanda? It's Will. Will Trent."

Her tone was terse. "I know who you are, Wilbur."

Will felt his body go rigid. Only Angie called him Wilbur. It was the name on his birth certificate.

Sara asked, "Is she okay?"

Will had to swallow before he could speak. "I think her wrist is broken."

"How's her respiration?"

He listened for the cadence of her breath, but all he could hear was his own blood pounding in his ears. Why was Amanda here? She should be out looking for the missing girl. She should be leading the team. She shouldn't be here. In this basement. With a hammer.

"Will?" Sara's tone was softer now. She was worried about him.

He asked, "How long before the ambulance gets here?"

"Not much longer. Are you sure you're all right?"

"I'm fine." Will put his hand on Amanda's foot again. He could feel a steady pulse near her ankle. He'd worked for this woman most of his career but still knew very little about her. She lived in a condo in the heart of Buckhead. She had been on the job longer than he had been alive, which put her age in the mid-sixties. She kept her salt-and-pepper hair coiffed in the shape of a football helmet and wore pantyhose with starched blue jeans. She had a sharp tongue, more degrees than a college professor, and she knew that his name was Wilbur even though he'd had it legally changed when he entered college and every piece of paper the GBI had on file listed his legal name as William Trent.

He cleared his throat again so that he could ask Sara, "Is there anything I should be doing?"

"No, just stay where you are." Sara used a raised, clear tone Will thought of as her doctor's voice. "Amanda. This is Dr. Linton. Can you tell me today's date?"

She groaned out a pained breath. "I told Edna to shore up those steps a million times."

Will sat back on his heels. Something sharp pressed against his knee. He felt blood sliding across his ankle, dripping through his sock. His heart was pounding so hard that he was sure Sara could hear it.

"Will," Amanda mumbled. "What time is it?"

Will couldn't answer her. His mouth felt wired shut.

Sara took over, saying, "It's five-thirty."

"In the evening," Amanda said, not a question. "We're at the children's home. I fell down the basement stairs." She lay there taking deep breaths of the pungent air. "Dr. Linton, am I going to live?"

"I'd be very surprised if you didn't."

"Well, I suppose that's as much as I can ask for right now. Did I lose consciousness?"

"Yes," Sara answered. "For about two minutes."

Amanda spoke more to herself. "I don't know what that means. Are you touching my foot?"

Will pulled away his hand.

"I can move my toes." Amanda sounded relieved. "My head feels like it's been cracked open." He heard movement, the rustling of clothes. "No, nothing sticking out. No blood. No soft spots. God, my shoulder hurts."

Will tasted blood. His nose was bleeding. He used the back of his hand to wipe his mouth.

Amanda let out another heavy sigh. "I'll tell you what, Will. You get past a certain age and a broken bone or a cracked head is no laughing matter. It's with you for the rest of your life. What's left of the rest of your life."

She was quiet for a few seconds. From the sound of it, she was trying to keep her breathing steady. Despite the fact that he was obviously not going to answer, she told Will, "When I joined the Atlanta Police Department, there was a whole division assigned to checking our appearance. The Inspection Division. Six full-duty officers. I'm not making that up."

Will glanced up at Sara. She shrugged.

"They would show up during roll call, and if you didn't fix what they told you to fix, you were suspended without pay."

He put his hand to his watch, wishing he could feel the second hand ticking by. Grady Hospital was only a few blocks away. There was no reason for the ambulance to be taking so long. They knew Amanda was a cop. They knew she needed help.

Amanda said, "I remember the first time I rolled up on a signal forty-five. Some jackass had a CB radio stolen out of his car. We were always getting forty-fives on CB radios. They had those big antennas pointing like arrows off their back bumpers."

Again, Will glanced up at Sara. She made a circling motion, indicating he should keep Amanda talking.

Will's throat was too tight. He couldn't force out the words, couldn't pretend that they were all just a bunch of friends who'd had a bad day.

Amanda didn't seem to need encouragement. She chuckled under her breath. "They laughed at me. They laughed at me when I got there. They laughed at me when I took the report. They laughed at me when I left. No one thought women should be in uniform. The station would get calls every week—someone reporting that a woman had stolen a squad car. They couldn't believe we were on the job."

Sara said, "I think they're here," just as Will heard the distant wail of a siren. "I'll go wave them down."

Will waited until Sara's footsteps were on the front porch. It took everything in him not to grab Amanda by the shoulders and shake her. "Why are you here?"

"Is Sara gone?"

"Why are you here?"

Amanda's tone turned uncharacteristically gentle. "I have to tell you something."

"I don't care," he shot back. "How did you know—"

"Shut up and listen," she hissed. "Are you listening?"

Will felt the dread come flooding back. The siren was louder. The ambulance braked hard in front of the house.

"Are you listening?"

Will found himself speechless again.

"It's about your father."

She said more, but Will's ears felt muffled, as if he was listening to her voice underwater. As a kid, Will had ruined the earpiece to his transistor radio that way, putting the bud in his ear, dunking his head in the bathtub, thinking that would be a cool new way to hear music. It had been in this very house. Two floors up in the boys' bathroom. He was lucky he hadn't electrocuted himself.

There was a loud thunk overhead as paramedics shoved open the front door. Heavy footsteps banged across the floor. The bright beam of a Maglite suddenly filled the basement. Will blinked in the glare. He felt dizzy. His lungs ached for breath.

Amanda's words came rushing back to him the same way sound had come back to his ears when he'd grabbed the sides of the tub and thrust his head above water.

"Listen to me," she'd ordered.

But he didn't want to. He didn't want to know what she had to say.

The parole board had met. They had let Will's father out of prison.

three

October 15, 1974

LUCY BENNETT

Lucy had lost track of time once the symptoms had subsided. She knew it took heroin three days to fully leave your bloodstream. She knew that the sweats and sickness lasted a week or more, depending on how far gone you were. The stomach cramps. The throbbing pain in your legs. The alternating constipation and diarrhea. The bright red blood from your lungs giving up the Drano or baby formula or whatever was used to cut down the Boy.

People had died trying to leave H on their own. The drug was vengeful. It owned you. It clawed into your skin and wouldn't let go. Lucy had seen its castoffs laid out in back rooms and vacant parking lots. Their flesh desiccated. Fingers and toes curled. Their nails and hair kept growing. They looked like mummified witches.

Weeks? Months? Years?

The stifling August heat had been broken by what could only be fall temperatures. Cool mornings. Cold nights. Was winter coming? Was it still 1974, or had she missed Thanksgiving, Christmas, her birthday?

Sands through the hourglass.

Did it really matter anymore?

Every day, Lucy wished that she was dead. The heroin was gone, but not a second went by when she wasn't thinking about that high. The transcendence. The obliteration. The numbing of her mind. The ecstasy of the needle hitting vein. The rush of fire burning through her senses. Those first few days, Lucy could still taste the H in her vomit. She'd tried to eat it, but the man had forced her to stop.

The man.

The monster.

Who would do something like this? It defied logic. There was no pattern in Lucy's life to explain why this was happening. As bad as some of her johns were, they always let her go. Once they got what they wanted, they tossed her back into the street. They didn't want to see her again. They hated the sight of her. They kicked her if she didn't move fast enough. They shoved her out of their cars and sped away.

But not him. Not this man. Not this devil.

Lucy wanted him to fuck her. She wanted him to beat her. She wanted him to do anything but the loathsome routine she had to endure every day. The way he brushed her hair and teeth. The way he bathed her. The chaste way he used the rag to wash between her legs. The gentle pats of the towel as he dried her. The look of pity every time her eyes opened and closed. And the praying. The constant praying.

"Wash away your sins. Wash away your sins." It was his mantra. He said nothing directly to her. He only spoke to God, as if He would listen to an animal like this man. Lucy asked why—why her? Why this? She screamed at him. She begged him. She offered him anything, and all he said was, "Wash away your sins."

Lucy had grown up with prayer. Over the years, she had often found solace in religion. The smell of a burning candle or the taste of wine could send her back to the church pew, where she happily sat between her mother and father. Her brother, Henry, would scribble crude drawings on the bulletin, bored nearly to death, but Lucy loved listening to the preacher extol the vast rewards of a godly life. On the streets, it gave her comfort to think about those sermons from long ago. Even as a sinner, she was not completely without salvation. The crucifixion meant nothing if not to redeem Lucy Bennett's soul.

But not like this. Never like this. Not the soap and water. Not the blood and wine. Not the needle and thread.

There was penance, and then there was torture.

four

July 7, 1975

MONDAY

Amanda Wagner let out a long sigh of relief as she drove out of her father's Ansley Park neighborhood. Duke had been in rare form this morning. He'd begun a litany of complaints the moment Amanda walked through his kitchen door and not stopped until she was waving goodbye from behind the wheel of her car. Feckless veterans looking for handouts. Gas prices through the roof. New York City expecting the rest of the country to bail them out. There was not one story in the morning paper about which Duke did not share his opinion. By the time he'd started listing the seemingly endless faults of the newly organized Atlanta Police Department, Amanda was only half listening, nodding occasionally to keep his temper from turning in the wrong direction.

She cooked his breakfast. She kept his coffee mug filled. She emptied his ashtrays. She laid out a shirt and tie on his bed. She wrote down directions for thawing the roast so she could fix his supper after work. Meanwhile, the only thing that made it all bearable was thinking about her tiny studio apartment on Peachtree Street.

The place was less than five minutes away from her father's house, but it might as well be on the moon. Stuck between the library and the hippie compound along Fourteenth Street, the apartment was one of six units in an old Victorian mansion. Duke had taken one look at the space and snorted that he'd had better accommodations on Midway during the war. None of the windows would properly close. The freezer wasn't cold enough to make ice. The kitchen table had to be moved before the oven door could be opened. The toilet lid scraped the side of the bathtub.

It was love at first sight.

Amanda was twenty-five years old. She was going to college. She had a good job. After years of begging, she'd finally managed by some miracle to persuade her father to let her move out. She wasn't exactly Mary Richards, but at least she wouldn't pass for Edith Bunker anymore.

She slowed her car and took a right turn onto Highland Avenue, then another right into the strip mall behind the pharmacy. The summer heat was almost suffocating, though it was only quarter till eight in the morning. Steam misted from the asphalt as she pulled into a parking space at the far end of the lot. Her hands were sweating so badly that she could barely grip the steering wheel. Her pantyhose were cutting into her waist. The back of her shirt stuck to the seat. There was a throbbing ache in her neck that was working its way up to her temples.

Still, Amanda rolled down her shirtsleeves and buttoned the tight cuffs at her wrists. She dragged her purse off the passenger's seat, thinking the bag got heavier every time she lifted it. She reminded herself that it was better than what she was wearing on patrol this time last year. Undergarments. Pantyhose. Black socks. Navy-colored, polyester-blend pants. A man's cotton shirt that was so big the breast pockets tucked below her waist. Underbelt. Metal hooks. Outer belt. Holster. Gun. Radio. Shoulder mic. Kel-Lite. Handcuffs. Nightstick. Key holder.

It was no wonder the patrolwomen of the Atlanta police force had bladders the size of watermelons. It took ten minutes to remove all the equipment from your waist before you could go to the bathroom—and that was assuming you could sit down without your back going into spasms. The Kel-Lite alone, with its four D-cell batteries and eighteen-inch-long shaft, weighed in at just under eight pounds.

Amanda felt every ounce of the weight as she hefted her purse onto her shoulder and got out of the car. Same equipment, but now that she was a plainclothes officer it was in a leather bag instead of on her hips. It had to be called progress.

Her father had been in charge of Zone 1 when Amanda joined the force. For nearly twenty years, Captain Duke Wagner had run the unit with an iron fist, right up until Reginald Eaves, Atlanta's first black public safety commissioner, fired most of the senior white officers and replaced them with blacks. The collective outrage had nearly toppled the force. That previous chief John Inman had done basically the same thing in reverse seemed to be a fact lost in everyone's collective memory. The good ol' boy network was fine so long as you were one of the lucky few who were dialed in.

Consequently, Duke and his ilk were suing the city for their old jobs back. Maynard Jackson, the city's first black mayor, was backing his man. No one knew how it would end, though to hear Duke talk, it was just a matter of time before the city capitulated. No matter their color, politicians needed votes, and voters wanted to feel safe. Which explained why the police force gripped the city like a devouring octopus, its tentacles spreading in every direction.

Six patrol zones stretched from the impoverished Southside to the more affluent northern neighborhoods. Spotted within these zones were so-called "Model Cities," precincts that served the more violent sections of the downtown corridor. There were small pockets of wealth inside Ansley Park, Piedmont Heights, and Buckhead, but a good many of the city's inhabitants lived in slums, from Grady Homes to Techwood to the city's most notorious housing project, Perry Homes. This Westside ghetto was so dangerous it warranted its own police force. It was the sort of job returning vets clamored for, more like a war zone than a neighborhood.

The plainclothes and detective units were posted across the zones. There were twelve divisions in all, from vice control to special investigations. Sex crimes was one of the few divisions that allowed women in any numbers. Amanda doubted very seriously her father would've let her apply for the unit had he still been on the force when she submitted her application. She cringed to think what would happen if Duke won his lawsuit and got reinstated. He'd likely have her back in uniform performing crossing-guard duties in front of Morningside Elementary.

But that was a long-term problem, and Amanda's day—if it was like any other—would be filled with short-term problems. The primary issue each morning was with whom she would be partnered.

The federal Law Enforcement Assistance Association grant that had created the Atlanta police sex crimes division required all teams to be comprised of three-officer units that were racially and sexually integrated. These rules were seldom followed, because white women could not ride alone with black men, black women—at least the ones who wanted to keep their reputations—did not want to ride with black men, and none of the blacks wanted to ride with any man who was white. Every day was a battle just to figure out who was going to work with whom, which was ludicrous considering that most of them changed partners once they were out on the streets anyway.

Still, there were often heated arguments about assignments. Much posturing was to be found. Names were called. Occasionally fists were employed. In fact, the only thing that the men of the sex crimes unit could agree upon as far as assignments were concerned was that none of them wanted to be stuck with women.

At least, not unless they were pretty.

The problem trickled down to other divisions as well. Every morning, Commissioner Reginald Eaves's daily bulletin was read at the beginning of roll call. Reggie was always transferring people around to fill whatever federal quota was being forced down their throats that day. No officer knew where he or she would land when they showed up for work. It could be the middle of Perry Homes or the living hell that was the Atlanta airport. Just last year, a woman had been assigned to SWAT for a week, which would've been a disaster if she'd actually had to do anything.

Amanda had always been on day watch, probably because her father wanted it that way. No one seemed to notice or care that she continued with the schedule even as Duke sued the city. Day watch, the easiest rotation, was from eight to four. Evening watch was four to midnight, and morning watch, which was the most dangerous, ran from midnight until eight in the morning.

The patrol officers worked roughly the same schedules as the detective and plainclothes divisions, less an hour on either side, which followed the old 7-3-11 railroad schedule. The thinking was that one would hand over to the other. This seldom happened. Most of the time when Amanda got into work, she'd run into a couple of suspects sporting black eyes or bloody bandages on their heads. They were generally handcuffed to the benches by the front door and no one could say exactly how they'd gotten there or with what they'd been charged. Depending on how a uniformed officer's arrests were looking that month, some of the prisoners were freed, then immediately arrested again for loitering.

As with most zone headquarters, Zone 1 was housed in a dilapidated storefront that looked like the sort of place the police should be raiding, not milling around inside of drinking coffee and trading war stories about yesterday's arrests. Located behind the Plaza Pharmacy and a theater specializing in pornographic films, the zone headquarters had been unceremoniously relocated to this location when it was discovered the previous HQ was located directly above a sinkhole. *The Atlanta Constitution* had had a field day with that one.

There were only three rooms in the building. The largest was the squad room, which had the sergeant's office cordoned off by a glass partition. The captain's office was far nicer, meaning that the windows actually opened and closed. Before the Fourth of July holiday, someone had broken the plate-glass window in front of the squad room in order to let in fresh air. No one had bothered to fix it, probably because they knew it would just be broken again.

The third room was the toilet, but it was shared, and it had been ensured that no woman would ever be able to sit down on the seat. The one time Amanda had walked into the bathroom, she'd ended up dry heaving behind the Plaza Theater while the grunts and moans of *Winnie Bango* reverberated through the cinder-block wall.

"Mornin', ma'am." One of the patrolmen tipped his hat as Amanda walked by.

She nodded in return, making her way past a cluster of familiar white Atlanta Police cruisers as she headed for the squad entrance. The stench of winos permeated the air, though the benches were absent any handcuffed vagrants. A veil of cigarette smoke hugged the stained drop ceiling. Every surface had a layer of dust, even the long cafeteria-style tables set out in crooked lines across the room. The podium in front was empty. Amanda looked at the clock. She had ten minutes to spare before morning roll call.

Vanessa Livingston was sitting in the back of the squad room going over paperwork. She was wearing gray slacks and the same ugly, black men's shoes they'd all been forced to wear when they were in uniform. Her light blue shirt was short-sleeved and she wore her dark hair in a pageboy that curved out widely at the sides.

Amanda had patrolled with Vanessa a few times back when they were both in uniform. She was a reliable partner, but she could be a little hippie-dippie and there were rumors going around that she was trim—code for women who made themselves sexually available to police officers. Amanda didn't have a choice but to sit by her. As usual, the squad room was divided into four quadrants. White and black either side, women in back, men in the front.

Amanda kept her gaze straight ahead as she walked through a cluster of uniformed men. They all waited until the last minute to let her pass. A group in the corner were working deadbolt locks. There were daily competitions to see who could pick a lock the fastest. A few officers were trading hot-loaded ammunition. Over the last two years, fourteen Atlanta cops had been shot dead. A faster bullet in your gun was not a bad idea.

Amanda dropped her purse onto the table as she sat down. "How are you?"

"I'm very well." Vanessa's voice was cheerful, as usual. "I lucked up with Inspection Division this morning."

"They've already left?"

Vanessa nodded. Amanda immediately unbuttoned her cuffs and rolled up her sleeves. The fresh air on her arms was almost enough to make her swoon.

Amanda asked, "It wasn't Geary?" There was no way Sergeant Mike Geary would've given Vanessa a pass. He didn't think women should be on the job, and he had the power to do something about it. For some reason, he particularly had it in for Amanda. She was one more citation away from a daylong suspension. She couldn't even think what she'd do for rent if that happened.

"Geary's out today." Vanessa stacked her reports together. "It was Sandra Phillips, the black chick keeps her head shaved like a man?"

"I have a class with her," Amanda said. Most everyone she knew was taking night courses at Georgia State. The federal government paid tuition and the city was forced to bump up your pay if you got a degree. This time next year, Amanda would be pulling in almost twelve thousand dollars.

Vanessa asked, "You have a good Fourth?"

"I took a few extra shifts," Amanda admitted. She'd volunteered for no other reason than she couldn't face a whole day of her father rehashing every story he'd read in the newspapers. Thank goodness the paper only came twice a day or he'd never sleep. "What about you?"

"Drank so much I crashed my car into a telephone pole."

"Is the car all right?"

"Fender's smashed, but it still drives." Vanessa made her voice low. "You heard about Oglethorpe?"

Lars Oglethorpe was one of Duke's friends. They'd both been fired the same day. "What about him?"

"State supreme court ruled in his favor. Full back pay and benefits. Reinstated rank. He's been assigned to his old uniformed squad. I bet Reggie had a cow when he heard."

Amanda didn't have time to answer. There was a series of masculine cheers as Rick Landry and Butch Bonnie walked into the squad. As usual, the homicide detectives were up against the clock. Roll call was scheduled to start in two minutes. Amanda reached into her purse and pulled out a stack of typed reports.

"You're a doll." Butch took the reports and tossed his notebook on the table in front of Amanda. "Hope you can read it."

She looked at his scrawl across the first page and frowned. "I swear sometimes you make this illegible on purpose."

"Gimme a call, sweetheart. Day or night." He gave her a wink as he followed Landry to the front of the room. "Night's preferable."

There were chuckles around the room, which Amanda pretended to ignore as she flipped through Butch's notes. The words got easier to read as she paged along. Butch and Rick worked homicide division. There was a job Amanda never wanted. Because she typed Butch's reports, she couldn't help but absorb some of the details. They had to tell relatives that their family members were murdered. They had to look at dead people and watch autopsies. Just reading about these things turned Amanda's stomach. There really were some jobs that only men could do.

Vanessa asked, "Did you hear we've got a new sergeant?"

Amanda waited expectantly.

"He's one of Reggie's boys."

Amanda suppressed a groan. One of Reginald Eaves's seemingly better ideas was to finally institute a written exam for promotions. Amanda had actually been foolish enough to believe she had a chance. When none of the black officers could pass the written exam, Eaves had thrown out the results and instituted an oral exam. Predictably, very few white officers were able to pass the orals. None of them had been women.

Vanessa said, "I hear he's from up North. Sounds like Bill Cosby."

They both turned around, trying to see into the sergeant's office. There were filing cabinets stacked in front of the glass partition. The door was open, but all Amanda could see was another filing cabinet and the edge of a wooden desk. A glass ashtray was on the leather blotter. A black hand reached over and tapped a cigarette against the glass. The fingers were slim, almost delicate. The nails were trimmed in a straight, blunt line.

Amanda turned back around. She pretended to read Butch's notes, but her mind wouldn't focus. Maybe it was the heat. Or maybe it was because she was sitting next to a mynah bird.

Vanessa said, "I wonder where Evelyn is?"

Amanda shrugged, still staring at the notes.

"I can't believe she came back," Vanessa continued. "She's gotta be trippin'."

Despite her best intentions, Amanda felt herself getting sucked back in. "It's been almost two years," she realized. Duke had been off the job eleven months. Evelyn had left to have her baby the year before that. The woman had just made plainclothes division. Everyone assumed that was the end of her working life.

Vanessa said, "If I had a husband and a kid, no way I'd show up at this dump every day. It'd be 'Good night, John-Boy' for me."

"Maybe she has to." Amanda kept her voice low so no one could hear her gossiping. "For the money."

"Her husband makes plenty of dough. He's sold insurance to half the force." Vanessa snorted a laugh. "That's probably the only reason she came back—to help him sell policies." Her teasing tone dropped. "You really should talk to him, though. He's got cheaper rates than Benowitz. Plus, you wouldn't be giving your money to a Jew."

"I'll ask Evelyn," Amanda said, though she liked Nathan Benowitz. Her Plymouth belonged to the city, but they all had to pay for their own car insurance. Benowitz had always been nice to Amanda.

"Shh," Vanessa hushed, though Amanda hadn't said anything. "He's coming."

The assembled officers quieted down as the new sergeant walked into the room. He was wearing their winter colors, dark navy pants and a matching long-sleeved shirt. He was very light skinned. He kept his hair shaved in a square military cut. Unlike everyone else, there was no visible sweat on the man's brow.

Amanda watched as he navigated the invisible line down the center of the squad where none of the tables touched. The new sergeant looked to be around thirty years old. He was fit and lean, his body more like a teenager's than a grown man's, but he still had to turn sideways to pass between the tables. Amanda noticed that the gap was tighter than usual. Pettiness was generally the only thing that compelled them all to work together. The black cops would hate the new man because he was from the North. The whites would hate him because he was one of Reggie's boys.

He stacked his papers against the podium, cleared his throat, and said in a surprisingly deep baritone, "I'm Sergeant Luther Hodge." He glanced around the room as if he expected someone to challenge him. When no one spoke, he continued, "I'll read the daily briefing before roll call, since there are a considerable number of transfers."

A groan went around the room, but all Amanda could think was how refreshing it was that someone had actually figured out it was better to announce transfers before taking roll.

Hodge read through the names. Vanessa was right that he sounded like Bill Cosby. He spoke carefully if not slowly. Every word was fully enunciated. The uniformed men in the front rows stared openly, as if they were watching a dog walk on its hind legs. Black or white, they were all straight off the farm or freshly discharged from military service. The majority of them spoke in the same heavy dialect that Amanda's country cousins used. She couldn't help staring at Hodge herself.

He finished reading out the lengthy transfers, then cleared his throat again. "Roll will be called in teams. Some of you will have to wait for your partners to come from other divisions. Please check with me to make certain that your partner is accounted for before you go out into the streets."

As if on cue, Evelyn Mitchell rushed into the squad room, glancing around with an almost panicked look in her eyes. Amanda was still in uniform when Evelyn got promoted to sex crimes, but the few times she'd seen her, the woman was always stylishly dressed. Today, she was carrying a large suede purse with an Indian pattern on the front and tassels hanging down from the wide gusset. She wore a navy skirt with a yellow blouse. Her blonde hair was cut to shoulder length and very flattering, reminiscent of the style worn by Angie Dickinson. Obviously, Amanda wasn't the only one thinking this. Butch Bonnie called out, "Hey, Pepper Anderson, you can cuff me anytime."

The men laughed in unison.

"I'm sorry I'm late," Evelyn told the new sergeant. "It won't happen again." She spied Amanda and Vanessa and headed toward the back table. Her heels made a clicking sound that echoed through the space.

Hodge stopped her. "I didn't catch your name, Detective."

His words seemed to suck all the air from the room. Heads swiveled around to Evelyn, who stood frozen beside Amanda. The dread coming off of her was as palpable as the heat.

Hodge cleared his throat again. "Am I missing something, Officer? I assume you're a detective since you're not in a patrolman's uniform?"

Evelyn opened her mouth, but it was Rick Landry who answered. "She's plainclothes, not detective."

Hodge persisted. "I'm not sure I understand the difference."

Landry jabbed his thumb toward the back of the room. The cigarette in his mouth bobbed as he spoke. "Well, ya see those two tits under her shirt?"

The room erupted in laughter. Evelyn clutched her purse to her chest, but she laughed along with them. Amanda laughed, too. The sound rattled in her throat like a drain.

Hodge waited for the chatter to die down. He asked Evelyn, "What's your name, Officer?"

"Mitchell," she provided, sinking down into the chair beside Amanda. "Mrs. Evelyn Mitchell."

"I suggest you avoid tardiness in the future, Mrs. Mitchell." He looked down at the roll sheet and checked off her name. "You'll be with Miss Livingston today." He went to the next name. "Miss Wagner, we'll put you with Detective Peterson, who'll be coming from—" Someone gave a loud wolf whistle. Hodge talked over it. "—from Zone Two."

Evelyn turned to Amanda and rolled her eyes. Kyle Peterson was a mess. When he wasn't trying to put his hand up your skirt, he was sleeping one off in the back of the car.

Vanessa leaned over and whispered to Evelyn, "I like your new cut. It's very chic."

"Thanks." She pulled at the back of her hair as if she wished she could make it longer. She asked Amanda, "Did you hear Oglethorpe got reinstated?"

"They gave him his old squad back," Vanessa supplied. "I wonder what that means for us?"

"Probably nothing at all," Evelyn murmured.

They all turned their attention back to the front of the room. There was a white man standing on the periphery, just inside the open doorway. He was around Amanda's age and wearing a sharp, powder blue three-piece suit. His sandy blond hair was long in the back, his sideburns untrimmed. His arms were crossed impatiently over his chest. The round paunch of his stomach stuck out below.

"Brass?" Vanessa guessed.

Evelyn shook her head. "Too well dressed."

"Lawyer," Amanda told them. She'd been to the downtown office of her father's lawyer enough times to know what they looked like. The nice suit was a giveaway, but the arrogant tilt to his chin was the only clue she needed.

"Detectives Landry and—" Luther Hodge seemed to realize no

one was paying attention to him anymore. He looked up from the
roll sheet and stared at the visitor for a few seconds before saying,
"Mr. Treadwell, we can talk in my office." He told the squad, "I'll be
a few minutes. If someone could take over?"

Butch jumped up. "I'll handle it."

"Thank you, Detective." Hodge seemed to miss the wary expres-
sions around the room. Putting Butch in charge of the schedule was
like putting a fox in charge of the henhouse. He would change the
assignments into his own version of *The Dating Game*.

Hodge made his way back to the rear of the room, angling his
lanky frame through the narrow dividing line. The lawyer, Treadwell,
followed along the outside wall. He lit a cigarette as he walked into
the office and shut the door.

Evelyn asked, "Wonder what that's about?"

"Never mind them," Vanessa said. "Why on earth did you come
back?"

"I like it here."

Vanessa pulled a face. "Come on, kid. The truth."

"The truth is really boring. Let's wait to see what the rumors say."
Evelyn smiled, then unzipped her purse and searched around inside.

Vanessa looked to Amanda for an explanation, but she could only
shake her head.

"Yassuh, yassuh," someone said.

Amanda saw a group of black patrolmen had taken it upon themselves to narrate the goings-on in Hodge's office. Amanda glanced at
Evelyn, then Vanessa. They all turned around for the full effect.

Behind the glass partition, Treadwell's mouth moved, and one of
the black cops said in a pompous voice, "Now, see here, boy, my
taxes pay your salary."

Amanda stifled a laugh. She heard this same phrase almost every
day—as if Amanda's taxes didn't pay just as much of her salary as the
next person's.

Hodge was looking down at his desk. There was a meekness to
the slump in his shoulders as his mouth moved. "Yassuh," the first
cop supplied. "I's'a gone look into it fo ya, suh. Yes indeedy-do."

Treadwell jabbed a finger at Hodge. The second cop grumbled, "This city is a mess, I say. What's the world coming to? The monkeys are running the zoo!"

Hodge nodded, his eyes still trained downward. The first cop offered, "Yassuh, it sho do be a mess. Cain't even eat my cone-bread without hearing 'bout thems po' white women what's gettin' harassed by Negro men."

Amanda chewed her bottom lip. There were a few nervous titters.

Treadwell's hand dropped. The second cop said, "I say, you damn niggers act like you own the place!"

No one laughed at that, not even the black officers. The joke had gone too far.

When Treadwell threw open the office door and stormed out, the room remained stiflingly silent.

Luther Hodge was a study in contained fury as he walked to the open door. He pointed at Evelyn. "You." His finger jabbed in Amanda and Vanessa's general direction. "And you. In my office."

Vanessa stiffened in her chair. Amanda put her hand to her chest. "Me or—"

"Do you women understand orders? In my office." He told Butch, "Continue roll call, Detective Bonnie. I shouldn't have to tell you twice."

Evelyn clutched her purse to her chest as she stood. The back of Amanda's legs felt cool as she rose to follow. She turned to Vanessa, who looked both guilty and enormously relieved. Evelyn was standing in front of Hodge's desk when Amanda joined her. He sat in his chair and started writing on a piece of paper.

Amanda turned to shut the door, but Hodge said, "Leave it open."

If Amanda thought she'd been sweating before, it was nothing compared to how she felt now. Evelyn was obviously feeling it, too. She nervously pulled at the back of her hair. The thin silver of her wedding ring caught the light from the overhead fluorescents. Butch Bonnie's dull monotone called out team assignments in the other room. Amanda knew that even with the door closed, Luther Hodge had heard the black officers making fun of him.

Hodge put down his pen. He sat back in his chair and looked at first Evelyn, then Amanda. "You two are on the sex crimes unit."

They both nodded, though he hadn't asked a question.

"There's been a signal forty-nine reported at this address." A rape. Hodge held out the sheet of paper. There was a moment's hesitation before Evelyn took it.

She looked down at the page. "This is in Techwood." The ghetto.

"That's correct," Hodge answered. "Take statements. Determine whether or not a crime has been committed. Make an arrest if necessary."

Evelyn glanced at Amanda. They were obviously wondering the same thing: what did this have to do with the lawyer who'd just been in here?

"Do you need directions?" Hodge asked, though, again, it wasn't really a question. "I assume you ladies know your way around the city? Should I have one of the squad cars provide you with an escort? Is that how this works?"

"No," Evelyn said. Hodge stared at her until she added, "Sir."

"Dismissed." He opened a file and began reading it.

Amanda looked to Evelyn, who nodded toward the door. They both edged out, not quite sure what had just happened. Roll call was finished. The squad room was empty but for a few stragglers who were waiting for their newly transferred partners to arrive. Vanessa was gone, too. Probably with Peterson. She would certainly enjoy the assignment more than Amanda.

"Can we take your car?" Evelyn asked. "I'm in the station wagon today and it's packed full."

"Sure." Amanda followed her into the parking lot. Evelyn wasn't lying. Boxes were crammed into every available space in her red Ford Falcon.

"Bill's mother moved in down the street this weekend. She's going to help take care of the baby while I'm at work."

Amanda climbed into her Plymouth. She didn't want to pry into Evelyn's private life, but the arrangement struck her as odd.

"Don't get me wrong," Evelyn said, settling into the passenger's seat. "I love Zeke and it was great spending this last year and a half with him, but I swear to God, one more day being stuck at home with a kid, and I'd end up swallowing a bucket of Valium."

Amanda had been about to put her key in the ignition, but she stopped. She turned to Evelyn. Most everything she knew about the woman had been filtered through her father. She was beautiful, which Duke Wagner didn't view as an asset for someone in uniform. "Opinionated" was the word that came up most often, with "pushy" serving a close second.

Amanda asked, "Your husband was okay with you working again?"

"He came around to it." She unzipped her purse and pulled out an Atlanta city map. "Do you know Techwood?"

"No. I've been to Grady Homes a few times." Amanda didn't mention that she mostly took calls from North Atlanta, where the victims were white and generally had mothers who offered sweet tea and talked about quickly putting this ordeal behind them. "How about you?"

"Somewhat. Your dad sent me there a few times."

Amanda pumped the gas as she turned the key. The engine caught on the second try. She kept her mouth closed as she backed out of the parking lot. Evelyn had been on patrol for most of her tenure under Duke Wagner. Her plainclothes promotion had been something he didn't agree with, but the winds were shifting by then and he had lost the battle. Amanda could easily see her father sending Evelyn out to the projects to teach her a lesson.

"Let's try to figure this out." Evelyn unfolded the map and spread it out on her lap. She traced her finger down and across to the area near Georgia Tech. The projects of Techwood were incongruous with the setting of one of the state's top technological universities, but the city was running out of places to house the poor. Clark Howell Homes, University Homes, Bowen Homes, Grady Homes, Perry Homes, Bankhead Courts, Thomasville Heights—they all had long waiting lists, despite the fact that they were effectively slums.

Not that any of them had started out that way. In the 1930s, the

city had built the Techwood apartment buildings on the site of a former shantytown called Tanyard Bottom. It was the first public housing of its kind in the United States. All the buildings had electricity
and running water. There was a school on site, a library and laundry
facilities. President Roosevelt had been at the opening ceremonies. It
had taken less than ten years for Techwood to revert back to its original shantytown state. Duke Wagner often said that desegregation
was the final nail in Techwood's coffin. No matter what the case,
Georgia Tech spent thousands of dollars a year hiring private security to keep students safe from their neighbors. The area was one of
the most dangerous in the city.

"Okeydokey." Evelyn folded the map, saying, "Get us to Techwood Drive and I can tell you where to go from there."

"The buildings don't have numbers." This was a problem not just
limited to the projects. When Amanda was in uniform, the first half
hour of most of her calls was wasted searching for the correct address.

"Don't worry," Evelyn said. "I've figured out their system."

Amanda made her way up Ponce de Leon Avenue, past old Spiller
Field where the Crackers used to play. The stadium had been torn
down to build a shopping mall, but the magnolia tree that had been
in center field was still there. She cut through a side alley by the Sears
building to get to North Avenue. Both Amanda and Evelyn rolled up
their windows as they approached Buttermilk Bottom. The shanties
had been torn down a decade ago, but no one had bothered to do
anything about the sewage problem. A sour smell filled Amanda's
nostrils. She had to breathe through her mouth for the next five
blocks. Finally, they were able to roll down the windows again.

"So," Evelyn said. "How's your father's case going?"

This was the second time she'd asked about it, which made
Amanda wary. "He doesn't really talk about it with me."

"That's good news about Oglethorpe, right? Good news for your
father?"

"I expect it is." Amanda stopped at a red light.

"What do you think this Techwood forty-nine has to do with Treadwell showing up?"

Amanda had been too flustered before to consider the question, but now she said, "Perhaps he was reporting a rape on behalf of a client."

"Lawyers in hundred-dollar suits don't have clients at Techwood." Evelyn rested her head against her hand. "Treadwell shows up bossing Hodge around. Hodge calls us in and bosses us around. There has to be a connection. Don't you think?"

Amanda shook her head. "I have no idea."

"He looked young, right? He must've just gotten out of school. His daddy's firm really got behind the mayor's election bid."

"Maynard Jackson?" Amanda asked. She hadn't really thought about white people supporting the city's first black mayor, but then, Atlanta's businessmen had never let race get in the way of making money.

Evelyn supplied, "Treadwell-Price was knee-deep in the campaign. Daddy Treadwell had his picture in the paper with Jackson the day he won. They had their arms around each other like two showgirls. Adam? Allen?" She blew out a stream of air. "Andrew. That's his name. Andrew Treadwell. Sonny boy must be a Junior. I bet they call him Andy."

Amanda shook her head slowly from side to side. She left politics to her father. "Never heard of any of them."

"Junior was certainly walking around with confidence. Hodge was terrified of him. Pantomime aside. Wasn't that a gas?"

"Yes." Amanda looked up at the red light, wondering why it was taking so long to change.

"Just pull through," Evelyn suggested. She noticed Amanda's worried expression and said, "Relax. I won't arrest you."

Amanda checked both ways twice, then a third time, before edging the Plymouth forward.

"Watch it," Evelyn warned. There was a Corvette cresting the hill on Spring Street. Sparks flew from under the engine as it scraped the asphalt and blew through the intersection. "Where's a cop when you need 'em?"

Amanda's calf ached from pounding the brake home. "My car insurance is with Benowitz, if you're trying to make your husband some money."

Evelyn laughed. "Benowitz isn't bad once you look past the horns."

Amanda couldn't tell if Evelyn was mocking her or stating her own opinion. She checked the light. Still red. She inched forward again, wincing as she pressed the accelerator. Amanda didn't feel her shoulders relax until they had passed the Varsity restaurant. And then they went back up again.

The smell engulfed the interior of the car as soon as they had crossed over the four-lane expressway. It wasn't sewage this time, but poverty, and people living stacked on top of one another like animals in crates. The heat was doing no one any favors. Techwood Homes was made of poured concrete with a brick façade, which breathed about as well as Amanda's nylons.

Beside her, Evelyn closed her eyes and took a few shallow breaths through her mouth. "Okay." She shook her head, then looked down at the map. "Left on Techwood. Right on Pine."

Amanda slowed the car to navigate the narrow streets. In the distance, she could see the brick row houses and garden apartments of Techwood Homes. Graffiti marred most surfaces, and where there was no spray paint, there was trash piled waist-high. A handful of children were playing in the dirt courtyard. They were dressed in rags. Even from a distance, Amanda could see the sores on their legs.

Evelyn directed, "Take a right up here."

Amanda went as far as she could go before the road became impassable. A burned-out car blocked the street. The doors were open. The hood was raised, showing the engine like a charred tongue. Amanda pulled onto a berm and put the gear in park.

Evelyn didn't move. She was staring at the children. "I'd forgotten how bad it is."

Amanda stared at the boys. They were all dark skinned and knobby kneed. They used their bare feet to kick around a flat-looking basketball. There was no grass here, only dry, red Georgia clay.

The kids stopped playing. One of the boys pointed to the Plymouth, which the city bought in lots and the population easily recognized as an unmarked police car. Another boy ran into the nearest building, dust kicking up behind him.

Evelyn huffed a laugh. "And there the little angel goes to alert the welcoming committee."

Amanda popped open the door handle. She could see the Coca-Cola tower in the distance, sandwiching the fourteen-block slum with Georgia Tech. "My father says Coke's trying to get the city to tear this place down. Move them somewhere else."

"I can't see the mayor throwing away the people who elected him."

Amanda didn't vocally disagree, but in her experience, her father was always right about these things.

"Might as well get this over with." Evelyn pushed open her door and got out of the car. She unzipped her purse and pulled out her radio, which was half as long as a Kel-Lite and almost as heavy. Amanda checked to make sure the zipper on her own bag was closed as Evelyn gave dispatch their location. Amanda's radio seldom worked, no matter how many times she changed the battery. She would've left it at home but for Sergeant Geary. Every morning, he made all the women dump out their purses so he could make sure they were properly equipped.

"This way." Evelyn walked up the hill toward the apartment block. Amanda could feel hundreds of sets of eyes tracking their movement. Given the setting, not many people were at work during the day. There was plenty of time to stare out the window and wait for something awful to happen. The farther away they got from the Plymouth, the sicker Amanda felt, so that by the time Evelyn stopped in front of the second building, she felt as if she might be ill.

"Okay." Evelyn pointed to the doorways, counting off, "Three,

four, five . . ." She mouthed the rest silently as she continued walking. Amanda followed, wondering if Evelyn knew what she was
doing or was just trying to show off.

Finally, Evelyn stopped again and pointed to the middle unit on
the top floor. "Here we are."

They both stared at the open doorway that led to the stairwell. A
single shaft of sunlight illuminated the bottom steps. The windows at
the front of the vestibule and on the upper landings were all boarded
over, but the metal-encased skylight provided enough light to see by.
At least so long as it was daytime.

"Fifth floor, penthouse," Evelyn said. "How'd you do on the fit-
ness exam?"

Another one of Reggie's new rules. "I barely clocked the mile."
They were given eight and a half minutes. Amanda had pushed it to
the last second.

"They gave me a pass on the pull-ups or I'd be at home right now
watching *Captain Kangaroo*." She gave a cheery smile. "I hope your
life doesn't depend on my upper body strength."

"Surely you can outrun me if it comes to that."

Evelyn laughed. "I'm planning on it." She zipped her purse, then
buttoned the flap closed. Again, Amanda made sure her purse was
closed tightly. The first thing you learned about going into the projects was you never left your bag open and you never put it down
anywhere. No one wanted to bring lice or cockroaches home to their
families.

Evelyn took a deep breath, as if she was about to dunk her head
underwater, then entered the building. The smell hit them both like
a brick to the face. Evelyn covered her nose with her hand as she
started up the steps. "You'd think sniffing a baby's diaper all day
would accustom me to the smell of urine. I suppose grown men eat
different foods. I know asparagus makes mine smell. I tried cocaine
once. I can't remember what my pee smelled like, but zow-ee, did I
not care one bit."

Amanda stood shocked at the bottom of the stairs, looking up at

Evelyn, who seemed not to realize that she'd just admitted to using an illegal narcotic.

"Oh, don't pimp me out to Reggie. I looked the other way on that red light." Evelyn flashed a smile. She turned the corner on the landing and she was gone.

Amanda shook her head as she followed her up the stairs. Neither of them touched the handrails. Cockroaches skittered underfoot. Trash seemed glued to the treads. The walls felt as if they were closing in.

Amanda forced herself to breathe through her mouth, just as she forced one foot after the other. This was crazy. Why hadn't they called for backup? Half of the signal 49s in Atlanta were reported by women who'd been raped in stairwells. They were as ubiquitous to the housing projects as rats and squalor.

As Evelyn rounded the next landing, she tugged at the back of her hair. Amanda guessed this was a nervous tic. She shared the anxiety. The higher up they climbed, the more her insides rattled. Fourteen cops killed in the last two years. Gunshots to the head. Sometimes to the stomach. One officer had lived for two days before finally succumbing. He'd been in so much pain you could hear his screams all the way downstairs in the Grady Hospital ER.

Amanda's heart clenched as she rounded the next landing. Her hands started shaking. Her knees wanted to give out. She felt seized by the desire to burst into tears.

Surely one of the patrol units had heard Evelyn call in their location to dispatch. The men seldom waited for any female officer to request backup. They just arrived on scene, taking over the case, shooing the women away like they were silly children. Normally, Amanda felt slightly irked by this macho grandstanding, but today, she would've welcomed them with open arms.

"This is crazy," she mumbled, rounding the next landing. "Absolutely crazy."

"Just a little bit farther," Evelyn happily called back.

It wasn't like they were undercover. Everyone knew there were two cops in the building. White cops. Female cops. The hum of televisions and whispered conversations buzzed around. The heat was as stifling as the shadows. Every closed door represented an opportunity for someone to jump out and hurt one or both of them.

"Okay, what've we got?" Evelyn asked no one in particular. "Four hundred forty-three rapes reported last year." Her voice clattered down the stairs like a bell. "One hundred thirteen were white women. What is that, a one-in-four chance of us being raped?" She looked back at Amanda. "Twenty-five percent?"

Amanda shook her head. The woman might as well be speaking in tongues.

Evelyn continued up the stairs. "Four times one hundred thirteen . . ." Her voice trailed off. "I was almost right. We have a twenty-six percent chance of being raped today. That's not high at all. That's a seventy-four percent chance of nothing happening."

The numbers, at least, made sense. Amanda felt an ounce of pressure lift off her chest. "That doesn't seem so bad."

"No, it doesn't. If I had a seventy-four percent chance of winning the Bug, I'd be down on Auburn right now betting my paycheck."

Amanda nodded. The Bug was a numbers game run out of Colored Town. "Where did you—"

There was a commotion down the hallway. A door slammed. A child screamed. A man's voice shouted for everyone to shut the hell up.

The pressure came back like a boulder dropping from the sky.

Evelyn had stopped on the stairs. She was looking directly down at Amanda. "Statistically, we're fine. More than fine." She waited for Amanda to nod before continuing the climb. Evelyn's posture had lost its certainty. She was breathing heavily. Suddenly, Amanda realized that the other woman had taken the lead. If there was something bad waiting for them at the top of the stairs, Evelyn Mitchell would meet it first.

Amanda asked, "Where did you get those numbers?" She'd never heard them before and frankly did not care. All she knew was that talking was the only thing keeping her from vomiting. "The reported rapes?"

"Class project. I'm taking statistics at Tech."

"Tech," Amanda repeated. "Isn't that hard?"

"It's a great way to meet men."

Again, Amanda didn't know if she was joking. Again, she didn't care. "How many of the perpetrators were white?"

"What's that?"

"Techwood is ninety percent black. How many of the rapists were—"

"Oh, right, right." Evelyn stopped at the top of the stairs. "You know, I can't recall. I'll look it up for you later. This is it." She pointed down the hallway. All the lights were blown out. The skylight cast everything in shadow. "Fourth door on the left."

"Do you want my Kel?"

"I don't think a light will make much difference. Ready?"

Amanda felt her throat work as she tried to swallow. There was an apple core on the floor that seemed to be moving. It was completely covered in ants.

Evelyn said, "Smell's not so bad up here."

"No," Amanda agreed.

"I suppose if you're going to relieve your bladder on the floor, you need not climb five flights of stairs to do it."

"No," Amanda repeated.

"Shall we?" Evelyn walked down the hall with renewed purpose. Amanda caught up with her in front of the closed door. A plastic cutout of the letter *C* was nailed to the wall. Taped just below the spyhole was a strip of notebook paper with blue capital letters written in a child's hand.

Amanda read, "Kitty Treadwell."

"The plot thickens." Evelyn took a deep breath through her nose. "You smell that?"

Amanda had to concentrate in order to discern the new odor. "Vinegar?"

"That's what heroin smells like."

"Don't tell me you've tried that, too?"

"Only my hairdresser knows for sure." She motioned for Amanda to stand to the side of the door. Evelyn took the opposite side. This marginally ensured their safety in case someone was standing behind the door with a loaded shotgun.

Evelyn raised her hand and knocked on the door with such force that the wood shook on its hinges. Her voice was entirely different—deeper, more masculine—when she shouted, "Atlanta Police Department!" She saw Amanda's expression and gave her a wink before banging again. "Open up!" she ordered.

Amanda listened to her own heartbeat, the quick gulps of breath. Seconds passed. Evelyn raised her hand again, then dropped it when a muffled woman's voice said, "Jesus," from behind the door.

There was a shuffling noise inside the apartment. A chain slid back. Then a lock turned. Then another lock. Then the handle moved as the thumb latch was toggled.

The girl inside was obviously a prostitute, though she was dressed in a thin cotton shift that was more appropriate for a ten-year-old girl. Bleach blonde hair hung to her waist. Her skin was so white it bordered on blue. Her age was between twenty and sixty. Track marks riddled her body—her arms, her neck, her legs, pricking open like wet, red mouths on the veins of her bare feet. Missing teeth gave her face a concave appearance. Amanda could see how the ball-and-socket joint in her shoulder worked as she folded her arms low on her waist.

Evelyn asked, "Kitty Treadwell?"

Her voice had a smoker's rasp. "Whatchu bitches want?"

"Good morning to you, too." Evelyn breezed into the apartment, which looked just as Amanda expected. Molded dishes filled the sink. Empty fast-food bags were everywhere. Clothes were strewn across the floor. There was a stained blue couch in the middle of the room with a coffee table in front. Syringes and a spoon rested on a dingy washrag. Matches. Pieces of cigarette filters. A small bag of dirty white powder was laid out beside two cockroaches that were either dead or so high they couldn't move. Someone had pulled the kitchen stove into the middle of the room. The oven door was open, the edge resting on the coffee table to support the large color television set on top.

"Is that Dinah?" Evelyn asked. She turned up the volume. Jack Cassidy was singing with Dinah Shore. "I just love her voice. Did you see David Bowie on here last week?"

The girl blinked several times.

Amanda checked for roaches before turning on the floor lamp. A harsh light filled the room. The windows were covered in yellow construction paper, but that only served to filter the bright morning sun. Perhaps that was why Amanda felt safer inside the apartment than she had in the stairwell. Her heartbeat was returning to normal. She wasn't sweating any more than dictated by the temperature.

"David Bowie," Evelyn repeated, turning off the TV. "He was on *Dinah* last week."

Amanda stated the obvious. "She's stoned out of her gourd." A heavy sigh came from deep inside her chest. They had risked their lives for this?

Evelyn patted the girl on the cheek. Her palm made a firm slapping sound against the skin. "You in there, sweetheart?"

"I'd soak that hand in Clorox," Amanda advised. "Let's get out of here. If this girl was raped, she probably deserved it."

"Hodge sent us here for a reason."

"He sent you and Vanessa here," Amanda countered. "I can't believe we've wasted our whole morning—"

"Fonzie," the girl mumbled. "He wa' talkin' to Fonzie."

"That's right," Evelyn said, smiling at Amanda as if she'd won a prize. "Bowie was on *Dinah* last week with Fonzie from *Happy Days*."

"I seen 'em." Kitty ambled over to the couch and collapsed onto the cushions. Amanda didn't know if it was the drugs or her circumstances that made the girl's speech almost unintelligible. She sounded as if someone had turned upside down the entire Flannery O'Connor canon and shaken her out. "I don'member what'e sang."

"You know, I don't either." Evelyn motioned for Amanda to check the rest of the place.

Amanda asked, "What am I looking for, back editions of *Good Housekeeping*?"

Evelyn smiled sweetly. "Wouldn't that be funny if you actually found some?"

"Just hilarious."

Reluctantly, Amanda did as she was asked, trying not to let her arms touch the walls of the narrow hallway as she walked to the back. The apartment was larger than her own. There was a proper bedroom separate from the living area. The door to the closet was off its hinges. Several torn black garbage bags seemed to hold the girl's clothing. The bed was a pile of stained sheets wadded up on the carpet.

Impossibly, the bathroom was even more disgusting than the rest of the apartment. Black mold had replaced the grout in the tile. The sink and toilet were serving double duty as ashtrays. The trashcan was overflowing with used sanitary napkins and toilet paper. The floor was smeared with something Amanda didn't want to know about.

Taking up every available surface were various personal grooming products, which, to Amanda's thinking, was the very definition of irony. Two cans of Sunsilk hairspray. Four Breck shampoo bottles at varying levels. A ripped box of Tampax. An empty bottle of Cachet by Prince Matchabelli. Two open pots of Pond's cold cream, both caked with a yellowed rind. Enough makeup to stock the Revlon counter at Rich's. Brushes. Pencils. Liquid eyeliner. Mascara. Two combs, both clumped with hair. Three very well used toothbrushes sticking out of a Mayor McCheese drinking glass.

The shower curtain was torn from the hooks, giving the cockroaches in the tub a clear view of Amanda. They stared at her intently as she shuddered uncontrollably. She gripped her purse, knowing she was going to have to shake it out before she even thought about putting it in the car.

Back in the living room, Evelyn had moved on from Arthur Fonzarelli to the reason for their visit. "Andy Treadwell is your cousin or your brother?"

"Uncah," the girl said, and Amanda assumed she meant the elder Andrew Treadwell. "Wha' time it is?"

Amanda looked at her watch. "Nine o'clock." She felt the need to add, "In the morning."

"Shee-it." The girl reached down between the couch cushions and pulled out a pack of cigarettes. Amanda watched as, entranced, the girl studied the pack of Virginia Slims as if they'd just fallen like manna from heaven. Slowly, she took out a cigarette. It was bent at an angle. Still, she grabbed the matches off the table and with shaking hands lit the cigarette. She blew out a stream of smoke.

"I hear those will kill you," Evelyn said.

"I's waitin'," the girl answered.

Evelyn countered, "There are faster ways."

"You stick aroun', you see how fast."

Amanda detected an edge to the girl's tone. "Why is that?"

"Them kids done seen ya pull up. My daddy gonna wanna know why two white bitches chattin' me up."

Evelyn said, "I think your uncle Andy is worried about you."

"He want his dick suck again?"

Amanda exchanged a look with Evelyn. Most of these girls claimed an uncle or father had abused them. Around the sex crimes units they called it an Oedipal complex. Not technically correct, but close enough, and obviously a waste of police time.

Kitty said, "You cain't arrest me. I ain't did nothin'."

"We don't want to arrest you," Evelyn tried again. "We were told by our sergeant that you'd been raped."

"S'what I get pay for, ain'it?" She blew out another plume of smoke, this one straight into their faces.

Evelyn's sunny disposition faltered. "Kitty, we need to speak with you and take a statement."

"Ain't ma problem."

"All right. We'll just leave then." Evelyn snatched the bag of heroin off the coffee table and turned on her heel.

If Amanda hadn't been so surprised to see Evelyn take the drugs, she would've been heading toward the door herself. As it was, she saw everything—the shock on the girl's face, the way she sprang from the couch, fingers out like the claws on a cat.

Seemingly of its own volition, Amanda's foot rose up. She didn't trip the girl. She kicked her in the ribs, sending her straight into the stove. The blow was hard. Kitty slammed into the television, breaking off the stove door. The TV cracked against the floor. Tubes popped. Glass shattered.

Evelyn stared at Amanda in visible shock. "What was that?"

"She was about to jump you."

"You certainly stopped her." Evelyn knelt down on the floor. She took a handkerchief out of her purse and handed it to the girl.

"Bitches," Kitty slurred. Her fingers went to her mouth. She pulled out one of her last remaining teeth. "Got damn bitches."

Evelyn stood back up, probably thinking it wasn't wise to kneel in front of an angry prostitute. Still, she said, "You need to tell us what's going on. We're here to help you."

"'uck you," the girl mumbled, fingers feeling around inside her mouth. Amanda saw old scars across her wrist where Kitty had tried to slice open the veins. "'et the 'uck outta 'ere."

Evelyn's voice turned hard. "Don't make us drag you to the station, Kitty. I don't care who your uncle is."

Amanda thought of her car, the time it would take to wash away the grime from the back seat. She told Evelyn, "You can't seriously be considering—"

"Like hell I'm not."

"There's no way I'm letting this—"

"Shut up!" the girl yelled. "I ain't even Kitty. I's Jane. Jane Delray."

"Oh for the love of—" Amanda threw her hands into the air. All the terror she'd experienced on the stairwell turned into anger. "We don't even have the right girl."

"Hodge didn't give a name. Just an address."

Amanda shook her head. "I don't know why we even listened to him. He's been here less than a day. The same as you, I might add."

"I was in uniform for three years before—"

"Why are you back?" Amanda demanded. "Are you here to do the job or is it something else?"

"You're the one who wants to hightail it out of here."

"Because this whore can't tell us anything."

"Hey!" Jane screamed. "Who you callin' a whore?"

Evelyn looked down at the girl. Sarcasm dripped from her voice. "Really, darling? You want to make that argument now?"

Jane wiped the blood from her mouth. "Y'all ain't from the gub-mint."

"Brilliant deduction," Evelyn said. "Exactly who from the government is looking for you?"

Her shoulders gave a slight shrug. "I might'a been down to the Five on account'a needin' s'money."

Evelyn put her hand to her head. "The Five" referred to the Five Points Station bus line that serviced the welfare office. "You were trying to cash Kitty's government assistance voucher."

Amanda asked, "Isn't it mailed?"

They both stared openly at Amanda. Evelyn explained, "The post office boxes here aren't exactly secure."

Jane said, "Kitty don't need it. She ain't never need it. She rich. Gotta family that's connected. Thass why you bitches here, ain't it?"

Evelyn asked, "Where is she now?"

"She be gone six months."

"Where did she go?"

"Dis'peared. Same wid Lucy. Same wid Mary. All dem jes up and dis'peared."

"These are working girls?" Evelyn asked. "Lucy and Mary?" The girl nodded. "Is Kitty on the game, too?" Again, the girl nodded.

Amanda had had quite enough of this. "Should I write this down for the newspaper? Three prostitutes are missing. Stop the presses."

"Ain't missin'," the girl insisted. "They gone. Real gone.

Dis'peared." She wiped blood from her lips. "They's all livin' here. They stuff's here. They's puttin' down roots. They's cashin' they vouchahs from the Five."

Amanda said, "Until you tried to get their vouchers instead."

"Y'ain't lissenin' to me," Jane insisted. "They all gone. Lucy been gone a year. She here one minute, then—" She snapped her fingers. "Poof."

Evelyn turned to Amanda, and in a deadly serious tone said, "We need to put out an immediate APB on a man wearing a cape and a magician's hat." She stopped. "Hold that. Let's check to see if Doug Henning's in town."

Amanda couldn't help herself. She laughed at the joke.

They all jumped when the front door slammed open. Wood splintered. The knob dug into the wall. Plaster shattered. The air seemed to shake.

A well-built black man stood in the doorway. He was out of breath, probably from running up the stairs. His thick sideburns grew into a goatee and mustache that circled his mouth. His pants and shirt were a matching lime green. He was obviously a pimp, and clearly furious. "Whatchu honky bitches doin' here?"

Amanda could not move. She felt as if her body had turned to stone.

"We were looking for Kitty," Evelyn answered. "Do you know Kitty Treadwell? Her uncle is a very good friend of Mayor Jackson's." Her throat worked as she swallowed. "That's why we're here. They asked us to come. The mayor's friend. They're very concerned that Kitty is missing."

The man ignored her, grabbing Jane up by her hair. She screamed in pain, her fingers digging into his hands as she tried to keep her scalp from ripping. "You been talkin' to the po-lice, gal?"

"Ain't say nothin'. Honess." Jane could barely speak from terror. "They jes' show up."

He shoved her out into the hall. Jane stumbled, falling against the wall before she found her footing.

"We're leaving now." Evelyn's voice was shaking. She edged toward the door, motioning Amanda to follow. "We don't want trouble."

The man shut the door. The sound was like a gunshot. He stared at Amanda for a few intent seconds, then Evelyn. His eyes looked as if they were on fire.

Evelyn said, "Our sergeant knows we're here."

He turned around and slowly slid the chain into the track. And then he locked the deadbolt. And then the next one.

"We talked to dispatch before we—"

"I hear ya, Mrs. Pig. Lessee can the mayor get here 'fore I'm through." He took the key from the lock and slid it into his front pocket. His voice went into a deep baritone. "You a fine-lookin' woman. You know that?"

He wasn't talking to Evelyn. His eyes were trained on Amanda. He licked his lips, his gaze lingering on her chest. She tried to back up, but he followed. Her legs hit the arm of the couch. His fingers touched the side of her neck. "Damn, gal. So fine."

Amanda fought a wave of dizziness. She reached down to her purse, fidgeting with the zip, trying to get it to open. "Call for backup."

Evelyn already had her radio in her hand. She clicked the button.

The man's hand circled Amanda's neck. His thumb pressed under her chin. "Radio ain't gone work up here. We too high for the antennies."

Evelyn furiously clicked the button. There was only static. "Shit."

"We gone have some fun, ain't we, Fuzzy?" His hand tightened around Amanda's throat. She could smell his cologne and sweat. There was a birthmark on his cheek. A patch of hair showed where his shirt was unbuttoned. Gold chains. A tattoo of Jesus with a crown of thorns.

"Ev . . . ," Amanda breathed. She could feel the outline of the revolver inside her purse. She tried to force her finger into the trigger guard.

"Mmm-hmm," the pimp moaned. He unzipped his pants. "Fine-lookin' woman."

"Eh-eh-ev . . . ," Amanda stuttered. His hand slipped under her skirt. She could feel his fingernails scrape her bare flesh, the pressure of him against her thigh.

Evelyn jammed the radio back into her purse and zipped closed the bag as if she was preparing to leave. Amanda panicked. And then gasped as Evelyn gripped the straps with both hands, swung around and smashed her bag into the side of the man's head.

Gun. Badge. Handcuffs. Kel-Lite. Radio. Nightstick. Nearly twenty pounds of equipment. The pimp collapsed to the floor like a rag doll. Blood spurted from the side of his head. There were deep cuts across his cheek where the Indian tassels had sliced open the skin.

Amanda grabbed her revolver out of her purse. The bag fell to the floor. Her hands shook as she tried to grip the gun. She had to lean against the arm of the couch so she wouldn't fall down.

"Christ." Evelyn stood over the man, mouth agape. The blood was really flowing now.

"My God," Amanda whispered. She pushed down her skirt. Her pantyhose were ripped from his prying fingernails. She could still feel his hand on her throat. "My God."

"Are you okay?" Evelyn asked. She put her hands on Amanda's arms. "You're okay, all right?" Slowly, she reached down for Amanda's revolver. "I've got this, okay? You're fine."

"Your gun . . ." Amanda was panting so hard she was going to hyperventilate. "Why didn't . . . Why didn't you shoot him?"

Evelyn chewed her bottom lip. She stared at Amanda for what seemed like a full minute before finally admitting, "Bill and I agreed that we shouldn't keep a loaded gun in the house because of the baby."

Words clogged Amanda's throat. She screamed, "Your gun isn't loaded!"

"Well . . ." Evelyn dug her fingers into the back of her hair. "It worked out, right?" She let out a strained laugh. "Sure, it worked out. We're both fine. We're both just fine." She looked down at the pimp again. His pants were splayed open. "I guess it's not true what they say about—"

"He was going to rape me! He was going to rape both of us!"

"Statistically . . ." Evelyn's voice trailed off before she admitted, "Well, yes. It was bound to happen. I didn't want to tell you before, but . . ." She picked up Amanda's purse from the floor. "Yeah."

For the first time in two months, Amanda wasn't hot anymore. Her blood had turned cold.

Evelyn kept babbling. She zipped Amanda's gun inside her purse, looped the strap over her shoulder. "We're both okay, though. Right? I'm okay. You're okay. We're all okay." She spotted a telephone on the floor by the couch. Her hand was shaking so hard that she dropped the receiver. It rattled in the cradle, dinging the bell. She finally managed to pick up the phone and put it to her ear. "I'll call this in. The boys will come running. We'll get out of here. We're both fine. All right?"

Amanda blinked sweat out of her eye.

Evelyn stuck her finger in the dial. "I'm sorry. I talk when I get nervous. It drives my husband crazy." The rotary slid back and forth. "What about those missing girls the whore mentioned? Do you recognize any of their names?"

Amanda blinked away more sweat. Her mind flashed up strange images. The disgusting bathroom. The shampoo bottles. The piles of makeup.

Evelyn said, "Lucy. Mary. Kitty Treadwell. Maybe we should write that down somewhere. I'm certain I'll forget the minute I get a drink in me. Two drinks. A whole bottle." She huffed out a short breath. "It's weird that Jane was worried about them. These girls usually don't worry about anything but keeping their pimps happy."

Three used toothbrushes in the glass. The long, dark hair clumped in one of the combs.

Amanda said, "Jane's hair is blonde."

"I wouldn't bet on that." Evelyn looked down at the unmoving man. "His wallet's in his back pocket. Could you—"

"No!" The panic came back in full force.

"You're right. Never mind. They'll ID him at the jail. I'm sure he has a record. Hey, Linda." Evelyn's voice wavered as she spoke into the phone. "Ten-sixteen, my location. Hodge sent us in on a forty-nine and it turned into a fifty-five." She looked at Amanda. "Anything else?"

"Tell them you're twenty-four," Amanda managed.

Duke Wagner was wrong about Evelyn Mitchell being pushy and opinionated.

The woman was just plain crazy.

five

Present Day

SUZANNA FORD

Zanna fell back on the bed, her feet still on the floor. She held up her iPhone and checked her messages. No texts. No voicemail. No email. The asshole was already ten minutes late. If she showed up downstairs without any money, Terry was going to beat her ass. Again. He seemed to forget it was his job to screen these losers. Not that Terry ever took the blame for anything.

She looked out the window at the downtown skyline. Zanna was born and raised in Roswell, half an hour and a lifetime away from Atlanta. Except for the buildings that had names on them, she had no idea what she was looking at. Equitable. AT&T. Georgia Power. All she knew was she was going to be seriously screwed if her john didn't show.

The plasma TV on the wall flashed on. Zanna had rolled over on the remote. She saw Monica Pearson behind the news desk. Some girl was missing. White, blonde, pretty. They sure as shit wouldn't care if Zanna was gone.

She flipped around the channels, trying to find something more interesting, finally giving up when she got into the triple digits. She tossed the remote onto the bedside table. Her arms itched. She wanted a cigarette. She wanted more than that.

If she thought about the meth long enough, she could taste the powder in the back of her throat. Her freaking nose was rotting from the inside, but she couldn't stop snorting the stuff. Couldn't stop thinking about the smash cut to her brain. The way it shook through her body. The way it made the world so much more bearable.

That wasn't going to happen for at least an hour. To tide herself over, she went to the minibar and took out four small bottles of vodka. Zanna downed them in quick succession, then filled the empties in the bathroom sink. She was stacking the bottles back in the refrigerator when there was a knock at the door.

"Thank Jesus," she groaned. She checked herself in the mirror. Not too bad. She could still pass for sixteen if the lights were turned down low enough. She twisted the wand to close the blinds and turned off one of the bedside lamps before answering the door.

The man was massive. The top of his head almost touched the doorway. His shoulders were nearly as wide as the frame. Zanna felt a stir of panic, but then she remembered Terry was downstairs, and that he had cleared this guy, and that whatever was about to happen wouldn't matter when that first huff of meth snaked into her brain.

She said, "Hey, Daddy," because he was older. Zanna didn't want to think about the geezer using his social security check to pay for this. She looked at his face, which was pretty smooth considering his age. His neck was a little scrawny. You could really tell it in his hands. Liver spots. The hair on his arms was white, though what was left on his head was sandy brown.

Zanna threw open the door. "Come in, big boy." She tried to swing her hips as she walked, but the carpet combined with her new high heels wasn't a good mix. She ended up having to brace herself against the wall. She turned around and waited for him to come in.

He took his time. He didn't seem nervous and God knew you didn't pop your first whore at his age. He glanced up and down the hallway before finally shutting the door behind him. He was still in good shape despite the years on him. His hair was in a military cut. His shoulders were square. World War II, she thought, then her middle school history came back to her and Zanna figured he wasn't old enough for that. Probably Vietnam. A lot of her customers lately were young guys just back from Afghanistan. She didn't know which was worse—the sad ones who tried to make love or the angry ones who wanted to hurt her.

She got straight to the point. "You a cop?"

He said what they always said. "Do I look like a cop?" But he unzipped his pants without prompting. It was the last vestige of democracy. Even undercover, a cop wasn't allowed to show you his junk. "All right?"

Zanna nodded, suppressing a shudder. He was huge. "Damn," she managed. "That looks fun."

The man zipped back up. "Have a seat." He indicated the chair. Zanna sat, legs apart, so he'd have a good view from the bed. Only, he kept standing. His shadow stretched across the room, nearly reaching the edge of the door.

"How do you like it?" she asked, though Zanna had a sneaking suspicion he liked it rough. She pulled in her shoulders, tried to look smaller than she already was. "You wanna be gentle with me. I'm just a girl."

His lip quivered, but that was the only reaction she got. He asked, "How did you get here?"

She thought he meant the literal path she'd taken—up Peachtree, left on Edgewood. Then she realized he meant her current state of employment.

Zanna shrugged. "What can I say? I love sex." That's what they wanted to hear. That's what they tried to tell themselves when they ripped you apart and threw money in your face—that you loved it, couldn't live without it.

"No," he said. "I want the real story."

"Oh, you know." She blew out a puff of air. Her story was so boring. You couldn't turn on the television without seeing some iteration of the same. Zanna hadn't been tossed out on the streets. She hadn't been abused. Her parents were divorced, but they were good people. The problem was Zanna. She'd started smoking weed so a boy would think she was cool. She'd started taking pills because she was bored. She'd started smoking meth to lose weight. And then it was too late to do anything else but hang on by her fingernails until the next hit.

Her mom let her live at home until she figured out Zanna was smoking more than Marlboros. Her dad let her live in his basement until his new wife found the blackened pieces of tinfoil that smelled like marshmallows. Then, they put her up in an apartment. Then they got all tough love, and two failed stints in rehab later, Zanna was out on the street, earning her fix between her legs.

"Tell me the truth," the man said. "How did you get here?"

Zanna tried to swallow. Her mouth was dry. She couldn't tell if it was from withdrawal or from the scary feeling she was getting off this guy. She told him what she knew he wanted to hear. "My daddy hurt me."

"I'm sorry to hear that."

"I didn't have a choice." She sniffed and looked down at the floor. She used the back of her hand to wipe away fake tears. Her jaw could've come unhinged like a boa constrictor's, so bored was Zanna with spinning this story. "I didn't have anywhere to go. I was sleeping on the streets. Sex is something I like. And I'm good at it, so . . ."

He kneeled down to look at her. Even on his knees, he was taller than her. Zanna glanced at him, then quickly looked away. It was shame this guy was looking for. Older generation. They lapped it up. Zanna could give him plenty of shame. Valerie Bertinelli. Meredith Baxter. Tori Spelling. Zanna had seen the look in every single Lifetime movie she'd ever watched.

She said, "I miss him. That's the sad part." She looked back up at the man, blinked her eyes a few times. "I miss my daddy."

He took her hand, gently sandwiching it between both of his. Zanna couldn't see anything but her wrist. His touch was light on her skin, but she felt like he'd trapped her. Her breath stuttered in her chest. Panic was a natural instinct she thought she'd learned to control. There was something about this man that set off what little warning system she had left.

He said, "Suzanna, don't lie to me."

Bile boiled up into her mouth. "That's not my name." She tried to pull away. His fingers clamped around her wrist. "I didn't tell you my name."

"Didn't you?"

She was going to kill that fucking pimp. He'd sell his mother for an extra twenty. "What did Terry tell you? My name is Trixie."

"No," the man insisted. "You told me your name is Suzanna."

She felt pain rush up her arm. She looked down. He held both her wrists in one hand. He leaned into her legs, trapping her against the chair. "Don't fight," he said, his free hand wrapping around her neck. The tips of his fingers touched in the back. "I want to help you, Suzanna. To save you."

"I-I-I'm not—" She couldn't speak. She was choking. She couldn't breathe. Panic jerked through her body like a live wire. Her eyes rolled upward. She felt a stream of urine dribble down her leg.

"Just relax, sister." He hovered above her. His eyes going back and forth as if he did not want to miss a second of her fear. A smile creased his lips. "The Lord will guide my hand."

six

Present Day

MONDAY

Sara walked through the Grady Hospital emergency room, trying not to get pulled away on cases. Even if she tattooed "off duty" on her forehead, the nurses wouldn't leave her alone. She shouldn't blame them. The hospital was notoriously understaffed and overburdened. There had not been a time in Grady's 120-year history when supply was able to keep up with demand. Working here was tantamount to signing away your life, which had been just what Sara needed when she'd taken the job. She hadn't really had a life back then. She was newly widowed, living in a different city, starting over from scratch. Throwing herself into a demanding job was the only way she'd been able to cope.

It was amazing how quickly her needs had changed in the last two weeks.

Or the last hour, for that matter. Sara had no idea what was going on between Will and Amanda. Their relationship had always puzzled her, but the exchange in the hallway before the stairs collapsed had been downright bizarre. Even after the fall, when it was clear that Amanda had been badly injured, Will seemed more intent on questioning the woman than helping her. Sara still felt shocked by his tone of voice. She'd never heard such coldness from him before. It was like he was another person, a stranger she did not want to know.

At least Sara had finally figured out the root of their conversation, though it was through no brilliant deduction of her own. The television over the nurses' station was always tuned to the news. Closed captioning scrolled mindlessly day and night. The missing girl from Georgia Tech had made the jump to the national news, courtesy of CNN, whose world headquarters was just down the street from the university. The video of Amanda leading the press conference played on an endless loop, reporters flashing up statistics and the sort of non-information required to fill twenty-four-hour programming.

The latest speculation held that perhaps Ashleigh Renee Snyder had faked her own abduction. Students claiming to be close friends of the missing girl had come forward, giving details about her life, Ashleigh's fears that her grades were slipping. Maybe she really was hiding somewhere. The theory was not completely without foundation. Georgia had a short history of women pretending to be kidnapped, the most famous being the so-called Runaway Bride, a silly woman who'd wasted several days of police time hiding from her own fiancé.

"Sara." A nurse rushed up with a lab report. "I need you to—"

"Sorry. I'm off duty."

"What the hell are you doing back here?" The woman didn't wait around for an answer.

Sara checked the board to see if Will had been assigned a room. Generally, a case as mundane as sutures would take hours to get to, but before Sara dealt with Amanda, she'd made certain the admitting nurse hadn't abandoned Will to the waiting room. He'd been assigned one of the curtains in the back. Sara felt her spine stiffen when she saw Bert Krakauer's name instead of her own adjacent to Will's.

She headed toward the back, a startling sense of ownership quickening her pace. The curtain was open. Will was sitting up in bed. A drape was around his foot. Worst of all, Krakauer had a pair of pickups in his hand.

"No-no-no," she said, jogging toward the two men. "What are you doing?"

Krakauer indicated the needle holder. "They didn't let you play with these in medical school?"

Sara gave him a tight smile. "Thanks. I'll take over from here." He took the hint, returning the instrument to the tray and taking his leave. Sara gave Will a sharp look as she closed the curtain. "You were going to let Krakauer sew you up?"

"Why not?"

"For the same reason you weren't left rotting in the waiting room." Sara washed her hands at the sink. "If someone broke into my apartment, would you let another cop investigate it?"

"I don't normally work burglaries."

Sara wiped her hands dry with a paper towel. Will wasn't normally this obtuse. "What's going on?"

"He said I need stitches."

"Not that." She sat down on the edge of the bed. "You've been acting strange since we got here. Is it Amanda?"

"Why? Did she say something to you?"

Sara had a creeping sense of déjà vu. She'd spoken briefly to Amanda and gotten the same question about Will. "What would Amanda tell me?"

"Nothing important. She wasn't making a lot of sense."

"She seemed pretty sharp to me." Sara resisted the urge to put her hands on her hips like a lecturing schoolmarm. "I saw Ashleigh Snyder on the news."

Will sat up. "Did they find her?"

"No. They're speculating that she might've staged her own kidnapping. One of her friends came forward and said she was about to flunk out of school."

Will nodded, but didn't offer his opinion.

"Are you working the case?"

"Nope." His tone was clipped. "Still keeping Atlanta's airport toilets safe from horny business travelers."

"Why aren't you on the kidnapping?"

"You'd have to ask Amanda."

Here they were, full circle again.

"Is she all right?" Will asked, though the question seemed obligatory. "Amanda, I mean."

Sara had never been good at staring contests, especially with someone as blatantly pigheaded as the man she'd been sleeping with for the last two weeks. "She has what's called a Colles' fracture. Ortho is reducing it right now. She'll get a cast. She's pretty banged up, but she'll be okay. Normally, she'd be sent home, but she lost consciousness, so she'll have to spend the night."

"Good." He stared at her blankly. Sara got the feeling that she might as well be talking to a brick wall. The tension between them was just as thick.

She took his hand. "Will—"

"Thanks for letting me know."

Sara waited for him to say more. Then she realized they only had twelve hours before it would be too late to suture his ankle. She slipped on a pair of surgical gloves. She could tell from the mess that Krakauer had already cleaned out the wound. "Your ankle is numb?"

Will nodded.

"Let's see what we have." She pressed her fingers around the open skin. The laceration was at least an inch long and half as deep. Fresh blood wept out when she forced together the skin. She asked, "You didn't think to tell me that a nail went into your ankle?"

"The other doctor said it barely needs a stitch."

"The other doctor is never going to have to see your ankle again." Sara rolled over the stool so she could sit down. She took the scalpel and used the edge to shape the jagged opening into an ellipse. "I'll make sure there isn't a scar."

"You know that doesn't matter."

Sara looked up at him. There were worse scars on his body. It was something they didn't talk about. One of the many things they didn't talk about.

She tried, again. "What's going on with you?"

Will shook his head, looking away. He was obviously still angry, but Sara had no idea why. There was no use asking him. As sweet and kind and gentle as Will Trent was, Sara had learned that he was about as forthcoming as an amnesiac with lockjaw.

She didn't know what else to do but start suturing. Her glasses were in her purse, which she assumed was still locked inside her car. Sara leaned in close and hooked the needle into the flesh just beneath Will's skin. The chromic thread dipped in and out as she placed a single row of interrupted sutures. Pull, knot, cut. Pull, knot, cut. Over the years, Sara's hands had performed this same action so many times that she went into autopilot, which, unfortunately, gave her mind plenty of time to wander.

The same question she'd been asking herself for the last two weeks popped into her head: What was she doing?

She liked Will. He was the first man Sara had really been with since her husband had died. She enjoyed his company. He was funny and smart. Handsome. Incredibly good in bed. He'd met her family. Her dogs adored him. Sara adored his dog. Over the last few weeks, Will had practically moved into her apartment, but in some ways, he still felt like a stranger.

What little he revealed about his past always came in sugarcoated sound bites. Nothing was ever too bad. No one was that horrible. To hear Will tell it, he'd lived a charmed life. Never mind the cigarette and electrical burns on his body. The jag to his upper lip where the skin had been busted in two. The deep gouge that followed his jaw-line. Sara kissed these places and rubbed her hands along them as if they didn't exist.

"Halfway there." Sara glanced up at Will again. He was still looking away.

She tied off the last knot and picked up a new needle threaded with Prolene. She started the running subcuticular row, zigzagging the thread back and forth, all the while berating herself for giving in to Will's silence.

When their relationship first started, none of this had mattered. There were far more interesting things Will could do with his mouth other than talk about himself. These last few days, his reticence had started to bother her. Sara found herself wondering if he was capable of giving more, and failing that, if she was willing to settle for less.

Even if by some miracle he decided to pour out his heart to Sara, there was still the larger problem of his wife. If Sara was being honest, she was afraid of Angie Polaski, and not just because the woman kept leaving nasty notes on the windshield of Sara's car. Angie lingered in Will's life like a vaporous poison. The joy that Sara felt as Will showed her around his old neighborhood had quickly dissipated when practically every memory he recalled had something to do with Angie. He didn't have to say her name. Sara knew that he was thinking about her.

Which left Sara questioning whether or not there was any space in Will's life for someone other than Angie Polaski.

"There." Sara pulled closed the skin and knotted the loop. "These need to stay in for two weeks. I've got some waterproof Band-Aids at home so you can shower. I'll get you some Tylenol for the pain."

"I've got some at home." He stared at his hands as he rolled down the leg of his pants. "I should probably stay there tonight." He slid on his sock, still not meeting her eyes. "I need to wash some of my shirts. Do the laundry. Check on the dog."

Sara stared openly. Will's jaw was clenched. He was a study in controlled anger. She wasn't sure if this was directed solely at Amanda anymore. "Are you mad at me?"

"No." The answer was short, quick, and obviously a lie.

"All right." Sara turned her back to him as she snapped off her gloves. She tossed them into the trashcan, then started cleaning up the suture kit. Behind her, she could hear Will moving around, probably looking for his shoe. Sara normally had a long fuse, but her bad day had made it considerably shorter. She reached under the bed and grabbed his shoe out of the basket.

She asked, "Do me a favor, sweetheart?"

He took his time answering. "What?"

"Don't talk about what happened tonight, all right?" She tossed the shoe in his general direction. He caught it with one hand, which only served to irritate her more. "Don't tell me what you think about Amanda, or the hammer, or what she was doing at the place where you grew up when she's supposed to be leading a case, and sure as hell let's not talk about whatever she said to you in the basement that has you so freaked out that you're emotionally catatonic. At least, more than usual." Sara stopped for a breath. "Let's just ignore everything. Okay?"

He stared at her for a few seconds, then said, "That sounds like an excellent idea." Will shoved his foot into his shoe. "I'll see you later."

"You bet." Sara looked down at the digital tablet as if she could actually read the words. Her fingers pressed random keys. She felt Will hesitate a moment, then he yanked back the curtain. His shoes snicked on the floor. Sara kept her head down, counting silently. When she reached sixty, she looked up.

He was gone.

"Asshole," Sara hissed. She slid the tablet onto the counter. Earlier, she'd felt tired, but now she was too wired to be anything but furious. She washed her hands. The water was hot enough to scald her skin, but she just scrubbed harder. There was a mirror over the sink. Her hair was a mess. Specks of dried blood dotted her sleeve. This was the first night she'd come straight home in her work clothes. For the last two weeks, she'd been showering at the hospital, changing into a dress or something more flattering, before seeing Will.

Was that part of the problem? Maybe the Amanda thing was another issue. There was an earlier moment on the street when Will had looked down at her. Sara had felt him taking in her scrubs, her hair, with a less-than-impressed expression. Will was always impeccably dressed. Maybe he was thinking that Sara hadn't made much of an effort. Or maybe it went back farther than that. He'd found her crying in her car. Was that what set him off? If so, why had he taken her to the children's home? The fact that he would share something so personal had made Sara feel as if their relationship was finally moving forward.

And here they were again, tripping over their feet as they took giant leaps back.

"Hey, you." Faith stood at the open curtain. Will's partner held her five-month-old daughter on one shoulder and a large diaper bag on the other. "What's going on?"

Sara cut straight to the point. "Do I look bad?"

"You're half a foot taller than me and ten pounds lighter. Do you really want to make me answer that question?"

"Fair enough." Sara held out her hands for Emma. "May I?"

Faith kept the baby on her shoulder. "Trust me, you don't want to be anywhere near this thing. I'm going to have to slap a hazmat sticker on her diaper."

The smell was pungent, but Sara took the baby anyway. It was a nice change to hold a healthy child in her arms. "I guess you're here to see Amanda?" Sara's husband had been a cop. She'd learned the rules long ago. If one of them was in the hospital, they were all in the hospital. "You just missed Will."

"I'm surprised he showed up. He hates this place." Faith took a diaper and some wipes out of her bag. "Do you know what happened to Amanda?"

"She fell on her wrist. She'll be in a cast for a while, but she's fine." Sara laid Emma down on the bed. Faith probably assumed Sara was working a shift. This was one of the problems with Will's myriad secrets—Sara found herself keeping them on his behalf. There was no way to tell Faith what had happened to Amanda without revealing why Sara had been there.

"Right on schedule." Faith indicated a group of older women who were clustered at the nurses' station. Except for a striking African American woman wearing a pink scarf around her neck, they were all dressed in monochromatic pantsuits and sporting the same short haircuts and ramrod-straight spines. "The good old gals," Faith explained. "Mom and Roz are already in with Amanda. I'm sure they'll be spinning war stories until the crack of dawn."

Sara wiped down Emma. The baby squirmed. Sara tickled her stomach. "How's it going with your mom in the house?"

"You mean do I want to strangle her yet?" Faith sat down on the stool. "I get maybe ten minutes, tops, every morning before Emma wakes up and I have to get her fed and ready and then get myself fed and ready and then my whole day starts and I'm at work and the phone is ringing and I'm talking to idiots who are lying to me and it's not until the next morning when I get that ten minutes to myself again."

Faith paused, giving Sara a meaningful look. "Mom's up at five o'clock every morning. I hear her poking around downstairs and I smell coffee and eggs and then I go down to the kitchen and she's all cheery and chatty and wants to talk about what she's got planned for the day and what she saw on the news last night and do I want her to cook me something for breakfast and what do I want for supper and I swear to God, Sara, I'm going to end up killing her. I really am."

"I have a mother, too. I completely understand." Sara slid a new diaper under the baby. Emma's feet kicked up as she tried to turn over. "What are you doing while Will's working at the airport?"

"I thought you knew."

"Knew what?"

"Amanda assigned him to toilet duty so my days are free to take Mom to her physical therapy appointments." Faith shrugged. "You know it's not the first time Mom or Amanda's bent the rules for each other."

"Amanda's not punishing Will because of his hair?"

"What's wrong with his hair? It looks great."

Yet again, Will's ability to read women was pitch-perfect. "I don't understand that relationship."

"Amanda and Will? Or Will and the world?"

"Either. Both." Sara buttoned up the onesie. She stroked her fingers along Emma's face. The baby smiled, showing two tiny white specks where her first pair of teeth were breaking through the bottom gum. Emma's eyes tracked Sara's fingers as they waved back and forth. "She's starting to be a real person."

"She's been laughing at me a lot lately. I'm trying not to take it personally."

Sara put Emma on her shoulder. The baby's arm looped around her neck. "How long has Will been working for Amanda?"

"As far as I know, he's followed her around his whole career. Hostage negotiation. Narcotics. Special crimes."

"Is that normal to stay with one boss your entire career?"

"Not really. Cops are like cats. They'd rather change owners than change houses."

Sara couldn't imagine Will asking to be transferred along with Amanda. He seldom sang her praises, and for Amanda's part, she seemed to delight in torturing him. Then again, if Will had one overriding characteristic, it was his resistance to change. Which fact Sara should probably take as a warning.

"Okay, my turn for questions." Faith crossed her arms. "Here's the big one: when are you going to grab him by the short hairs and tell him to get a fucking divorce?"

Sara managed a smile. "It's very tempting."

"Then why don't you?"

"Because ultimatums never work. And I don't want to be the reason he leaves his wife."

"He wants to leave her."

Sara didn't state the obvious. If Will really wanted to be divorced, then he would be divorced.

Faith hissed air through her teeth. "You probably shouldn't take advice from a woman who's never been married and has one kid in college and another in diapers."

Sara laughed. "Don't sell yourself short."

"Well, it's not like the good guys are lining up to date a cop, and I'm certainly not attracted to the type of useless asshole who'd want to marry a female police officer."

Sara couldn't argue with her. Not many men possessed the temperament for dating a woman who could arrest them.

"Does Will talk to you?" Faith amended, "I mean, about himself. Has he told you anything?"

"Some." Sara felt unreasonably guilty, as if it was her own fault that Will was so closed off. "We just started seeing each other."

"I've got this long list of questions in my head," Faith admitted. "Like, what happened to his parents? Where did he go when he aged out of the system? How did he manage college? How did he get into the GBI?" She studied Sara, who just shrugged. "Statistically, kids in state care have an eighty percent chance of getting arrested before they turn twenty-one. Sixty percent of them end up staying inside."

"Sounds about right." Sara had seen this scenario play out again and again with her kids in the ER. One day she was treating them for an earache, the next they were handcuffed to a gurney awaiting transport to jail. Will's transcendence of this soul-killing pattern was one of the things that she most admired about him. He had succeeded despite the odds.

Which Sara was fairly certain Will would not want her discussing with Faith. She changed the subject. "Are you working this Ashleigh Snyder case?"

"I wish," Faith said. "Though I don't see there's much hope. It hasn't broken on the news yet, but she's been missing for a while, and those so-called friends of hers who're hogging the camera have no idea."

"How long?"

"Since before spring break."

"That was last week." The ER had seen a resulting spike in alcohol poisoning and drug-induced psychosis. "No one noticed she was gone?"

"Her parents thought she went to the Redneck Riviera, her

friends thought she was with her parents. Her roommate waited two days to report her missing. She thought Ashleigh had met a guy and didn't want to get her in trouble."

"So there's no chance she's faking it?"

"There was a lot of blood in her bedroom—on the pillow, the carpet."

"The roommate didn't think that was odd?"

"My son's that age. They're professionally obtuse. I doubt a spaceship landing on his forehead would strike him as odd." Faith returned to their earlier conversation. "Can you look at Will's medical records?"

Sara felt caught out by the question.

Faith added, "His juvenile files are sealed—trust me, I've tried—but there has to be something at Grady from when he was a kid."

A deep blush worked its way up Sara's chest and face. She'd actually considered this once, but common sense had won out. "It's illegal for me to access anyone's records without their permission. Besides—"

Sara stopped talking. She wasn't being completely honest. She'd made it as far as the records department. One of the secretaries had pulled Will's patient chart. Sara hadn't touched the file, but the name on the label listed him as Wilbur Trent. Will's license gave his legal name as William Trent. Sara had seen it the other night when he'd opened his wallet to pay for dinner.

So why had Amanda called him Wilbur?

"Hello?" Faith snapped her fingers. "You in there?"

"Sorry. I zoned out." Sara shifted Emma onto her other shoulder. "I'm just . . ." She tried to remember what they'd been talking about. "I'm not going to spy on him." That, at least, was the truth. Sara wanted to know about Will because they were lovers, not because she was writing a salacious exposé. "He'll tell me when he's ready."

"Good luck with that," Faith said. "Meanwhile, if you find out anything good, let me know."

Sara chewed her lip as she stared at Faith. The overwhelming urge to strike a bargain started to well up from deep inside. Amanda showing up at the children's home. The hammer. Will's unexplained anger. His sudden desire to be alone.

Faith was whip-smart. She'd worked as a homicide detective on the Atlanta police force before becoming a special agent with the GBI. She'd been Will's partner for two years. Faith's mother was one of Amanda's oldest friends. If Sara shared what had happened at the children's home tonight, maybe Faith could help Sara put together the clues.

And then Will really would be lost to her forever.

"Faith," Sara began. "I'm glad we're friends. I like you a lot. But I can't talk about Will behind his back. He has to always know I'm on his side."

She took it better than Sara expected. "You're far too healthy to be in a relationship with a cop. Especially Will."

The thought occurred to Sara that they might not even be in a relationship anymore, but she said, "Thank you for understanding."

Faith waved to an older woman who was standing at the nurses' station. No pantsuit—she was dressed in jeans and a flowery blouse—but there was the unmistakable air of a police officer about her. It was the way she looked around the room, noting the good guys, singling out the possible bad ones. The woman waved at Faith, checked the patient board, then escorted herself toward Amanda's room.

"She trained with Mossad after 9/11," Faith provided. "Two kids. Three grandkids. Divorced five times. Twice from the same man. And did it all without ever wearing a pantsuit." Faith sounded reverential. "She's my role model."

Sara cradled Emma so she could look at her face. There was a soft, powdery scent coming off her, a mixture of baby wipes and sweat. "Your mom's a pretty good role model, too."

"We're too different." Faith shrugged. "Mom's quiet, methodical, always in charge, and I'm 'oh my God, we're all going to die.'"

The evaluation was strange coming from a woman who kept a loaded shotgun in the trunk of her car. Sara said, "I feel safe knowing you're with Will." Faith would never know what kind of compliment Sara had paid her. "You're pretty good under fire."

"Once I stop freaking out." She pointed toward Amanda's room. "You could blow up a bomb right now and as soon as the dust cleared, all of them would still be right there, guns drawn, ready to fight the bad guys."

Sara had seen Amanda in some tough situations. She didn't doubt it one bit.

"Mom told me when they joined up, the first question on the polygraph was about their sex lives. Were they virgins? If not, how many men had they been with—was it more than one? Was it less than three?"

"Is that legal?"

"Anything's legal if you can get away with it." She grinned. "They asked mom if she was joining the force so she could have sex with policemen. She told them it depended on what the policeman looked like."

Sara asked, "What about Amanda?" The fall in the basement had her recalling her early days on the force. Maybe there was a reason. "Was she always a cop?"

"Far as I know."

"She never worked for children's services?"

Faith narrowed her eyes. Sara could practically see her detective's brain click on. "What are you getting at?"

Sara kept her attention on Emma. "I was just curious. Will hasn't told me much about her."

"He wouldn't," Faith said, as if she needed reminding. "I grew up with Amanda. She dated my uncle for years, but the idiot never asked her to marry him."

"She never got married? Had kids?"

"She can't have children. I know she tried, but it wasn't in the cards."

Sara kept her gaze on Emma. There was one thing she shared with Amanda Wagner. It wasn't the kind of club you bragged about belonging to.

Faith said, "Can you imagine her as a mother? You'd be better off with a dingo."

Emma hiccupped. Sara rubbed her tummy. She smiled at Faith, wishing—longing—to talk to her, but knowing she could not. Sara had not felt this cut off in a long while.

Of course, she could always call her mother, but Sara wasn't up for a lecture about right and wrong, especially because Sara could clearly see the difference, which made her less the subject of a torrid love affair and more like a woman who had resigned herself to being a doormat. Because that was exactly what Cathy Linton would say: why are you giving a man everything when he won't or can't give you anything in return?

Faith asked, "Was that you or Emma?"

Sara realized she'd grunted. "Me. I just figured out my mother was right about something."

"God, I hate when that happens." Faith sat up straight. "Speaking of . . ."

Evelyn Mitchell was standing by the nurses' station. The woman was cut from the same cloth as her friends: matching pantsuit, trim figure, perfect posture even though she couldn't stand without crutches. She was obviously looking for her daughter.

Faith reluctantly stood. "Duty calls." Her feet dragged the floor as she headed toward the nurses' station.

Sara held up Emma and touched her nose to the baby's. Emma showed both rows of gums, squealing in delight. If there was any question about how good a mother Faith Mitchell was, one need only look at her happy baby. Sara kissed Emma's cheeks. The little girl giggled. A few more kisses and she started snorting. Her feet kicked in the air. Sara kissed her again.

"His *what*?" Faith shouted.

Her voice echoed through the ER. Both mother and daughter stared openly at Sara. From this distance, they could've been twins. Both around the same weight and height. Both with blonde hair and a familiar set to their shoulders. Faith's expression was troubled, and Evelyn's was as inscrutable as usual. The older woman said something, and Faith nodded before heading toward Sara.

"Sorry." Faith held out her hands for Emma. "I need to go."

Sara passed her the baby. "Is everything okay?"

"I don't know."

"Is it Ashleigh Snyder?"

"No. Yes." Faith's mouth opened again, then closed. Obviously, there was something wrong. Faith didn't shock easily, and Evelyn Mitchell wasn't one to casually dole out information.

Sara said, "Faith, you're scaring me. Is Will all right?"

"I don't—" She stopped herself. "I can't—" Again, she stopped. Her lips pressed together in a thin white line. Finally, she said, "You were right, Sara. Some things we have to keep separate."

For the second time that night, a person keeping a secret turned their back on Sara and walked away.

seven

July 11, 1975

FRIDAY

Amanda scanned through her women's studies textbook, marking the paragraphs she needed to know for her evening class. She was sitting in the passenger's seat of Kyle Peterson's Plymouth Fury. The police radio was turned down low, but her ear had been trained long ago to tune out anything but the pertinent calls. She turned the page and started to read the next section.

> To understand the far-reaching effects of the sex/gender system, one must first deconstruct the phallic hypothesis in relation to the unconscious.

"Brother." Amanda sighed. Whatever the hell that meant.

The car shook as Peterson turned over in the back seat. Amanda studied his reflection in the visor mirror, willing him not to wake.

She'd already wasted nearly an hour this morning slapping away his hands, then another half hour had been consumed with apologies so that he would stop sulking. Thank God the flask in his pocket had been full enough to knock him out or Amanda would've never found time to read her assignment.

Not that she understood a word of it. Some of the passages were downright obscene. If these women were so eager to find out how their vaginas worked, they should start shaving their legs and find themselves husbands.

The radio clicked. Amanda heard the in-and-out of a man's voice. There were pockets all over the city where the radios had little or no reception, but that wasn't the problem. A black officer was calling for backup, which meant the white officers were blocking the transmission by clicking the buttons on their mics. In the next hour, a white officer would call for help and the blacks would do the same.

And then someone with the *Atlanta Journal* or *Constitution* would write an article wondering why there had been a recent spike in crime.

Amanda checked on Peterson again. He'd started snoring. His mouth gaped open beneath his shaggy, untrimmed mustache.

She read the next paragraph, then promptly forgot everything it said. Her eyes blurred from exhaustion. Or maybe it was irritation. If she never read the words "gynecocratic" and "patriarchy" again, it would be too soon. Send Gloria Steinem into Techwood Homes and see if she still thought women could run the world.

Techwood.

Amanda felt the panic rising up like bile. The pimp's hand around her throat. The feel of his erection pressing against her. The scrape of his fingernails as he tried to pull down her hose.

She gritted her teeth, willing her heart to settle. Deep breaths. In and out. Slow. "One . . . two . . . three . . ." She whispered off the seconds. Minutes passed before she was able to unclench her jaw and breathe normally again.

Amanda had not seen Evelyn Mitchell in the four days since the awful ordeal. The other woman hadn't shown up for roll call. Her name wasn't on the roster. Even Vanessa couldn't find her. Amanda found herself hoping that Evelyn had come to her senses and gone back home to take care of her family. It was hard enough for Amanda to force herself out of bed every morning. She couldn't imagine the dread she'd feel leaving her family, knowing the sort of world into which she was thrusting herself.

But then, Evelyn wasn't the only officer who'd disappeared. The new sergeant, Luther Hodge, had been summarily transferred. His replacement was a white man named Hoyt Woody. He was from North Georgia, and his thick hill accent was made all the more unintelligible by the toothpick he kept in his mouth at all times. The tensions around the squad were still there, but they were the usual kind. Everyone was more comfortable with a known entity.

At least Hodge's disappearance wasn't into thin air. Vanessa had made more phone calls, which revealed the sergeant had been transferred to one of the Model City precincts. Not only was it a downward move, it took him out of Amanda's circle. Unfortunately, she hadn't the nerve to go to Hodge's new station and ask him why they'd been sent to Techwood Homes on such a fool's errand.

Not that Amanda wasn't capable of other useless errands. The last few days had been a test of her two warring sides. She longed to put the whole Techwood ordeal behind her, but her curiosity would not let it go. Her sleepless nights were not just filled with fear. They were filled with questions.

Amanda wanted to think that her cop's curiosity had been piqued, but the honest truth was that she was coasting on nothing more than woman's intuition. The whore who was living in Kitty Treadwell's apartment had put the bug in Amanda's ear. Something wasn't right there. She could feel it in her bones.

Which is why Amanda had done some poking around that had exacerbated her already frayed nerves. Stupid poking around that would probably get back to her father and land her in hot water not just with Duke, but with the higher-ups in the police force.

Amanda closed her textbook. And she especially hadn't the stomach to read Phyllis Schlafly's rebuttal to the Equal Rights Amendment. Amanda was sick and tired of being told how to live her life by women who never had to write their own rent checks.

"What's the skinny?"

Amanda jumped so hard she nearly slammed her book into her face. She shushed Evelyn Mitchell, then turned around to check on Peterson.

"Sorry," Evelyn whispered. She put her hand on the door handle, but Amanda slammed down the lock. Evelyn stood outside the car, unmoved. "You know the window is down, right?"

Behind her, Vanessa Livingston giggled.

Reluctantly, Amanda unlocked the door and got out of the car. She whispered, "What do you want?"

Evelyn whispered back, "We're trading. You for Nessa."

"No way." The brass wouldn't care, but Amanda had no intention of ever partnering with Evelyn Mitchell again. She started to get back into the car. Evelyn caught her arm, and Vanessa squeezed past, slipping into the seat and carefully latching the door.

Amanda stood in the empty parking lot, wanting to slap them both.

Evelyn told Vanessa, "We'll be back in a few hours."

"Take your time." Vanessa checked Peterson. "I don't think he's going anywhere."

Evelyn used her finger to swipe the side of her nose, à la Robert Redford in *The Sting*. Vanessa did the same.

"This is ridiculous," Amanda muttered, reaching into the car to retrieve her purse and textbook.

"Oh, cheer up," Evelyn said. "Maybe we'll find some mud for you to stick in."

Evelyn drove her Ford Falcon up North Avenue. The station wagon was now devoid of moving boxes and filled with various baby items. Except for the radio on the seat between them, there was nothing that would indicate a police officer drove this car. The vinyl seat felt sticky under Amanda's legs. As an only child with no cousins, she was seldom around children. Amanda could not help but think that Zeke Mitchell had secreted a vile substance onto the vinyl.

"Pretty day," Evelyn said.

She had to be joking. The noontime sun was so intense that Amanda's eyes were watering. She shielded her eyes from the glare.

Evelyn reached into her purse and slipped on a pair of Foster Grants. "I think I have another pair." She dug around in her bag.

"No, thank you." Amanda had seen the same glasses at Richway. They cost at least five dollars.

"Suit yourself." Evelyn zipped closed her purse. She drove like an old woman, slowing for yellow lights, letting anyone pass who showed the slightest desire. She kept one foot on the gas and one on the brake. By the time they pulled into the Varsity drive-in, Amanda was ready to grab the wheel and push her out of the car.

Evelyn mumbled, "Steady, Freddy." With great concentration, she angled the Falcon into a parking spot close to the North Avenue entrance. The brakes squealed as she pumped the pedal, inching up slowly until she felt the tires bump against the barrier. Finally, Evelyn shifted the gear into park. The engine knocked when she turned off the ignition. The car shook.

Evelyn turned in her seat, facing Amanda. "Well?"

"Why did you bring me here? I couldn't possibly eat."

"I think I prefer when you're not speaking to me."

"Your wish is my command," Amanda snapped back. But then she couldn't help herself. "You almost got me raped."

Evelyn leaned back against the door. "In my defense, both of us were going to be raped."

Amanda shook her head. The woman was incapable of taking anything seriously.

Evelyn said, "We made it through okay."

"Spare me your positive energy."

Evelyn was silent. She turned back around. She kept her hands in her lap. Amanda stared straight ahead at the menu board. The words jumbled around senselessly. In her head, Amanda listed again all the things she had to do before she could go to sleep tonight. The more she thought about it, the harder the tasks seemed. She was too tired to do any of it. She was too tired to even be here.

"Damn, gal." Evelyn's voice was deep, an approximation of the pimp's baritone. "You a fine-lookin' woman."

Amanda gripped the textbook in her lap. "Stop it."

Evelyn, as usual, was oblivious. "You is fi-ine."

Amanda turned her head away, leaning her chin on her hand. "Please, be quiet."

"Gone get me some'a that hog tush."

"Oh, for God's sakes," Amanda sputtered. "He didn't say that!" Her lips were trembling, but for the first time in four days it wasn't because she was forcing back tears.

"Mmm-hmm," Evelyn goaded, moving her hips obscenely in the seat. "Fine-lookin' woman."

Amanda couldn't stop her lips from curving upward. And then, she was laughing. There was no controlling it, even if she tried. Her mouth opened wide. She felt a lessening of pressure not just from the sound, but from the release of air that had been trapped in her lungs like a poison. Evelyn was laughing, too, which seemed the funniest part of all. Before long, they were both doubled over in their seats, tears streaming down their faces.

"Afternoon, ladies." The carhop was at Evelyn's window. His hat was rakishly tilted to the side. He slapped a number card on their windshield and smiled at them both as if he was in on the joke. "What'll ya have?"

Amanda wiped tears from her eyes. For the first time in days, she was hungry. "Bring me a Glorified Steak and some strings. And a P.C."

Evelyn said, "I'll have the same. Add a fried pie."

"Wait," Amanda called him back. "I'll have a fried pie, too."

Evelyn was still chuckling when he left. "Oh, Lord." She sighed. She tilted the mirror and used the tip of her pinky finger to fix her eyeliner. "Lord," she repeated. "I haven't been able to even think about eating since . . ." She didn't have to finish the sentence. Neither of them would have to finish that sentence ever again.

Amanda asked, "What did your husband say?"

"There are some things I don't share with Bill. He likes to think I'm Agent 99, hiding safely behind the scenes while Max Smart does all the real work." She gave a short laugh. "It's not too off the mark. You know, they never even say her name on that dumb show. She's just a number."

Amanda didn't respond. It sounded like a chapter in her women's studies book.

Evelyn waited a beat. "What did your father say?"

"I wouldn't be here if I'd told him." Amanda picked at the edge of her book. "Hodge got transferred to Model City."

"Where do you think I've been?"

Amanda felt her jaw drop. "They assigned you to Model City?"

"Hodge won't even talk to me. Every morning, first thing, I go into his office and I ask him what happened, who we ticked off, why he sent us to Techwood in the first place, and every day, he tells me to get the hell out of his office."

Amanda couldn't help but be impressed by the other woman's brashness. "You think you're being punished?" she asked. "That can't be true. The brass didn't move me. I was there, same as you."

Evelyn seemed to have an opinion on the matter, but she kept it to herself. "The boys took care of that pimp for us."

Amanda felt her heart go into her throat. "You didn't tell anyone?"

"No, of course not, but you don't have to be Columbo to figure it out—a pimp bleeding on the floor with his winky hanging out and both of us looking like we're about to have heart attacks."

She was right. At least Evelyn had saved them some face by managing to knock him out before the cavalry arrived.

"They let him out of jail long enough to get picked up again. Apparently, he resisted arrest. Up and down Ashby Street. Ended up in the hospital."

"Good. Maybe he learned his lesson."

"Maybe," Evelyn said, sounding doubtful. "He thought I'd just stand there while he raped you, waiting for my turn."

"He's probably done it hundreds of times before. You saw how Jane was with him. She was terrified."

Evelyn nodded slowly. "Dwayne Mathison. That's his name. He's been jammed up a couple of times for roughing up his girls. He runs mostly white women—tall blondes who used to be pretty. Goes by the name Juice."

"Like the football player?"

"Except one's a Heisman winner and the other likes to beat on women." Evelyn tapped her finger against the textbook in Amanda's lap. "This is surprising."

She covered the book with her hands, embarrassed. "It's a required course."

"Still, it's not a bad thing to know what's going on in other places."

Amanda shrugged. "It won't change anything."

"Don't you think it's kind of inevitable? Look at what happened to the coloreds." She indicated the restaurant. "Nipsey Russell used to be a curb man here, and now you can't turn on the TV without seeing his face."

This was true enough. Amanda didn't know which infuriated her father more, seeing Russell on every game show or finding Monica Kaufman, the new black anchor, on the Channel 2 news every evening.

Evelyn said, "Mayor Jackson's not doing such a bad job. Say what you will about Reggie, but the city hasn't burned down. Yet."

The carhop was back with their food. He hooked the tray through Evelyn's window. Amanda reached for her purse.

Evelyn said, "I've got this."

"I don't need you to—"

"Consider it buying your forgiveness."

"It's going to take more than that."

Evelyn counted out the dollar bills and left what seemed like a very generous tip. "What are you doing tomorrow?"

If her Saturday was like any other, Amanda would spend the day cleaning her father's house, then cleaning her own apartment, then while away the evening with Mary Tyler Moore, Bob Newhart, and Carol Burnett. "I hadn't thought about it."

Evelyn handed over her food. "Why don't you come to my house? We're having a barbecue."

"I'll have to check my schedule," Amanda managed, though she didn't think her father would approve. She was actually worried that he'd heard something. Without prompting, he'd seen fit to warn her off Evelyn Mitchell every morning this week. "Thank you for the invitation, though."

Evelyn said, "Well, let me know. I'd love for you to meet Bill. He's just—" Her voice took on a dreamy quality. "He's just the best. I know you'd like him."

Amanda nodded, unsure of what to say.

"You date much?"

"All the time," she joked. "Men just love it when they find out you're a cop." They loved it as they ran screaming for the door. "I'm too busy to date right now, anyway. I'm trying to finish my degree. There's just a lot going on."

Evelyn obviously saw right through her. "Working around jerks like Peterson all day, you forget what a nice, normal guy is like." She paused. "There are some good ones out there. Don't let the Neanderthals get you down."

"Mm-hm." Amanda put a french fry in her mouth, then another, until Evelyn did the same.

They both ate in silence, sticking their cups on the dashboard, balancing the paper containers in their laps. For Amanda's part, the greasy french fries and hamburger were exactly what she needed. The iced chocolate milk was as sweet as a dessert, but she ate the fried pie anyway. By the time she was through, she felt slightly nauseated again, but this time it was overindulgence rather than fear turning her stomach.

Evelyn transferred their empty containers back to the window tray. She put her hand to her stomach and groaned. "*Mamma mia, that's a spicy meatball.*"

"I put a new bottle of Alka-Seltzer in my purse this morning."

Evelyn waved over the carhop and ordered two cups of water. "I'm beginning to think you and I are a bad influence on each other."

Amanda's eyelids dipped into a lengthy blink. "This is the first time I've ever wanted to be in the car with Peterson so I could lay down and go to sleep."

"You'd wake up with him on top of you." Evelyn tugged at the back of her hair. She was silent a few seconds, then asked, "Say, why do you think Hodge sent us to Techwood?"

Not for the first time, Amanda felt the danger behind her question. It was clear that someone very high up was pulling strings. Both Evelyn and Hodge had been transferred. There was no telling what would happen to Amanda, especially if anyone found out what she'd been doing.

Evelyn prodded, "Come on, girl. I know you've been thinking about it."

"Well." Amanda tried to make herself stop there, but she continued, "The guy in the blue suit bothers me. And not just because he's a lawyer."

"I know what you mean," Evelyn agreed. "He walked into the station like he owned it. He yelled at Hodge. You don't get to do that to a cop, even if you're white and in a fancy blue suit."

"Hodge called him by name. That's what he said during roll call: 'Mr. Treadwell, we can talk in my office.'"

"And then they went into the office, and Treadwell started ordering him around right off the bat."

"Evelyn, you're missing the point. Think about what you told me before. Andrew Treadwell, Sr., has friends in high places. He had his picture in the paper with Mayor Jackson. He worked on the campaign. Why would he reach out to a lowly sergeant with no pull who's only been in charge for less than an hour?"

She nodded. "Okay. You're right. Keep going."

"Treadwell-Price specializes in construction law. Andrew Senior is negotiating all those contracts for the new subway system nobody wants."

"How'd you hear that?"

"I went down to the newspaper and looked through some of the back issues."

"They let you do that?"

Amanda shrugged. "My dad worked on that kidnapping case last year." An editor from the paper had been held for a million-dollar ransom. One of Duke's last official duties was transporting the money from the C&S vault to the drop location. "I told them who I was and they let me look through the archives."

"Your father doesn't know you were there?"

"Of course not." Duke would've been livid that Amanda hadn't cleared it with him first. "He'd ask me what I was up to. I didn't want to open that can of worms."

"Phew." Evelyn leaned her head back against the seat. "What you found out is certainly interesting. Anything else?"

Amanda hesitated again.

"Come on, darlin'. You can't be a little pregnant."

Amanda sighed to make her reluctance known. She had a sneaking suspicion she was just stirring up trouble. "The man who was talking to Hodge isn't Treadwell Junior. According to the newspaper, Treadwell Senior has one child, a daughter."

Evelyn sat up again. "Named Kitty? Or Katherine? Kate?"

"Eugenia Louise, and she's at some girls' school in Switzerland."

"So, not shooting up Boy at Techwood."

"Boy?"

"It's what Negroes call heroin. Thank you." The carhop was back with their water. Amanda unscrewed the cap from the bottle of Alka-Seltzer and dropped two tablets into each cup. The fizzing was a welcome sound.

Evelyn said, "So, there's no Treadwell Junior. I wonder who the man in the blue suit was? And why Hodge thought he was Treadwell?" Evelyn smiled. "I'm sure Hodge thinks we all look alike."

Amanda smiled, too. "Blue Suit has to be a lawyer. Maybe he's from the firm and Hodge just assumed his name was Treadwell. But that doesn't make sense, either. We've already established Andrew Treadwell wouldn't send his minion to talk to a brand-new zone captain. He'd go straight to the mayor. The more delicate the situation, the more likely he'd be to let as few people know as possible."

Evelyn made the obvious connection. "Which means either Blue Suit was taking initiative to help the boss or he was looking to make trouble."

Amanda wasn't so sure about that, but she said, "Either way, Hodge wasn't telling him what he wanted to hear. Blue Suit was angry when he left. He yelled at Hodge, then stormed out of the building."

Evelyn circled back to her earlier theory. "Blue Suit pressured Hodge to send us out to check on Kitty Treadwell. Treadwell isn't a common name. She has to somehow be related to Andrew Treadwell."

"I couldn't find a connection in the newspapers, but they don't keep all the back issues and they're a bear to search through."

"Treadwell-Price is in that new office building off Forsyth Street. We could sit outside during lunch. These guys don't brown-bag it. Blue Suit will have to come out sooner or later."

"And then what?"

"We show him our badges and ask him some questions."

Amanda didn't see that working. The man would probably laugh in their faces. "What if it gets back to Hodge that you're snooping around?"

"I don't think he cares so long as I stay out of his office and stop asking him questions. What about your new sergeant?"

"He's one of the old guard, but he barely knows my name."

"Probably drunk before lunchtime," Evelyn said. She was likely correct. Once the older sergeants got past their morning duties, you were hard-pressed to find one behind his desk. There was a reason half the force could be found napping during shift. "We can get together Monday after roll call. They don't care what we do so long as we're on the streets. Nessa's okay with Peterson."

Amanda was slightly worried about how good Vanessa was being with Peterson, but she let it slide. "Jane wasn't the only girl living in that apartment. There were at least two others."

"How do you get that?"

"There were three toothbrushes in the bathroom. All of them well used."

"Jane didn't have that many teeth."

Amanda stared into the fizzing seltzer. Her stomach was too full to laugh at Evelyn's jokes. "Half of me thinks I'm crazy for wasting so much time tracking down a story off a junkie prostitute."

Evelyn sounded apologetic. "You're not the only one who's been wasting time."

Amanda narrowed her eyes at the other woman. "I knew it. What've you been up to?"

"I talked with a friend I know at the Five. Cindy Murray. She's a good girl. I described Jane to her. Cindy says maybe she remembers her coming in last week. Lots of girls try to pick up vouchers that don't belong to them. They have to show two forms of ID—a license, a blood donor card, electric bill, something with their picture and address on it. If Jane is the girl Cindy was thinking of, she tried to pass herself off with someone else's license. When Jane saw the jig was up, she went bonkers. Started screaming and making threats. Security had to throw her out into the street."

"What happened to the license?"

"They toss 'em into a box, wait to see if anyone tries to claim them. Cindy says there's at least a hundred licenses already. They tear them in half and throw them away at the end of every year."

"Are the welfare rolls organized by names or by addresses?"

"Numbers, unfortunately. Too many of them have the same last name or live at the same address, so they all get assigned an individual number."

"Social security number?"

"No such luck."

"It's got to be on computers, right?"

"They're in the process of changing over from punch cards to magnetic tape," Evelyn answered. "Cindy says it's a mess. She's basically working with a hammer and chisel while the boys try to figure it out. Which means even if we had access to the information, which they probably won't give us, we'd have to do it all by hand: get the welfare roll number first, then cross-reference the number to the name, then verify the name against the address, then match both against the benefits logs that verify whether the girls have collected their vouchers in the last six months, which we could then use to compare to the names on the licenses." Evelyn stopped for a breath. "Cindy says we'll need a staff of fifty and about twenty years."

"How long until the computers are up and running?"

"I don't think it would matter." Evelyn shrugged. "They're computers, not magic beans. We'd still have to do most of it by hand. Assuming they'd give us access. Does your father know anyone down at the Five?"

Duke would've taken a blowtorch to the Five if they let him. "It wouldn't matter. We can't even start the whole process until we find out Kitty Treadwell's roll number." Amanda tried to think this through. "Jane said three women were missing: Kitty Treadwell, Lucy, and Mary."

"I already checked missing persons in Zones Three and Four," Evelyn provided. "No Kitty Treadwell. No Jane Delray—which I thought I'd check on while I was there. What I did find were a dozen Lucys and about a hundred Marys. They never clean out their files. Some of these girls have died of old age by now. They've been missing since the Depression." She offered, "I can go to the other zones next week. Do you know Dr. Hanson?"

Amanda shook her head.

"Pete. Runs the morgue." She saw Amanda's expression. "No, he's a good guy. Kind of what you'd expect from a coroner, but very nice. I know a gal works for him, Deena Coolidge. She says he lets her do things sometimes."

"What things?"

Evelyn rolled her eyes. "Not what you're thinking. Lab things.

Deena's real into that stuff. Likes chemistry. Pete's teaching her how to do the tests and some of the lab work on her own. She's going to Tech at night, too."

Amanda could guess why Dr. Hanson was letting her do these things, and it probably wasn't out of the kindness of his heart. "Did you check the DNF?"

"The what?"

The dead Negro file. Duke had told Amanda about the running list of unsolved black homicides. Amanda offered, "I'll check it."

"Check what?"

She changed the subject. "Do we know if the apartment is in Kitty's name?"

"Oh!" Evelyn seemed impressed. "That's a very good question." She grabbed one of the napkins off the dashboard and wrote herself a note. "I wonder if the number you get assigned for Section Eight housing is the same as the one they give you for collecting welfare vouchers? Do you know anyone at the Housing Authority?"

"Pam Canale." Amanda checked the time. "I need to study for my class tonight, but I can call her first thing Monday."

"You can tell me what you find out when we're staking out Mr. Blue Suit. Also—" She scribbled something else on the napkin. "Here's my number at home so you can let me know about tomorrow. The barbecue."

"Thank you." Amanda folded the napkin in two and stuck it in her purse. There was no lie she could tell Duke that could explain such a long absence. He was always calling her apartment to make sure she was home. If Amanda didn't pick up by the second ring, he hung up and drove over.

"You know," Evelyn began, "I read an article in the paper about this guy out West who's been killing college students."

"These girls aren't college students."

"Still, we've got three missing."

"This isn't Hollywood, Evelyn. There aren't serial killers lurking around Atlanta." Amanda changed the subject back to something more plausible. "I've been thinking about Kitty's apartment. There were three trash bags full of clothes in the bedroom. No woman can afford that many clothes, especially if she's living in the projects." Amanda felt her stomach rumble. She had forgotten about the paper cup in her hand. She downed the seltzer in one swallow and suppressed the resulting belch. "There was a lot of makeup in the bathroom, too. Way too much for one girl. Even a prostitute."

"Jane wasn't wearing any makeup. There was no smeared mascara under her eyes. I can't see her cleaning up with cold cream every night."

"There was cold cream in the bathroom," Amanda recalled, "but suffice it to say, no one was using it. There were used sanitary napkins in the trashcan, but a box of Tampax was on the shelf. So, obviously, someone was staying there who wasn't on the game. Maybe a little sister. Maybe even Kitty Treadwell."

Evelyn put the cup to her lips. "Why do you think that?"

"You can't wear Tampax if you're a virgin. So—"

Evelyn choked on the seltzer. The water spurted from her mouth and nose. She grabbed at the napkins on the dashboard, coughing so hard it sounded as if her lungs were trying to come out of her mouth.

Amanda patted her back. "Are you all right?"

She put her hand to her mouth and coughed again. "Sorry. Went down the wrong way." She coughed a third and fourth time. "What's that?"

Amanda looked out into the street. An Atlanta Police cruiser zoomed by, lights rolling, no siren. The next cruiser was the opposite: siren blaring, lights off.

"What on earth . . . ," Amanda began.

Evelyn turned up the police radio. All they could hear was the usual chatter, followed by mics being clicked so that the speakers could not be heard. "Idiots," Evelyn mumbled, turning the volume back down. Another cruiser screeched by. "What could it be?"

Amanda was sitting up in her seat, straining to see what was happening. Then she realized there was an easier way. She tossed her paper cup out the window and pushed open the door. By the time she reached the sidewalk, another car zoomed past, this one a Plymouth Fury like her own.

Evelyn joined her on the sidewalk. "That was Rick and Butch." Homicide. "They're going to Techwood. All of them are going to Techwood."

Neither woman said what they were thinking. They headed toward the station wagon. Amanda edged Evelyn toward the passenger's side, saying, "I'll drive."

Evelyn didn't offer protest. She rode shotgun as Amanda backed up the car, then headed up North Avenue. They turned on Techwood Drive. A police cruiser blew past on Amanda's left as she turned onto Pine.

Evelyn grabbed the dashboard. "My Lord. Why are they in such a hurry?"

"We'll find out soon enough." Amanda pulled up onto the familiar berm. There were already five cruisers and two unmarked Plymouths. Today, no children were playing in the courtyard of Techwood Homes, though their parents had finally made an appearance. Shirtless men in tight jeans stood with cans of beer in their hands. Most of the women were just as scantily clad, but a few looked as if they'd just returned home from office work. Amanda checked her watch. It was past one o'clock. Maybe they'd come home for lunch.

"Amanda." Evelyn's tone held a low tremor. She followed the other woman's gaze to the second apartment block on the left. A group of patrolmen were clustered outside the door. Butch Bonnie pushed past them as he ran out into the courtyard. He fell to his knees and spewed vomit onto the ground.

"Oh, no." Amanda searched in her bag for a tissue. "We can get some water from—"

Evelyn stopped her with a firm hand. "Stay exactly where you are."

"But he—"

"I mean it," she said, her voice taking on a tenor Amanda had not heard before.

Rick Landry exited the building next. He used his handkerchief

to wipe his mouth, then tucked it into his back pocket. Had his partner still not been vocally ill, Landry probably would've never noticed
Amanda and Evelyn. As it was, he walked right over to them.

"What the hell are you broads doing here?"

Amanda opened her mouth, but Evelyn beat her to a response.
"We had a case here earlier this week. Top floor. Apartment C. Prostitute named Jane Delray."

Landry stuck his tongue into his cheek as he stared first at Evelyn,
then Amanda. "And?"

"And, obviously something happened here."

"It's Techwood, darlin'. Something happens here all the time."

"Top floor?" Evelyn asked. "Apartment C?"

"Wrong and wrong," Landry said. "Behind the building. Suicide.
Jumped off the roof and went splat."

"Fuck!" Butch Bonnie gave a heave that rivaled the sound of a pig
rutting in the wild. Landry's gaze faltered. He didn't quite look back
at his partner, but he wouldn't look at Evelyn or Amanda, either.

"You." Landry motioned over one of the uniformed patrolmen.
"Get all these people outta here. Looks like we're filming a damn
Tarzan movie." The cop rushed to disperse the group of onlookers.
There were yells and protests.

Evelyn said, "Maybe someone saw—"

"Saw what?" Landry interrupted. "They probably didn't even
know her. But, give 'em another minute, they'll all be wailin' and
howlin' and flappin' their gums about what a tragedy it is." He shot
Evelyn a look. "You should know better than that, Mitchell. Never
let 'em crowd up. They get too emotional and pretty soon you're
callin' in SWAT to thin 'em out."

Evelyn spoke so quietly that Amanda could barely hear her. "We'd
like to see the body."

"We what?" Amanda's voice trilled around the words.

Landry grinned. "Looks like Ethel ain't up for this, Lucy."

Evelyn didn't back down. She cleared her throat. "We're working
a case, Landry. Same as you."

"Same as me?" he echoed, incredulous. He glanced back at Butch, who was sitting back on his heels, chest heaving. Amanda could see the glint of the revolver he kept on his ankle. "You girls need to toddle on back and—"

"She's right." Amanda heard the words clear as a bell. They were spoken in her own voice. They had come out of her own mouth.

Evelyn seemed just as surprised as Amanda.

"We're working a case," Amanda told him. That was *exactly* what they were doing. They'd just spent the last half hour in the car talking it through. Something was going on with these women—Kitty, Lucy, Mary, and now possibly Jane Delray. Right now, Amanda and Evelyn were the only two officers on the entire force who even knew—or apparently cared—that they were missing.

Landry lit a cigarette. He let out a stream of smoke. "Same as me, huh?" he repeated, but this time he was laughing. "You skirts working homicide now?"

Evelyn shot back, "You just said it was a suicide. What are you doing here?"

He didn't like that. "You want some balls, Mitchell, you can always suck on mine."

Amanda looked down at the ground so her expression wouldn't give her away.

"I'm fine with my husband's, thank you." Evelyn reached into her purse and pulled out her Kel-Lite. "We're ready when you are."

Landry ignored her, telling Amanda, "Come on, gal. This ain't no place for you. That body's a mess. Guts all over the place. Nasty stuff. Too nasty for a lady to handle." He tilted his chin toward Butch, not stating the obvious. "Go on, get back in your car and scoot off. Nobody'll think nothin' about it."

Amanda felt her stomach start to unclench. He was giving them an out. A graceful exit. No one would know they had asked to see the body. They could leave with their heads held high. Amanda was about to take him up on the offer, but then Landry added, "God knows, I don't want your old man coming after me with his shotgun for scaring his baby girl."

There was an odd tingling in Amanda's spine. She felt as if every vertebra was locking into place. She spoke in a shockingly certain tone. "You said the victim is behind the building?"

Evelyn appeared just as surprised as Landry when Amanda started walking toward the apartment building. She kept pace with Amanda, whispering, "What are you doing?"

"Keep walking," Amanda begged her. "Please keep walking."

"Have you ever seen a dead body?"

"Never close up," Amanda admitted. "Unless you count my grandfather."

Evelyn muttered a curse. She spoke in a hoarse whisper. "Whatever you do, don't get sick. Don't scream. For God's sake, don't cry."

Amanda was ready to do all three and she hadn't even seen the body yet. What in the name of God was she thinking? Landry was right. If Butch Bonnie hadn't been able to handle it, there was no way in hell either of them would be able to.

"Listen to me," Evelyn ordered. "If you break, they'll never trust you again. You might as well join the typing pool. You might as well slit your wrists."

"I'm okay," she said, then because she knew Evelyn needed to hear it, she told her, "You're okay, too. You're absolutely okay."

Evelyn's heels kicked up dust as she walked beside Amanda. "I'm okay," she repeated. "You're right. I'm okay."

"We're both okay." So much sweat was dripping down Amanda's back that it was pooling into her underwear. She was glad she was wearing a black skirt. She was glad she had taken that Alka-Seltzer. She was very glad that she wasn't alone as she walked into the dark building.

The vestibule was cast in more shadow than Amanda remembered. She glanced up the stairwell. One of the panes in the skylight had been broken. A piece of wood was nailed in its place. They both stopped at the metal exit door at the end of the hall, waiting for Landry.

He put his hand on the door but didn't open it. "Lookit, girls, playtime is over. Go back to taking reports on poor little sluts got mixed up with the wrong fella and cried wolf."

"We're working a case," Evelyn told him. "It might have something to do with—"

"Whore took a long walk off a short plank. You seen this dump. I'm surprised everybody here don't jump off the roof."

"We still—"

He said, "Just turn around and walk back. This has gone far enough."

"I was—"

"Stop!" Landry banged his fist against the door. "Just shut your fucking mouth!" he shouted. "I told you to leave and you'd better goddamn leave."

Evelyn was visibly startled, but she tried, "We just—"

"You want me to make you?" He snatched the Kel-Lite out of Evelyn's hand and jabbed it into her chest. "You like that?" He jabbed her again, then again, until her back was to the wall. "Not so mouthy now, are you?"

Amanda tried, "Rick—"

"Shut up!" There was a flash of white skin as he jammed the flashlight up Evelyn's skirt and pressed it between her legs. He warned, "Unless you want that for real, you better do as I damn well say. You hear me?"

Evelyn didn't speak. She could only nod. Her hands shook as they went up in surrender.

"Don't fuck around with me," Landry warned. "You got that?"

"She's sorry," Amanda said. "We're both sorry. Rick, please. We're sorry."

Slowly, he pulled the flashlight out from under Evelyn's skirt. With one hand, he flipped it around and held out the handle to Amanda. He told her, "Get her the hell out of here."

Which is exactly what Amanda did.

eight

MONDAY

The cabdriver gave Will a dubious look as he stopped in front of 316 Carver Street. "You sure this is the place, man?"

"I'm sure." Will checked the meter and handed him a ten. "Keep the change."

The guy seemed reluctant to take the money. "I know you're a cop and all, but that don't make much matter after dark. You feel me?"

Will opened the door. "I appreciate the warning."

"You sure you don't want me to wait?"

"No, but thank you." Will got out of the car. Still, the man dawdled. It wasn't until Will walked toward the side of the building that the cab slowly pulled away.

Will watched the taillights disappear down the street. Then he turned and picked his way past the tall weeds and brambles as he headed to the rear of the children's home. Between the moon and the streetlights, he had a pretty clear path to the back of the house. He stepped around syringes and condoms, broken glass and piles of trash.

He remembered Sara's earlier warning about all the dangers inside the house. She'd been full of observations tonight. And pretty pissed off. Will couldn't blame her. He was pretty pissed off himself. He was actually furious.

Hell, he was still furious.

Will's fists clenched as he rounded the house. He knew he was in an almost delirious state of denial about what was really bothering him. His father out of prison. That monster breathing free air. Will pushed this back down, just as he'd been pushing it down since he first found out.

The entire time Sara was stitching up his ankle, the only thing Will could think about was going into Amanda's hospital room and beating the truth out of her. Why did the parole board let his father out of prison? Why did Amanda find out before Will? What else was she hiding from him?

She had to be hiding something. She always hid something.

And she would die before she let Will in on it. She was tougher than any man Will had ever known. She wasn't exactly a liar, but she did things with the truth that made you think you were losing your mind. Will had given up on trying to be direct with Amanda a long time ago. Fifteen years of studying her personality had revealed nothing but the fact that she lived for subtleties and riddles. She delighted in tricking him. For every question Will had, she'd have another question, and pretty soon they'd be talking about things that would probably make him wish he hadn't gotten out of bed this morning. Or this year. Or ever in his life.

Why was she at the children's home tonight? What was she looking for? How much did she know about his father?

Will could already guess Amanda's answers. She was out for an evening drive. Who didn't enjoy a leisurely romp through the ghetto when they were supposed to be working a kidnapping case? She saw

Will and Sara inside the house and wondered why they were there. Is it wrong to be curious? Of course she knew about his father. She was his boss. It was her job to know everything about Will.

Except for one thing. The old broad had knocked her head hard enough to lose her legendary control.

"I told Edna to shore up these steps a million times."

Edna, as in Mrs. Edna Flannigan.

Amanda was in the middle of a high-profile case. The press was all over her. The director of the GBI was probably breathing down her neck. Yet, she'd stopped everything, grabbed a hammer, and headed here. There was only one way to get an honest answer about what she'd been up to, and Will was going to tear apart the children's home with his bare hands if that's what it took to find it. And then he was going to throw it right back into Amanda's face.

He stared at the back of the house. There had been a deck here at one time, but now there was only a gaping hole where a basement window used to be. The paramedics hadn't been able to take Amanda out through the interior doorway. Instead, they'd kicked out the plywood covering the basement windows and chipped away the brick to enlarge one of the openings.

Will looked up at the streetlight. Moths fluttered around, creating a strobe. He looked back at the window opening.

In retrospect, there were better ways to do this. Will could've asked the cabdriver to drop him at home, which was less than a mile away. There were lots of tools in Will's garage. Two sledgehammers, several pry bars, even a jackhammer he'd picked up secondhand at the Habitat Store. They were all well worn and well used. Will had bought his house for back taxes on the courthouse steps. It had taken him three years and every spare dime to turn it back into a home.

The hardest part was convincing the drug addicts that the house was under new ownership. The first six months, Will had to sleep with his shotgun beside his sleeping bag. When he wasn't tearing down walls and soldering copper pipe, he was going to the door and telling whoever had knocked that they would have to find somewhere else to smoke crack.

Which was actually good preparation for what Will was about to do.

He climbed in through the opening. The strobing streetlight illuminated most of the basement. Will used his cell phone to supplement its reach, picking his way past the broken stairs. Amanda Wagner was the very definition of preparedness. Will couldn't imagine her going into the dark basement without her Maglite. He spotted the familiar metallic blue casing over by a set of empty shelves. He pressed the button. The flashlight was small enough to fit in his pocket, but the LCDs glowed like a headlamp on an old Chevy.

Will hadn't exactly been honest with Sara. He'd spent his fair share of time down in the basement with Angie. Of course, he hadn't been on his elbows and toes taking measurements, but his memory of the place had somehow reduced it to a shoebox when in fact it was as large as the upper floors.

Will ran his hand along the exterior walls. Smooth plaster was interrupted every sixteen inches by bumps from the studs underneath. A dividing wall split the center of the room. This construction was newer. The Sheetrock was edged with black mold. Chunks were missing at the bottom. Pairs of oddly spaced, yellow pine two-by-fours showed at the base like legs below a petticoat.

There was a small room in the back with a sink and toilet, probably for the help. The walls were exposed lumber with knotty pine paneling on the outside. Will checked behind the fixtures. With his foot, he kicked apart the P-trap under the sink. Nothing was in the drain.

He took off the lid on the toilet tank and found it empty. The bowl was filled with black water. He glanced around for something to search with other than his hand. The old knob-and-tube wiring hung limply from the joists. He pulled out a long section, folded it in lengths until it was stiff enough, and checked the bowl. Other than a noxious odor, there was nothing.

Overhead, the flashlight picked up spiderwebs and termite damage in the floor joists as he walked around the room. The wooden storage shelves were empty. The coal chute was filled with black dust along with a couple of syringes and a used condom. He used the Maglite to examine the flue. Bird droppings. Scratches. An animal had been trapped inside at some point. Will closed the metal door and twisted the handle to lock it into place.

He took off his suit jacket and hung it from a nail in one of the joists. His Glock stayed on his belt where it was handy. He found Amanda's hammer by the stairs. It had never been used. The price tag was still on. Midtown Hardware. Forty bucks.

Will slipped the Maglite into his back pocket. The streetlight was enough for now. He studied the hammer. Forged blue steel with a smooth face and nylon end cap. Shock-reduction grip. It was a brick-layer's tool, not something a framer would use. Will assumed Amanda had bought it for form, not function. Or maybe she'd picked it off the shelf because the blue matched her flashlight. Either way, there was a well-balanced heft to the tool. The claw was sharp and busted cleanly through the plaster when Will slammed it into the exterior wall.

He pulled back the hammer and pounded it into the wall again, enlarging the hole. He punched out a chunk of plaster. It crumbled between his fingers. There was horsehair in the mix, tiny, silk strands that had held together the clay and limestone for almost a century.

Will chipped away a large enough section to reach his hand behind the lath. The wood was rotted, still wet from rain that had poured through the foundation. He should probably be wearing gloves and goggles, or at least a mask. There was undoubtedly mold behind the plaster, maybe fungus from dry rot. The odor inside the wall was dank, the way houses smelled when they were dying. Will used the claw hammer to pry away another chunk of plaster. Then another.

Slowly, he made his way around the perimeter of the basement, pulling down the plaster chunk by chunk, row by row. Then removing the lath, then brushing out the shredded newspapers that had been used for insulation, then moving on to the next section.

He gripped Amanda's Maglite between his teeth when the street-light couldn't reach the darkest corners. A white powder permeated the air. His eyes watered from the grit. His nose started to run from the dust and mold. The work wasn't difficult, but it was tedious and repetitive, and the temperature of the basement seemed to rise with every step as Will worked his way around the room. He was sweating profusely by the time he pounded off the last chunk of plaster. Again, the lath came apart in his hand, like wet paper. He used the claw hammer to pull out the rotted wood. As he had done with every section thus far, Will shone the flashlight onto the bare opening.

Nothing.

He pressed his palm to the cold wall. There was only a thin layer of brick holding back the dirt around the foundation. Will had broken through some sections to check anyway, then stopped for fear he might cause a cave-in. He took his phone out of his pocket and looked at the time. Two minutes past midnight. He'd been doing this for three hours.

All for nothing.

Will pushed away from the wall. He coughed and spit out a wad of plaster.

Three hours.

No scribbled notes, no hidden passages. No severed hands or bags of magic beans. As far as he could tell, nothing had been disturbed inside the walls since the house had been built. The wood was so old he could see the hatch marks where the axes had hewn down the studs from larger trees.

Will coughed again. The dust would not clear in the airless room. He used the back of his hand to wipe sweat off his forehead. His muscles were aching from the constant hacking of the hammer. Still, he started on the dividing wall down the center of the room. In many ways, the Sheetrock was harder to take down than the plaster. The paper was damp, but the gypsum was soaked through. The wall came down in tiny pieces. The pink insulation was filled with crawling bugs Will tried not to get in his mouth and nose. The studs were rotting from the floor up.

Another forty minutes went by.

Again, there was nothing.

Which meant that the niggling question that had been bouncing around Will's brain for the last two hours probably had to be asked: Why hadn't he started out on the floor?

Amanda had bought a bricklayer's hammer. The basement floor was comprised entirely of paved brick. Will recognized the Chattahoochee Brick Company logo on some of the pieces. It was similar to the brick in his own home—fired from red Georgia clay in an Atlanta manufacturing plant that had been turned into loft apartments during the financial boom times.

Will gripped the hammer in his hand. He'd thought Amanda had bought it because it was blue. He could hear her grating voice in his head: *I thought you were a detective.*

Will hadn't exactly been tidy as he'd destroyed the basement. There wasn't an inch of floor that was clean. He put his back to the corner and looked out into the room. Without the wall down the center, it was easy to plan the grid pattern. Each brick was approximately eight by four inches. He could clear out five-by-nine rows, which would roughly be three-by-three-feet sections. In a fifteen-hundred-square-foot room, that would take approximately eleventy billion years.

He kicked away debris with his foot, then got down on his knees to start on the first section. There was no pleasure in knowing that he'd devised a logical plan for tearing up the basement floor. Will swung the hammer in tight arcs, using the claw to pry up pieces of brick, squinting his eyes to keep out flying shards. Of course the brick didn't come up easily. It was too late for easy. The clay was old. The firing technique back in the thirties wasn't exactly scientific. Immigrants had probably worked sunup to sundown, backs and knees bent as they filled wooden forms with clay that would be air-dried, then fired in a kiln.

The first row of bricks crumbled under the hammer's claw. The edges were weak. They would not hold the center. Will had to use his bare hands to scoop out the pieces. Finally, by the third row, he had found a more successful system. He had to use precision with every swing of the hammer in order to wedge the claw into the cracks. Sand was packed into the joints. It got into Will's eyes, flew up into his mouth. He clenched his teeth. He thought of himself as a machine as he worked back and forth across the room, clearing each section brick by brick, digging a few inches into the dirt to see what was underneath.

He was a third of the way through when the futility overwhelmed him. He kicked away the debris covering the next section, then the next. He used Amanda's Maglite to study each crack and crevice. The bricks were tight. Nothing had disturbed them—not in Will's life-time, or the building's lifetime, or at any time at all.

Nothing. Just like the walls. There was nothing.

"Dammit!" Will flung the hammer across the room. He felt a tearing in his bicep. The muscle spasmed. Will clutched his arm. He stared into the loam, the useless fruits of his labor.

Will thought about his revenge fantasies from the Grady ER. His mind flashed up an image of Amanda—terrified, willing to answer any question he asked. He'd been in plenty of fights during his life-time, but he'd never used his fists on a woman. Amanda was probably sleeping like a baby back in her hospital bed while Will was chasing ghosts that he wasn't even sure he wanted to find.

He clenched his hands. There were tiny rips up and down his fingers—like paper cuts, only deeper. His sutured ankle felt like it was on fire. He tried to stand, but his knees wouldn't hold him. He forced himself up to standing. This time he stumbled. He grabbed onto one of the studs. A splinter dug into his palm. He screamed just to let out some of the pain. There was not a muscle in his body that did not ache.

All for nothing.

Will took his handkerchief out of his pocket and wiped his face. He grabbed his jacket off the nail. The streetlight was no longer strobing when he pulled himself out of the basement. The air was so crisp that he started coughing. He spit out more chunks of plaster.

Will went to the faucet in the middle of the yard. It was the same one he'd used as a kid during the summer months when Mrs. Flannigan locked them all out of the house and told them not to come back until suppertime. The pump handle was nearly rusted through.

Carefully, Will moved the lever up and down until a thin stream of water came out of the spigot. He put his mouth to the water and drank until he felt knives in his stomach. Then he put his head under the stream and washed off the grime. His eyes stung from the water. There were probably chemicals in there that he didn't want to know about. A tannery had operated down the street when he was growing up. Will had probably drunk enough benzene to fill a cancer ward.

Another souvenir from his childhood.

He pushed himself up, using the pump for leverage. The handle snapped off. Will could only shake his head. He tossed the handle into the yard and started the long walk home.

Will sat at his kitchen table, hands clutching a blue file folder. His eyes wouldn't stay open. He was punch-drunk from exhaustion. He hadn't bothered to go to bed. By the time he got home, it was already three in the morning. He had to leave by four to get to the airport in time for the business travelers. He'd taken a shower. He'd cooked a breakfast he couldn't eat. He'd walked the dog around the block. He'd shined his scuffed shoes. He'd put on a suit and tie. He'd used Bactine on the thousands of tiny cuts and blisters on his hands. He'd wiped away the weird pink fluid seeping through the Band-Aid on his ankle.

And now he couldn't make himself get up from the table.

Will picked at the edge of the file folder. His mother's name was neatly typed on the label stuck to the tab. Will had seen the letters so many times that they were burned into his retinas. He was twenty-two years old before he finally gained access to her information. There was a lot of paperwork that had to be filled out. He'd had to go down to the courthouse. There were other things, too, all of which involved navigating the juvenile justice system. The biggest obstacle was Will. He'd had to get to a point in his life where the prospect of going before a judge didn't bring on a cold sweat.

Betty came in through the dog door. She gave Will a curious look. The dog was adopted, an embarrassingly tiny Chihuahua mix that had come to Will through no fault of his own. She put her front feet on his thigh. She looked perplexed when Will didn't lean back to let her into his lap. After a while, she gave up, circling the floor three times before settling down in front of her food bowls.

Will let his gaze fall back to the file, his mother's name. The black typed letters were sharp on the white label. Not that it was white anymore. Will had rubbed his fingers along her name so many times that he'd yellowed the paper label.

He opened the file. The first page was what you'd usually find in a police report. The date was followed by the case number at the top. Then there was the section for the more salient details. Name, address, weight, height, cause of death.

Homicide.

Will stared at his mother's picture. Polaroid. It was taken years before her death. She was thirteen, maybe fourteen. As with the label, the photo was yellowed from being handled so much. Or maybe age had broken down the processing chemicals. She was standing in front of a Christmas tree. Will had been told the camera was a gift from her parents. She was holding up a pair of socks, probably another gift. There was a smile on her face.

Will wasn't the type of man to stare in the mirror, but he'd spent plenty of time examining his features one by one, trying to find similarities between himself and his mother. They had the same almond shape to their eyes. Even in the faded photo, he could see the color was the same blue. His blond hair was sandy, shaded more toward brown than his mother's almost yellow curls. One of his bottom teeth was slightly crooked like hers. She was wearing a retainer in the photo. The tooth had probably been pulled back into line by the time she was murdered.

Will lined up the photo to the edge of the front page, making sure to keep the paper clip in the same spot. He turned to the second page. His eyes couldn't focus on the words. The text jumped around. Will blinked several times, then stared at the first word of the first line. He knew it by heart, so it came easy to him.

"*Victim.*"

Will swallowed. He read the next words.

". . . *was found at Techwood Homes.*"

Will closed the file. There was no need to read through the details again. They were ingrained in his memory. They were a part of his waking existence.

He looked at his mother's name again. The letters weren't so crisp this time. If his brain hadn't filled in the words, he doubted he'd be able to make them out.

Will had never been much of a reader. The words moved around the page. The letters transposed. Over the years, he'd figured out some tricks to help him pass for more fluent. A ruler under a line of text kept one row from blending in with another. He used his fingers to isolate difficult words, then repeated the sentence in his head to test for sense. Still, it took him twice as long as Faith to fill out the various reports that had to be submitted on a daily basis. That a person like Will had chosen a career that relied so heavily on paperwork was something Dante could've written about.

Will was in college by the time he figured out that he had dyslexia. Or, rather, he had been told. It was the fifteenth anniversary of John Lennon's death. Will's music appreciation professor was talking about how it was believed that Lennon had dyslexia. In great detail, she described the signs and symptoms of the disorder. She could've been reading from the book of Will's life. In fact, the woman had basically delivered a soliloquy directly to Will on the gift of being different.

Will had dropped the class. He didn't want to be different. He wanted to blend in. He wanted to be normal. He'd been told most of his school life that he didn't fit into the classroom structure. Teachers had called him stupid. They'd put him in the back of the room and told him to stop asking questions when he would never understand the answers. Will had even been called to the principal's office his junior year and had been told that maybe it was time for him to drop out.

If not for Mrs. Flannigan at the children's home, Will probably would have left school. He could vividly remember the morning she'd found him in bed rather than waiting outside for the school bus. Will had seen her slap other kids plenty of times. Nothing bad, just a smack on the bottom or across the face. He'd never been hit by her before, but she slapped him then. Hard. She had to stand on her tiptoes to do it. "Stop feeling sorry for yourself," she'd commanded. "And get your ass on that bus before I lock you in the pantry."

Will could never tell this story to Sara. It was yet another part of his life she would never understand. She would see this as abuse. She would probably say it was cruel. For Will, it had been exactly what he needed. Because if Mrs. Flannigan hadn't cared enough to climb those stairs and push him out the front door, no one else would have bothered.

Betty's ears perked up. Her tags jingled on her collar as she turned her head. A low growl came out of her throat. Will heard a key in the front door lock. For just a second, he thought it might be Sara. He was overwhelmed by a feeling of lightness. And then he remembered that Sara didn't have a key to his house. And then the darkness came back when he remembered why. Sara didn't need a key. They didn't spend much time here. They always stayed in her apartment because at Will's, there was the constant threat of Angie walking in on them.

"Willie?" Angie called as she made her way through the living room. She paused at the open kitchen doorway. Angie had always embraced her feminine side. She favored figure-hugging skirts and shirts that showed her ample cleavage. Today, she was wearing a black T-shirt and jeans that hung low on her hips. She had lost weight in the three weeks since he'd last seen her. The pants were loose, but not on purpose. Will could see a black thong peeking over the top of the waistband.

Betty started growling again. Angie hissed at the dog. Then she looked at Will. Then she looked at the light blue file folder in his hand. She asked, "Reading up, baby?"

Will didn't answer.

Angie walked to the refrigerator and took out a bottle of water. She unscrewed the cap. She took a long swig as she studied Will. "You look like shit."

He felt like shit. All he wanted to do was put his head down on the table and sleep. "What do you want?"

She leaned back against the counter. He should've been surprised by her words, but then, nothing Angie said ever really surprised him. "What are we going to do about your father?"

Will stared down at the file. The kitchen was quiet. He could hear the whistling sound of Betty's breathing, the tinkle of the tags on her collar as she settled back down.

Angie had never been good at waiting him out. "Well?"

Will didn't have an answer for her. Eighteen hours of thinking about it pretty much nonstop hadn't brought any solutions. "I'm not going to do anything."

Angie seemed disappointed. "You need to call your girlfriend and ask for your balls back."

Will glared at her. "What do you want, Angie?"

"Your father's been out for almost six weeks. Did you know that?"

Will felt his stomach clench. He hadn't bothered to look up the details in the state database, but he'd assumed the release was recent, in the last few days, not almost two months ago.

She said, "He's sixty-four now. Diabetic. Had a massive heart attack a few years ago. Old people are expensive to take care of."

"How do you know all this?"

"I was at his parole hearing. Thought I'd see you there, but no." She raised an eyebrow, waiting for him to ask the obvious question. When Will didn't, she volunteered, "He looks good for his age. Been keeping in shape. I guess the heart attack scared him." She smiled. "You've got his mouth. The same shape to your lips."

"Is there a point to this?"

"The point is, I remember our promise."

Will looked down at his hands. He picked at a torn cuticle. "We were kids back then, Angie."

"Put a knife in his throat. Jam a crowbar in his head. Shoot him up with H and make it look like an accident. That was your favorite one, right?" She leaned down, inserting herself in his line of sight. "You pussin' out on me, Wilbur?" He moved away from her. "Do I need to remind you what happened to your mother?"

Will tried to clear his throat, but something got stuck.

Angie dragged over a chair and sat a few inches away from him. "Listen, baby, you can have all the fun you want with your little doctor friend. You know I've had my share. But this is business. This goes back to you and me and a promise we made to each other." She waited another beat, then said, "What happened to your mother, what happened to you—all because of that bastard—we can't just let that go, Will. He has to pay."

Will's cuticle started to bleed, but he couldn't stop picking at the skin. Angie's words stirred up something familiar inside of him. The anger. The rage. The need for revenge. Will had spent the last ten years of his life trying to let that go, and now Angie was shoving it back in his face.

He told her, "You're not in a position to talk to me about broken promises."

"Ashleigh Snyder."

Will's head jerked up, surprised to hear her mention the missing girl.

Angie smiled as she tapped her finger on his mother's file. "You're forgetting that I know everything, baby. Every detail. Every last drop. You think he's changed his ways? You think he's too old to get around? Let me tell you, honey, he's been busy inside. He could out-run you, out-jump you, out-kill you. Just looking at him made me scared, and you know I don't scare easy."

Will looked at her finger. The nail polish was chipped.

"Are you listening to me, Will?"

He waited for her to stop touching his mother's file.

Slowly, she moved her hand away.

Angie had helped him fill out the paperwork to get the documents. Angie had been the first to show him his mother's photograph. Angie had read the autopsy report aloud when Will, so upset he could barely function, was unable to make sense of it. Lacerations. Abrasions. Scratches. Tears. Wounds. The indescribable rendered in cold, medical language. Like Will, Angie knew every word. She knew every awful thing. She knew the pain and the misery, just like she knew when she finished telling Will what had happened to his mother, he had been so violently ill that he'd started coughing up blood.

She said, "He's holed up at the Four Seasons on Fourteenth. I guess his money earned some interest over the years."

"You've been watching him?"

"I've got a friend in security keeping an eye on him for me." She pursed her lips. "It's not a bad life. Five-star hotel. He uses the gym every morning. He orders room service. He goes for walks. He hangs out at the bar."

Will pictured every single tableau. The thought of this man living such an easy life put a fist in his stomach.

"It's all right," she soothed. Will couldn't stop looking at the file. His hands were gripping the edge. "It's me, baby. You don't have to pretend with me."

He flinched as Angie's fingers traced down his neck, his back. Her fingernails lined up with the scars that mottled his skin. "You can talk to me about it. I was there. I know what went down. I'm not going to judge you." Will shook his head, but she kept touching him, her hand going to the front of his chest, tips of her fingers finding the perfectly round circles where the tip of a burning cigarette had seared into his flesh. Her mouth was at his ear. "You think this would've happened to you if your mother had been around? You think she would've let them hurt her baby boy?"

This was what they had talked about for hours, days, weeks, years. The things that had been done to them. The things they would do to pay those people back. Childhood revenge fantasies. That's all they were. And yet, it felt so good to give in to them now. So nice to enjoy the fantasy of doing to that bastard what the state had refused to do.

"Let me take care of it," Angie said. "Let me make it all better for you."

Will was so tired. He felt incapacitated. Every inch of his body was sore. His brain was filled with static that wouldn't go away. When Angie pressed in closer, all he could think was how good it felt to be near another person. This was what being with Sara had done to Will. She'd taken away his ability to be alone. She'd broken through his solitude. She'd dragged him into a world where he didn't just want things—he needed them. He needed to be touched. He needed to feel her arms around him.

"Poor baby," Angie said. She kissed his ear, his neck. Will felt a familiar stirring in his body. When she slipped her hand inside his shirt, he didn't stop her. When her mouth found his, he didn't stop her. His hand went to her breast. She pressed closer against him.

But she tasted like nothing. Not mints or honey or those little sour candies Sara liked. Angie's hands rested on his shoulders, palms flat, not wrapped around the back of his neck. Not pulling him closer. Pushing him away.

Will tried to kiss her again. Angie moved back out of his reach, just as he knew she would. That's how she worked. Once she got something, she didn't want it anymore.

Will breathed out a heavy sigh. "I don't love you." He corrected, "I'm not in love with you."

She crossed her arms as she sat back in the chair. "Am I supposed to be hurt by that?"

Will shook his head. He didn't want to hurt her. He just wanted her to stop.

"Get real, baby. Sara may be all lovey-dovey now and telling you she wants to know all about you, but what's she really gonna do with that knowledge?"

He couldn't answer the question, but he knew one thing for certain. "She won't use it against me."

"That's sweet, but tell me this: how's she gonna go to sleep beside you every night knowing your father's DNA is swirling around inside you? Nature trumps nurture, baby. Sara's a doctor. Eventually she's gonna start to wonder what you're really capable of." She leaned closer. "Think about the terror you're gonna see in her eyes."

Will stared at her. There was a nasty twist to her mouth, a hollow look to her eyes. She wasn't just thinner. She was almost gaunt. For as long as Will had known her, Angie had always worn her makeup heavy—not because she needed to, but because she wanted the cover. Thick black eyeliner around her eyes. Dark brown eye shadow with a sparkle of glitter. Deep red lipstick. Blush on her high cheekbones. Her curly brown hair draped along the sides of her face. Her lips were a perfect bow tie. She was tall and thin with breasts that spilled out of the tight shirts she favored. She was the sort of woman that made men cheat on their wives. Literally. Angie loved taking things away from other people. She was a temptress. She was a siren. She was a thief.

She was also high as a kite. Her pupils were blown wide open.

He asked, "Are you taking pills again?" He tried to take her hand, but she jerked away. "Angie?"

She pushed herself up from the table and went back to the sink.

Will sat back in the chair. "What are you doing, Angie?"

She didn't answer him. Instead, she stared out the kitchen window. Her shoulder blades were sharp. The skull and crossbones tattoo she'd gotten when she was eighteen had faded to a light blue.

Will put his hand in his pocket. He felt the cold metal of his wedding ring. Sara kept her husband's wedding ring in a small wooden box on the mantel over the fireplace. Her ring was in there, too. They were tied together with a white ribbon, resting on a pillow of blue satin.

Will repeated, "What are you doing, Angie?"

Her shoulders went up. "I guess this is what happens to me without you."

"You've been without me lots of times."

"We both know this is different."

He couldn't argue with the truth. "Please stop hurting yourself."

"I will when you stop fucking your girlfriend."

Angie walked out of the kitchen. She picked up her purse where she'd dropped it on the couch. She turned around at the front door and blew him a kiss.

And then she was gone.

Will pressed his forehead to the table. The Formica was cold against his skin. Betty's paws tapped on his leg again. He let her into his lap. Her fur was wiry under his hand. She licked his fingers.

Angie's mother had killed herself with drugs. It was a twenty-seven-year-long suicide. That was what brought Angie to the children's home. Deidre Polaski had spent more than half of Angie's life in a vegetative coma, warehoused in a state hospital. She'd finally died a few months ago. Maybe that's what had gotten Angie back on the pills. Maybe she needed an escape.

Or maybe Will was to blame.

Three weeks ago in this very kitchen, Angie had put Will's gun in her mouth. She'd threatened to kill herself before. It was her go-to strategy when nothing else was working. Will thought about the wedding ring in his pocket. Maybe he was keeping it for the same reason Sara kept her husband's. Will had been mourning Angie for years. The only difference was that she hadn't died yet.

His phone rang. Not his cell, which was charging on his desk, but the landline. Will lifted his head from the table, but couldn't make himself stand. Maybe it was Sara calling. Though Will was pretty sure it was his responsibility to call her, not the other way around. He had stormed out last night. He had pissed her off. He had kissed Angie.

Will put his hand to his mouth. There was lipstick on his fingers. Jesus Christ, what had he done? Sara would be devastated. She would—Will didn't even want to think about what she would do. It would be the end of them. It would be the end of everything.

The phone stopped ringing. The house was completely silent. He could feel his heart jackhammering in his chest. There was no saliva left in his mouth. Betty stirred in his lap.

What the hell had he done?

His cell phone started chirping. Will had never seen himself as a coward, but the lure to just sit there and do nothing was strong. Unfortunately, he didn't have the willpower.

Will put Betty on the floor. He felt like he was dragging through quicksand as he walked into the living room. He picked up his cell phone, expecting to see Sara's number, but there was Amanda's instead.

He considered for a moment not answering the call, but if the last twenty-four hours had taught him anything, it was that Amanda always knew how to track him down.

Will grabbed his car keys and flipped open the phone. "I'm on my way to the airport."

"Stay where you are." Amanda's tone was off. "We found a body. Faith is on her way to pick you up."

Will braced his hand on the desk. His head started pounding. "Where?"

Amanda hesitated, something Will had never heard her do before. "Faith will loop you in on the details."

"Where?"

"You know where." Will made her say it. "Techwood."

nine

November 15, 1974

MARY HALSTON

Mary had been robbed at the Union Mission last night, which was not unusual, but still annoyed her. It wasn't money that was stolen—her pimp kept all of that—but a locket that her high school boyfriend had given her. Jerry. He'd gone to Nam straight out of school. He'd held his own against Charlie, but got hooked on H so bad that he couldn't pass the drug test to get back into the U.S. Took him six more months of rotting in the jungle before he could get clean, then the minute the plane touched down, he grabbed Mary and a bag of H, and another six months later, Jerry was dead with a needle in his arm and Mary was face down in an alley gritting her teeth, praying for it to be over fast.

She preferred not to look at their faces. Their beady eyes. Their wet lips. Their brown teeth. She felt like their images were etched into a part of her brain that she would be able to access one day and then—puff. She would ignite like a Roman candle and flame out forever.

Mary had read a crazy book one time about scientists slicing off your retinas and sticking them into a big TV that showed everything you'd ever seen in your entire life. The book was a gas, but creepy, because Mary didn't want to think about her life. Strange she'd read the thing in the first place. Mary's speed was more the Dana Girls and Nancy Drew. She'd been on a sci-fi kick after watching *2001: A Space Odyssey*. Not really watching it, because Jerry's hands were down her pants the entire time, but she got the gist of the movie: human beings were totally screwed by 2001.

Not that she would live to see it happen. Mary was nineteen years old. When she wasn't sleeping on a cot at the Union Mission, she was trolling the streets for trade. She'd lost some teeth. Her hair was coming out in clumps. She wasn't good enough to stand on the street corners. She had to walk around during the day looking for lawyers and bankers who turned her around and smashed her face into the wall while they did their business. It kind of reminded her of the way you held a kitten. Grab it by the back of the neck and it goes limp. None of these assholes were limp, though. That was for damn sure.

Mary darted into an alley and sat down by the Dumpster. Her feet hurt. There were blisters on her heels because her shoes were too tight. Not really her shoes. Mary wasn't just a victim at the Union Mission. She took what she needed, and she'd needed shoes. White patent leather. Chunky heel. They were very stylish, the sort of thing Ann Marie might wear to an audition on *That Girl*.

She heard heavy footsteps making their way toward her. Mary looked up at the man. It was like staring up at a mountain. He was tall with broad shoulders and a pair of hands that could easily snap her neck.

He said, "Good morning, sister."

And that was the last thing she heard.

ten

July 12, 1975

SATURDAY

Amanda had never been particularly adept at lying, especially where her father was concerned. Since childhood, Duke could look at her a certain way and Amanda would burst into tears, pouring out her soul no matter the consequences. She couldn't even begin to predict how angry he would be if he found out Amanda was spending the afternoon at Evelyn Mitchell's house. It reminded her of all those stories from the Nixon scandal. The cover-up always brought you down.

And this one was a doozy. Not only had Amanda completely fabricated a church function, she'd dragged Vanessa Livingston into the mix, exacting a promise that the other woman would support the story no matter what. Amanda could only hope that Duke was too wrapped up in his court case to dig too deeply into her story. He'd been on the phone with his lawyer all morning. The state supreme court's decision for Lars Oglethorpe had shifted the winds at police headquarters. Duke had barely registered Amanda's presence as she cleaned his house and ironed his shirts.

All she wanted to do now was see Evelyn with her own two eyes to make certain the other woman was all right. After leaving Techwood yesterday, neither of them had said a word to each other. Evelyn had dropped off Amanda at the station and driven away without even saying goodbye. What Rick Landry had done to her in the hallway seemed to be stuck in her throat.

Amanda pulled out onto Monroe Drive. She wasn't often on this side of Piedmont Heights. In her mind, she still thought of it as barren farmland, though the area had been given over to industry some time ago. As a child, she'd visited Monroe Gardens with her mother, where they'd peruse the nursery for hours picking out pansies and roses to plant in the backyard. The land had been turned into office buildings for the Red Cross, but she could still recall the rows of daffodils.

She took a left onto Montgomery Ferry. Plaster's Bridge narrowed the road to one lane. The Plymouth's tires bumped over the rutted concrete. A cold sweat came on as she passed Ansley Golf Club, even though she knew her father wasn't playing today. She followed the dogleg to Lionel Lane and went right on Friar Tuck, which cut straight through the heart of Sherwood Forest.

Evelyn's house was one of those ranch-style homes they'd built by the thousands for returning veterans. One story with a carport on the side, just like the house next door, which in turn was an exact duplicate of the next house, and the next.

Amanda parked on the street behind Evelyn's station wagon and checked herself in the rearview mirror. The heat had done her makeup no favors. Her hair was flat and lifeless. She had planned on washing it today, but the thought of sitting under the dryer was nauseating and she couldn't let her hair dry naturally because it would sour.

She cut the engine and heard the whir of a circular saw. The driveway was taken up with a black Trans Am and a convertible Ford Galaxie like Perry Mason used to drive. As she approached the house, Amanda saw that a shed was being built on the open side of the carport. The wall supports and roof were up, but little else. There was a man in the carport leaning over a piece of plywood resting on a pair of sawhorses. He was dressed in cutoff jeans and no shirt. The logo on his orange sun visor was easily recognizable, though it wasn't until Amanda was halfway up the drive that she could make out the Florida Gator.

"Hello!" he called, setting down the saw. Amanda guessed this was Bill Mitchell, though she realized that somewhere in the back of her mind she had imagined a more glamorous man. He was plain looking, about Evelyn's height with wispy brown hair and a bit of a belly. His skin was bright red from the sun. There was a welcoming smile on his face, though Amanda felt immensely uncomfortable talking to a man who wasn't fully clothed.

"Amanda." He held out his hand as he walked toward her. "I'm Bill. So pleased to meet you. Ev's told me a lot about you."

"You as well." Amanda shook his sweaty hand. Sawdust was stuck to his chest and arms.

"Let's get out of this sun. It's a scorcher." He cupped his hand to her elbow as he led her into the shade of the carport. Amanda saw a picnic table laid out in the backyard. The Weber was already belching smoke. She felt a brief flash of guilt. She'd been so worried about Evelyn's state of mind that she'd forgotten this was a party. She should've brought a hostess gift.

"Bill?" Evelyn came into the carport holding a jar of mayonnaise. She was barefoot, dressed in a bright yellow sundress. Her hair was perfect. She wasn't wearing any makeup, but she didn't seem to need any. "Oh, Amanda. You made it." She handed the mayonnaise to her husband. "Sweetheart, put a shirt on. You're red as a lobster."

Bill rolled his eyes at Amanda. He popped open the jar before handing it back to his wife.

Evelyn asked Amanda, "Did you meet Kenny? Bill, where's Kenny?" She didn't give him time to answer. "Kenny?"

"Under here," a deep voice called from beneath the shed. Amanda saw a pair of hairy legs, then cutoff jeans, then a man's naked torso as Kenny pushed himself out from beneath the plywood floor. He smiled at Amanda, said, "Hello," then told Bill, "Looks like we could use some more bracing."

Evelyn explained, "They're building a shed so we have a safe place to keep my gun."

"And potting soil," Kenny added. He held out his hand to Amanda. "Kenny Mitchell. I'm this character's brother."

Amanda shook his hand. It was warm. The palms were rough. She felt herself blushing in the heat. Kenny Mitchell was the most beautiful man she'd ever seen outside of a Hollywood movie. His chest and stomach rippled with muscles. His mustache was trimmed above what could only be called sensual lips.

He said, "Ev, you didn't tell me your friend was so pretty."

The blush ignited into a raging fire.

"Kenny!" Evelyn chastised. "You're embarrassing her."

"Sorry, ma'am." He winked at Amanda as he dug into his pocket and pulled out a packet of cigarettes. Amanda forced herself not to look at the trail of hair that started at his navel and worked its way down.

Evelyn said, "Kenny's a pilot with Eastern. He looks like that hunk from the Safeguard commercials, doesn't he?" She motioned for Amanda to follow her into the house. "We'll leave the boys to it."

Bill stopped them, telling Amanda, "Thanks for taking care of my girl yesterday. She's an awful driver. Too busy checking her makeup to look at the road."

Evelyn spoke before Amanda could. "I told him about almost hitting that man in the street." She put her hand to her chest, the exact spot where Rick Landry had jabbed her with the Kel-Lite. "The steering wheel left a terrible bruise."

"You should be more careful." Bill patted his wife on her bottom. "Now, get inside before I ravage you."

Evelyn kissed his cheek. "Be sure to drink plenty of Coke. You don't want to get dehydrated in this heat." She hugged the mayonnaise jar to her stomach as she walked across the carport. Amanda followed her into the house. Her plan was to ask Evelyn why she had lied to her husband, but the cool temperature inside left her momentarily speechless. For the first time in months, Amanda wasn't sweating.

"You have air-conditioning?"

"Bill bought it when I got pregnant, and neither one of us can give it up." Evelyn put the jar on the counter by a large Tupperware bowl that was already filled with chopped potatoes, eggs, and peppers. She stirred in the mayonnaise, saying, "Potato salad is the only thing I can make. I'm not a fan, but Bill loves it." The smile on her face seemed almost rapturous. "Isn't he wonderful? He's a perfect Libra."

Bill was a very happy Libra, judging by Evelyn's beautiful home. The kitchen was extremely modern—white laminate countertops with matching avocado green appliances. The chrome handles on the cabinets gleamed in the sunlight. The linoleum had a subtle flower pattern. The Perma-Prest ruffled curtains on the window filtered a soft light. There was a room off the kitchen with a washer and dryer. A pair of toddler's jeans hung from the indoor clothesline. It was the sort of thing Amanda thought only existed in magazines.

Evelyn put the potato salad in the refrigerator. "Thanks for not telling Bill about—" She put her hand to her chest. "He would only worry."

"Are you all right?"

"Oh." She sighed, but she didn't add more. She put the mayonnaise by the salad, but stopped shy of shutting the refrigerator door. "You want a beer?"

Amanda had never tasted beer in her life, but obviously Evelyn needed something. "All right."

Evelyn took two cans of Miller out of the door. She pulled the rings and tossed them into the trashcan. She was handing Amanda one of the cans when the circular saw started up again. "In here." Evelyn waved for Amanda to follow her through the dining room, then into a large foyer.

The living room was a step down. The temperature was almost frigid, courtesy of the large air-conditioning unit mounted into one of the windows. Amanda felt the sweat on her back start to chill. Her shoes sank into the lush ocher-colored carpet. The ceiling was beautifully textured. There was a chintz green and yellow sofa. Matching wingback chairs framed the sliding glass doors. The hi-fi was softly playing a track from McCartney. One wall was taken up entirely with books. A console television the size of a baby carriage served as a centerpiece. The only thing out of place was the large tent in the middle of the room.

"We sleep in here because of the AC," Evelyn explained, taking a place on the couch. Amanda sat down beside her. "We had the unit in the bedroom, but that wasn't fair to Zeke, and his crib is too big to fit in our room, so . . ." She took a healthy drink of beer.

Amanda grasped at conversational straws. She was awful at small talk. "How old is he?"

"Almost two." Evelyn groaned, and Amanda gathered this was a bad thing. "When he was little, Bill would stick him in the bottom drawer of the bureau and shut it when we needed privacy. But now that he's walking around—" She indicated the tent. "Thank God he's a heavy sleeper. Though you wouldn't know it this morning. He was screaming his head off. Bill took him off to his mother's before I started screaming, too. I'll change the record over." She got up and walked to the stereo. "Have you heard what John Lennon's doing?"

It sounded like he'd put a cat in a bag and swung it around a small room, but Amanda mumbled, "Yes. It's very interesting."

"I think Bill loaned the album to Kenny." She started thumbing through the records, talking to herself. Or maybe she was talking to Amanda. It didn't seem to matter that Evelyn wasn't getting a response. "Simon and Garfunkel?" she asked, but she was already putting on the record.

Amanda stared at the cocktail table, trying to think of a good excuse to leave. She could not remember a time in her life when she'd ever felt so out of place. She wasn't used to socializing, especially not with strangers. There was church, work, school, and her father. Not much else fit between. Evelyn was obviously fine after yesterday's experience. She had her husband and her brother-in-law. She had her living room sex tent and her beautiful home. She had her *Cosmo* magazine on the cocktail table where anyone could see it.

Amanda felt her cheeks burning again as she scanned the lurid headlines. It would be just her luck that lightning would strike them both right now and her father would find her in Evelyn Mitchell's house with a can of beer in her hand and a *Cosmopolitan* magazine in front of her.

Evelyn sat back down on the couch. "You okay?"

Amanda said, "I should leave."

"But you just got here."

"I just wanted to make sure you were okay after what Rick—"

"You smoke?" She reached for a metal box on the cocktail table.

"No, thank you."

"I gave them up when I got pregnant with Zeke," Evelyn admitted. "For some reason, I couldn't stand the taste anymore. Funny, I used to love it." She returned the box to its place. "Please don't leave, Amanda. I'm so glad you're here."

Amanda felt embarrassed by the statement. And trapped. Now she couldn't leave without being rude. She returned to the subject of Evelyn's child because that seemed the only safe topic. "Is Zeke a family name?"

"It's Ezekiel. I tried not to let Bill shorten it, but . . ." Her voice trailed off. "Bill's only criteria for picking a name was asking how it would sound coming out of the stadium speakers when he's playing for Florida." Instead of laughing at her joke, she went uncharacteristically quiet. She studied Amanda.

"What is it?"

"Are we still going to do our thing?"

Amanda didn't have to ask what thing. They were going to stake out the office building to find Mr. Blue Suit. Amanda was going to make a call to the Housing Authority. Evelyn was going to check missing persons reports at the other zones. Yesterday, this had seemed

like a solid plan. From this distance, it appeared amateur and dangerous. "Do you think we should go through with it?"

"Do you?"

Amanda could not answer her. After what had happened with
Rick Landry, she was scared. She was also worried about all the
snooping around she'd done thus far. They had both made calls to
people they had no business talking to. Amanda had spent a full
morning reading back issues of the *Journal* and the *Constitution*. If
Duke was right about getting his job back, the first thing he'd do
was find out what Amanda had been up to. And he would not be
happy.

Evelyn began, "You know, I was thinking . . ." She put her hand
to her chest. Her fingers picked at one of the pearl buttons. "What
Landry did to me. What Juice tried to do to you. It's funny how,
black or white, they go straight for what's between our legs. That's
the sum total of our worth."

"Or lack of it." Amanda finished the beer. She felt lightheaded.

Evelyn asked, "Why did you sign up for the job? Was it your
dad?"

"Yes," she answered, though that was only partly true. "I really
wanted to be a Kelly girl. Work in a different office every day. Go
home to a nice apartment." She didn't completely sketch out the fantasy. There would be a husband there, maybe a child, someone she
could take care of.

Amanda admitted, "I know it sounds flighty."

"It sounds better than my reason." Evelyn sat back against the arm
of the couch. "I used to be a mermaid."

"A what?"

She laughed, seemingly delighted by Amanda's surprise. "Ever
hear of Weeki Wachee Springs? It's about an hour outside Tampa."

Amanda shook her head. She'd only been to the Florida Panhan-
dle.

"They gave me the job because I could hold my breath for ninety
seconds. And these." She indicated her breasts. "I swam all day." She

floated her arms up through the air. "And drank all night." Her arms went down. She was smiling.

All Amanda could think to say was, "Does Bill know?"

"Where do you think we met? He was visiting Kenny at McDill Air Force Base. It was love at first sight." She rolled her eyes. "I followed him to Atlanta. We got married. I was bored staying home all day, so I decided to try for a job with the state." She smiled, as if in anticipation of a funny story. "I went downtown to the courthouse to fill out an application. I'd seen an ad in the paper that the tax commissioner was hiring, only I went into the wrong room. And there was this man in a patrol uniform. Such an ass. He took one look at me and said—" she puffed out her chest, " 'Little gal, you gots the wrong place. This here room is for the po-lice, and I can tell just by lookin' at ya that you ain't got it in ya.' "

Amanda laughed. She was a very good mimic. "What did you do?"

"Well, I was furious." Evelyn straightened her shoulders. "I said, 'No, sir, you're the one who's wrong. I'm here to join the police, and I have every right to take the test.' " She sank back down. "I assumed I wouldn't pass, but a week later, they called me to come back in for the interview. I wasn't sure whether or not I should go. I hadn't even told Bill. But I showed up for the interview, and I guess I passed that, because they told me to report to the academy the following week."

Amanda couldn't imagine such brazenness. "What did Bill say?"

"He said, 'Have fun and be careful.' " She held out her hands in an open shrug. "And that's how I became a police officer."

Amanda shook her head over the story. At least it was better than Vanessa's, who'd seen a sign on the bulletin board inside the jail, where she was being processed for a DUI.

Evelyn said, "I wasn't sure I could go back after Zeke." She took a deep breath. "But then I thought about how good it feels when I roll up on a call and a woman sees that I'm in charge, and she sees that her boyfriend or husband or whoever's been whaling on her has to answer *my* questions. It makes me feel like I'm doing something. I guess it's how the coloreds feel when a black cop shows up. They feel like they're talking to somebody who understands them."

Amanda had never thought about it that way, but she supposed it made sense.

"I want to do this. I really want to do it." Evelyn took her hand. There was an urgency to her tone. "Those girls. Kitty, Mary, Lucy, Jane—rest her soul. They aren't very different from us, are they? Someone along the way decided that they don't matter. And that made it true. They *don't* matter. Not in the scheme of things. Not when the Rick Landrys of the world can say a Jane Delray commit-ted suicide and the only problem is who's gonna clean up the mess."

Amanda didn't respond, but Evelyn had gotten good at reading her moods.

"What is it?"

Amanda told her, "It wasn't Jane."

"What do you mean? How do you know that?"

"I type all of Butch's reports. It wasn't Jane who jumped off the building. The woman's name is Lucy Bennett."

Evelyn looked confused. She took a moment to process the infor-mation. "I don't understand. Did someone identify her? Did her family come forward?"

"They found Lucy's purse in apartment C on the fifth floor."

"That's Jane's place."

"Butch's notes say that the victim was the only inhabitant. Her purse was on the couch. He found her license and made a positive ID."

"Did they do fingerprints?"

"Lucy doesn't have a record. There are no fingerprints to match up."

"That doesn't add up. She's a whore. They all have records."

"No, it doesn't add up." Unless she was new to the game, there was no way Lucy Bennett had avoided an arrest. Some of the girls voluntarily gave themselves up to spend the night in jail. It kept them safe when their pimps were mad.

"Lucy Bennett. Her license was in her purse?" Evelyn thought it through. "There's no way Jane would leave a license lying around like that. She said those girls have been missing for months, Lucy for a full year. Jane was trying to get their government vouchers. Either Lucy's license is in Jane's possession or it's in a cardboard box at the Five."

Amanda had already considered this. "Butch always gives me evidence receipts so I can note them in the report." The purse had been taken to central lockup, where the desk sergeant catalogued every item that went into storage. "According to the receipt, Lucy's purse didn't have a license."

"The desk sergeants never lie about that. It's their ass if something goes missing."

"Right."

"Was there cash in the wallet?"

Amanda was relieved not to be the naïve one for a change. Every purse or wallet homicide checked into lockup was miraculously absent any cash.

"Never mind," Evelyn allowed. She repeated the girl's name. "Lucy Bennett. All this time I assumed it was Jane."

"Does the name mean anything to you? Do you remember a Lucy Bennett from any of the missing persons reports?"

"No." Evelyn chewed her lip. She stared blankly at Amanda. Finally, she said, "Do you mind if I introduce you to someone?"

Amanda felt a familiar sense of dread. "Who?"

"My neighbor." She got off the couch. She took Amanda's beer can and put it beside hers on the table. "She's worked with APD for years. Her husband's been banished to the airport. Drinks too much. A real piece of work." She walked toward the sliding glass door. Amanda had no choice but to follow her. Evelyn kept up her chatter as she walked across the backyard. "Roz is a bit grumpy, but she's a good gal. She's seen her share of dead bodies, believe you me. Does it bother you that she's Jewish?"

Amanda couldn't figure out which tangent to start with. "Why would it bother me?"

Evelyn hesitated before she continued her trek across the yard. "Anyway, Roz is a crime scene photographer. She develops all the photos at her house. They won't have her at headquarters because she's too mouthy. I think she's been doing the job for ten years now. I'm sure your father's mentioned her?"

Amanda shook her head when Evelyn glanced back.

Evelyn continued, "I saw her earlier this morning and she was already in a state." They made their way past a green Corvair parked in the carport. The home was set up similar to Evelyn's, except there was a screened porch between the carport and house.

Evelyn lowered her voice. "Don't say anything about her face. Like I said, her husband's a real piece of work." She pushed open the screen door and tapped her fingers on the kitchen window. "Hello?" she called, her tone upbeat. "Roz? It's Ev again." After a few seconds without a response, she told Amanda, "I'll go around to the front."

"I'll be here." Amanda rested her hand on the washing machine that took up half the porch. Her sense of discomfort started to amplify as she thought about what she was doing. Amanda had never been inside a Jew's home before. She didn't quite know what to expect.

Evelyn was right; Amanda didn't get out much. She hadn't been to a party in years. She didn't drop in on neighbors. She didn't sit around plush living rooms listening to records and drinking alcohol. There were very few dates in her past. Any boy who wanted to ask her out had to go through Duke first. Not many had survived his scrutiny. There was one boy in high school who'd managed to persuade Amanda to go all the way. Three times, and then she couldn't take it anymore. She'd been so terrified of getting pregnant that the whole ordeal was only slightly more pleasant than getting a tooth drilled.

Evelyn was back. "I know she's here." She knocked on the kitchen door this time. "I don't know why she isn't answering."

Amanda looked at her watch, praying she could think of a good excuse to leave. Standing next to Evelyn Mitchell only heightened her sense of mortification. She felt like an old maid. The clothes

Amanda was wearing—a black skirt, short-sleeved white cotton shirt, heels and pantyhose—exemplified the difference. Evelyn looked like a carefree flower child. Kenny must have taken one look at Amanda and pegged her for exactly what she was: a square.

"Hello?" Evelyn knocked on the door again.

From inside the house, a voice called, "Hold your horses, for God's sakes."

Evelyn grinned at Amanda. "Don't let her get to you. She can be nasty."

The door swung open. An older woman dressed in a brown housecoat and slippers glared at them. Her face was a mess: broken lip, blackened eye. "Why'd you knock on the front door, then run around to the side?"

Evelyn ignored her question. "Roz Levy, this is my friend Amanda Wagner. Amanda, this is Roz."

Roz narrowed her eyes at Amanda. "Duke Wagner's girl, right?"

Normally, people said this with respect. There was something close to hate in the woman's voice.

Evelyn said, "She's a good gal, Roz. Give her a break."

Roz was unmoved. She asked Amanda, "You know they call you Wag, right? Always waggin' your tail, tryin' to please."

Amanda felt sucker-punched. Her stomach dropped.

"Oh, hush up, Roz." Evelyn grabbed Amanda's arm and pulled her inside the house. "I want Amanda to see the photos you showed me."

"Doubt she can handle it."

"Well, I think you'll be surprised. Our gal can handle more than you think." She squeezed Amanda's arm as she dragged her through the kitchen.

The house was nothing like Evelyn's. There was no coolness from a running air conditioner. As a matter of fact, it felt as if all the air had been pulled out. Heavy brown curtains lined all the windows, blocking the sun. The living room was sunken, three steps down, and decorated in more dark browns. Evelyn pulled Amanda past a large couch that stank of body odor. Beer cans were on the floor beside a reclining chair. Cigarette butts spilled from the ashtray. Three steps back up. Evelyn forced Amanda to walk down the hallway. She only let go when they were in Roz Levy's spare bedroom.

As with the rest of the house, the room was dark and airless. The closet door hung open. A red lightbulb hung from a cord over various trays and chemicals. A rumpled daybed held cameras of all shapes and sizes. The desk was overflowing with paperwork. There were tennis rackets and roller skates in small piles around the room.

"She does yard sales," Evelyn explained. "The first time Bill met her, he said she reminded him of the guy who works for Baroness Bomburst in *Chitty Chitty Bang Bang*." She saw Amanda's expression and said, "Sweetie. Don't be upset. She says awful things sometimes. That's just her way."

Amanda crossed her arms, feeling exposed. Wag. She'd never heard the nickname before. She knew that people around the station considered her a goody-two-shoes. Amanda had come to terms with the reputation. There were worse things they could call her. She wasn't trim. She wasn't bad at her job. She was helpful. Courteous.

They called her Wag because she was always trying to please people.

Amanda's throat worked as she tried to swallow back tears. She *did* try to please people. Please her father by doing everything he told her to. Please Butch by typing his reports. Please Rick Landry by taking Evelyn away from Techwood. Why had Amanda done that? Why hadn't she told Landry to stop? He had practically assaulted Evelyn with her own flashlight. She was bruised on her chest and God only knew where else. And Amanda's response had been to grab her and run away like a puppy with its tail between its legs.

Wagging her tail.

Roz Levy finally deigned to join them. Amanda saw the reason for her delay when she entered the room. She'd stopped to get a Tab.

"So." Roz pulled the ring from the can. She dropped it into a mason jar on the desk. "You gals playing cops and robbers today?"

"I told you we're working a case." Evelyn's voice was surprisingly terse.

"Look at this one," Roz told Amanda. "Thinks they're gonna let her work homicide one day."

Amanda said, "Maybe they will."

"Ha." She didn't really laugh. "Women's lib, right? You can do anything you want so long as you do exactly as you're told."

Evelyn snapped, "We're out there on the streets every day just the same as they are."

"You gals just watch. Think you're hot shit because they let you go to the academy, gave you a badge and a gun. Mark my word. They only let you climb high enough so it breaks your back when you fall." She took a sip of her Tab. Her next words were addressed to Amanda. "You think your old man's gonna win his case?"

Amanda said, "If you're curious, you should ask him yourself."

"I already got one black eye, thank you very much." She put the Tab to her forehead. The can was cold. Sweat dripped down the sides. She glared at Amanda. "What's your problem?"

"Nothing. I'm just starting to understand why your husband beats you."

Evelyn gasped.

Roz glared at her. "That so?"

Amanda bit her tongue to stop the apology that wanted to come. She forced herself to stare the woman straight in the eye.

Roz gave a sharp laugh. "Ev's right. You're tougher than you look." She drank from the can, wincing as the liquid went down. There were yellowed bruises around her neck. "Sorry about before. I've been having hot flashes all morning. Turns my bitch on."

Amanda looked at Evelyn, who shrugged.

"The change. You'll find out for yourselves soon enough." Roz went inside the closet and started going through a stack of photos. "Shit. I left them in the kitchen."

Amanda waited until she left the room. "Tell me what she's talking about?"

"I think it's something old Jewish women get."

"Not that. Have you heard other people calling me that name? Wag?"

Evelyn had the grace not to look away. It was Amanda who couldn't hold her gaze. She stared into the closet, the stacks of photographs showing gory scenes in sharp Kodachrome.

"Photos," Amanda mumbled. Now it made sense. That's why Evelyn had brought her here. "Roz was the crime scene photographer at Techwood yesterday."

"The pictures are bad. Really bad. Jane—I mean Lucy—jumped from the top floor."

"The roof," Amanda provided. She had all the details from Butch's report. "There's an access ladder at the end of the hall. It goes up to a trapdoor in the roof. Lucy managed to bust off the padlock. Butch thinks she used a hammer. They found one on the floor at the bottom of the ladder. Lucy went to the roof and jumped."

"Where would she get a hammer?"

"There weren't any tools lying around the apartment," Amanda remembered. "Maybe the repairmen used it for the broken skylight?"

"I suppose you'd need a hammer for that." Evelyn sounded dubious. "Can a hammer bust a padlock?"

"Hammer?" Roz Levy was back. She held a manila envelope in her hand. "Those jackasses think she banged open the roof access with a hammer? Why not just jump out the window? She's on the top floor. They think she's so stoned she doesn't take the easy way out?" She started to open the envelope, but stopped. Her eyes drilled into Amanda. "If you throw up on my carpet, you're going to have to clean every inch. I don't care if you have to use a toothpick."

Amanda nodded, even as she felt a wave of nausea building. Her stomach was already sour. She dreaded to think what the beer would taste like coming back up.

"Are you sure?" Roz asked. "Because I'm not cleaning up after you. It's bad enough I have to clean up after that jackass I married."

Amanda nodded again, and the older woman pulled out the photographs. They were image side down.

Roz said, "A fall that high, you land on your feet, your intestines squirt out your ass like icing from a pastry bag."

Amanda pressed her lips together.

"Your ears bleed. Your face rips off your skull like a mask. Your nose and mouth and eyes—"

"Oh, for goodness sakes." Evelyn snatched the photos from Roz's hand. She showed them to Amanda one by one. "Breathe through your mouth," she coached. "Nice and easy. In and out."

Amanda did just that, taking in gulps of stale air. She expected to faint. Honestly, she expected to end the afternoon on her hands and knees with a toothpick cleaning Roz Levy's shag carpet. But neither of those things happened. The photos were unreal. What had happened to Lucy Bennett was too horrific for Amanda's brain to accept that she was still looking at an actual human being.

Amanda took the photos from Evelyn. They were in vivid color, the flash so bright that every single detail was on display. The girl was fully clothed. The material of her red-checkered cotton shirt was stiff, glued to her skin. Her skirt was hanging down, the waistband broken. Amanda assumed this was subsequent to the fall, as was the girl's missing left shoe.

She studied Lucy Bennett's face. Roz had been right about a lot of things, but none more so than what jumping from a five-story building did to the skin on your skull. Lucy's flesh looked to be dripping from the bone. Her eyes bulged from their sockets. Blood poured from every opening.

It looked fake, like something out of a horror movie.

Evelyn asked, "You okay?"

Amanda said, "Now I see why you thought this was Jane Delray." Except for the bleached blonde hair, the Halloween mask of her face could've belonged to any girl walking the street. The track marks up her arms were the same. The open wounds on her feet. The red pricks along her inner thigh.

Evelyn said, "I wonder if she has family."

Roz stated the obvious. "Everyone has family. Whether they admit it or not is an entirely different question."

Amanda ran through the pictures again. There were only five of them. Three were of the girl's face—left, right, center. One showed a close-up of her mangled body, probably taken from a ladder. The last was a more widely framed shot with the Coca-Cola building on the horizon. Lucy's hand was turned out, her wrists exposed.

Amanda asked Roz, "Do you have any more photos?"

The older woman smiled. One of her upper teeth was missing. "Look at the bloodlust. Who would've guessed it?"

Amanda made her request more specific. "Do you have any close-ups of her wrists?"

"No. Why?"

"Does that look like a scar to you? There, along her wrist?" She showed Evelyn the photo.

Evelyn squinted, then shook her head. "I can't tell. What are you getting at?"

"Jane had scars on her wrist."

"I remember." Evelyn studied the photo more carefully. "If this is Lucy Bennett, why would she have scars on her wrists like Jane Delray?"

"Whoring's not exactly something to live for." Still, Roz opened one of her desk drawers and found a magnifying glass. Each woman took turns holding the glass to the picture.

Finally, Evelyn said, "I still can't tell. It looks like a scar, but maybe it's the light?"

"That's my fault." Roz sounded uncharacteristically apologetic. "My flash was acting up and Landry was pushing me to hurry so he could clock in to his other job."

Amanda supplied, "Butch didn't say anything in his notes about scars."

"That idiot wouldn't." Contrary to her words, Roz Levy seemed delighted. "All right, Wag. Time to see what you're really made of."

Another wave of dread washed over Amanda. She felt as if she was on a roller coaster.

Evelyn said, "Roz, there's no need to—"

"Shut your pie hole, blondie." Roz cackled like a witch. "Pete's cutting up your dead whore this afternoon. You hotshot lady dicks want, I can make a call and get you a ringside seat to the autopsy."

Amanda knew some of the patrolmen used the morgue as their crack, or on-duty hiding place, especially during the summer. It was easier to sleep in an air-conditioned building, so long as you didn't mind laying up next to a dead body.

She'd been to the Decatur Street building many times to pick up reports and drop off evidence, but she'd never before been into the back. Just the thought of what went on there gave Amanda the heebie-jeebies. Still, she kept her mouth closed as Evelyn led her deep inside the building, even though every step felt as if it was ratcheting down a clamp around her rib cage.

The two beers Amanda drank on the drive over were not helping matters. Instead of relaxed, she felt both lightheaded and extremely focused. It was a miracle she hadn't driven her Plymouth up a telephone pole.

"Do you know Deena?" Evelyn asked, pushing open a swinging door. They were in a small lab. Two tables were shoved into opposite corners in the back of the room. There was a microscope on each. Various medical tools were laid out beside them. A large window took up the back wall. The hospital-green curtains were pulled back to show what must be the autopsy room. Yellow tile ran along the floor and up to the ceiling. There were two metal sinks. Two scales that seemed more appropriate for a grocer's produce section.

And a body. A green drape covered the figure. A large light like a dentist used was overhead. One hand dropped down beside the table. The fingernails were bright red. The hand was turned inward. The wrist did not show.

Evelyn said, "I hate autopsies."

"How many have you seen?"

"I don't actually look at them," she confessed. "You know how you can blur your eyes on purpose?"

Amanda nodded.

"That's what I do. I just blur my eyes and say 'mm' and 'yes' when they ask questions or point out something interesting, and then I go to the bathroom afterward and throw up."

That seemed like as good a plan as any. They heard footsteps in the hallway behind them.

Evelyn said, "Deena's got a bad scar on her neck. Try not to stare."

"A what?" Evelyn's words got jumbled up in Amanda's brain, so they didn't make sense until a striking black woman came through the door. She was wearing a white lab coat over blue jeans and a flowing orange blouse. Her hair was in full Afro. Blue eye shadow adorned her eyelids. The skin around her neck was marred as if by a noose.

"Hey, Miss Lady," Deena said, setting down a tray on one of the tables. There were slides laid out, splatters of white and red sandwiched between the glass. "What are you doing here?"

Evelyn said, "Roz called in a favor for me."

"Why you still talkin' to that nasty old Jew?" She smiled warmly at Amanda. "Who's your pretty friend?"

Evelyn looped her arm through Amanda's. "This is Amanda Wagner. She's my partner now."

The smile dropped. "Any relation to Duke?"

For the first time in her life, Amanda felt the compulsion to lie about her father. Maybe if they'd been alone, she would have, but she confessed, "Yes. I'm his daughter."

"Hm." She shot Evelyn a look and turned back around to her slides.

"She's all right," Evelyn said. "Come on, Dee. Do you think I'd bring someone here who'd—"

The woman spun back around. Her lip trembled with rage. "You know how I got this?" She pointed to the ugly scar on her neck. "Working at the cleaners down on Ponce, pressing Klan robes nice and stiff for people like your daddy."

Evelyn tried, "That's hardly her fault. You can't blame her for her father's—"

Deena held up a hand to stop her. "One day, my mama got her

arm caught in one'a the machines. Ain't no way to turn 'em off. Mr. Guntherson's too cheap to pay for an electrician. I grab the cord and it swings back on my neck. Live wires. Boom, there's an explosion— one'a them transformers gives out. Shut down the whole block for two days. Saved my life, but not my mama's."

Amanda didn't know what to say. She'd been to that same dry cleaners many times, had never given a thought to the black women working in the back. "I'm sorry."

Evelyn said, "She can't control what her father does."

Deena leaned back against the table. She crossed her arms. "You remember what I told you about my scar, Ev? I said I'd cover it up the day it don't matter anymore." She glared at Amanda. "It still matters."

Evelyn stroked Amanda's back. "This is my friend, Deena. We're working a case together, trying to find some missing women." Her words were rushed. "Kitty Treadwell. Someone named Mary. They might be connected to Lucy Bennett."

"You check the dead nigger file?" She was talking to Amanda. "That's what y'all call it, right? The DNF? Got one at every station house. Ain't that right, Wag?"

Amanda was too embarrassed to look at her. She told Deena, "I think you probably know that I lost my mother, too." What had happened to Miriam Wagner was common knowledge around the force. With enough whiskey in him, Duke relayed the story with a heady machismo. Amanda said, "You're not the only one here with scars."

Deena tapped her fingers on the table. The staccato started strong, then died down to nothing. "Look at me."

Amanda forced herself to look up. It had been so easy with Roz, but with the old Jew, there had been a sense of righteousness. Now, there was only guilt.

Deena studied her for a bit longer. The anger that had burned so hotly in her eyes started to fade. Finally, she nodded. "All right," she said. "All right."

Evelyn slowly exhaled. She had a tight smile on her face. As usual, she tried to smooth things over. "Dee, did I tell you what Zeke did the other day?"

Deena turned back to the trays. "No, what'd he do?"

Amanda didn't listen to the story. She stared back into the morgue. Her mind was still clouded from the beer, or maybe just the traumas of the day. She felt as if something was shifting inside of her. The last few days had called into question the previous twenty-five years of her life. Amanda wasn't sure whether or not this was a good thing. Truthfully, she wasn't sure about anything anymore.

"Hello-hello!" a man's voice boomed from inside the morgue.

"That's Pete," Evelyn supplied.

The coroner was pudgy, with a ponytail and beard that looked days past washing—as did his tie-dyed T-shirt and faded, torn blue jeans. His white lab coat was tight through the sleeves. A cigarette dangled from his lip. He stood at the window, showing his yellow teeth. Amanda was not one to believe in vibes, but even with a thick piece of glass between them, she could almost feel the creepiness radiating off Pete Hanson's body.

He said, "Deena, my love, you're looking beautiful as ever this afternoon."

Deena laughed even as she rolled her eyes. "Shut up, fool."

"Only a fool for you, my dear."

Evelyn supplied, "They do this all the time."

"Oh." Amanda tried to pretend she heard white men flirting with black women every day.

"Come on, Dee." Pete tapped on the window. "You gonna let me buy you that drink?"

"Meet me outside at ten-after-never." She snatched the drapes closed. "Y'all go on in." She told Amanda, "When you throw up, aim for the floor drain. It's easier to hose down that way."

"Thank you," Amanda managed.

She followed Evelyn into the autopsy room. The temperature was as cold as expected, but it was the odor that caught Amanda off guard. It was clean, like Clorox and Pine-Sol mixed with apples; nothing like what she expected.

There had been two calls during her uniform days wherein she was sent out to take a missing persons report and found that person not far from the house. One had been a man who'd been locked in his trunk. The other had been a child who'd gotten trapped inside an old refrigerator on the family's shed porch. Each time, Amanda had taken one whiff and called for backup. She did not know what happened to the cases. She was at the station filling out reports by the time the bodies were removed.

"Who is this elegant lady?" Pete Hanson asked, his eyes on Amanda.

"This is—"

"Amanda Wagner," Amanda told him. "I'm Duke Wagner's daughter."

He paused a beat. "So you are," he finally said. "Duke's quite a character, isn't he?"

Amanda shrugged. She was bruised enough about her father for one day.

"Pete." Evelyn put on her cheery voice again, but her fingers snaked into her hair, giving a telltale sign of her discomfort. "Thanks so much for letting us watch. We were in Lucy's apartment last Monday. We never met her, but it was quite a shock to learn about the suicide."

"Lucy?" Pete's brow furrowed. "Where did you get that?"

"It was in Butch's report," Amanda supplied. "He ID'd her off her license."

Pete walked over to a large, cluttered desk underneath the window. There were piles of papers stacked in a hodgepodge, but he somehow found the right one.

Smoke drifted from his cigarette as he read the preliminary report. The paper was thin. Amanda recognized Butch Bonnie's scrawl reversed on the back where he'd turned the carbon paper the wrong way.

"Bonnie. Not the sharpest tack in the box, but at least it wasn't that jackass Landry." Pete put the report back on his desk. "In a case like this, the license ID is a last resort. I generally prefer dental records, fingerprints, or a family member coming in before I feel comfortable signing off on the identity." He explained, "Learned my lesson in Nam. You don't send someone home in a body bag unless you know the right family's waiting on the other end."

Amanda found relief in his words. For all his eccentricities, the man was at least good at his job.

"So." Pete flicked ash off his cigarette. "What's Kenny been up to? I haven't seen him around."

"This and that," Evelyn said. She was watching Pete's every move—the way he wiped his nose with a tissue from his pocket, the bobbing of his cigarette as he talked. Meanwhile, she pulled so hard at her hair that Amanda was certain she was going to yank some out. "He's working with Bill on a shed at the house today." She chewed her lip for a few seconds. "We're having a barbecue later. You should come."

Pete smiled at Amanda. "Will you be there?"

She got a sinking feeling. It was her lot in life to be attracted to the Kenny Mitchells of the world while the Pete Hansons were the only ones who ever bothered to ask her out. "Maybe," she managed.

"Excellent." He rolled over a metal tray. There were scalpels, scissors, a saw.

Evelyn stared at the instruments. Her face was pale. "You know, maybe I should give Bill a call. We dashed out without telling him when we'd be back."

This wasn't actually the truth. Evelyn had been clear that they weren't sure what time they would return. Bill, unsurprisingly, had been very accommodating to his beautiful wife.

"I should go call," Evelyn repeated. She practically ran out of the room.

Which left Amanda alone with Pete.

He was looking at her, but this time she saw the kindness in his eyes. "She's a great lady, but this is one of the more challenging spectator sports."

Amanda swallowed.

"Would you like me to take you through the process?"

"I—" She felt her throat tighten. "Why do you have to do an autopsy if it's a suicide?"

Pete considered her question before walking across the room. There was a light box mounted on the wall. He flipped the toggle, and the lights flickered on. "The word 'autopsy' means, literally, 'to see for oneself.'" He waved her over. "Come, my dear. Contrary to rumor, I don't bite."

Amanda tried to conceal her trepidation as she joined him. The X-ray showed a skull. The holes where the eyes and nose were supposed to go looked eerily empty.

"Do you see here?" he asked, pointing to the neck on the X-ray. Pieces of vertebrae flexed apart the way a cat's paw opened when you pressed the pad. "This bone here is called the hyoid. That's pronounced 'hi-oid.' It's horseshoe shaped, and free-floats at the anterior midline between the chin and thyroid." He showed on his own neck. "Here."

Amanda nodded, though she wasn't quite sure she grasped the point of his lecture.

"The wonderful thing about your neck is that you can move it up and down and side to side. The cartilage helps make that possible. The hyoid itself is fairly fascinating. It's the only jointless bone in your entire body. Supports your tongue. Jiggles when you move it. Now, as I said, it's right here—" He pointed to his neck again. "So, if someone is choked with a ligature, you'll generally find bruising around the hyoid. But here"—he moved his fingers up—"is where you'll find bruising if someone is hanged, above the hyoid. That's a classic sign of hanging, actually. I'm sure you'll see it more than once in your career."

"You're saying she tried to hang herself first?"

"No." He pointed to the X-ray of the neck. "See this darker line here that bisects the hyoid?" Amanda nodded. "That indicates a fracture, which tells me she was choked, probably with great force."

"Why great force?"

"Because she's a young woman. Your hyoid starts out as two pieces. The bone doesn't fully fuse until around the age of thirty. Feel for yourself."

She thought he meant for her to touch his neck. Amanda desperately did not want to touch him. Still, she started to reach out.

Pete smiled, saying, "I believe you have your own neck."

"Oh. Right." Amanda laughed through her discomfort. She gently touched her fingers to her throat. She palpated the area, feeling things shift back and forth. The noise clicked in her ears.

Pete said, "You can feel there's a lot of movement in there. So, you'd have to have significant pressure to fracture the hyoid."

He motioned her to follow him over to the body. He stubbed out his cigarette in an ashtray on the table. Without preamble, he pulled back the sheet, exposing Lucy Bennett's head and shoulders. "See these bruises here?"

Amanda felt her eyes blur, but not on purpose. She blinked, focusing only on the neck. There were deep purple and red marks around the woman's throat. They reminded her of Roz Levy. "She was choked."

"Correct," Pete agreed. "Her attacker wrapped his hands around her neck and strangled her. See the fingerprints here?"

Amanda leaned in for a closer look. Now that he'd put the thought into her head, she could see the individual strands of bruises that formed the fingers of a hand.

"Carotids," Pete explained. "Arteries. One on each side of the neck. They deliver oxygenated blood to the brain. Very important. No oxygen, no brain."

"Right." Amanda remembered the lesson from her police academy days. They got to watch the men learn how to do choke holds one morning.

"Now." Pete wrapped both his hands loosely around the woman's neck. "See where my hands are?" Amanda nodded again. "See how pressing her carotid arteries in order to strangle her exerts enough force on the front of the neck to fracture the hyoid?" Again, she nodded. "Which tells me that this woman was strangled into unconsciousness."

Amanda looked back at the X-ray. "The fall from the roof wouldn't break the bone?"

"You'll see when I open the neck that it's highly improbable."

Amanda could not suppress the shudder that came.

"You're really doing quite well."

Amanda ignored the compliment. "Could she live with a broken hy . . ."

"Hyoid."

"Right. Could she live with that?"

"Most certainly. A hyoid fracture or break isn't necessarily fatal. I saw it often in Nam. The officers were trained in hand-to-hand combat, which of course they loved showing off. You hit a man here—" he chopped at his own neck—"with your elbow or even an open hand, and you can stun him or, with enough force, break the bone." He cupped his hand to his chin like a tweedy college professor. "You feel a very distinctive sensation when you run your fingers along the neck, as if hundreds of bubbles are bursting under the skin. This comes from the air leaking out of the larynx into the tissue planes. In addition to the obvious panic, there's tremendous pain, bleeding, bruising." He smiled. "It's a nasty little injury. Almost totally incapacitating. They'll just lay there wheezing high up in their throats, praying for someone to help them."

"Are they able to scream?"

"I'd be shocked if they could manage more than a hoarse whisper, but people surprise you sometimes. Everyone is different."

Amanda tried to process all this new information. "But what you're saying is that Lucy Bennett was choked." She remembered Pete's earlier terminology. "Strangled to death."

He shook his head and shrugged at the same time. "I'll need to see the lungs. Strangulation causes aspiration pneumonitis—the inhalation of vomit into the lungs. The gastric acids eat into the tissue. This gives us something of a timeline. The more tissue damage, the longer she was alive. Was she strangled into unconsciousness and then thrown off the roof or was she strangled to death and then thrown off the roof?"

"Why does it matter?" Either way, Lucy had been murdered.

"When you catch your perpetrator, you're going to want to know the details of the crime. That way, you can make sure you've got the right guy and not some nut looking for a headline in the newspaper."

Amanda didn't see a scenario where she would be catching any perpetrator. She wasn't even sure why Pete was answering her questions. "But why would the killer give details of the crime? That would just make the case against him stronger."

"He won't realize he's walking into the trap you set." Pete told her, "You are a lot smarter than he is. Your perpetrator is a man who cannot control himself."

Amanda considered the statement, which didn't strike her as wholly true. "He was smart enough to try to cover the crime."

"Not as smart as you think. Throwing her off the roof was risky. It called attention to the crime. It opened up the possibility of witnesses. Why not leave her in the apartment and let a neighbor report the smell a few days—weeks—later?"

He was right. Amanda remembered the Manson murders, the way the bodies were posed. "Do you think the killer was sending a message?"

"Possibly," Pete allowed. "We can also assume that he knew the victim fairly well."

"Why do you say that?"

Pete gripped his hands around the top of the sheet. "Remember to breathe." He pulled away the covering, exposing the rest of the body.

Amanda put her hand to her mouth. Nothing rushed up her throat. She didn't pass out. She wasn't even woozy. As with Roz Levy's photos, she expected a violent reaction inside her body but was met instead with steely resolve. That same locking sensation from Techwood ran up Amanda's spine. Her stomach actually stopped churning. Instead of fainting, she felt her vision sharpen.

Amanda had never seen another woman entirely nude before. There was something sad about the way her breasts hung to the side. Her stomach was saggy. Her pubic hair was short, as if it had been trimmed, but the hair on her thighs was grotesquely unshaven. Blood and viscera leaked between her legs. Her body had been pummeled. Bruises blackened her stomach and ribs.

Pete said, "In order to hurt somebody like this, you have to hate them. And hate does not come without familiarity. Just ask my ex-wife. She tried to strangle me once."

Amanda glanced up at him. There was no suggestion behind his smile. He wasn't just creepy, he was downright strange. And polite. Amanda could not recall the last conversation she'd had with a man where she wasn't constantly interrupted or talked over.

Pete said, "You could be very good at this."

Amanda didn't know if that was much to write home about. It certainly wasn't conversation for the dinner table. "Can you tell me anything about the nail polish?"

He took a latex glove out of his pocket. "Why don't you tell me?"

Amanda didn't want to, but she took the glove. She tried to shove her hand into the stiff latex.

"Wipe your palm first," Pete advised.

Amanda wiped her sweaty hand on her skirt. The glove was still a tight fit, but once she managed to force her fingers into the tips, the rest of her hand easily followed.

Gently, she reached out for Lucy's hand. The skin felt cold through the glove, or maybe Amanda was just imagining that. Instead of being limp, the body was stiff.

"Rigor mortis," Pete explained. "The skeletal muscles contract, locking the joints. Onset varies depending on temperature and lesser factors. It starts in as little as ten minutes and lasts for up to seventy-two hours."

"You can tell how long she's been dead by how stiff she is."

"Precisely," he confirmed. "By the time I got to our victim yesterday afternoon, she had been dead approximately three to six hours."

"That's quite a window."

"Science is not as precise as we'd like to believe."

Amanda tried to turn the arm. It wouldn't move.

"Don't worry about being gentle. She can't feel pain anymore."

Amanda heard the sound of her throat working as she swallowed. She wrenched up the arm. There was a loud popping sound that sent a knife into Amanda's chest.

"Breathe in and out," Pete advised. "Remember, it's just tissue and bone."

Amanda swallowed again. The sound echoed in the room. She looked at Lucy Bennett's fingers. "There's something under her fingernails."

"Very good catch." He went over to the cabinet in the corner. "We can send it to the lab for analysis."

Amanda wished she had Roz Levy's magnifying glass. It wasn't grime under the girl's fingernails. "What do you think it is?"

"If she fought back, it's probably skin scratched off her attacker. Let's hope she managed to draw blood." Pete was back with a glass slide and something that looked like an oversized toothpick. "Hold her steady." Pete scraped the wooden pick under the fingernail. A long piece of skin came out. "If there's enough blood in this skin tissue, and you find a suspect, we can analyze his blood and see if it's the same type, whether he's a secretor or nonsecretor."

"We'd need more than blood to convict him."

"The FBI is doing amazing work with enzymes right now." He tapped the skin tissue onto the slide. "In ten years' time, they'll have samples from everyone in America stored on thousands of different computers all around the country. All you'll have to do is send the sample around to each computer and bingo, within months you'll know your perpetrator's name and address."

"You should tell that to Butch and Rick." The two homicide detectives would probably laugh in his face. "This is their case."

"Is it really?"

She didn't bother answering the question. "I guess I don't have to tell you how much trouble Evelyn and I would be in if they found out we were down here poking around."

Pete put the slide on the counter. "You know, the GBI can't find enough women to meet their quotas. They're going to lose their federal grants if they don't fill up the slots by the end of the year."

"I work for the Atlanta Police Department."

"You don't have to."

Pete obviously didn't know Duke Wagner as well as everyone else she'd met today. Forget Butch and Rick. Her father would have a canary if he knew Amanda was at the morgue. Touching a dead person. Talking to a hippie about leaving her steady job to be the token woman on the state's police force.

In for a penny, she supposed. There was still the reason they'd come here in the first place. Amanda turned the woman's hand out, exposing the wrist to the light. There they were—the familiar white scars. "She tried to kill herself before."

"Maybe," Pete allowed. "A lot of young women cut themselves. Generally, it's for attention. Your victim was obviously an addict. You can see that from the track marks. If she wanted to kill herself, she would've doubled down with the needle and her old friend H."

Amanda realized, "You washed her."

"Yes. We took photographs and X-rays, then we cut off her clothes and washed her down in preparation for the procedure. She'd urinated on herself—an unfortunate by-product of strangulation. Though one could point out this pales in comparison to the intestinal prolapse." He added, "I should point out that she was remarkably clean considering her occupation and addiction."

"What do you mean?"

"There was the expected results of the fall—picture a water balloon being dropped from that height—but in my experience, addicts don't favor bathing. The natural oils clog the skin. They think it holds the drug in longer. I'm not sure if there's a scientific basis for that, but someone who injects drain cleaner into their veins isn't necessarily troubled by facts. You can see the trimming—" He indicated the short pubic hair. "That's unusual, but I've seen it before. Some men are drawn to women who appear more infantilized."

"Child molesters?"

"Not necessarily."

Amanda nodded, though her eyes avoided the area Pete was talking about. Instead, she studied Lucy's hands again. The fingernail polish was perfect except for the chip. The strokes were even. It had taken a lot of time and patience to apply such a thick coat. Even Amanda, who buffed and clear-coated her nails in front of the television every night, couldn't manage such an expert job.

Pete asked, "Did you find something else?"

"Her fingernails."

"Are they fake? I've been seeing a lot of those plastic ones out of California lately."

"It looks like—" Amanda shook her head. She didn't know what it looked like. The nails were trimmed in a straight line. The cuticles were neat. The red polish was evenly within the margins. She'd never met a woman who could afford a professional manicure. She doubted a dead prostitute would be the first.

Amanda walked around the table and looked at Lucy's other hand. Again, the polish was perfect, as if someone else had applied it for her.

Amanda opened her mouth to speak, then stopped herself.

"Go on," Pete said. "There are no silly questions in here."

"Can you tell if she's left- or right-handed?"

Pete beamed at Amanda as if she was his star pupil. "There will be more muscle attachment to the bone on the dominant side."

"From holding a pen?"

"Among other things. Why are you asking?"

"When I paint my fingernails, one side always looks better than the other. With her, both sides look perfect."

He smiled again. "This, my dear, is why more women should be in my field."

Amanda doubted any sane woman would ever do this job—at

least not one who ever wanted to get married. "Maybe she has a friend who painted her fingernails?"

"Do women really groom one another? I assumed *Behind the Green Door* was taking cinematic liberties."

Amanda ignored the observation. She carefully put Lucy's hand back down on the table. It was so easy to focus on the parts rather than the whole. She'd let herself forget that Lucy Bennett was an actual human being.

This was to be blamed in part because Amanda had not yet looked at the girl's face. Amanda forced herself to do so now. She felt her early steeliness, but there was a tandem emotion of what could only be called curiosity. With the blood washed from Lucy's face, she looked different. As in Roz's photo, the skin still hung loosely to the side, but something beyond the obvious was not right.

"Could you . . ." Amanda didn't want to sound morbid, but she pushed through it. "Can I see her teeth?"

"Most of them were broken in the fall. What are you getting at?"

"The skin on her face. Is it possible to move it back to—"

"Oh, of course." Pete went to the head of the table. He gripped the loose flesh of the cheek and forehead and pulled it back over her skull. Lucy had bitten her lip in the fall. Pete returned it to the proper position. He used his fingers to tack the skin into place around the eyes and nose, like a baker kneading dough. "What do you think?"

Amanda realized it was exactly as she had expected. This woman was not Lucy Bennett. The scars on her wrist weren't the only indication. The open sores on her feet had a familiar pattern, like a constellation of stars. Barring that, there was the face, which clearly belonged to Jane Delray. "I think we need to get Evelyn back in here."

"How intriguing."

Amanda left the room through the swinging doors. The lab was empty, so she pushed open the other set of doors leading into the hallway. Evelyn was several yards ahead, close to the entrance. She was talking with a man wearing a navy blue suit. He was tall, over six feet. His sandy brown hair touched his collar. The tailoring of his clothes was obviously professional. The jacket curved into his back. The flared pants hovered over his white loafers. He was finishing a cigarette when Amanda joined them. Evelyn shot her a look, her eyes practically bulging from their sockets.

She was talking to Mr. Blue Suit.

"Mr. Bennett." Evelyn's voice was pitched higher than usual, though she was doing a good job of hiding her excitement. "This is my partner, Miss Wagner."

He barely glanced at her, keeping his eyes on his white loafers as he stamped out the cigarette. "As I said, I just want to see my sister and leave."

"We had a few more questions," she began, but Bennett cut her off.

"Is there a man I can talk to? Someone in charge?"

Amanda thought of Pete. "The coroner is in the back."

Bennett's lips twisted in distaste, whether at the thought of the coroner or what he saw in Amanda, she wasn't sure. And it really didn't matter. The only thing she could focus on was how arrogant and unlikable he was.

Amanda said, "Dr. Hanson is preparing the body. It'll only be a few more minutes."

Evelyn picked up the lie. "You won't want to see her how she is now, Mr. Bennett."

"I don't want to see her period," he snapped back. "As I told you, Mrs. Mitchell, my sister was a drug addict and a whore. What I'm doing here is a mere formality so that my mother can have some peace at the end of her life."

"His mother has cancer," Evelyn explained.

Amanda let a few seconds pass out of respect for the man's mother, but she couldn't stop herself from asking, "Mr. Bennett, can you tell us when was the last time you saw your sister?"

He glanced away. "Five, maybe six years?" He looked down at his watch. It was a furtive movement, as obvious as Evelyn tugging the back of her hair. "I really do not appreciate your wasting my time. Shall I go back to the coroner?"

"Just another minute." Amanda had never been good at spotting a liar, but Bennett was as easy to read as an open book. "Are you sure that's the last contact you had with your sister?"

Bennett took a pack of Parliaments from his breast pocket and shook out a cigarette. A large gold college ring was on his middle finger. UGA Law School. Class of '74. The Georgia Bulldog was etched into the red stone.

Amanda asked, "Mr. Bennett, are you sure about the timing? It seems like you've had contact with Lucy more recently."

He showed a flash of guilt as he jammed the cigarette between his lips. "I mailed her a letter to the Union Mission. It was perfunctory, I assure you."

"On Ponce de Leon?" Amanda asked. The Ponce Union Mission was the only homeless facility that allowed women.

Bennett said, "I tried to find Lucy when our father passed away. My mother had it in mind that she'd joined the hippie movement— you know, just dropped out for a while. She thought Lucy would want to come home, go to college, live a normal life. She could never accept that Lucy chose to be a whore."

Evelyn asked, "When did your father pass?"

Bennett flicked his gold lighter, taking his time to light the cigarette. He didn't speak again until he'd blown out a stream of smoke. "It was a few weeks after I graduated from law school."

"Last year?"

"Yes. July or August. I can't recall." He inhaled deeply on the cigarette. "Lucy was never really a good girl. I suppose she fooled us all, right up until she ran off with some greaser to Atlanta. I'm sure you've heard this story more than a dozen times." He exhaled, smoke curling from his nostrils. "She was always too willful. Stubborn."

Amanda asked, "How did you know to mail the letter to the Union Mission?"

Bennett seemed irritated that she wouldn't let him change the subject. "I made some calls to some people. They said that Lucy probably would've ended up there."

Amanda wondered who these people were. She took a chance. "Are you a litigator, Mr. Bennett?"

"No, I do tax abatement. I'm a first-year associate at Treadwell-Price downtown. Why do you ask?"

So, Evelyn was right. He'd obviously gotten his boss to make a phone call. "Did you hear back from your sister?"

"No, but the man working there assured me that he gave the letter to Lucy. For whatever that's worth."

"Do you remember the man's name?"

"Trask? Trent?" Bennett blew out a plume of smoke. "I don't know. He was very unprofessional. Dirty clothes. Hair unkempt. Frankly, there was an odor about him. I imagine he's a marijuana smoker."

"You met him in person?"

"You can't trust these people." He sucked on the cigarette. "I thought I might find Lucy there. What I found was a bunch of disgusting whores and drunkards. Just the sort of place I knew Lucy would end up."

"Did you see her?"

"Of course not. I doubt I would even recognize her."

Amanda nodded, though this seemed like an odd statement coming from a man who was about to identify his dead sister's body.

Evelyn asked, "Do you know a young woman named Kitty Treadwell?"

He narrowed his eyes. Smoke drifted from the tip of his cigarette. "What do you know about Kitty?" He didn't let them answer. "You two ladies should mind where you stick your noses. They're liable to get cut off."

The front doors slammed open. Rick Landry and Butch Bonnie walked into the hallway. Both men scowled when they saw Amanda and Evelyn.

"Finally," Bennett mumbled.

Landry was visibly furious. He stomped forward, demanding, "What the hell are you two slits doing here?"

Amanda was standing beside Evelyn. It didn't take much to get in front of her, blocking Landry in the process. "We're investigating our case."

Landry didn't bother responding to her statement. He turned, his shoulder bumping into Amanda's so hard that she had to step back. "Hank Bennett?"

Bennett nodded. "Are you in charge?"

"Yes," Landry said. "We are." He crowded out Amanda, forcing her to step back again as he inserted himself between her and Bennett. "I'm sorry about your loss, sir."

Bennett waved his hand, as if it was nothing. "I lost my sister a long time ago." Again, he checked his watch. "Can we get this over with? I'm late for supper."

Landry walked him down the hallway. Butch took up the rear. He glanced back at Amanda and Evelyn. He gave Amanda an unwelcome wink. She waited until they disappeared behind the door.

Evelyn hissed out air between her teeth. She put her hand to her chest. She was shaking.

"Come on." Amanda grabbed Evelyn's hand. The other woman was resistant. Amanda had to pull her down the hallway. She pushed ajar the door to the lab just as the three men were walking into the morgue.

Amanda waited until they were inside before opening the door. She kept her knees bent, as if she was sneaking around. The curtains on the large picture window were still drawn.

Evelyn whispered, "Amanda—"

"Shh," Amanda shot back. Carefully, she parted the drapes a few inches. Evelyn joined her as they peered through the window.

Pete Hanson stood with his back to the far wall. His arms were crossed. He'd struck Amanda as a very easygoing fellow, but there was something in his posture that indicated he was very unhappy.

Landry and Butch had their backs to the window. Hank Bennett stood opposite, the dead girl between them. He was looking down at the victim's face.

Apparently, Evelyn was, too. She whispered, "That's Jane Delray," at the same moment Hank Bennett said, "Yes, that's my sister."

eleven

April 15, 1975

LUCY BENNETT

There was another girl in the next room. The old one was gone. She hadn't been bad, but this one was awful. Constantly crying. Sobbing. Begging. Pleading.

She sure as hell wasn't moving. Lucy could guarantee that. None of them moved. The pain was too excruciating. Too unspeakable. It took your breath away. It blacked you out.

At first, it was impossible not to try. Claustrophobia took over. The unreasonable fear of suffocation. It started in the legs like the cramps from withdrawal. Your toes curled. Your muscles ached to contract. It worked its way through your body like a violent storm.

Last month, a tornado had hit the Governor's Mansion. It started in Perry Homes, but no one cared about that. The Governor's Mansion was different. It was a symbol, meant to show businessmen and visiting dignitaries that Georgia was the heart of the New South.

The tornado had other ideas.

The roof had been torn off. The grounds damaged. Governor Busbee said that he was saddened by the destruction. Lucy had heard him say so on the news. It was a special bulletin cut between the re-play of the top-forty countdown. Linda Ronstadt's "When Will I Be Loved," then the governor saying they were going to rebuild. A phoenix rising from the ashes. Hopeful. Certain.

Back when it got really cold, the man had started to let Lucy listen to the transistor radio. He kept it turned down low so the other girls couldn't hear. Or maybe he kept it low special for Lucy. She would listen to the news, tales of the whole wide world spinning by. She would close her eyes and feel the ground moving underneath her.

Lucy didn't like to think too much about it, but she could tell she was his favorite. It reminded her of the games she and Jill Henderson used to play in elementary school. Jill was good with her hands. She'd take a sheet of notebook paper and fold it into triangles. What was it called?

Lucy tried to think. It didn't help that the other girl was sobbing so hard. She wasn't loud, but she was consistent, like a kitten mewing.

Cootie Catchers. That was it.

Jill would slide her fingertips into the folded sections. There were words written on the inside. You asked who liked you. Who was going to marry you. Were you going to be happy? Were you going to have one kid or two?

Yes. No. Maybe. Keith. John. Bobby.

It wasn't just the radio that made Lucy feel special. The man spent more time with her. He was gentler with her than he was before— than he was with the other girls, because Lucy could hear it.

How many other girls had there been? Two, three? All weak. All familiar.

The new girl in the other room should stop fighting back. She should just give in and he would make it all better. Otherwise, she would end up like the girl before. And the one before that. Nothing would get better. Nothing would change.

Things had changed for Lucy. Instead of the pieces of Vienna sausage and stale bread he'd shoved between her teeth in the early days, he was letting her feed herself. She sat on the bed and ate McDonald's hamburgers and french fries. He would sit in the chair, knife in his lap, watching her chew.

Was it Lucy's imagination, or was her body healing itself? She was sleeping more deeply now. Those first weeks—months?—she'd had nothing to do but sleep, but back then, every time she found herself nodding off, she'd jerk awake in panic. Now, oftentimes when he came into the room, he had to wake her.

Gentle nudge of the shoulder. Stroke along the cheek. The warm feel of the washcloth. The careful tending of her body. He cleaned her. He prayed over her. He made her whole.

Back on Juice's corner, the girls would trade stories about the bad johns out there. Who to watch out for. Who you would never see coming. There was the one who stuck a knife in your face. The one who tried to put his whole fist inside you. The one who wore a diaper. The one who wanted to paint your fingernails.

In the scheme of things, was this guy really that bad?

twelve

present day

TUESDAY

The morning sun was just winking open its eye when Will raked back the passenger's seat in Faith's Mini. A body had been found, probably the missing Georgia Tech student, and he was wasting time adjusting knobs on a clown car so that his head wouldn't press against the roof.

Faith waited until he was putting on his seatbelt to speak. "You look awful."

Will glanced at her. She was wearing her GBI regs: khaki pants, navy blue shirt, and her Glock strapped to her thigh. "Thank you."

Faith backed the car down the driveway. The wheels bumped over the curb. She didn't say anything else, which was unusual. Faith tended to chat. She tended to pry. For some reason, she was doing neither this morning. Will should've been worried about this, but there were only so many burdens he could take on at once. His useless night in the basement. His argument with Sara. The fact that his father was out of prison. Whatever Amanda was hiding from him. That there was a dead body at Techwood. That he had kissed his wife.

Will put his fingers to his mouth again. He'd wiped off Angie's lipstick with a paper towel, but he could still taste the bitter chemical residue.

Faith said, "There's an accident on this side of North Avenue. Do you mind if I take the long way through Ansley?"

Will shook his head.

"Did you not get any sleep last night?"

"Off and on."

"You missed a place on your—" She touched the side of her cheek. When Will didn't respond, she flipped down the visor in front of him.

Will stared at his reflection in the mirror. There was a small strip of beard he'd missed with the razor this morning. He looked at his eyes. They were bloodshot. No wonder people kept telling him he looked bad.

"This Techwood murder," Faith began. "Donnelly was the first responder."

Will flipped up the visor. Detective Leo Donnelly had been Faith's partner when she worked homicide with the APD. He was slightly annoying, but his greater sin was mediocrity. "Have you talked to him?"

"No. Just Amanda." She paused, as if to give Will the opportunity to ask what Amanda had said. After a few silent seconds, she told him, "I know about your father."

Will stared out the window. Faith had taken more than the long way. There were better routes to bypass North Avenue on the way to Techwood. She had navigated the back roads to Monroe Drive. They were skirting Piedmont Park and heading toward Ansley. It was six o'clock in the morning. There was no accident on North.

She said, "Mama told me last night. She needed me to make a phone call."

Will watched the houses and apartment buildings go by. They passed the vet's office where Betty got her shots.

"There's a guy I used to date way back when. I think you met him once. Sam Lawson. He's a reporter for the *AJC*."

The Atlanta Journal-Constitution. Will didn't want to think about the why behind Evelyn Mitchell's request. He assumed Amanda was making some kind of Machiavellian move, trying to get ahead of whatever the paper was going to print. Sara read the *AJC* every morning. She was the only person Will knew who still got the paper delivered. Was this how Sara was going to find out? Will could imagine the phone call. If she called. Maybe she wouldn't. Maybe Sara would see this as an easy opportunity to get out of whatever they had started.

Faith said, "That's how Amanda found out about your father's parole." She paused, again anticipating a response. "Sam called her office and asked for a quote. He wanted to know how she felt about him getting out." Faith stopped at the red light. "He's not going to run the story. I fed him some details on a biker gang APD busted for running crank out of a charter school. It's a front-page story. Sam won't circle back."

Will stared at the darkened strip of Ansley Mall. The upscale stores weren't open yet. Their lights glowed in the low dawn. He felt a strange sensation, like he was being driven to the hospital for surgery. Some part of his body would be removed. He would have to recover from that. He would have to find a way to acclimate his senses so they did not feel the gaping hole.

Faith asked, "What did you do to your hands?"

Will tried to bend his fingers. It hurt just flexing them. His ankle throbbed with every beat of his heart. His basement excursion was being felt by every joint in his body.

"Anyway." Faith swung through the steep curve that took them up Fourteenth Street. "I looked up his case."

Will was more than familiar with his father's crimes.

"He dodged a bullet. *Furman v. Georgia* was in the early seventies."

"Seventy-two," Will provided. The landmark Supreme Court case had temporarily suspended the death penalty. A few more years either side and Will's father would've been put to death by the State of Georgia.

He said, "Gary Gilmore was the first man executed after Furman."

"Spree killer, right? Up in Utah?" Faith loved reading about mass murderers. It was an unfortunate hobby that often came in handy.

Will asked, "Is it a spree if it's only two people?"

"I think two qualifies so long as the timing is close."

"I thought that it had to be three."

"I think that's just for serial killers." Faith took out her iPhone. She typed with her thumb as she waited to make an illegal turn onto Peachtree.

Will stared up Fourteenth Street. He couldn't see the hotel from his vantage point, but he knew that the Four Seasons was two blocks away. That was probably why Faith was making the turn. She knew that his father was staying at the hotel. Will wondered if he was still in bed. The man had been in prison for over thirty years. It was probably impossible for him to sleep late. Maybe he'd already ordered his breakfast from room service. Angie said he used the gym every morning. He was probably running on the treadmill, watching one of the morning shows and planning his day.

"Here we go. Two or more qualifies as a spree." Faith dropped her iPhone back into the cup holder and turned against the light. "Can we talk about your father now?"

Will said, "Did you know that Peachtree Street is Georgia's continental divide?" He pointed to the side of the road. "Rain that falls on that side of the road goes to the Atlantic. Rain on this side goes to the Gulf. Maybe I've got the sides mixed up, but you get the gist."

"That's fascinating, Will."

"I kissed Angie."

Faith nearly ran up onto the sidewalk. She jerked the car back into the lane. She was silent for a while before she muttered, "You fucking idiot."

That felt more like it.

"What are you going to do?"

"I don't know." He stared out the window again. They were heading toward the thick of downtown. "I think I have to tell Sara."

"No, you most certainly do not," she countered. "Are you crazy? She'll kick your ass to the curb."

She probably should. There was no way that Will could explain to Sara that the oldest cliché in the world happened to be true this one time: the kiss meant nothing. For Will's part, it had been a reminder that Sara was the only woman he wanted to be with; maybe the first woman he'd ever *really* wanted to be with. For Angie's part, the kiss had been tantamount to a dog raising its leg on a fire hydrant.

Faith asked, "Do you want to be with Angie?"

"No." He shook his head. "No."

"Was there anything else?"

Will remembered he'd touched her breast. "Not—" He wasn't going to get into specifics with Faith. "There was no contact between—"

"Okay, I get it." She turned onto North Avenue. "Jesus, Will."

He waited for her to continue.

"You can't tell Sara."

"I can't hide things from her."

She laughed so loud his ears hurt. "Are you kidding me? Does Sara know about your father? Does she know that he—"

"No."

Faith did not bother to hide her incredulity. "Well then, don't let this be the one thing you tell her the truth about."

"It's different."

"Do you think Angie will tell her?"

Will shook his head. Angie's moral code wasn't easily decipherable, but Will knew she would never tell Sara about the kiss. It was much better to use it to torture Will.

Faith cut straight to the point. "If it's not going to happen again and it didn't mean anything, then you're just going to have to live with the guilt. Or live without Sara."

Will couldn't talk about this anymore. He stared out the window again. They were stopped at a red light. The lights were on at the Varsity. In a few hours, the curb men would be out sweeping the lot, slapping numbers on cars and taking orders. Mrs. Flannigan used to bring the older kids to the Varsity once a month. It was a reward for good behavior.

Faith asked, "Have you ever tried to talk to the detectives who worked your mother's case?"

"One disappeared. Somebody thought he moved to Miami. The other died from AIDS in the early eighties."

"Did either of them have family?"

"No one I could find." Honestly, Will hadn't looked that hard. It was like picking at a scab. There came a point when you started to draw blood.

"I can't believe how many conversations I've had with you over the last two years, and you never told me about this."

Will left her to wonder why on her own.

Faith crossed the interstate. The athlete dorms that had been built for the Olympics had the Georgia Tech logo on them now. The old stadium was being remodeled. The streets were freshly paved. Brick inlays carpeted the sidewalks. Even this early in the morning, students were out jogging. Faith turned at the next light. She was more than familiar with the area. Her son was currently enrolled at Georgia Tech. Her mother had gotten her doctorate here. Faith had finished her four-year degree at the university so she could qualify for employment with the GBI.

Faith slid a piece of notebook paper out from her visor. Will saw that she'd scribbled directions on it. She slowed the car, mumbling, "Centennial Park North . . . here we go." Finally, she turned onto a side street, downshifting as they went up a hill. The area was filled with upscale brick apartment buildings and townhouses. The cars on the street were nice—newer Toyotas and Fords with an occasional

BMW thrown in. The grass was trimmed. The eaves and windows
were painted a crisp white. Satellite dishes dotted every other bal-
cony. The compound was designed to be mixed income, which
meant a handful of poor people lived in the less desirable units and
the rest went for top dollar. Will imagined that some of the better-
off students lived here rather than the dorms, where Faith's son re-
sided.

"Zell Miller Center," Faith read from the sign. "Clark Howell
Community Building. Here we go." She slowed the car to a crawl.
The directions weren't really needed anymore. Two cruisers blocked
the street. Police tape cordoned off a group of residents. Most were
in pajamas and robes. A few of the joggers had stopped to find out
what was happening.

Faith had to drive down several blocks to find a space. She pulled
up onto a berm and jerked up the parking brake. She asked Will, "Are
you okay?"

He was going to ignore the question, but that didn't seem fair.
"We'll see," he managed, then got out of the car before she could say
anything else.

The streetlights were still on, supplementing the rising sun. Two
newscopters hovered overhead. Their whirring blades chopped the
air into white noise. More reporters were camped out down the road.
Cameras were set up on tripods. Reporters were checking their
makeup, scribbling their notes.

Will didn't wait for Faith. He headed back toward the crime scene,
where he could see Amanda Wagner was waiting.

Her arm was in a sling, the only indication that she'd spent the
night in the hospital. She stood on the sidewalk dressed in her usual
monochromatic skirt, blouse, and jacket. Two burly patrolmen were
looking down at her, nodding as she gave them orders. They looked
like football players huddled before a snap.

As Will and Faith approached Amanda, the patrolmen jogged off
toward the bystanders, probably to get names and photos so they
could run them through the database. Amanda was old school with
all her investigations. She didn't rely on a blood sample or a stray hair

to sway a jury. She worked the case until she got a resolution that no logical human being could ever doubt.

She also didn't bother with small talk. "I don't want you here."

"Then why did you call me?"

"Because I knew you wouldn't stay away."

Amanda didn't wait for a response. She turned on her heel, heading toward the community building. Will easily matched her brisk pace. Uncharacteristically, Faith kept her distance, trailing several feet behind.

Amanda said, "We're covered up in red tape. As you know, this whole area used to be a slum. The state emptied it out for the Olympics. The city got its finger in the pie. Tech got a piece of it. The Parks Department had its say. The Housing Authority. The Historical Register, which is a joke if there ever was one. We've got more jurisdictions than news vans. APD is supplementing for now, but it's our techs and our ME handling the evidence."

"I want to sit in on the autopsy."

"It'll be hours before—"

"I'll wait."

"Do you really think that's a good idea?"

Will thought it was a terrible idea, but that wasn't going to stop him. "You need to bring him in for questioning."

"Why would I do that?"

The fact that her voice sounded so reasonable made Will want to punch her. "You read my father's file."

She stopped, looking up at him. "Yes."

"You think it's a coincidence that he got out of prison and a dead student was found dumped at Techwood?"

"Coincidences happen all the time." Her usual certainty was showing some cracks. "I can't bring him in without probable cause, Will. Due process? The Fourth Amendment? Any of these inalienable rights ringing a bell?"

"That's never stopped you before."

"I've found it's within the purview of rich white men to avoid such unpleasantries."

Will realized that she'd backed him into a corner. "Still—"

"There's nothing more to say." Amanda continued walking. "We have a tentative ID on Ashleigh Snyder. They found her purse in the Dumpster. Her credit cards were there but her license was missing. So was her cash."

"That sounds familiar."

"Bless the Sunshine Laws." Georgia's freedom of information act was one of the most liberal in the country. Inmates were especially fond of the law.

Will said, "He's staying at the Four Seasons Hotel."

"I'm aware of that," she acknowledged. "We lost track of him for two hours yesterday afternoon, but I've made certain that won't happen again."

"He's been out almost two months."

Amanda didn't immediately answer. "I've never understood time off for good behavior. It's prison. Shouldn't you be on your best behavior at all times?"

"No one told me when he got out."

"That's the thing about having a sealed juvenile record, Will. They aren't allowed to notify you unless you ask them to."

"He was supposed to die in there."

"I know."

One of the patrolmen called out, "Dr. Wagner?"

Amanda said, "You two go on." She waited for the cop to join her.

Will kept walking. Faith had to jog to keep up. She asked, "What was that about?"

He could only shake his head as they entered the mouth of the parking lot. The ground sloped downward. In the back of the lot, a group of detectives formed a half circle around the body. The woman was in front of a large Dumpster area. Brick walls horseshoed the metal container. The tall metal doors stood open. The lock was hanging off the latch, the ring broken. Someone had already marked it with a yellow tag so it could be catalogued as evidence.

Will glanced around, feeling watched. Or maybe he was just being paranoid. He scanned the area. The community center was on the opposite side of the parking lot. More apartments edged the perimeter. Their white garage doors were like teeth against the gum of the red brick. There was a playground in the distance, with brightly colored tunnels and swings. The Coca-Cola building loomed on the horizon.

If he squinted at the view back across the interstate, he could pick out the familiar salmon-colored façade of the Four Seasons Hotel.

"Another case solved by the glorious GBI." Leo Donnelly laughed around the cigarette in his mouth. As usual, the homicide detective was dressed in a tan suit that was probably already wrinkled when he picked it up off the floor this morning. His new partner, a young guy named Jamal Hodge, nodded at Faith.

Leo winked at her. "Lookin' good across the chest, Mitchell. I guess you're still nursing?"

"Fuck off, Leo." Faith took her notebook out of her purse. "When'd the call come in?"

Leo pulled out his own notebook. "Four thirty-eight in the cheery a.m. Janitor comes on shift, sees her and freaks. His name's Otay Keehole."

"Utay Keo," Jamal corrected.

"Lookit Poindexter here." Leo shot him a nasty look. "Ooo-Tay is a student at Tech. Twenty-four years old. Lives with his baby mama. No priors."

Faith asked, "How's he look for this?"

Jamal supplied, "Not likely."

Leo made a show of closing his notebook. He took a drag on his cigarette, staring at Jamal. "Janitor's two years out of Cambodia. Works off his student visa. Voluntarily submitted to fingerprinting and DNA. No record. No motive. I'm sure he's popped a few whores in his day—who hasn't?—but he doesn't even have a car. Took the bus here."

Will asked, "You ID'd the victim off her credit cards?"

Jamal held out his hands, indicating Leo should answer.

"We're pretty sure it's Snyder," Leo said. "Face is a mess, but the blonde hair is a giveaway."

Will asked, "Have you notified the family?"

"Mom's dead. Daddy's flying back from a business trip in Salt Lake. Should be here this afternoon."

Jamal added, "We asked for dental records."

"Great, thanks," Faith mumbled. She was probably thinking about the father's long flight home, the moment at the morgue when his life would forever be changed.

They all turned back to the Dumpster. The crowd had dispersed so the crime scene techs could begin the arduous process of cataloguing the scene.

Will looked down at the woman's twisted body. Long blonde hair draped across her face. She was on her back. Her arms were turned, wrists open to the sky. Her face was a bloody pulp, probably unrecognizable to even her closest friends. Her fingernails were painted bright red. Blood glued her clothes to her skin. Will could guess what was underneath the tight T-shirt and flowered skirt.

Leo said, "Here's something you don't see every day: guy pummeled her gut until her intestines shit out. You can't find that kind of thing on YouTube." He chuckled to himself. "At least, not until I figure out how to work the camera on my phone."

"Lord help us," Jamal muttered. He headed toward Charlie Reed, the GBI crime scene investigator.

"Come on, Hodge," Leo called to his back. "It's funny."

Faith said, "Smart, Leo. You really want to piss off the deputy chief's grandson?"

Will glanced at Faith. Her voice sounded a little shaky. She had never been good around bodies, but through sheer determination she held her own. One crack in her shell and Leo or someone like him would turn Faith into a joke every squad room was laughing about by morning roll call. Faith had once told Will that working with Leo

CRIMINAL 201

was like watching a wind-up monkey that couldn't quite get the cymbals to meet.

Will knew better than to ask if she was okay. Instead, he knelt beside the body, keeping his distance so he wouldn't taint the area. The crime scene photographers weren't waiting for the sun. Their digital cameras and computers were laid out on a folding table. One of the women turned on the diesel generator. The xenon lights flickered. The victim's hand showed stark against the asphalt. Her red manicured nails glistened as if they were still wet.

Faith asked Leo, "What's this building? Is it still a community center?"

"Dunno." Leo shrugged. "Guess they named it after that guy on the radio."

Will stood up too quickly. He fought a wave of dizziness. "Clark Howell was the publisher of *The Atlanta Constitution*."

"No shit?" Leo asked.

"He's chock-full of fascinating trivia today," Faith said. "Do you have any leads?"

"What's it to you?"

Faith put her hands on her hips. "Don't be an asshole, Leo. You know this is a state case. Do you have any leads, or should I ask Jamal?"

Leo reluctantly offered, "I made some calls, checked with downtown. There's nobody on our books what would knock the shit out of a girl like this." He laughed at his own joke. "Literally."

"She have any enemies?"

"Y'all should know more about that than me."

"What about a drug problem?"

Leo sniffed, rubbing his nose. "Nothing serious, from what I've heard."

"Coke or meth?"

"She's a student. What do you think?"

"Meth," Faith said. "And watch the generalities, Leo. My kid goes to Tech. He doesn't hit anything harder than Red Bull."

"Sure."

"Faith," Amanda called. She was at the edge of the parking lot, waving them over. Faith shot Leo a nasty look as they headed toward Amanda.

Leo yelled at their backs, "No, don't thank me, Officers. It was my pleasure."

Amanda was digging around in her purse when they joined her. She pulled out her BlackBerry. The case was still cracked from her fall. She scrolled through her emails while she talked. "Patrol found a jogger who saw a suspicious green minivan circling the area shortly after four this morning."

"He just came forward?" Faith looked at her watch. "Was he jogging for two hours?"

"That sounds like a good question to start with. He lives there, apartment two-six-twenty." Amanda indicated the building across the street. "Make sure you get him on paper. All the t's crossed and i's dotted."

Will said, "I'll talk to him." He made to go, but Amanda stopped him.

"Faith, you do this."

Faith gave him a look of apology before heading toward the apartment building.

Amanda held up a finger, silencing Will. She read a few more emails before dropping her BlackBerry into her purse. "You know you can't work this case."

"I don't see how you're going to stop me."

"This has to look good on paper. We can't have it falling apart in court."

"It held up in court the last time and he still got out."

"Welcome to the criminal justice system. I rather thought you were familiar with it by now."

Will stared across the interstate. Rush hour was gearing up. Cars were starting to clog the fourteen lanes. He saw a sign for one of the Emory hospitals. Sara had gone to Emory University. Grady was part of their teaching system. She would be getting ready for work right now. Showering, drying her hair. Will usually walked the dogs before he left. He wondered if she missed that.

Amanda said, "Give me time to do this right, Will. It has to be done right."

Will shook his head. He didn't care about the means, just the end. "We need to work his case from the beginning."

"What do you think I've been doing?" she asked. "I've had two teams on this since I found out. We're dealing with a thirty-plus-year time gap in a city that tears itself down every five years. His old stomping ground is currently a twelve-story office complex."

"I'll check it. Faith can go with me."

"It's already been checked top to bottom."

"Not by me."

She wasn't looking at him. Like Will, she was staring over the interstate. "Motive, means, and opportunity." It was Amanda's mantra.

Will said, "You know he's got all three."

She gave a tight nod of her head. If Will hadn't been watching, he would've missed it. He studied her profile. She seemed to be as tired as he was. There were dark circles under her eyes. Her makeup was caked into the creases around her eyes and mouth.

She said, "I have to say, I love what you did with the basement."

Will's hands clenched. The cuts opened up along his fingers.

"Did you find what you were looking for?"

His jaw popped when he opened his mouth to speak. "Why were you there?"

"That's a very interesting question."

"How long have you known about my father?"

"You work for me, Will. It's my job to know everything about you."

"Why did that reporter call you?"

"It makes for a good story, I suppose—your chosen path of law and order. Your rise from the ashes. Atlanta's symbol is the phoenix. What a fitting dovetail."

He turned and headed toward North Avenue, the bridge over the interstate. Amanda's stride was half as long as Will's. She had to work to match his pace.

She asked, "Where are you going?"

"To talk to my father."

"To what end?"

"You've read his file. You know he has a pattern. He kills one, he keeps one. He's probably already picked her out."

"Shall I put out an APB on a missing prostitute?"

She was mocking him. "You know he's looking for another girl."

"I told you we've got eyes on him. He hasn't left his room."

"Except for yesterday afternoon."

She stopped trying to keep up. "You will *not* talk to him."

Will turned around. Amanda never raised her voice. She didn't scream. She didn't stamp her foot. She never cursed. She managed to scare everyone by reputation. For the first time in fifteen years, he saw through her. She was nothing, really. An old woman with her arm in a sling and secrets she would carry to her grave.

She said, "I've issued a standing order to have you arrested the minute you step one foot in that hotel. Understood?"

He stared his hate into her. "I should've left you to rot in that basement."

"Oh, Will." Her voice was filled with regret. "I have a feeling that by the end of this, we're both going to wish you had."

thirteen

SUZANNA FORD

She missed *Dancing with the Stars*. She missed Bobo, her little dog who'd died when she was ten. She missed her grandmother, who'd died when Suzanna was eleven, and her grandfather, who'd died a few months later. She missed Adam, the goldfish who'd died the night they brought him home from the store. Suzanna had found him in the tank just floating on his side. His eye was blank. She could see her reflection in it.

Suzanna called the store to complain.

"Just flush 'em down the toilet," the manager said. "Come by tomorrow and we'll give you a new one."

Suzanna had felt uneasy at the prospect. It felt wrong. Did Adam mean nothing? Was he that replaceable? Just plop another fish in the tank and forget he even existed? Call that one Adam, too. Feed him

Adam's food. Let him swim through Adam's secret treasure box and pink coral castle?

In the end, there was nothing else to do. Suzanna flushed him down the toilet. As the water circled around the bowl, she saw his fin flip up. The glass orb of his eyeball turned to her, and she had seen something like panic.

In her dreams, Suzanna was the fish. She was Adam One, because of course the temptation was too great—they had gone back the next day and gotten a free Adam Two.

That was the entirety of the dream:

Suzanna One, helpless, staring up at the ceiling as she spun, spun, spun quickly down the drain.

fourteen

July 14, 1975

MONDAY

Amanda leaned against her Plymouth as she waited for Evelyn in the parking garage of the Sears building. The air did not move in the underground facility. The coolness afforded from the poured concrete walls was no match for the scorching heat. Even at seven in the morning, Amanda could feel sweat dripping down her neck and into her collar.

Neither she nor Evelyn had been up for the barbecue after leaving the morgue on Saturday evening. Hank Bennett. The misidentified girl. The red fingernails. The broken hyoid bone. It was a lot to process, and neither of them seemed up to having a coherent conversation. They'd both talked in monosyllables, Amanda because of the things she'd seen with Pete Hanson, and Evelyn—most probably—because she'd been unsettled about seeing Rick Landry again. No matter their reasons, Evelyn had gone home to her husband and Amanda had gone home to her empty apartment.

If Sunday brought anything, it was a welcome sense of normalcy. Amanda had cooked breakfast for her father. They'd gone to church. She'd cooked Sunday dinner. All the while, Duke had been notably more cheerful. He'd made a few jokes about the preacher. He was feeling bullish on his case. He'd spoken with his lawyer again. Lars Oglethorpe's reinstatement was definitely good news for the men Reginald Eaves had fired.

Amanda doubted it was good news for her.

Evelyn's station wagon made a tight turn, the tires squealing against the concrete. She backed into the space beside the Plymouth, calling through the open window, "Did Kenny call you yesterday?"

Amanda felt a shock of panic. "Why would Kenny call me?"

"I gave him your number."

For a few seconds, Amanda was too flustered to do anything but stare. "Why would you give him my phone number?"

"Because he asked for it, silly. Why do you sound so surprised? And why are you just standing there?"

Amanda shook her head as she got into the car. Men like Kenny Mitchell didn't ask for her phone number. "That's very nice of you to put him up to this, but let's not waste time on something that's not going to happen."

"You can—" Evelyn stopped, but only for a moment before she blurted out, "You can wear Tampax, right?"

Amanda pressed her fingers into her eyelids, not caring whether or not she smudged her makeup. "If I say yes, can we please change the subject?"

Evelyn wouldn't be daunted. "You know, Pete's a real doctor. He can write you a prescription, no questions asked, and if you slip the guy at the Plaza Pharmacy a few extra bucks, he won't be a jerk about it."

Amanda fanned her face. The heat was even more stifling inside the car. She tried not to think about her telephone ringing in her empty apartment yesterday.

"It's legal now, sweetheart. You don't have to be married to get birth control anymore."

Amanda's laugh was genuine this time. "I think you're jumping to a lot of conclusions."

"Maybe, but it's fun, isn't it?"

It was humiliating, actually, but Amanda tried to hide that fact by looking at her watch again. "Did this consume your entire Sunday, or did you manage to think at all about what we've been doing?"

Evelyn rolled her eyes. "Are you kidding? It's all that's been on my mind for the last week. I was so distracted this morning I put salt instead of sugar in Bill's coffee. Poor man drank half the cup before he realized what I'd done." She paused for a breath. "What about you?"

"I've been going over Butch's notes." Amanda pulled the homicide detective's notebook out of her purse. "See this here?" She pointed to the page for Evelyn's benefit. The letters *CI* were circled twice.

"Confidential informant," Evelyn said. She flipped back through the notebook. "Does he say anything else about it? A name, maybe?"

"Nothing, but a lot of Butch's cases rely on CIs." Most of them did, actually. The man was very good at finding criminals and low-lifes who were willing to parlay information into a get-out-of-jail-free card. "He never names his sources."

"Oh, that's sneaky." She scanned the pages, stopping on a crude drawing of the apartment where Jane Delray had lived. "He left out the bathroom. Did he even search the place?" She answered her own question. "Of course he didn't. Why would he?"

Amanda checked the time again. She didn't want to be late for roll call. "We should go over what we're doing today. I can call my friend at the Housing Authority when I get to work. Maybe we can find out who rented that apartment."

Evelyn paused for a moment as she switched gears. "I'll call Cindy Murray at the Five and see if she has time to check the confiscated-license box for a Lucy Bennett. At least we'll have a photograph of her."

"I don't know what good it'll do. Pete will have to sign off on the ID. It came from her own brother." Neither she nor Evelyn had the nerve to contradict Hank Bennett's identification of his sister. "Bennett hasn't laid eyes on her in five or six years. Do you think he knew it wasn't Lucy?"

"I think all he cared about was not being late for his dinner date."

They were both silent. Amanda felt a ping-pong sensation inside her head. Thoughts kept bouncing around, getting lost. It was just too much to keep up with.

Evelyn was obviously feeling the same. She said, "Bill and I started a puzzle last night—bridges of the Pacific Northwest. Zeke picked it out for Father's Day last month—and I thought, 'This is exactly how I've felt all week. Like there are all of these different little pieces to a puzzle floating around out there, and if I could only put them together, maybe I'd be able to see the full picture.'"

"I know what you mean. All I do is ask myself questions, and I can't seem to get a satisfactory answer to any of them."

"Hey, I've got a crazy idea."

"You cannot imagine my surprise."

Evelyn gave her a sarcastic grimace, then leaned into the back seat of the station wagon.

"What are you doing?"

She snaked her body around into the back seat. Her legs went up. Amanda swatted the woman's feet out of her face. She scanned the parking lot, praying they were not being watched.

"Evelyn," she said. "What on earth?"

"Got it." Finally, she shimmied back into her seat. She had a pack of construction paper in her hands. "Zeke's crayons melted into the carpet. Bring your pen." She pushed open the door.

Amanda got out of the car and followed her around to the front of the wagon. Evelyn took a piece of paper off the top of the pack and, using Amanda's pen, wrote, "HANK BENNETT" on the page. Next, she took another page and wrote, "LUCY BENNETT," then on another put, "JANE DELRAY." She added "MARY" and "KITTY TREADWELL" into

the mix, then "HODGE," "JUICE/DWAYNE MATHISON," and finally, "AN-
DREW TREADWELL."

"What are you doing?" Amanda asked.

"Puzzle pieces." She spread the multicolored pages out on the
Falcon's hood. "Let's put it together."

Amanda took in the disparate words. The idea wasn't so crazy
after all. "We should do it chronologically." She moved the names
around as she spoke. "Hank Bennett came into the station, and then
Sergeant Hodge sent us to Techwood. Make a new one for Tech."
Evelyn scribbled the word onto a new sheet. "We need to subcatego-
rize these." Amanda took the pen and started filling in details: dates,
times, what they'd been told. The Fury's engine clicked in the heat.
The metal hood singed her skin.

Evelyn suggested, "I'll make a timeline."

Amanda handed her the pen. She pointed to the different pages as
she called out the sequence. "Hank Bennett goes to Sergeant Hodge
last Monday. Hodge immediately sends us out to Techwood to take a
rape report." She looked at Evelyn. "Hodge won't tell us why he sent
us in the first place. Obviously, there wasn't a rape. Why did he send
us there?"

"I'll ask him again this morning, but he wouldn't tell me the last
four times."

Amanda felt the need to tell her, "You were very brave to do
that."

"Fat lot of good it did." Evelyn waved away the compliment.
"Juice, the pimp, doesn't belong in here."

"Unless he's the one who killed Jane."

"That doesn't seem likely. Juice was probably in jail when it happened. Or having the crap beaten out of him for resisting arrest."

"Okay, let's push him up here as a remote possibility." Amanda
moved Juice to the periphery. "Next: We're at the apartment in
Techwood. Jane tells us that there are three girls missing: Lucy Bennett, Kitty—who we later find out is Treadwell—and a girl named
Mary, last name unknown."

"Right." Evelyn wrote down the information, shooting their names off Jane Delray's.

"Then, a few days later, Jane is murdered."

"But she was misidentified as Lucy," Evelyn corrected. "I'll put an asterisk beside her name, but we should keep it this way just for clarity's sake."

"Right. A person who is thought to be Lucy Bennett is murdered."

"I wonder if the brother had a big life insurance policy on her?"

Amanda supposed being married to an insurance man put these ideas into Evelyn's head. "Is there a way to check? A registry?"

"I'll ask Bill, but just talking it out, I think given Lucy's life, why murder her when she would eventually kill herself with drugs?" Evelyn looked down at the timeline. "It's not much of a motive."

"Motive." There was something they hadn't considered. "Why would someone want to murder Jane?"

"Are we assuming the killer knew it was Jane whom he was murdering?"

Amanda's head was starting to hurt. "I think we have to assume that until we find out otherwise."

"Okay. Motive. Jane was very annoying."

"True," Amanda agreed. "But the last person she annoyed other than us was Juice, and if there's one thing I know about pimps, it's that they don't kill their girls. They want them working. They're product."

"I'll call the jail and see when Juice got out, just to make triple sure." Evelyn tapped the pen against her chin. "Maybe the murderer was someone who saw Jane talking to us at Techwood? The whole compound lit up when we arrived. There's no way it wasn't broadcast to the rooftops that Jane was talking to two police officers."

Amanda felt unsettled by the thought that she might've been partly responsible for the girl's death. "Write that down as a possibility."

"I hate to think we had anything to do with it. Then again, she wasn't exactly baking cookies for the PTA."

"No," Amanda agreed, but Evelyn had only seen the pictures. "Have you ever had a manicure?"

Evelyn looked at her fingernails, which were clear-coated, just like Amanda's. "Bill treated me to one last Christmas. I can't say that I enjoyed having a stranger touch my hands."

"Jane's fingernails were perfect. They were filed and polished. I couldn't've done a better job myself."

"That manicure was ridiculously expensive. I can't imagine Jane having the money."

"No, and if she did, she'd spend it on drugs, not getting her fingernails polished." Amanda remembered, "Pete said something interesting about the attacker. He said the man was angry, uncontrolled."

"How in the world can he tell that?"

"From the way Jane looked. She was beaten all over." Amanda tried to think it through, but she found it was easier to talk it out to Evelyn. "I guess we should be asking ourselves what kind of person is capable of this. And then, ask how he would do it. He obviously used his fists, but he had the hammer, too. He busted open the lock on the access door to the roof. But then, we need to consider how he was able to get the better of someone like Jane. She wasn't bright, but she was street-smart."

"Who, how, and why," Evelyn summarized. "Those are very good questions. If Juice isn't the answer to them, then who is? Someone Jane has seen before. A regular customer who knows where she lives." Evelyn tapped the pen again. "But, then, this is what we're saying: He knocked on the door. He gave her a manicure. Then he threw her off the roof."

"He strangled her before he threw her off the roof."

Evelyn asked, "Pete told you that?" Amanda nodded. "That seems like a more plausible scenario. Jane screamed like a stuck pig when you kicked her, and that was barely a tap."

"You didn't say that at the time."

"I was scared," Evelyn admitted. "I'm sorry."

"It's all right," Amanda told her. "Maybe we could ask around and see if any johns are into choking."

"I know a gal who works undercover downtown. I'll see what she knows. But even if there is a guy out there who likes choking women—and something tells me there's more than one—how are we going to find his real name? And if by some miracle we do find his name, how on earth would we link him to Jane?"

Amanda offered, "Pete scraped some skin out from under Jane's fingernails. He said he could match the blood type against a suspect. See if he's a secretor or a nonsecretor."

"Eighty percent of the population has secretor status. Nearly forty percent is type O-positive. That's hardly narrowing it down."

"I didn't know that," Amanda admitted. Evelyn was much better at statistics than she was. "Let's go back to the puzzle before we're both late for work." Amanda picked up where they'd left off in the timeline. "Next, we met Mr. Blue Suit, aka Hank Bennett, at the morgue. He admits he hasn't seen his sister in years, which might explain why he couldn't identify her."

"Or, he's just too arrogant to admit that he can't."

That seemed far more likely. "I still find it odd that Lucy Bennett didn't have a record. She's been on the game at least a year, probably more."

"Neither does Kitty Treadwell." Evelyn looked sheepish. "I radi-oed dispatch on my way here. They ran through all the variations for me. There was no record for a Kitty Treadwell."

"How about Jane Delray?"

"She had two pick-ups several years ago, but nothing recently."

"Then her fingerprints are on file."

Evelyn frowned. "No, they're not. I asked. A lot of the older rec-ords have been purged."

"That's convenient." Amanda updated the information under each girl's name. "We need to work on Andrew Treadwell. He's a lawyer. He's a friend of the mayor's. What else do we know about him?"

"Jane intimated that he was Kitty's uncle. She point-blank said that Kitty was rich, that her family was connected."

Amanda said, "That article in the newspaper listed Andrew Treadwell as having only one daughter."

"He's one of the top lawyers in the city. He's politically powerful. If he has a daughter who's been pimped out on the streets by a black man, do you really think that's something he'd advertise? He'd more likely use his money and influence to keep her hidden away."

"You're right," Amanda allowed. She stared down at the diagram. "Don't you think it's odd that Lucy and Kitty are both out on the street and one of them has a brother working for the other's uncle?"

"Maybe they met at a self-help group." Evelyn smiled. "Whores Anonymous."

Amanda rolled her eyes at the joke. "Are we still assuming that Andrew Treadwell is the one who sent Hank Bennett to talk to Hodge last Monday?"

"I am. Are you?"

Amanda nodded again. "Which may support your theory that Andrew Treadwell doesn't want it to get out that he's related to Kitty. We could be looking at it wrong. Who does Treadwell want to hide the relationship from if not his buddies at City Hall?"

"Bennett is quite a piece of work," Evelyn mumbled. "He's one of the most arrogant asses I've met. And that's saying a lot considering the guys we work with."

Amanda tried to recall Hank Bennett's terse answers to their questions outside the morgue. She should've written them down. "Bennett said he sent his sister a letter at the Union Mission. Do you remember him saying when?"

"Yes. He mailed the letter to the Mission when his father passed away last year—this time last year. Which reminds me: Jane said Lucy has been missing for about a year."

Amanda wrote down this information under Lucy's name. "When you asked Bennett if he knew the name Kitty Treadwell, he told us to watch where we put our noses."

"Trask," Evelyn remembered. "That was the man he talked with at the Union Mission."

"He said Trask or Trent," Amanda corrected. The exchange stuck in her head because her mother's maiden name was Trent.

"We have to call him something for now," Evelyn pointed out.

"Trask," Amanda suggested.

"Okay, Trask told Bennett that he gave the letter to Lucy, which means he must know Lucy. If he works at the Union Mission, he might know all of our girls. Oh, Amanda—" She sounded devastated. "Why didn't we think to go to the Union Mission in the first place? All the hookers go there when they need a break. It's their Acapulco."

"The mission is just up the street," Amanda reminded her. "We can still talk to Trask, see if he remembers anything about Lucy—or Jane."

"If we're lucky, they'll tell us Lucy's alive and well and on such-and-such corner, and why are people saying she's been murdered." Evelyn looked at her watch. "I have to check in at Model City, but I could meet you there in half an hour."

"That should give me enough time to call the Housing Authority and figure out what I'm going to do with Peterson."

"I'm sure Vanessa won't mind taking him."

Amanda tucked her pen back in her purse. "I feel that's a bad situation brewing."

"Maybe. Listen, I'll try to question Hodge again, but I doubt that'll get me anywhere." She scooped up the pieces of construction paper and stacked them together. "I just have such a bad feeling about all of this."

"What do you mean?"

"I think Lucy Bennett's dead either way."

"Possibly, but it could be drugs, not malfeasance."

"Have you read about all those girls in Texas who disappeared around the I-45 corridor?"

"What?"

"A dozen or more," Evelyn told her. "They're not even sure where the bodies are."

"Where do you hear these things?"

There was no shame in her smile. "*True Crime* magazine."

Amanda sighed as she watched Evelyn climb into her station wagon. "I'll see you at the mission."

"Deal." Evelyn slowly pulled out of the parking space. "And I wouldn't worry too much about Vanessa," she called through the open window. "Who do you think told me about the guy behind the counter at the Plaza Pharmacy?"

"Mandy!" Vanessa called as soon as she walked into the station.

Amanda pushed her way through the crowd. The station was full. Roll call was a few minutes off. Amanda glanced into the sergeant's office, but it was empty.

"Hurry!" Vanessa was sitting in back again, practically bouncing in her chair. She was wearing slacks and a flowery blouse. Her gun was holstered on her hip. She was dressed in men's shoes. Amanda was beginning to wonder if she was worried about the wrong sex where Vanessa was concerned. At least she was still wearing a bra.

"Lookit what I got." Vanessa held up a credit card as if it was a bar of gold. Amanda recognized the logo of the Franklin Simon department store. And then her jaw dropped at the punch-typed gold letters spelling out VANESSA LIVINGSTON underneath.

"How did you . . ." Amanda sank down in her chair. She was almost afraid to touch the card. Then she did. "Is it real?"

"Yep." Vanessa beamed.

Amanda could not stop staring at the card. "Is this a joke?" She glanced around to see if anyone was watching. No one seemed to care. "How did you get this?"

"Rachel Foster over in dispatch told me about it. All you have to do is show them six months' worth of pay stubs."

"Are you kidding me?" Amanda hadn't been able to get her apartment without Duke guaranteeing the rent. If not for the city providing her a car, she'd be on foot. "They just gave it to you? Just like that?"

"That's right."

"They didn't ask to speak to your husband or your father or—"

"Nope."

Amanda was still dubious. She handed back the card. Franklin Simon was all right, but they were doomed to bankruptcy if they were handing out credit so freely. "Listen, can you do me a favor today and ride with Peterson?"

"Sure."

"Don't you want to know why?"

The guttural sound of someone vomiting filled the room. It was joined by other men making similar disgusting noises. Butch Bonnie walked into the station, his fists held up as if he was Muhammad Ali. Amanda had forgotten how ill he'd been at the crime scene last Friday. Obviously, the rest of the squad had not. People clapped and laughed. There were even cheers from the black side of the room. Butch did a sort of victory spin as he made his way toward Amanda.

He leaned on the table. "Hey, gal, you got my stuff for me?"

Amanda reached into her bag for the typed report. She dropped the pages on the table beside him.

"Why you bein' so cold?" he asked. "You on the rag?"

"It's what your partner did to Evelyn Mitchell," Amanda shot back. "He's an animal."

Butch scratched the side of his cheek. He looked rough. His clothes were wrinkled. His face was unshaven. There was a distinct odor of alcohol and stale cigarettes sweating from his pores.

Amanda stared straight ahead. "Is there anything else?"

"Jesus, Mandy. Cut him some slack. His wife's been giving him enough crap at home. He don't need to come to work and catch lip off another skirt."

She forced herself not to soften. "Your notes had a factual error."

Butch tossed a cigarette into his mouth. "Whattaya talkin' about?"

"You said you ID'd Lucy Bennett off a license in her purse. The evidence receipt didn't list a license of any type."

"Shit," he mumbled, then, "S'cuse the language." He skimmed his notebook, compared it to her typed report. "Yeah, I see it."

"How did you ID the victim?"

He lowered his voice. "Off a CI."

"Who?"

"Never you mind who," he told her. "Just fix the report."

"You know they can't change the evidence receipt. The carbons are in triplicate."

"Then change the report so it says someone recognized her." He handed back the typed report. "There was a witness on scene. Call him Jigaboo Jones. I don't care. Just make it work."

"Are you sure?" she asked. "You're the one whose signature goes at the bottom."

He looked nervous, but said, "Yeah, I'm sure. Just do it."

"Butch—" She stopped him before he could leave. "How did Hank Bennett find out his sister was dead? You usually specify that in your notes, but this time, there's nothing." Amanda pressed a bit harder. "Lucy didn't have a record, so it seems strange that you and Landry were able to locate next of kin so quickly."

He stared at her, unblinking. She could almost see the wheels turning in his head. She didn't know if Butch was just now asking himself the question or wondering why Amanda had posed it. Finally, he told her, "I don't know."

She studied him, trying to detect duplicity. "It seems like you're telling me the truth."

"Jesus, Mandy, hanging around Evelyn Mitchell's turning you into the wrong kinda gal." He pushed himself up from the table. "Get that report back to me first thing tomorrow morning." He waited for her to nod, then went to the front of the room.

"Wow," Vanessa said. She'd been strangely quiet. "What's going on with you and Butch?"

Amanda shook her head. "I need to make a phone call."

There were two telephones in the front of the room, but Amanda didn't want to make her way through the crowd. Nor did she want to run into Rick Landry, who'd just walked into the station. The clock on the wall was straight up at eight o'clock. Sergeant Woody was still not here. Amanda wasn't surprised. Woody had a reputation for hitting the bars before work. She might as well use his office.

Nothing much had changed since Luther Hodge had vacated the space. Paperwork was scattered across the blotter. The ashtray was brimming over. Woody hadn't even bothered to get a new mug for his coffee.

Amanda sat down behind the desk and dug into her purse for her address book. The black leather was cracked and peeling. She thumbed to the C's and traced her finger down to Pam Canale's number at the Housing Authority. They weren't close friends—the woman was Italian—but Amanda had helped Pam's niece out of some trouble a few years ago. Amanda was hoping the woman wouldn't mind returning the favor.

She checked the squad room before dialing Pam's number, then waited while the call was transferred.

"Canale," Pam said, but Amanda hung up. Sergeant Luther Hodge was heading back toward the office. His office.

She stood from the desk so fast that the chair hit the wall.

"Miss Wagner," Hodge said. "Has there been a promotion about which I am uninformed?"

"No," she said, then, "Sir." Amanda scuttled around the desk. "I'm sorry, sir. I was making a phone call." She stopped, trying to appear less flustered. The fact was that she was stunned. "Did you get transferred back here?"

"Yes, I did." He waited for her to move out of his path so that he could sit down. "I suppose you think I'm holding water for your father."

Amanda had been about to leave, but she couldn't now. "No, sir. I was just making a phone call." She remembered Evelyn, her boldness in confronting Hodge. "Why did you send me to Techwood last week?"

He had been about to sit at his desk. He paused midair, hand holding back his tie.

"You told us to investigate a rape. There was no rape."

Slowly, he sat down. He indicated the chair. "Have a seat, Miss Wagner."

Amanda started to close the door.

"Leave that open."

She did as she was told, sitting opposite him at the desk.

"Are you trying to intimidate me, Miss Wagner?"

"I—"

"I realize your father still has many friends in this department, but I will not be intimidated. Is that clear?"

"Intimidated?"

"Miss Wagner, I may not be from around here, but I can tell you one thing for sure. One thing you can take straight back to your daddy: this nigger ain't goin' back into the fields."

She felt her mouth working, but no words would come out.

"Dismissed."

Amanda couldn't move.

"Should I repeat my order?"

Amanda stood. She walked toward the open door. Her competing emotions compelled her to keep moving, to work this out in private, to formulate a more reasoned response than what actually came out of her mouth. "I'm just trying to do my job."

Hodge had been writing something on a piece of paper. Probably a request to have her transferred to Perry Homes. His pen stopped. He stared at her, waiting.

Words got jumbled in her mouth. "I want to work. To be good at . . . I need to be good at . . ." She forced herself to stop speaking long enough to collect her thoughts. "The girl you sent us out to interview. Her name was Jane Delray. She wasn't raped. She wasn't injured. There wasn't a scratch on her. She was fine."

Hodge studied her a moment. He put down his pen. He sat back in his chair, his hands clasped in front of his stomach.

"Her pimp came in. His street name is Juice. He chased Jane out of the apartment. He made suggestive overtures toward me and Evelyn. We arrested him."

Hodge continued to stare at her. Finally, he nodded.

"Last Friday, this woman was found dead at Techwood Homes. Jane Delray. It was reported as a suicide, but the coroner told me that she was strangled, then thrown from the building."

Hodge was still looking at her. "I think you're mistaken."

"No, I'm not." Even as Amanda said the words, she questioned herself. Was she certain that the victim was not Lucy Bennett? How was it possible to tell whether or not the corpse at the morgue was truly Jane Delray? Hank Bennett had been equally as certain that he was identifying his sister. But the face, the track marks, the scars on her wrists.

Amanda said, "The victim was not Lucy Bennett. It was Jane Delray."

Her words floated up into the stale air. Amanda fought the urge to equivocate. This was the hardest lesson they had learned at the academy. It was a woman's nature to be diminutive, to make peace. They'd spent hours raising their voices, giving orders rather than making requests.

Hodge steepled his fingers. "What's your next step?"

She let some of the breath out of her lungs. "I'm meeting Evelyn Mitchell at the Union Mission. All the streetwalkers end up there eventually. It's like their Mexico." Hodge's brow furrowed at the analogy. Amanda kept talking. "There has to be someone at the Union Mission who knew the girls."

He kept studying her. "Did I mishear a plural?"

Amanda bit her lip. She longed for Evelyn's presence. She was so much better at this. Still, Amanda couldn't give up now. "The man you spoke to last Monday. The lawyer in the blue suit. His name is Hank Bennett. You thought he was sent by Andrew Treadwell." Hodge didn't disagree, so she continued. "I imagine he was here looking for his sister, Lucy Bennett."

Hodge supplied, "And then, less than a week later, he found her."

His statement hung between them. Amanda tried to analyze its meaning, but then a more pressing issue presented itself. Rick Landry barreled into the office. He reeked of whiskey. He threw his cigarette on the floor. "Tell this fucking broad to keep her nose out of my case."

If Hodge was surprised, he didn't show it. Instead, he asked in a perfectly reasonable voice, "And you are?"

Landry was visibly taken aback. "Rick Landry. Homicide." He glared at Hodge. "Where's Hoyt?"

"I imagine Sergeant Woody is drinking his breakfast downtown."

Again, Landry was taken off guard. It was commonly held on the force that a man's drinking problem was his own business. "This is a homicide case. Ain't got nothin' to do with her. Or that mouthy bitch she's been hangin' around with."

"Homicide?" Hodge paused just a moment longer than necessary. "I was under the impression that Miss Bennett committed suicide." He pushed through the paperwork on his desk, taking his time finding what he was looking for. "Yes, here's your preliminary report. Suicide." He held out the paper. "Is that your signature, Officer?"

"Detective." Landry snatched the report out of his hand. "It's what you said, preliminary." He wadded the paper into a ball and stuck it in his pocket. "I'll give you the final report later."

"So, the case is still open? You believe Lucy Bennett was murdered?"

Landry glanced back at Amanda. "I need more time."

"Take all the time you need, Detective." Hodge held out his hands as if he was placing the world at Landry's feet. When the man did not leave, he asked, "Is there anything else?"

Landry glowered at Amanda before making his exit. He slammed the door behind him. Hodge looked at the closed door, then back at Amanda.

She asked, "Why did Hank Bennett come here last Monday?"

"That sounds like a very good question."

"Why did he want you to send us to Kitty's apartment?"

"Another good question."

"You didn't give us a name, just an address."

"That's correct." He picked up his pen. "You can skip roll call."

Amanda remained seated. She didn't understand.

"I said you can skip roll call, Miss Wagner." He went back to his paperwork. When Amanda didn't leave, he glanced up at her. "Don't you have a case to work?"

She stood, using the arm of the chair to leverage herself up. The door was stuck. She had to jerk it open. Amanda kept her gaze ahead as she walked through the squad room and out the door. Her resolve almost broke when she was pulling the Plymouth out of the parking lot. She could see the squad through the broken pane of glass in the storefront. A few of the patrolmen watched her leave.

Amanda pulled out onto Highland. Her breathing didn't return to normal until she was on Ponce de Leon heading toward the Union Mission. By her watch, she had another ten minutes before Evelyn joined her. Maybe Amanda could use the time to figure out what had just happened. The problem was that she didn't know where to begin. She needed time to digest it all. She also still needed to make a phone call.

The Trust Company branch on the corner of Ponce and Monroe had a bank of pay phones outside the building. Amanda pulled into the parking lot. She backed her car into a space and sat with her hands still wrapped around the wheel. None of this made sense. Why was Hodge speaking in riddles? He didn't seem to be afraid of much. Was he trying to help Amanda or trying to discourage her?

She found some coins in her wallet and grabbed her address book. Two of the pay phones were out of order. The last one took her dime. She dialed Pam's number again and listened to the rings. At twenty, she was about to give up, but Pam finally answered.

"Canale." She sounded even more harried than before.

"Pam, it's Amanda Wagner."

A few seconds passed before Pam seemed to recognize her name. "Mandy. What's going on? Oh, crap, don't tell me something's wrong with Mimi?"

Mimi Mitideri, the niece who'd almost run off with a Navy cadet. "No, nothing like that. I was calling to see if you could do me a favor."

She seemed relieved, though her day was probably filled with people asking for favors. "What do you need?"

"I was wondering if you could look up a name for me, or an apartment." Amanda realized she wasn't being very clear. She hadn't thought through the conversation. "There's an apartment at Techwood Homes—apartment C. It's on the fifth floor in the row of buildings—"

"Whoa, let me stop you there. There's no C at Techwood Homes. They're numbered."

Amanda resisted the temptation to ask her where one might find these numbers. "Could you look up a name, then? A Katherine or Kate or Kitty Treadwell?"

"We don't go by names. We go by roll numbers."

Amanda sighed. "I was afraid you'd say that." She felt the uselessness of the situation sitting like an elephant on her chest. "I'm not even sure if I've got the right name. There are—were—at least three girls living there. Maybe more."

"Wait a minute," Pam said. "Are they related?"

"I doubt it. They're working girls."

"All in the same unit?" Pam asked. "That's not allowed unless they're related. And even if they are, none of those gals ever want to room together. They lie all the time." There was a noise on Pam's end of the line. She covered the mouthpiece for a few seconds and had a muffled conversation with another person. When she came back on the line, her voice was clearer. "Tell me about the apartment. You said it was on the top floor?"

"Yes. Fifth floor."

"Those are one-bedroom units. A single girl wouldn't get that housing assignment unless she has a child."

"There was no child. Just three women. I'm guessing it was three. Maybe there were more."

Pam groaned. When she spoke, her voice was barely more than a whisper. "My supervisor can be persuaded sometimes."

Amanda was going to ask what she meant, but then it hit her.

Pam sounded bitter. "They should put me in charge. I wouldn't trade a top-floor apartment for a blow job."

Amanda gave a shocked laugh—as if such a thing was possible. "Well, thank you, Pam. I know you've got work to do."

"Let me know if you get the unit number. Maybe I can track it back from there. Might take me a week or two, but I'll do it for you."

"Thank you," Amanda repeated. She hung up the phone. Her hand stayed on the receiver. Her mind had been working on other things while she was talking to Pam Canale. It was like looking for your keys. The minute you stopped trying to find them, you remembered where you'd left them.

But there was only one way to be certain.

Amanda put another dime in the slot. She dialed a familiar number. Duke Wagner was never one to let a phone ring more than twice. He picked up almost immediately.

"Hey, Daddy," Amanda managed, but then she didn't know what else to say.

Duke sounded alarmed. "Are you all right? Did something happen?"

"No, no," she told him, wondering why she had called her father in the first place. This was sheer lunacy.

"Mandy? What's going on? Are you at the hospital?"

Amanda rarely heard her father panicked. Nor had she ever considered the fact that he might be worried about the job she was doing, especially since he was no longer there to protect her.

"Mandy?" She heard a chair slide across the kitchen floor. "Talk to me."

She swallowed back the uneasy realization that for just a moment, she had enjoyed scaring her father. "I'm fine, Daddy. I just had a question about—" She didn't know what to call it. "About politics."

He sounded relieved and slightly irritated. "This couldn't wait until tonight?"

"No." She looked out at the street. Cars were backing up at the light. Businessmen were going to work. Women were taking their children to school. "We had a new sergeant last week. One of Reggie's boys."

Duke made a sharp comment about this, as if his feelings weren't already known.

"He got transferred after just one day. Hoyt Woody was moved into his position."

"Hoyt's a good man."

"Well." Amanda didn't finish her thought. She found the man unctuous and off-putting, but that was not the point of this conversation. "Anyway, after a few days, Hoyt got transferred back out, and now the old sergeant, Reggie's boy, got moved back in."

"And?"

"Well," she repeated. "Doesn't that strike you as odd?"

"Not particularly." She heard him light a cigarette. "It's how the system works. You get one guy in to do one thing, then move in another to do something else."

"I'm not sure I follow."

"You gotta star pitcher, right?" Duke always favored baseball metaphors. "Only he can't swing a bat. You got it?"

"Yes."

"So you send in a pinch hitter."

"Oh." She nodded, understanding.

Duke still didn't think she got it. "There's something going on in your squad. Reggie's boy wouldn't follow orders, so they sent in Hoyt to take care of business." He laughed. "Typical. Send in a white man when you need the job done right."

Amanda held the phone away from her mouth so he wouldn't hear her sigh. "Thanks, Daddy. I should get back to work."

Duke wouldn't let her off that easy. "You're not getting mixed up in something you shouldn't?"

"No, Daddy." She tried to think of something else to say. "Be sure to put the chicken back in the refrigerator around ten. It'll spoil if you leave it out all day."

"I heard you when you told me the first six times," he snapped. Instead of hanging up, he said, "Be careful, Mandy."

She rarely heard such compassion in his voice. Unaccountably, tears came into her eyes. Butch Bonnie was right about one thing. It was close to that time of month for Amanda. She was turning into a hormonal mess. "I'll see you tonight."

She heard a click as Duke hung up the phone.

Amanda returned the receiver to the cradle. Back in her car, she took a handkerchief out of her purse and wiped her hand. Then she patted dry her face. The sun was unrelenting. She felt as if she was melting.

A honking sound ripped through the quiet of her car. Evelyn Mitchell's Ford Falcon had stopped for a yellow light. A delivery truck sped around her. The man stuck his hand out in an obscene gesture.

"For goodness sakes," Amanda mumbled, turning the key in the ignition. She pulled out onto the road and followed Evelyn three blocks down Ponce de Leon to the Union Mission. Evelyn took a slow, wide turn into the parking lot so she could back into an empty space. Amanda swung her Plymouth around and was getting out of the car by the time Evelyn turned off the engine.

Amanda said, "You're going to get yourself killed driving that slowly."

"You mean driving the speed limit? That truck driver—"

"Almost killed you," Amanda quipped. "I'm going to take you out to the stadium this weekend and give you a proper lesson."

"Oh." Evelyn seemed pleased. "Let's make a day of it. We can go to lunch and do some shopping."

Amanda was startled by her eagerness. She changed the subject. "Hodge is back at my station."

"I thought it was strange that he wasn't at Model City this morning." Evelyn closed her car door. "Why did they send him back?"

Amanda debated whether or not to reveal that she'd called her father. She decided against it. "It's possible the brass transferred in Hoyt Woody to do their dirty work."

"Why would they send in a white man? Wouldn't one of Reggie's boys be better for this sort of thing? Keep it in the family, as it were?"

She had raised a good point, but then, Evelyn didn't suffer from

Duke's color blindness. Hoyt Woody would do as he was told in hopes of ingratiating himself with the brass. Luther Hodge might not be as malleable.

Amanda said, "I imagine Woody was sent in for the same reason Hodge sent two women out to talk to Jane. We're expendable. No one really listens to us."

"That's true enough." Evelyn shrugged because there was nothing they could do about it. "So, Hodge was replaced for a few days by someone who would do their dirty work, then he was slotted back in."

"Exactly." Amanda said, "Your friend at the Five said she called security on Jane Delray when she tried to cash Lucy's vouchers. Security is run out of the Five Points precinct. Whoever hauled Jane out of the building would've written her up on an incident card." The cards were part of a larger system used to track petty criminals who weren't yet worth arresting. "The cards are fed into a daily report that goes up the chain of command. Someone high up would know that Jane was trying to use Lucy's name."

Evelyn came to the same conclusion as Amanda had. "We were sent to Techwood to scare Jane into silence."

"We did a great job, didn't we?"

Evelyn put her hand to her temple. "I need a drink. This is giving me a migraine."

"Well, this should make your head hurt even more." Amanda told her about the phone call with Pam Canale, the dead end she'd hit. Then she relayed the cryptic conversation she'd had with Sergeant Hodge.

"How strange," was all Evelyn could manage. "Why won't Hodge answer our questions?"

"I think he wants us to keep working this case, but he can't appear to be encouraging us."

"I think you're right." Evelyn said, "Maybe Kitty didn't get that top-floor apartment with sexual favors. Maybe her uncle or daddy pulled some strings."

"If Kitty is the black sheep of the Treadwell family, I can certainly see Andrew Treadwell trying to keep her from making trouble. He sets her up in an apartment with her own kind. He gets her on the welfare rolls. He makes sure she's got just enough money to stay out of his hair."

"There's no way we can talk to Andrew Treadwell. We wouldn't make it as far as the lobby."

Amanda didn't bother to agree with the obvious.

Evelyn said, "I talked to my gal in undercover. It's just what I thought: it'd be easier to find a man who *doesn't* like choking whores."

"That's depressing."

"It is if you're a whore." Evelyn added, "I told her to ask around if anybody likes painting fingernails."

"Smart thinking."

"We'll see if it pans out. I told her to call me at home. I'd hate for any of this to go out on the radio."

"Did you find out whether or not Juice was in jail when Jane was murdered?"

"He was at Grady getting fitted with a resisting-arrest turban."

Amanda had heard the terminology before. There were a lot of prisoners who woke up in the Grady ER with no recollection of how they'd gotten there. "That's hardly an alibi. He could walk in and out of the hospital without anyone noticing."

"You're right," Evelyn agreed.

Amanda blinked at the sweltering sun. "We could stand out here all day talking ourselves into circles."

"Right again. Let's get this part over with." Evelyn indicated the flat, one-story building in front of them. The Union Mission had been a butcher's shop at one time.

Amanda said, "Acapulco. Where did you get that?"

"I saw a spread in *Life* magazine. Johnny Weissmuller has a place there. It was gorgeous."

"You and your magazines."

Evelyn grinned, then turned serious as she looked up at the building. "How are we going to handle this? As far as anyone knows, Lucy Bennett committed suicide."

"I think that's the story we should stick to, don't you?"

"I don't think we have a choice."

Amanda was used to not having a lot of choices, but it had never grated the way it did lately. She walked toward the front entrance. She could hear funk music playing on a radio. There were metal bars across the glass storefront. Rows of empty beds filled the front space, at least twenty deep and four across. The girls weren't allowed to stay here during the day. Ostensibly, they were supposed to be out look-ing for jobs. The front door was propped open and the smell of the building airing out was as unpleasant as anything Amanda had smelled in the last week.

"Help you?" a man called over the music. He was dressed like a hippie, wearing sunglasses even though he was indoors. His sandy blond mustache was long and droopy. A brown fedora was pulled low on his head. He was extremely tall and lanky. His walk was more of an amble.

Evelyn mumbled, "He looks like Spike, Snoopy's brother."

Amanda didn't share that she'd been thinking the same thing. She called to the man, "We're looking for a Mr. Trask?"

He shook his head as he walked over. "No Trask here, ladies. I'm Trey Callahan."

"Trey," Evelyn and Amanda said in unison. At least Bennett had been close. There was no telling what he thought Amanda and Eve-lyn were called. If he gave it any thought at all.

"So." Callahan flashed a laconic smile, tucking his hands into his pockets. "I'm guessing one of the girls is in trouble, in which case, I probably can't help you. I'm neutral, like Switzerland. You dig?"

"Yes," Evelyn said. Like Amanda, she had to look up at the man. He was at least six feet tall. "Maybe this will change your mind: We're here about Lucy Bennett."

His easygoing demeanor dropped. "You're right. I'll do anything I can to help. God rest her troubled soul."

Amanda said, "We were hoping you could tell us about her. Give us an idea of who she was, with whom she associated?"

"Let's go to my office." He stood to the side, indicating they should go first. Despite his hippie appearance, someone had managed to teach him manners.

Amanda followed Evelyn into Callahan's office. The space was small but cheerful. The walls were painted a bright orange. Posters from various funk bands were pinned around the room. She catalogued the items on his desk: a framed photograph of a young woman holding a Doberman puppy. A rusted Slinky. A thick stack of typewriter paper held together by a rubber band. There was a sweet odor in the air. Amanda glanced at the ashtray, which looked recently emptied.

Callahan turned off the transistor radio on his desk. He indicated a set of chairs and waited for Evelyn and Amanda to sit before dragging his own chair out from behind the desk and sitting adjacent to them. It was a tactful move, Amanda realized. He'd managed to put them all on the same level.

Evelyn took a spiral-bound notebook out of her purse. She was very businesslike. "Mr. Callahan, you work here in what capacity?"

"Director. Janitor. Job counselor. Priest." He held out his hands, indicating the office. Amanda realized he was bigger than she first thought. His shoulders were broad. His frame filled the chair. "It doesn't pay much, but it gives me time to work on my book." He placed his palm on top of the stacked typewriter pages. "I'm doing an Atlanta version of *Breakfast of Champions*."

Amanda knew better than to engage him about the project. Her professors at school could wax on for hours. "Are you the only one who works here?"

"My fiancée works the night shift. She's finishing her nursing degree at Georgia Baptist." He pointed to the framed photo of the woman and the dog, flashing a used-car salesman's smile. "Trust me, ladies, we're all aboveboard here."

Evelyn wrote this down, though it was hardly germane. "Can you tell us about Lucy Bennett?"

Callahan seemed troubled. "Lucy was different from the usual clientele. She spoke properly, for one. She was tough, but there was a softness underneath." He indicated the outer room, all the empty beds. "A lot of these girls come from troubled families. They've been injured in some way. In a bad way." He paused. "You picking up what I'm putting down?"

"I feel you," Evelyn offered, as if she spoke jive every day. "You're saying Lucy wasn't like the other gals?"

"Lucy had been hurt. You could tell that about her. All of these girls have been hurt. You don't end up on the streets because you're happy." He leaned back in the chair. His legs were spread wide. Amanda could not help but be fascinated by the way a change of posture turned him from a boy into a man. Initially, she'd assumed he was her age, though looking at him now, he seemed closer to thirty.

Evelyn asked, "Did Lucy have any friends?"

"None of these girls are really friends," Callahan admitted. "Lucy chilled with her group. Their pimp was Dwayne Mathison. Goes by the name Juice. Though I'm not telling you anything you don't already know."

Amanda picked at an invisible piece of lint on her skirt. The ghetto gossip mill was more streamlined than the APD's. She guessed Callahan knew that Juice had almost assaulted them.

Evelyn asked, "When's the last time you saw Lucy?"

"Over a year ago."

"You seem to remember a lot about her."

"I had a soft spot for her." He held up his hand. "Not what you're thinking. It was nothing like that. Lucy was smart. We talked about literature. She was a voracious reader. Had these dreams about giving up the life and going to college one day. I told her about my book. Let her read some pages, even. She was down with it, you know? Got what I was doing." He shrugged. "I was trying to help her, but she wasn't ready for it."

"Did she ever have contact with her family?"

His hands gripped the arms of the chair. "That why y'all are here?"

Evelyn was better at sounding clueless than Amanda. "I don't understand."

"Lucy's brother. He send you here to tell me to keep my mouth shut?"

"We don't work for Mr. Bennett," Amanda assured the man. "He told us that he came here looking for his sister. We're simply following up."

Callahan didn't answer immediately. "Last year. Guy comes in here throwing his weight around. He was dressed real fly. Arrogant as hell." That sounded like Hank Bennett all right. "Wanted to know did I give Lucy the letter he mailed."

"Did you?"

"Of course I did." His grip loosened. "Poor thing couldn't bring herself to open it. Her hands were shaking so hard I had to put it in her purse for her. I never found out if she read it. She disappeared a week, maybe two weeks, later."

"When was this?"

"Like I said, about a year ago. August, maybe July? It was still hot as Hades, I remember that."

"You haven't seen Hank Bennett before or since?"

"I count myself lucky for that." He shifted in the chair. "Man wouldn't even shake my hand. I guess he was scared the groovy would rub off."

Evelyn asked, "I know it's been a while, but do you remember the other girls Lucy hung around with?"

"Uh . . ." He pushed up his sunglasses and pressed his fingers into his eyes as he thought it out. "Jane Delray, Mary something, and . . ." He dropped the glasses back down. "Kitty somebody. She wasn't here much—most nights, she was over at Techwood, but I got the feeling that wasn't a permanent situation. I never got her last name. She was a lot more like Lucy than the other girls. Not a stranger to the King's English, if you catch my drift. But they hated each other. Couldn't stand to be in the same room together."

Amanda didn't let herself look at Evelyn, but she could feel her own excitement reflecting off the other woman. "This place at Techwood—did Kitty have an apartment there?"

"I dunno. Could be. Kitty's the type of gal who's good at getting what she wants."

"Did Lucy and Kitty know each other from before?"

"I don't think so." He silently considered the question, then shook his head. "They were just the kind of girls who couldn't get along with each other. Too much alike, I expect." He leaned forward. "I'm a student of sociology, you dig? All good writers are. That's the focus of my work. The streets are my dissertation, if you will."

Evelyn seemed to understand exactly what the man was saying. "You have a theory?"

"The pimps know how to pit these types against each other. They make it clear only one can be their number one girl. Some of the gals are okay with being second string. They're used to being kicked down, you dig? But then some of them want to fight for the top. They'll do whatever it takes to be number one. Work harder. Work longer. It's survival of the fittest. They gotta be on that number one podium. Meanwhile the pimps just sit back and laugh."

Sociology be damned. Amanda had figured that out back in high school. "When's the last time you saw Kitty?"

"Maybe a year ago?" he guessed. "She wasn't spending much time here. That's around the time the church off Juniper opened up a soup kitchen. I think that was more Kitty's scene. Less competition there, anyway."

Evelyn asked, "Do you remember if Kitty stopped coming here before or after Lucy disappeared?"

"After. Maybe a couple of weeks? Not as long as a month. They might remember her at the church. Like I said, that was more Kitty's scene. She was fascinated by redemption. I gathered she had a religious upbringing. For all her faults, Kitty's a prayerful woman."

Amanda had a hard time imagining a streetwalker feeling close to the Lord. "Do you know the name of the church?"

"No idea, but it's got a big black cross painted on the front. Run by a tall brother, real clean-cut. Well spoken."

"Brother," Evelyn echoed. "You mean he's Negro?"

Callahan chuckled. "No, sister. I mean he's a brother in Christ. At the end of the day, we all shuffle off the same mortal coils."

"*Hamlet,*" Amanda said. She'd studied Shakespeare two quarters ago.

Callahan lifted up his sunglasses and winked at her. His eyes were bloodshot. The lashes reminded her of the teeth on a Venus flytrap. "'Be all my sins remembered,' fair Ophelia."

Amanda felt a flash of embarrassment.

Thankfully, Evelyn took over. "This man at the church. Do you know his name?"

"No idea. Kind of an asshole, if you ask me. Wants to argue about books and shit but you can tell he's never read one in his life." Callahan dropped his sunglasses back into place. "You know, I really thought Lucy would tell me goodbye before she left. Like I said, we had a thing. A platonic thing. Maybe she was too ashamed. These girls don't usually stay put for long. Their pimp gets tired of them not earning enough. He trades them off to the next guy down the line. Sometimes, they just move on. A few go back home, if their families will have them. The rest end up down at the Gradys."

"Gradys," Amanda repeated. It was strange to hear this word coming out of a white man's mouth. Only the blacks called Grady Hospital the Gradys. The name dated back to when the hospital wards were segregated. Amanda asked, "What about Jane Delray? Have you ever heard of her?"

Callahan gave a surprised laugh. "That sister is crazy mean. She'd cut you just as soon as look at you."

"Why do you say that?"

"Jane was always fighting with the girls. Always stealing their stuff. I finally had to ban her from the mission, and I don't like to do that to any of them. This is their last resort. They can't come here, there's nowhere else for them to go."

"They can't go to the soup kitchen?"

"Not if they're messed up. Brother won't let them through the door." Callahan shrugged. "It's not a bad policy. When these girls come in high, they're more prone to make trouble. But I can't just lock the door and leave them on the street."

"They can't get assistance from the Housing Authority?"

"Not if they've got prostitution on their record. The HA screens them out. They don't want girls setting up their businesses on the public dime."

Amanda tried to process the information. She was glad Evelyn was writing this down. "Is there anything else you can remember about Lucy?"

"Just that she was a good girl. I know it's hard for you to believe, especially working for the po-lice. But all of them started out good. They made a bad choice somewhere along the line, and then they made another one, and pretty soon their lives were nothing but bad choices. Lucy especially. She didn't deserve to go out like that." His hands gripped the chair again. His voice took on a hard edge. "I don't like to break on a brother, but I hope they fry him for this."

Amanda asked, "What do you mean?"

"It's already out." Callahan indicated the radio. "Heard it on the radio before you ladies walked in. Juice was arrested for killing Lucy Bennett. He gave a full confession." The phone on his desk started ringing. "Excuse me," he apologized, leaning over to lift the receiver.

Amanda didn't trust herself to look at Evelyn.

Callahan used his hand to cover the mouthpiece on the phone. "I'm sorry, ladies. This is one of our donors calling. Was there anything else you needed from me?"

"No." Evelyn stood up. Amanda followed suit. "Thank you for your time."

The sun was so bright when they walked out of the building that Amanda's eyes teared up. She shaded herself with her hand as they walked into the parking lot.

"Well." Evelyn slipped on her Foster Grants. "Arrested."

"Arrested," Amanda echoed. "And confessed."

They both stood by the cars, stunned silent.

Finally, Amanda said, "What do you make of that?"

"I'm flummoxed," Evelyn admitted. "I suppose Juice could've done it. Might've done it." She contradicted herself. "Then again, it's not that hard to get a confession, especially for Butch and Landry."

Amanda nodded. At least once a week, Butch and Landry showed up for roll call with cuts and bruises on their knuckles. "You said it yourself: Juice could've slipped out of the hospital, murdered Jane, and climbed back in bed with no one realizing he was gone." Amanda leaned against her car, then thought better of it when the heat singed through her skirt. "Then again, Trey Callahan just confirmed Juice was pimp to both Lucy Bennett and Jane Delray. He would know the difference between the two girls. Why would he confess to killing one when it was the other?"

"I doubt very seriously Rick Landry is letting him get his story out." She added, "A black man kills a white woman? That's a hummy if there ever was one."

She was right. The case would hum right through City Hall. Juice would be in prison before the year was out—if he lived that long.

Both women were silent again. Amanda couldn't recall a time she'd been more shocked.

And then Evelyn topped it. "Do you think we could speak to him?"

"Speak to whom?"

"Juice."

The question was as crazy as it was dangerous. "Rick Landry would string us up alive. I didn't want to tell you, but he was very angry this morning. He complained to Hodge right in front of me about us interfering in his case."

"What did Hodge say?"

"Nothing, really. The man speaks in riddles. Every question I asked, he just said, 'That's a good question.' It was maddening."

"That's his way of telling you to ignore Rick and to keep moving forward." Evelyn held up her hands to stop Amanda's protest. "Think about it: If Hodge wanted you to stop looking into this, he would've ordered you to stop. He could've assigned you to crossing duty. He could've benched you and made you file all day. Instead, he told you to skip roll call and meet up with me." She smiled appreciatively. "It's very clever, really. He doesn't tell you what to do, but he makes you want to do it."

"It's annoying, is what it is. Why can't he just speak directly? What's wrong with that?"

"He was already transferred to Model City for four days. I imagine he's making sure he doesn't get sent back."

"Meanwhile, it's my head on the chopping block."

Evelyn seemed to be gauging her own words. "He's probably afraid of you, Amanda. You must know that a lot of people are."

Amanda could've been knocked down with a feather. "Whatever for?"

"Your father."

"That's just silly. Even if my father cared about such things, I'm not a tattletale."

"They don't know that." Evelyn's voice was gentle. "Sweetheart, it's just a matter of time before your father's back in uniform. He still has a lot of powerful friends. There's bound to be payback. Do you really think people shouldn't be afraid?"

Amanda didn't want to admit that she was right about Duke, even while she was wrong about the rest. "I don't know why we're even having this conversation. Juice has been arrested for murder. The case is closed. We'd turn the whole department against us if we made trouble."

"You're right." Evelyn looked out into the street, the cars rushing by. "We're probably fools to care. Juice was going to rape us. Jane hated us on sight. Lucy Bennett was a junkie and a prostitute whose own brother couldn't stand to be in the same room with her." She nodded back at the mission. "No matter how well read Snoopy's brother says she was." She took off her sunglasses. "What was with that Ophelia line, anyway?"

"It's from *Hamlet*."

"I'm aware of that." Evelyn sounded testy. "I *do* read more than magazines, you know."

Amanda considered it wiser to hold her tongue.

Evelyn put her sunglasses back on. "Ophelia was a tragic figure. She had an abortion and killed herself by falling from a tree."

"Where do you get that she had an abortion?"

"She took rue. It's an herb women used to bring about miscarriages. Shakespeare had her passing out flowers and she—" Evelyn shook her head. "Never mind. The point is, are you going to go to the jail or not?"

"Me?" Amanda's mind couldn't handle these sudden shifts. "Alone?"

"I told Cindy I'd go to the Five and check the license box for Lucy's ID."

"That's very convenient."

"Bubba Keller is one of your father's poker buddies, right?"

Amanda wondered if she was making an allusion to the Klan. "What does that have to do with anything?"

"Keller runs the jail."

"And?"

"And, if *you* go to the jail and ask to speak with Juice, it's no big deal. If you go to the jail with *me* and ask to speak to Juice, it gets back to your father."

Amanda didn't know what to say. She felt caught out, as if Evelyn was suddenly privy to all the lies Amanda had told Duke over the last week.

"It's all right," Evelyn said. "We all have to answer to someone."

Evelyn didn't seem to have to answer to anybody. Amanda said, "Let me get this straight: you want me to waltz into the jail and ask to speak to a prisoner who's just been arrested for murder?"

Evelyn shrugged. "Why not?"

fifteen

Present Day

SUZANNA FORD

Zanna woke with a start. She couldn't move. She couldn't see. Her throat ached. She could barely swallow. She turned her head back and forth. A pillow cupped her head. She was lying down. She was in bed.

She tried to say "help," but her lips would not move. The word got trapped in her mouth. She tried again.

"Help . . ."

She coughed. Her throat was bone dry. Her eyes throbbed in her head. Every movement sent pain shooting through her body. She was blindfolded. She didn't know where she was. All she remembered was the man.

The man.

His weight shifted on the bed as he stood up. They weren't in the hotel room anymore. The low rumble of traffic weaving through downtown had been replaced by two noises. The first one was a hum, like the white-noise machine they bought her grandmother for Christmas one year. It kept up a steady hushing sound.

Hush, little baby . . . don't say a word . . .

The other noise was harder to place. It was so familiar, but every time she thought she had it pinned down, it would change. A whistling sound. Not like a train. Like air sucking through a tunnel. An underwater tunnel. A pneumatic tube.

There was no regularity to it. It only served to make her feel more out of body. More out of place. She didn't even know if she was still in Atlanta. Or Georgia. Or America. She had no idea how long she'd been out. She had no sense of time or place. She knew nothing but the fear of anticipation.

The man started mumbling again. There was the sound of a faucet turning on. The splash of water in a metal bowl.

Zanna's teeth started chattering. She wanted meth. She needed meth. Her body was starting to convulse. She was going to lose it. She was going to start screaming. Maybe she should scream. Maybe she should shout so loud that he had to kill her, because she had no doubt that's what this man was going to do. It was only a matter of the hell he would put her through first.

Ted Bundy. John Wayne Gacy. Jeffrey Dahmer. The Night Stalker. The Green River Killer.

Zanna had read every book Ann Rule had ever written, and when there wasn't a book, there was a TV movie or an Internet site or a *Dateline* or a *20/20* or a *48 Hours,* and she remembered every lurid detail about every sadistic freak who had ever kidnapped a woman for his own demonic pleasure.

And this man was a demon. There was no arguing with that. Zanna's parents had given up on church when she was a kid, but she had lived in Roswell long enough to recognize a stray verse, the cadence of scripture. The man mumbled prayers and he beseeched God for His forgiveness, but Zanna knew that no one was listening except the Devil himself.

The water turned off. Two footsteps, and he was back on the bed. She felt the weight of him as he sat down beside her. More water dripping. Loud drops into the bowl.

Suzanna flinched as the warm, wet rag washed along her skin.

sixteen

Present Day

TUESDAY

Sara's knees protested as she worked her way around the living room, dipping a washcloth into the bowl of vinegar and hot water, then washing down the baseboards section by maddening section.

Some women sat around watching TV when they were upset. Others went shopping or gorged themselves on chocolate. It was Sara's lot in life that she cleaned. She blamed her mother. Cathy Linton's response to any ailment was generally hard labor.

"Ugh." Sara sat back on her heels. She wasn't used to cleaning her own apartment. She was dripping sweat despite the low temperature on her thermostat. The climate was not being appreciated by anyone. Her greyhounds were huddled on the couch as if they were in the middle of an arctic winter.

Technically, Sara was supposed to be at work right now, but there was an unspoken rule in the ER that any person could leave if three really horrendous things happened to them during one shift. Today, Sara had been kicked in the leg by a homeless man, narrowly avoided being punched in the face by the mother of a boy who was so high he'd defecated on himself, and had her hand vomited on by one of the new interns. All before lunchtime.

If Sara's supervisor hadn't told her to leave, she was fairly certain she would've quit. Which was probably why Grady had the rule in the first place.

She finished the last section of baseboard and stood up. Her knees were wobbly from being bent for so long. Sara stretched out her hamstrings before she walked toward the kitchen with the rag and bowl. She dumped the vinegar solution down the drain, washed her hands, then picked up a dry rag and a can of Pledge to begin the next phase.

Sara looked at the clock on the microwave. Will still had not called. She imagined he was sitting on a toilet at Hartsfield-Jackson Airport waiting for a business traveler to tap his foot under the stall. Which meant there was plenty of time for him to dial her phone number. Maybe he was sending a message. Maybe he was trying to tell her that what they had was over.

Or maybe Sara was reading too much into his silence. She had never been good at playing games in relationships. She preferred to be direct. Which was at the very root of their problems.

What she desperately needed was a second opinion. Cathy Linton was at home, but Sara had a feeling her mother's reaction would be similar to the one she had the time Sara was ill from eating an entire package of Oreos. Sure, she'd held back Sara's hair and patted her back, but not without first demanding, "What the hell did you think would happen?"

Which was exactly what Sara kept asking herself. The worst part was that she was turning into one of those annoying people who got so caught up whining about a bad situation that they forgot they were actually capable of doing something about it.

Sara cleared off the mantel for dusting. She gently held the small cherrywood box that had belonged to her grandmother. The hinge was coming apart. Sara carefully opened the lid. Two wedding rings rested on the satin pillow.

Her husband had been a cop, which was basically where the similarity between Jeffrey and Will ended. Or maybe not. They were both funny. They had the same strong, moral character that Sara had always been attracted to. They were both drawn to duty. They were drawn to Sara.

That was one thing about Jeffrey that was completely different from Will. He had made no equivocations about wanting Sara. It was clear from the beginning that he was going to have her. He'd strayed once, but Jeffrey had dragged himself through broken glass to win her back. Not that Sara expected the same kind of dramatic gestures from Will, but she needed a stronger sign of commitment than just showing up in her bed every night.

Sara had fallen in love with her husband because of his beautiful handwriting. She'd seen his notes written in the margin of a book. The script was soft and flowing, unexpected for someone whose work required him to carry a gun and occasionally use his fists. Sara had never seen Will's handwriting, except for his signature, which was little more than a scrawl. He left her Post-it notes with smiley faces on them. A few times, he'd sent her a text with the same. Sara knew Will read the occasional book, but mostly stuck with audio recordings. As with many things, his dyslexia wasn't something they talked about.

Could she love this man? Could she see herself being part of his life—or, at least the part of his life that he allowed her to see?

Sara wasn't sure.

She closed the box and returned it to its proper place on the mantel.

Maybe Will didn't want her. Maybe he was just having fun. He still kept his wedding ring in the front pocket of his pants. Sara had been pleased when he'd shown up with his finger bare, but she wasn't stupid. Neither was Will, which was why it was puzzling that he kept the ring in an area where her hands usually ended up.

Sara hadn't realized she was falling in love with Jeffrey when she'd opened that book and seen his writing. It was only later when she looked back that she realized what was happening. There were memories of Will that gave her heart that familiar tug. Watching him wash dishes at her mother's kitchen sink. The way he listened so intently when she talked about her family. The look on his face the first time he'd really made love to her.

Sara leaned her head against the mantel. Given enough idleness and time, she could talk herself into either loving or hating the man. Which was why she wished he would just bite the bullet and call her.

The phone rang. Sara jumped. She felt her heart thumping as she walked toward the phone, which was equal parts stupid and foolish. She'd gone to medical school, for the love of God. She shouldn't be so easily swayed by coincidence. "Hello?"

"How is my favorite student?" Pete Hanson asked. He was one of the top ME's in the state. Sara had taken several courses from him when she was medical examiner for Grant County. "I hear you're playing hooky from school."

"Mental health day," she admitted, trying to hide her disappointment that it wasn't Will on the other end of the line. Then, because Pete never just called her out of the blue, she asked, "Is something wrong?"

"I have some news, my dear. It's fairly private, so I'd prefer to deliver it in person."

Sara glanced around the apartment, which was upside down. Pillows on the floor. Rugs rolled up. Dog toys scattered around. Enough fur to build a new greyhound. "Are you at City Hall East?"

"As always."

"I'm on my way."

Sara ended the call and tossed the receiver onto the couch. She checked her reflection in the mirror. Her hair was frizzed with sweat. Her skin was blotchy. She was wearing jeans that were torn at the knees and a Lady Rebels T-shirt that had looked great back when she was in high school. Will worked in the same building as Pete, but he was on the Southside all day, so there was no chance of running into him. Sara grabbed her keys and left the apartment. She took the steps down to the lobby, and didn't stop until she saw her car.

There was another note tucked under the windshield wiper. Angie Trent had changed things up. Along with the familiar "Whore," the woman had kissed the white notebook paper with her heavily lipsticked mouth.

Sara folded the note in two as she got into her car. She rolled down the window and tossed the paper into the trashcan by the automatic gate. Sara supposed Angie parked on the street and walked under the gate to put these notes on her car. Up until a few years ago, Angie had been a cop. Apparently, she had been one of the best undercover agents that the Vice Squad had ever had. Like many former police officers, she didn't worry about petty crimes such as trespassing and terroristic threats.

A horn beeped behind her. Sara hadn't noticed the gate go up. She waved her hand in apology, pulling out into the street. If thinking about Will was a futile endeavor, thinking about his wife was a lesson in self-hatred. There was a reason Angie had so easily passed for a high-class call girl. She was tall and curvy and had that secret pheromone that let every interested man—or woman, if the stories were true—know that she was available. Which was why Will was going to be wearing a condom until his final blood test came back.

That was, if they lasted that long.

City Hall East was less than a mile from Sara's apartment. Housed in the old Sears department store building on Ponce de Leon Avenue, the space was as sprawling as it was dilapidated. The metal windows and cracked brickwork had been pristine at one time, but the city hadn't the money to maintain such a vast structure. It was one of the largest buildings by volume in the southeastern United States, which only partially explained why half the complex stood vacant.

Will's office was on one of the upper floors that had been taken over by the Georgia Bureau of Investigation. The fact that Sara had never seen his office was one of the many things she tried to push from her mind as she navigated the large loop down to the underground parking lot.

Despite the mild climate, the parking garage was not as cool as it should've been, considering it was belowground. The morgue was even more subterranean, but like the garage, was mildly warmer than expected. There must've been something wrong with the air circulation, or maybe the building was so old that it was doing its best to force the inhabitants to let it go.

Sara took the cracked concrete stairs down to the basement. She could smell the familiar odors of the morgue, the caustic products that were used to clean the floors and the chemicals used to disinfect the bodies. Back in Grant County, Sara had taken the part-time job of medical examiner to help buy out her retiring partner at the children's clinic. The work in the morgue was sometimes tedious, but generally a lot more fascinating than the tummy aches and sniffles she treated at the clinic. That Grady Hospital was only marginally more challenging was yet another thought she pushed from her mind.

Pete Hanson's office was adjacent to the morgue. Sara could see him through the open door. He was bent over his desk, which was piled high with papers. His filing system wasn't one Sara would've chosen, but many times, she'd seen Pete pluck exactly what he needed from a random pile.

She knocked on the door as she walked into the office. Her hand stopped midair. He'd lost weight recently. Too much weight.

"Sara." He smiled at her, showing yellow teeth. Pete was an aging hippie who refused to give up his long braided hair, even though there was considerably less of it. He favored loud Hawaiian shirts and liked to listen to the Grateful Dead while he performed procedures. As medical examiners went, he was fairly typical, which was to say the bottled specimen of an eighteen-year-old victim's heart that he kept on a shelf above his desk was only in aid of his favorite joke.

She set it up for him. "How are you doing, Pete?"

Instead of telling her that he had the heart of an eighteen-year-old, Pete frowned. "Thanks for coming by, Sara." He indicated an empty chair. Pete had obviously prepared for her. The papers and charts that were normally piled on the chair had been placed on the floor.

Sara sat down. "What's wrong?"

He turned back to his computer and tapped the space bar on his keyboard. A digital radiograph was on the screen. The frontal chest X-ray showed a large white mass in the middle portion of the left lung. Sara looked at the file name at the top. Peter Wayne Hanson.

"SCLC," he told her. Small-cell lung cancer, the deadliest kind.

Sara felt like she'd been punched in the gut. "The new protocol—"

"Doesn't work for me." He clicked the file closed. "It's already metastasized to my brain and liver."

Sara delivered bad news to her patients on a daily basis. She seldom found herself on the other end. "Oh, Pete, I'm so sorry."

"Well, it's not the best way to go, but it beats slipping in the tub." He sat back in his chair. She saw it clearly now—the gauntness in his cheeks, the sallow look in his eyes. He indicated the jar on the shelf. "So much for my eighteen-year-old heart."

Sara laughed at the inappropriate humor. Pete was a great doctor, but his best trait was his generosity. He was the most patient and giving teacher Sara had ever had. He was delighted when a student managed to pick up on a detail he'd missed—a rare trait among physicians.

He said, "At the very least, it's given me a wonderful excuse to take up smoking again." He mimicked puffing a cigarette. "Unfiltered Camels. My second wife hated them. You've met Deena, right?"

"I only know her by reputation." Dr. Coolidge ran the forensics lab at GBI headquarters. "Do you have any plans?"

"You mean a bucket list?" He shook his head. "I've seen the world—at least the parts of it I want to see. I'd rather make myself as useful as I can with what little time I have left. Maybe plant some trees at my farm that my great-grandchildren will climb on. Spend time with my friends. I hope that includes you."

Sara willed herself not to tear up. She looked down at the cracked tile floor. There was so much asbestos in the building, she wouldn't be surprised to learn that Pete's cancer was down to more than cigarettes. She glanced at the pile of papers by the chair. A manila envelope was on top of the pile, faded red tape sealing it closed. The evidence was old. Deep creases maintained the accordion fold of the envelope. The areas that weren't yellowed with age were smeared black.

Pete followed her gaze. "Old case."

Sara noted the date, which was over thirty years ago. "Very old case."

"We were lucky they found it in evidence, though I'm not sure if we'll need it after all." He picked up the envelope and put it on his desk. The black dust transferred to his fingers. "The city used to purge closed cases every five years. We did some crazy stuff back then."

Sara could tell the case meant something to him. She knew the feeling. There were still victims she'd worked on back in Grant County that would haunt her memories until the day she died.

Pete asked, "How are things at Grady?"

"Oh, you know." Sara didn't know what to say. She was called "bitch" so often that she turned her head whenever anyone yelled the word. "Swimming pools and movie stars."

"In nearly fifty years, I've not once had a patient talk back or file a complaint against me." He raised an eyebrow. "You know they'll need someone to take my place when I'm gone."

Sara laughed, then saw that he wasn't joking.

"Just a thought," he told her. "But this brings me to a favor I need to ask."

"What can I do?"

"I've got a case that just came in. It's very important. It has to hold up."

"Does it have anything to do with that?" She indicated the dirty envelope on his desk.

"Yes," he admitted. "I can do all the heavy lifting, but I need to make sure that six months, a year from now, someone's around to testify."

"You've got dozens of people working under you."

"Just four at the moment," he corrected. "Unfortunately, none of them possess the length and breadth of your experience."

"I don't—"

"You're still credentialed. I checked with the state." He leaned forward. "I'm not a duplicitous man, Sara. You know that about me. So you'll understand that I'm being brutally honest when I tell you that this is a dying man's last request. I need you to do this for me. I need you to go to court. I need you to speak directly to a jury and put this man back where he belongs."

Sara was momentarily at a loss. This was the last thing she'd been expecting. Her apartment looked as if it had been hit by a tornado. She still had Will to deal with. She was dressed more suitably for a pickup softball game than for work. Still, she knew that she didn't have a choice. "There's already a suspect?"

"Yes." He shuffled the papers around and found a yellow file folder.

Sara scanned the preliminary report. There wasn't much. A dead Jane Doe had been found outside a Dumpster in a fairly upscale part of town. She'd been beaten to death. Her wallet was absent cash. The bruising around her wrists and ankles indicated that she'd been tied up, possibly kidnapped.

Sara looked up at Pete. She had an awful, sinking feeling. "The missing Georgia Tech student?"

"We don't have positive ID yet, but I'm afraid so."

"Death penalty case?" Pete nodded. "Is the body here?"

"They brought her in half an hour ago." Pete looked up at the doorway. "Hello, Mandy."

"Pete." Amanda Wagner's arm was in a sling. She looked worse for the wear, though she still kept up the formalities. "Dr. Linton."

"Dr. Wagner," Sara returned. She couldn't help but look over the woman's shoulder for Will.

Amanda asked Pete, "Did Vanessa come by?"

"First thing this morning." He explained to Sara, "The fourth Mrs. Hanson."

Amanda said, "Dr. Linton, I hope we can avail ourselves of your expertise?"

Sara felt a bit managed. She asked the obvious question. "Is this Will's case?"

"No. Agent Trent is absolutely not assigned to this case. Which doesn't explain why I've spent the last three hours of my day walking up and down every hallway in a twelve-story office building talking to people who have better things to do than watch us chase our tails." She paused for a breath. "Pete, when did we get so old?"

"Speak for yourself. I always told you I was going to die young."

She laughed, but there was a sad edge to the sound.

"I can still remember the first time you came into my morgue."

"Please, let's not get maudlin. Try to go out with some dignity."

He grinned like a cat. There was a moment between them, and Sara wondered if Amanda Wagner had fallen somewhere along the timeline of the many Mrs. Hansons.

The moment passed quickly. Pete stood from his desk. He reached out, bracing himself against the chair. Sara jumped up to help him, but he gently pushed her away. "Not to that point yet, my dear." He told Amanda, "You can use my office. We'll go ahead and get started."

Pete indicated that Sara should leave ahead of him. She pushed open the doors to the morgue, resisting the urge to hold them for Pete. He seemed more diminished in the large tiled room. The office had served as a buffer against his wasted appearance. In the bright lights of the autopsy theater, there was no hiding the obvious.

"A bit cool in here," Pete mumbled, taking his white lab coat off the hook. He went to the cabinet and handed Sara one of his spares. His name was stitched over the pocket. Sara could've wrapped the coat around her body twice. But then, so could Pete.

"Our victim." He indicated a draped body in the center of the room. Blood had permeated the sheet, which was unusual. Circulation stopped when the heart stopped beating. Blood congealed. Sara couldn't help but feel some guilty excitement. She relished a difficult case. Working at Grady, dealing with the same types of ailments and injuries over and over again, could become a bit mind-numbing.

Pete said, "We've already photographed and X-rayed her. Sent her clothes to the lab. Do you know we used to just cut them off and throw them in a bag? And rape cases." He laughed. "My God, the science was flawed from the beginning. There was no taking the victim's word for it. If we didn't find semen in the suspected attacker's underwear, then we couldn't legally sign off on a charge of rape."

Sara didn't know what to say. She couldn't imagine how awful things used to be. Thankfully, she didn't have to.

Pete looped his braid on top of his head and pulled on an Atlanta Braves baseball hat. He was in his element inside the morgue, visibly more animated. "I remember the first time I talked to an odontologist about bite marks. I was certain we were looking at the future of crime solving. Hair fibers. Carpet fibers." He chuckled. "If I have one regret about my impending doom, it's that I won't live to see the day when we've got everyone's DNA on an iPad, and all we have to do is scan some blood or a piece of tissue and up pops a current location for our bad guy. It'll end crime as we know it."

Sara didn't want to talk about Pete's impending doom. She busied herself with her hair, tightening the band, tucking it into a surgeon's cap so she wouldn't contaminate anything. "How long have you known Amanda?"

"Since dinosaurs walked among us," he joked. Then, in a more serious tone, he said, "I met her when she started working with Evelyn. They were both a couple of pistols."

The description struck Sara as odd, as if Amanda and Evelyn had run around Atlanta like two Calamity Janes. "What was she like?"

"She was interesting," Pete said, which was one of his highest compliments. He looked at Sara's reflection in the mirror over the sink as he washed his hands. "I know it wasn't great when you came up in medical school—what were there, a handful of women?"

"If that," Sara answered. "But this last class was over sixty percent." She didn't mention that the ones who weren't taking time off to have children were mostly funneling themselves into pediatrics or gynecology, the same as they had when Sara was an intern. "How many women were on the force when Amanda joined?"

He squinted as he thought about it. "Less than two hundred out of over a thousand?" Pete stepped back so Sara could wash her hands. "No one thought women should be on the job. It was considered man's work. There was all kinds of grumbling about how they couldn't protect themselves, didn't have the *cojones* to pull the trigger. The truth was that everyone was secretly terrified they'd be better. Can't blame 'em." Pete winked at her. "The last time women were in charge, they outlawed alcohol."

Sara smiled back at him. "I think we should be forgiven one mistake in almost a hundred years."

"Perhaps," he allowed. "You know, you listen to my generation these days, we were all free-loving hippies, but the truth is there were more Amanda Wagners than there were Timothy Learys, especially in this part of the country." He gave her a twinkling smile. "Not to say it entirely passed us by. I lived in a glorious singles complex off the Chattahoochee. Riverbend. Ever hear of it?"

Sara shook her head. She was enjoying Pete's reminiscing. His cancer was obviously compelling him to put his life in perspective.

"A lot of airline pilots lived there. Stewardesses. Lawyers and doctors and nurses, oh my." His eyes lit up at the memory. "I had a nice side business selling penicillin to many of the fine Republican men and women currently running our state government."

Sara used her elbow to turn off the faucet. "Sounds like crazy times." She had come of age during the AIDS epidemic, when free love started exacting its price.

"Crazy indeed." Pete handed her some paper towels. "When was *Brown v. the Board of Education*?"

"The desegregation case?" Sara shrugged. Her high school history class was some time ago. "Fifty-four? Fifty-five?"

Pete said, "It was around that time that the state required white teachers to sign a pledge disavowing integration. They would lose their jobs if they refused."

Sara had never heard of the pledge, but she wasn't surprised.

"Duke, Amanda's father, was away when the pledge was circulating." Pete blew into a pair of powdered surgical gloves before putting them on. "Miriam, Amanda's mother, refused to sign the pledge. So her grandfather—a very powerful man. He was a higher-up with Southern Bell—sent her off to Milledgeville."

Sara felt her lips part in surprise. "He committed his daughter to the state mental hospital?"

"The facility was basically a warehouse back then, mostly for vets and the criminally insane. And women who wouldn't listen to their fathers." Pete shook his head. "It broke her. It broke many people."

Sara tried to do the math. "Was Amanda born yet?"

"She was around four or five, I'd guess. Duke was still in Korea, so his father-in-law was in charge. I gather no one told Duke what was really going on. The minute he was back in Georgia, he grabbed Amanda and signed his wife out of Milledgeville. Never talked to his father-in-law again." Pete handed Sara a pair of gloves. "Everything seemed fine, and then one day, Miriam went out into the back garden and hanged herself from a tree."

"That's awful." Sara pulled on the surgical gloves. No wonder Amanda was so closed down. She was worse than Will.

"Don't let it soften you toward her too much," Pete warned. "She lied to you in my office. She wanted you here for a reason."

Instead of asking what reason, Sara followed his gaze to the door. Will was there. He stared at Sara in utter shock. She had never seen him look so awful. His eyes were bloodshot. He was rumpled and unshaven. His body swayed from exhaustion. His pain was so obvious that Sara could almost feel her heart breaking.

Her instinct was to go to him, but Faith was there, then Amanda, then Leo Donnelly, and Sara knew that a public display would only make things worse. She could read it in his face. He looked absolutely stricken to find her there.

Sara glared at Pete, making sure he knew that she was furious. Amanda may have lied about this being Will's case, but Pete was the one who had lured Sara to the morgue. She snapped off the gloves as she walked toward Will. He obviously didn't want Sara to see him like this. She planned to take him into Pete's office to explain what had happened and apologize profusely, but Will's expression stopped her.

Close up, he looked even worse. Sara had to force herself not to put her hands to his face, rest his head on her shoulder. Exhaustion radiated from his body. There was so much pain in his eyes that her heart broke all over again.

She kept her voice low. "Tell me what you need me to do. I can leave. I can stay. Whatever is best for you."

His breathing was shallow. He gave her such a look of desperation that Sara had to fight to keep herself from crying.

"Tell me what to do," she begged. "What *you* need me to do."

His gaze settled on the gurney. The victim on the table. He mumbled, "Stay," as he walked into the room.

Sara let out a stuttered breath before she turned around. Faith couldn't look at her, but Amanda held her gaze. Sara had never understood Will's mercurial relationship with his boss, but at that moment, she ceased caring. There was not another person on the planet right now whom Sara despised more than Amanda Wagner. She was obviously playing some kind of game with Will, just as it was obvious that Will was losing.

"Let's begin," Pete suggested.

Sara stood to Pete's side, opposite Will and Faith, her arms crossed. She tried to calm her anger. Will had told her to stay. Sara could not guess the reason why, but she didn't need to add more tension to the room. A woman had been murdered. That should be the focus.

"All right, ladies and gentlemen." Pete used his foot to tap on the Dictaphone to record the procedure. He called out the usual information—time of day, persons present, and the victim's tentative identity of Ashleigh Renee Snyder. "ID has yet to be confirmed by family, though of course we'll follow with dental records, which have already been digitized and sent to the Panthersville Road lab." He asked Leo Donnelly, "Is the father en route?"

"Squad car's picking him up from the airport. Should be any minute now."

"Very good, Detective." Pete gave him a stern look. "I trust you're going to keep any wry comments or off-color jokes to yourself?"

Leo held up his hands. "I'm just here for the ID so I can turn over the case."

"Thank you."

Without preamble, Pete grabbed the top of the sheet and pulled back the drape. Faith gasped. Her hand went to her mouth. Just as quickly, she forced her arm back down to her side. Her throat worked. She didn't blink. Faith had never had the stomach for these things, but she seemed determined to hold her own.

Unusually, Sara shared her discomfort. After all these years, she'd thought herself anesthetized to the horrors of violence, but there was something gut-wrenching about the state of the woman's body. She hadn't just been killed. She'd been mutilated. Bruises blackened her torso. Tiny red edemas cracked the skin. One of her ribs had punctured through the flesh. Her intestines hung between her legs.

But that wasn't the worst of it.

Sara had never been one to believe in the concept of evil. She always thought the word was an excuse—a way to explain away mental illness or depravity. A safe word to hide behind rather than face the truth that human beings were capable of despicable acts. That not much kept us from acting on our baser urges.

Yet, "evil" was the only word that came to mind when Sara looked down at the victim. It wasn't the bruises, the punctures, even the bite marks that were shocking. It was the methodical slices along the insides of the woman's arms and legs. It was the crisscross pattern that traced up her hips and torso in an almost ruler-straight line. Her attacker had ripped the flesh the same way you would rip out a seam in a dress.

And then there was her face. Sara could not begin to understand what had been done to her face.

Pete said, "The X-rays show the hyoid bone was broken."

Sara recognized the familiar bruising around the woman's neck. "Was she thrown off a building after she was strangled?"

Pete said, "No. She was found outside a one-story building. The intestinal prolapse is likely from premortem external trauma. A blunt object, or a fist. Do these striations look like finger marks to you, perhaps from a closed fist?"

"Yes." Sara pressed her lips together. The force of the blows must have been tremendous. The killer was obviously fit, probably a large man, and undoubtedly filled with rage. For all the world had changed, there were still men out there who absolutely despised women.

"Dr. Hanson," Amanda asked, "for the benefit of the tape, what would you estimate is the time of death?"

Pete smiled at the question. "I would guess anywhere between three and five o'clock this morning."

Faith volunteered, "The witness who saw the green van was out jogging around four-thirty. He doesn't know the make or model." She still couldn't look at Sara. "We've put out an APB, but it's probably a dead end."

"Four-thirty this morning certainly works for me," Pete said. "As you all know, time of death is not an exact science."

Amanda huffed, "Just like old times."

"Dr. Linton?" Pete motioned for Sara to join him. "Why don't you take the left side and I'll take the right?"

Sara pulled on a fresh pair of gloves. Will stepped back as she made her way around the table. He was being too quiet. He wouldn't meet her questioning gaze. Sara still felt the need to do something for him, but there was an equally overwhelming pull to do right by the dead woman. Something told her that the latter would aid in the former. This was Will's case, no matter what lies Amanda had told. He obviously felt some emotional attachment. Sara had never seen anyone look so bereft.

And she understood why Pete wanted to make sure someone he trusted was able to testify. Every inch of the victim's body screamed for justice. Whoever had attacked and murdered Ashleigh Snyder had not just wanted to hurt her. He'd wanted to destroy her.

Sara felt a subtle shift in her brain as she prepared herself for the procedure. Juries had watched enough *CSI* to understand the basic tenets of autopsy, but it was the medical examiner's job to guide them through the science behind each finding. The chain of custody was sacrosanct. All the slide numbers, tissue samples, and trace evidence would be catalogued into the computer. The lot would be sealed with tamper-proof tape that could be opened only inside the GBI lab. Trace evidence and tissue would be profiled for DNA. The DNA would hopefully be matched to a suspect, and the suspect would be arrested based on incontrovertible evidence.

Pete asked Sara, "Shall we begin?"

There were two Mayo trays prepared with identical instruments: wooden probes, tweezers, flexible rulers, vials and slides. Pete's had a magnifying glass, which he held to his eye as he leaned over the body. Instead of starting at the top of the head, he studied the victim's hand. As with the legs and torso, the flesh along the inside of her arm, from her wrist to her armpit, was ripped open in a straight line. It continued in a U to her upper torso, then followed down to her hips.

"You haven't washed her?" Sara asked. The skin looked scrubbed. There was a faint odor of soap.

"No," Pete answered.

"She looks clean," Sara noted for the tape. "The pubic hair is shaved. No stubble on the legs." She used her thumb to press the skin around the eyes. "Eyebrows tweezed into an arch. Fake eyelashes."

Sara concentrated on the scalp. The roots were dark, the remaining strands a choppy yellow and white. "She has blonde hair extensions. They're attached close to the scalp, so they must be new." Sara used the fine-toothed comb as best she could, working around the weave to remove any particles from the hair. The white paper under the girl's head showed dandruff and pieces of asphalt. Sara set the specimens aside for processing.

Next, she examined the hairline, checking for needle punctures and other marks that didn't belong. She used an otoscope to examine the nostrils. "There's some nasal corrosion. The membrane is torn, but not perforated."

"Meth," Pete guessed, which was probable, given the victim's age. He raised his voice. Either the Dictaphone was old or he wasn't used to using it. "The fingernails are professionally manicured. The nails are painted a bright red." He suggested to Sara, "Dr. Linton, perhaps you can check your side?"

Sara picked up the woman's hand. The body was in the early throes of rigor mortis. "Same on this hand. Manicured. Same polish." She didn't know why Pete was drawing such close attention to the fingernails. You couldn't throw a rock in Atlanta without hitting a nail salon.

He said, "The pedicure color is different."

Sara looked at the girl's toes. The nails were painted black.

Pete asked, "Is it normal for the toes to be different from the nails?"

Sara shrugged, as did Faith and Amanda.

"Well," Pete said, but the opening refrain from "Brick House" cut him off.

"Sorry." Leo Donnelly took his phone out of his pocket. He read the caller ID. "It's the patrolman I sent to the airport. Daddy Snyder's probably outside." He answered the phone as he walked out the door. "Donnelly."

The room was quiet except for the hum of the motor on top of the walk-in refrigerator. Sara tried to get Will's attention, but he just stared at the floor.

"Jesus Christ." Faith wasn't cursing Donnelly—she was looking at the victim's face. "What the hell did he do to her?"

There was a click as Pete's foot tapped off the Dictaphone. He spoke to Sara, as if she'd been the one to ask the question. "Her eyes and mouth were sewn shut." Pete had to use both hands to hold open one of the torn eyelids. They were shredded in thick strips like the plastic curtain inside a butcher's freezer. "You can see where the thread ripped through the skin."

Sara asked, "How do you know this?"

Pete didn't answer the question. "These lines along her torso, inside her arms and legs—a thicker thread was used to keep her from moving. I imagine an upholstery needle was used, probably a waxed thread or maybe a silk-blend yarn. We'll probably find plenty of fibers to analyze."

Pete handed Sara the magnifying glass. She studied the lacerations. As with the victim's eyes and mouth, the skin was ripped apart, flesh hanging down in even intervals. She could see the red dots where the thread had gone in. Not once. Not a few times. The circles were like the holes in Sara's earlobes where she'd gotten her ears pierced when she was a child.

Amanda said, "She must've ripped herself away from the mattress, or whatever she was sewn to, when he started beating her."

Pete expounded on the hypothesis. "It would be an uncontrollable response. He punches her in the stomach, she curls up into a ball. Mouth opens. Eyes open. And then he punches her again and again."

Sara shook her head. He was jumping to some pretty quick conclusions. "What am I missing?"

Pete tucked his hands into the empty pockets of his lab coat, silently watching Sara with the same careful intensity he used when he was teaching a new procedure.

Amanda supplied, "This isn't our killer's first victim."

Sara still didn't understand. She asked Pete, "How do you know?"

Will cleared his throat. Sara had almost forgotten he was in the room.

He said, "Because the same thing was done to my mother."

seventeen

June 15, 1975

LUCY BENNETT

Father's Day. It was all over the radio. Richway was having a special sale. Davis Brothers was offering an all-you-can-eat buffet. The disc jockeys were talking about their favorite gifts from years past. Shirts. Ties. Golf clubs.

Lucy's dad was easy to buy for. They always got him a bottle of scotch. Then two weeks would pass and if there was anything left in the bottle, they'd all get a drink on the Fourth of July while they watched the fireworks explode over Lake Spivey.

Lucy's dad.

She didn't want to think about him. About anyone she used to know.

Patty Hearst was suddenly in the news again. Her trial was still a year off, but her defense had decided to leak details about the kidnapping. Lucy already knew what went down with that crazy chick. It happened back when Lucy was on the street. There was no one else to talk about it with back then. Except for Kitty, none of the girls even knew Hearst's name. Or maybe Kitty was lying. She was good at lying, pretending she knew things when all it was in the end was an excuse to lure you in so she could stab you in the back like a sneaky little bitch.

After Hearst, there was a reporter with the *Atlanta Constitution* who'd been kidnapped. They demanded a million bucks for his release. They claimed to be from the SLA, too. What they were was idiots. They got snatched up by the cops. They didn't spend a dime of that money.

A million dollars. What would Lucy do with that kind of dough?

The only bank in town who'd had the ransom cash on hand was C&S. Mills Lane was the bank president. His picture was in the paper a lot. He was the same guy who helped the mayor build the stadium. Not the black mayor, but the one who ran against Lester Maddox.

Lucy felt the gurgle of laughter in her throat.

The Pickrick. Maddox's restaurant on West Peachtree. He kept axes on the wall. Rumor was he'd smash one through the head of any nigger who dared walk through the front door.

Lucy tried to imagine Juice going through the front door. An ax in his head. Brains spattered everywhere.

Washington-Rawson. The slum they'd torn down to build the Atlanta Stadium. Lucy's dad told her the story. They were there for a baseball game. The Braves. Chief Noc-a-Homa with his crazy big face running around with an ax he could've stolen from Lester Maddox. Lucy's dad said the stadium was supposed to revitalize the area. There were almost a million and a half residents in the city limits, most of them living on government vouchers. If Atlanta couldn't strong-arm the nigras out of the city, then they'd just pave over them.

The SLA paved over Patty Hearst. They were a cult. They brainwashed her. Or so said a doctor on the radio. The shrink was a woman, so Lucy took her opinion with a grain of salt, but she claimed that it only took two weeks for a person to become brainwashed.

Two weeks.

Lucy had lasted at least two months. Even after the H had worn off. Even after she had stopped longing for the high. Even after she had learned not to move, not to breathe too deep or too long. Even after she had stopped caring that she had sores on her back and legs from laying for so long in her own piss and shit.

She'd glowed with hate whenever he came into the room. She'd flinched when he touched her. She'd made sounds in her throat, used words that even without moving her mouth, she knew he could understand.

Satan.

Devil.

I'll kill you dead.

Motherfucker.

And then suddenly, he'd stopped coming. It had to be only a few days. You couldn't live without water for more than two, three days, tops. So maybe he'd been gone three days. Maybe when he'd come through the door, she'd been crying. Maybe when he brushed back her hair, she didn't flinch. Maybe when he washed her, she didn't tense up. And maybe when he finally got on top of her, finally did the things that Lucy had expected him to do from day one, she'd felt herself responding.

And then maybe when he left again, she sobbed for him. Longed for him. Begged for him. Missed him.

Just like she'd done with Bobby, her first love. Just like she'd done with Fred, the guy who cleaned planes at the airport. Then Chuck, who managed the apartment complex. Then countless others who had raped her, beat her, fucked her, left her on the side of the road for dead.

Stockholm syndrome.

That's what the woman doctor on CBS Radio called it. Walter Cronkite introduced her as a noted authority. She worked with victims of cults and mind-control experiments. She seemed to know what she was talking about, but maybe she was just making excuses, because what she was saying didn't entirely track.

At least not to Lucy.

Not to the girl who slept in her own excrement. Not to the girl who couldn't move her arms or legs. Not to the girl who couldn't open her mouth unless it was cut open for her. Couldn't blink without the razor sharp edge of his pocketknife slicing through the tiny stitches of thread.

The second Lucy saw an opening, the minute she saw even the sliver of a chance, she would escape. She would run to her freedom. She would crawl on her hands and knees back home. She would find her parents. She would find Henry. She would go to the cops. She would rip her body from this mattress and find a way to get home.

Patty Hearst was a stupid bitch. She was in a closet, but no one held her down. She had a chance. She had ample opportunity. She'd stood with a rifle in that bank, yelling SLA bullshit, when she could've just run out the door and asked for help.

If Lucy had a rifle, she'd use it to shoot the man in the head. She'd pound in his skull with the stock. She'd rape him with the long barrel. She'd laugh when the blood poured from his mouth and his eyeballs popped out.

And then she'd find that woman doctor from the radio and tell her that she was dead wrong. Patty Hearst wasn't helpless. She could've gotten away. She could've bolted at any time.

But then the doctor might point out that Lucy had something Patty Hearst did not.

Lucy wasn't alone anymore. She didn't need Bobby or Fred or Juice or her father or even Henry ever again. She no longer marked time by the feel of warm sunlight rising or falling across her face or the seasonal change in temperature. She marked her passage not in days, but in weeks and months and the cresting swell of her belly.

It would happen any day now.

Lucy was going to have a baby.

eighteen

July 14, 1975

MONDAY

Captain Bubba Keller was one of Duke's poker buddies, which meant that he likely had his white robe pressed at the dry cleaner where Deena Coolidge's mother had died. Keller's wife would be the one dropping off his laundry. He probably had no idea who cleaned it.

Amanda had never given much thought to her father's Klan affiliation. The Klan still controlled the Atlanta Police Department when men like Duke Wagner and Bubba Keller joined. Membership was compulsory, the same as paying dues to the Fraternal Order of Police. Neither man had likely objected. They were both of German descent. They had both joined the Navy in hopes of being sent to the Pacific rather than having to fight in the European theater. They both wore their hair in tight military cuts. Their pants were always creased. Their ties were always straight. They took charge of things. They

opened doors for ladies. They protected the innocent. They punished the guilty. They understood right and wrong.

That is to say, they were right and everyone else was wrong.

Back in the late sixties, Police Chief Herbert Jenkins had drummed
the Klan out of the force, but most of the men with whom Duke
played poker still honored the former affiliation. As far as Amanda
could tell, membership consisted solely of sitting around and grous-
ing about how much things had changed for the worse. All they
could talk about was the good old days—how much better things
had been before the coloreds ruined everything.

What they didn't acknowledge was that the things that made it
bad for them made it better for everyone else. Over the last few days,
Amanda had found herself thinking that injustice was never more
tragic than when you found it knocking at your own door.

She tried to keep this in perspective as she walked into the Atlanta
Jail. Captain Bubba Keller took pride in his post, though the Decatur
Street building was despicable, worse than anything you'd find in At-
tica. Bats hung from the ceiling. The roof had gaping holes. The concrete floor was crumbling. During the winter, prisoners were allowed
to sleep in the hallways rather than risk freezing to death inside their
cells. Last year, a man had been rushed to Grady after being attacked
by a rat. The creature chewed off most of his nose before the guards
managed to beat it off with a broom.

The most surprising part of that story was not that there was a
broom at the jail, but that a guard had noticed something was amiss.
Security was lax. Most of the men were already inebriated when they
showed up for work. Escapes were routine, a problem compounded
by the fact that the secretarial pool was adjacent to the cells. Amanda
had heard horror stories from some of the typists about rapists and
murderers running past their desks on their way out the front doors.

"Ma'am," a patrolman said, tipping his hat to Amanda as she
walked up the stairs. He took a deep breath of fresh air as he headed
toward the street. Amanda imagined she'd do the same thing when
she left this nasty place. The smell was almost as bad as the projects.

She smiled at Larry Pearse, who ran the property room from behind a caged door. He gave her a wink as he sipped from his flask. Amanda waited until she was on the stairs to look at her watch. It wasn't yet ten in the morning. Half the jail was probably lit.

The whir of Selectrics got louder as Amanda headed toward the typing pool. This had been her dream job, but now she couldn't imagine sitting behind a desk all day. Nor could she imagine working for Bubba Keller. He was lecherous and bombastic, two things he didn't bother to hide from Amanda, despite being close friends with Duke.

She often wondered what would happen if she told her father that Keller had grabbed her breast on more than one occasion, or about the time he'd pushed her up against the wall and whispered filthy things in her ear. Amanda wanted to think that Duke would be angry. That he would end the friendship. That he would pop Keller in the nose. The possibility that he might not do any of these things was likely what kept her from telling him.

True to form, she could hear Keller's raised voice over the hum of typewriters. His office faced the typing pool, which was large and open. Sixty women sat behind rows of desks, diligently typing, pretending that they couldn't hear what was going on a few yards away. Holly Scott, Keller's secretary, stood in his open doorway. She was wise not to go in. Keller's face was bright red. He waved his arms in the air, then swooped down his hand and pushed all the papers onto the floor.

"You goddamn do that!" he yelled. Holly mumbled something back, and he picked up his telephone and threw it against the wall. The plaster cracked, sending down a rain of white powder. "Clean up this mess!" Keller ordered, grabbing his hat and stomping out of his office. He stopped when he saw Amanda. "What the hell are you doing here?"

The lie came without much thought. "Butch Bonnie asked me to check—"

"I don't care," he interrupted. "Just don't be here when I get back."

Amanda watched him push his way toward the exit. He was the

very definition of a bull in a china shop. Desks were shoved out of the way. Stacks of paper were knocked onto the floor. There were sixty women seated at sixty desks, working on sixty typewriters and trying their darndest not to be singled out.

And then finally, there was an audible, collective sigh of relief as Keller left the room. The typewriters were momentarily silenced. Someone screamed back in the cells.

Holly said, "Good night, Irene."

Titters of laughter went around the room. The typewriters whirred back into motion. Holly waved Amanda back into Keller's office.

"Goodness," Amanda said. "What was that about?"

Holly bent over, picking up a broken bottle of Old Grand-Dad bourbon. "I just lost it."

Amanda knelt down to help her pick up the scattered papers. "Lost it how?"

"We're all trying to get Reggie's new handbook typed for the printer." Holly tossed the broken glass into the trashcan. "We're on deadline. The brass is breathing down our necks. Breathing down Keller's."

"And?"

"And so Keller thinks that's the perfect time to call me into his office and tell me to show him my tits."

Amanda sighed. She was familiar with the request. It was usually followed by a disturbing laugh and a groping hand. "And?"

"And, I told him I was going to file a complaint against him."

Amanda picked up the telephone. The plastic was cracked, but it still had a dial tone. "Would you really do it?"

"Probably not," Holly admitted. "My husband told me if he does it again, to just get my purse and leave."

"Why don't you?"

"Because that asshole's one more tantrum away from a heart attack. I'm going to outlive him if it kills me." She scooped up the last of the papers. There was a smile on her face. "What're you doing here, anyway?"

"I need to talk to an inmate."

"White or black?"

"Black."

"Good. There's an awful case of lice being passed around." Everyone knew the coloreds didn't get lice. "Keller's going to have to set off a can of DDT back there. It's the third time this year. The smell is just awful." Holly took a pen off the desk and held it over a sheet of paper. "Who's the girl?"

Amanda felt a thickness in her throat. "Male."

Holly dropped the pen. "You want to go back there and talk to a black man?"

"Dwayne Mathison."

"My God, Mandy. Are you crazy? He killed a white woman. He already confessed."

"I just need a few minutes."

"No." She vehemently shook her head. "Keller would have my scalp. And rightfully so. I've never heard anything so crazy. Why on earth would you want to talk to him?"

Not for the first time, Amanda realized that she would be better served to plan out her explanations in advance. "It's for one of my cases."

"What case?" Holly sat down at the desk to organize the papers. There were two more bottles of bourbon on the blotter, one of them almost empty. The cut-crystal glass between them showed a permanent ring from Keller's constantly replenishing his drink throughout the day. Crude renderings of a penis and a pair of breasts were carved into the soft wood of the desk.

Holly looked up at her. "What is it?"

Amanda pulled around another chair, just as Trey Callahan had this morning at the Union Mission. She sat across from Holly. Their knees were almost touching. "There are some missing girls."

Holly stopped collating. "You think the pimp killed them, too?"

Amanda didn't outright lie. "Maybe."

"You should tell Butch and Rick. It's their case. And you know they're going to hear about this." She put one hand on her heart and held up the other, as if swearing allegiance. "They won't hear about it from me or my girls, but you know it'll get around."

"I know." There was nothing more prevalent in any police force than gossip. "But I want to do it."

"Mandy." Holly shook her head, as if she couldn't understand what had happened to her friend. "Why are you inviting trouble?"

Amanda stared at her. Holly Scott had a dancer's lean body. She ironed her long red hair straight. Her makeup was expertly applied. Her skin was perfect. Even in this miserable heat, she could be photographed for a magazine ad. That she took near-perfect dictation and could type 110 words a minute were probably factors Keller had not even considered when he'd hired her.

Amanda reached back and closed the door. The typewriters were just as loud, but it engendered a feeling of confidentiality.

She told Holly, "Rick Landry threatened me." She didn't feel right bringing Evelyn's name into this, but Amanda was telling the truth when she said, "He called me a slit in front of my boss. He cursed at me. He told me I should stay the . . . the F away from his case."

Holly's lips pressed together in a straight line. "Aren't you going to listen to him?"

"No," Amanda said. "I'm not. I'm tired of listening to them. I'm tired of being scared of them and doing all their bidding when I know better than they do."

The words were said quietly, but there was an air of revolution about them.

Holly nervously glanced over Amanda's shoulder. She was afraid of being heard. She was afraid of being any part of this. Still, she asked, "Have you ever been into men's holding?"

"No."

"It's awful down there. Worse than the women's side."

"I assumed it would be."

"Rats. Feces. Blood."

"Don't oversell it."

"Keller will be furious."

Amanda forced up her shoulders in a shrug. "Maybe this will give him that heart attack you've been waiting for."

Holly stared at her for a good long while. Her blue eyes glistened with tears that did not fall. She was visibly afraid. Amanda knew she had a kid and a husband who worked two jobs so they could live in the suburbs. Holly went to school at night. She helped out at church on Sundays. She volunteered at the library. And she came here five days a week and put up with Keller's advances and innuendo because the city was the only employer around that followed the federal law mandating women be paid the same salary as men.

And yet, Holly held Amanda's gaze as she reached over for the phone on Keller's desk. Her finger found the dial. There was a slight tremor in her hand. She didn't have to look down as she dragged the rotary back and forth. Holly put through calls for Keller all day long. She was silent as she waited for the line to engage. "Martha," she said. "This is Holly up in Keller's office. I need you to have a prisoner transferred to holding for me."

Amanda watched her carefully as Holly relayed Dwayne Mathison's information. She had to shuffle through the papers from Keller's desk to get his arrest record, which had his booking number. Her hands steadied as they performed the familiar task. Her nails were short and clear-coated, like Amanda's. Her skin was almost as white as Jane Delray's, though of course absent any track marks. Amanda could see the thin blue lines of the veins in the back of the other woman's hand.

She looked down at her own hands, which were clasped in her lap. Her nails were neatly trimmed, though she hadn't bothered with polish the night before. The skin along the side of her palm was scratched. Amanda didn't remember injuring herself. Maybe she'd scraped off the skin while she was cleaning her father's house. There was a piece of metal sticking out of the refrigerator that always caught her hand when she cleaned it out.

Holly put down the phone. "He's being transferred. It'll be about ten minutes." She paused. "I can call them back, you know. You don't have to go through with this."

Amanda had other things on her mind. "Can I use the phone while I wait?"

"Sure." Holly groaned as she hefted the phone around. "I'll be outside. I'll let you know when they're ready."

Amanda found her address book in her purse. She should be scared about coming face-to-face with Juice again, but looking at her scratched hand had put a question in her mind.

She kept an index card in the back of her address book that listed the numbers she used on a daily basis. Butch was constantly leaving out details in his notes. Amanda had to call the morgue at least once a week. She usually talked to the woman who handled the filing, but today she asked for Pete Hanson.

The phone was picked up on the third ring. "Coolidge."

Amanda considered hanging up, but then she had a flash of paranoia, as if Deena Coolidge could somehow see her. The jail was only a few buildings down from the morgue. Amanda glanced around nervously.

Deena said, "Hell-o?"

"It's Amanda Wagner."

The woman let some time pass. "Uh-huh."

Amanda looked out into the typing pool. All the women were hard at work, backs straight, heads slightly tilted, as they typed the pages of a handbook that would more than likely be used as toilet paper by half the force and target practice by the other. "I had a question for Dr. Hanson," Amanda said. "If he's around?"

"He's in court all day testifying on a case." Deena seemed to lose some of her wariness. "May I help you with something?"

Amanda closed her eyes. This would be so much easier with Pete. "I had a question about the piece of skin found under the victim's fingernail." Amanda looked down at the scratch on her palm. "I was wondering—" She couldn't do this. Maybe she would wait for Pete. He would probably be back in the office tomorrow. Jane Delray wouldn't be any more dead by then.

Deena said, "Come on, girl. Don't waste my time. Spit it out."

"Pete found something under the girl's fingernail on Saturday."

"Right. Skin tissue. She must've scratched her assailant."

"Did you analyze it yet?"

"Not yet. Why?"

Amanda shook her head, wishing she could just melt into the chair. It was probably best to just blurt it out. "If the attacker was Negro, wouldn't the skin under the girl's fingernail be black?"

"Hm." Deena was quiet for a few seconds. "Well, you know, Pete's got this special light. You shine it on the skin sample and it glows this kind of orange if it's from a Negro."

"Really?" Amanda had never heard of such a thing. "Did he test the skin yet? Because I think—"

At first, she thought Deena was crying. Then Amanda realized the woman was laughing so hard that she had started gulping for air.

"Oh, very funny," Amanda said. "I'm hanging up now."

"No, wait—" Deena was still laughing, though she was obviously trying to get it under control. "Wait. Don't hang up." She kept laughing. Amanda looked down at Keller's desk. Cigarette butts spilled out of the ashtray. His coffee cup was rimmed in an orange nicotine stain. "Okay," Deena said. "All right." And then she started laughing again.

"I'm really hanging up now."

"No, wait." She coughed a few times. "I'm good now. I'm good."

"I was asking a sincere question."

"I know you were, honey. I know." She coughed again. "Listen, you know that Pure and Simple lotion ad, shows the different layers of skin?"

Amanda couldn't tell whether or not she was setting up another joke.

"I'm serious, girl. Listen to me."

"Okay, I know the ad."

"The skin basically has three layers. All right?"

"All right."

"Usually, when you scratch someone, you get the upper dermis, which is white no matter who you are. In order to get the pigmented layer of skin, the black part, you'd have to scratch to the subcutis, which means the fingernail would have to go deep enough to cause some serious bleeding. And it wouldn't be a sliver of skin you'd have to scrape out from under the fingernail. It'd be a chunk."

Amanda detected Pete's patient teaching tone in the woman's words. "So, there's no way to tell if the girl from Friday scratched a black assailant or a white one?"

Deena was quiet again, though this time, she wasn't laughing. "You're talking about that pimp they arrested for killing that white girl, aren't you?"

Amanda saw a guard standing by Holly's desk. He was gangly, with an untrimmed mustache and dark hair. Holly waved Amanda over. Juice was ready.

"Amanda?" Deena asked. "I'm not playing now. You best think about what you're doing."

"I assumed you'd be eager to help one of your own kind."

"That murdering bastard ain't got nothing to do with me." She lowered her voice. "I'm eager to keep my head attached to my shoulders, is what I am."

"Well, thank you for answering my question."

"Wait."

Holly's waving took on an urgency. She was probably afraid Keller would return. Amanda held up her finger, indicating she needed a minute. "What is it?"

"Be careful. The same people protecting you right now are gonna be the same ones coming after you when they find out what you're doing."

There was a long silence after that. Both of them reflected on the words.

"Thank you." Amanda tried not to read anything into Deena's gruff goodbye. She hung up the phone. Her heart was thumping in her chest. The woman was right. Duke would be furious if he knew what Amanda was doing. So would Keller. So would Butch and

Landry and possibly Hodge. Add the whole department to that if they found out she was trying to help a black man get out of jail. A black man who'd already confessed to murder.

Holly came to the doorway. "Hurry up, Mandy. Phillip's going to take you down and stay with you." She lowered her voice. "He's not so bad."

Amanda felt the urge to flee. Her bravado was going up and down like a piston engine. "I'm ready."

She stood from the desk. She forced a smile onto her face as Phillip came into the office. He was wearing the dark blue uniform of the prison guards, a set of keys hanging from one side of his belt and a nightstick dangling from the other.

He was younger than Amanda, but he talked to her as if she was a child. "You sure you wanna be doing this, gal?"

Amanda swallowed past the lump in her throat. She wished that Evelyn were there to give her strength. Then she felt guilty, because Evelyn had been taking the brunt of the anger lately—not just from Rick Landry, but from Butch and whoever had transferred her into Model City.

Maybe Evelyn was right. Maybe people were careful with Amanda because they were afraid of Duke. Instead of being afraid of him herself, Amanda should be taking advantage of it. At least for as long as she could.

"I'm not sure we've met." Amanda walked toward the man, hand extended. "I'm Amanda Wagner. Duke's daughter."

His eyes shifted to Holly, then to Amanda as he shook her hand. "Yeah, I know Duke."

"He's friends with Bubba." Amanda never called Keller by his first name, but the guard needn't know that. She took her purse out of the chair and dug around for the new pen and spiral-bound notebook she'd brought from home. She handed her bag to Holly. "Mind holding on to this for me?"

Holly stared wide-eyed as Amanda walked out of the office. She forced herself to keep a steady pace as she passed through the typing pool. The constant spinning and pecking of the Selectric balls seemed to match the erratic beats of her heart, but Amanda forced herself to keep walking. Going into the men's jail was likely the same as going into a swimming pool. You either jumped in and experienced that quick shock of cold or you dragged it out, walking in slowly, your skin prickling with goose bumps, your teeth chattering.

Amanda jumped right in.

She held on to the railing as she walked down the stairs. She didn't wait for Phillip to open the door. She pushed it with the palm of her hand. The cells. Holly was right. The men's side was far worse than the women's. Large cracks split the walls. Pigeons cooed from the rafters; their droppings littered the concrete floor. She stepped over a passed-out wino leaning against the wall. She ignored the catcalls and the stares. She kept her posture straight, her eyes ahead, until Phillip spoke.

"It's on the left."

Amanda stopped in front of a door. Someone had used a knife to carve INTERRORGATION into the thick lead paint. There was a square window at eye level, though the glass was nearly opaque with grime.

Phillip took out a set of keys and searched for the right one. He swayed slightly, obviously from drink. Finally, he found the correct key. He slid it into the lock and pushed open the door. Amanda turned around, preventing him from going in.

She said, "I've got it from here."

He laughed, then saw she was serious. "Are you nuts?"

"I'll call you if I need you."

"That ain't gonna be enough time." He indicated the door. "This thing locks when you close it. I can leave it cracked so—"

"Thank you." She pulled one of Rick Landry's moves, closing the space between them, forcing him back without having to touch him. The last thing she saw of Phillip was the shocked expression on his face when she closed the door.

The clicking of the latch echoed in the room. She caught a glimpse of the guard's blue hat, just the rim, in the window, but nothing else.

And then she turned around.

Dwayne Mathison was sitting at the table. A bloody white bandage was wrapped around his head. One of his eyes was swollen shut. His nose was broken. He had pulled back his chair several feet, so it was almost touching the wall. Amanda recognized his clothes as the same he'd had on last week, though they were stained with blood and dirt now. His legs were wide apart. His arm hung over the back of the chair, fingers nearly touching the floor. She could see the Jesus tattoo on his chest. The mole on his cheek. The hate in his eyes.

"Whatchu doin' here, bitch?"

It was a good question. Amanda had never before interviewed a suspect in a proper interrogation room. She was usually in the suspect's home. His parents were in the room, sometimes a lawyer. The boys were always contrite, terrified to be talking to a police officer, though relieved it was just a woman. Their fathers assured Amanda that it would never happen again. Their mothers revealed salacious details about the girl who'd made the allegations. Generally, it was over in less than an hour and the boy was left to get on with his life.

So what was she doing here?

Amanda hugged her notebook to her chest, then regretted the move. Juice would think she was covering her breasts. He would think she was scared. Both of which were true, but she couldn't let him know that. She dropped her arms as she walked to the table. The room was small. It was just a few steps. She dragged back the empty chair and sat down. Juice was watching her the way an animal studies prey. Amanda pulled the chair closer to the table, though every muscle in her body was tingling with the desire to flee.

In seconds, he could lurch across the table and snap her neck. He could punch her. Beat her. Try to rape her again. Amanda had always worried that if something bad happened—a man broke into her apartment in the middle of the night, an attacker cornered her in an alley—she would not be able to scream. She hadn't screamed before when Juice had threatened her. Could she scream now if he lunged for her? Would Phillip even hear her? If he did, would he be able to find his keys in time to stop the worst of it?

Amanda couldn't generate enough saliva in her mouth to swallow. She opened her notebook. "Mr. Mathison, I understand that you've confessed to the murder of Lucy Bennett?"

He didn't answer.

Water dripped from a hole in the ceiling. The drops had puddled on the floor. There was a dead rat in the corner, its neck broken by a trap. Cobwebs filled the corners. The air stank of sweat mixed with the distinctive ammonia smell of dried urine.

She said, "Mr. Math—"

"Mm-mm." Juice slowly licked his tongue along his top lip. "You still a fine-lookin' woman." He made a tsking noise. "Shoulda took you when I had the chance."

Incongruously, Amanda felt a smile wanting to come to her lips. She could hear Evelyn's voice, the way she'd mimicked Juice when they were at the Varsity.

Her tone was surprisingly strong when she said, "Well, you lost your chance." Amanda clicked her pen so she could take notes. "What happened to Jane Delray?"

He made a noise somewhere between a grunt and a groan. "Why you askin' after that bitch?"

"I want to know where she is."

He held his hand up above his head and whistled like a dive-bombing airplane as he dropped it to the table.

Amanda looked at his hand. Two of his fingers were taped together with surgical tape. There were no scratches on his hands, his bare arms. "You confessed to killing Lucy Bennett."

"I confessed to keepin' my black ass outta the 'lectric chair."

"The death penalty is no longer legal."

"They say they gone bring it back for me."

Given the circumstances, Amanda didn't doubt that the state would try. Everyone knew it was only a matter of time before Old Sparky was powered back up again.

She said, "We both know you didn't kill that woman."

"Wished I woulda."

"Why didn't you?"

"Why you here, bitch? Why you care what happen to a nigger?"

"I don't, actually." Amanda was startled by the truth of her own words. "I care about the girls."

"'Cause they white."

"No." Again, she told him the truth. "Because they're girls. Because no one else cares about them."

He looked at her. Amanda hadn't realized until that moment that Juice had been avoiding her eyes. She stared back at him, wondering if she was the first woman who'd had the courage to do so. He must have a mother somewhere. A sister. He couldn't rape and whore out every woman he met.

Juice tapped his hand on the table. Amanda didn't look away, but Juice did. "You're like her."

"Like who?"

"Lucy." He kept tapping his fingers on the tabletop. "She strong. Too strong. I break her down. But she always get back up."

"Was Kitty like that, too?"

"Kitty." He snorted. "That bitch near about broke *me,* you hear what I'm sayin'? Had to beat her down and keep her down." He pointed at Amanda. "You run them gals long enough, you see the strongest one's the one what's gonna be most loyal. All's you gotta do is find you way in."

"I'll keep that in mind if I ever decide to trick out women."

He put his palms flat on the table and leaned toward her. "I trick you out, bitch. Gimme five minutes with that fine white ass." He started thrusting his hips, banging against the table. "Dig my hands in that juicy white meat. Stick it in ya till ya cryin'." He banged harder against the table, punctuating each thrust with a deep moan. It was a guttural sound that made her note the dark bruises on his throat.

She asked, "Would you choke me?"

"I choke you, bitch." He pushed one last time against the table. "I choke you till you come so hard you pass out."

"Do you like being choked?"

"Shit." He crossed his arms over his chest. His biceps were huge. "Ain't nobody chokin' this brother."

Amanda remembered something Pete had said in the morgue. "Did you urinate on yourself?"

"I ain't piss myself." He tilted up his chin defensively. "Who told you that?"

Amanda felt a smug smile on her lips. "You just did."

He stared at the wall.

"The apartment at Techwood. That's Kitty's, isn't it?"

He didn't answer.

"I can stay here all day," she told him, and in that moment, Amanda could see herself doing just that. Bubba Keller would have to drag her from this room. She would sit here staring down this disgusting pimp for as long as it took. "The apartment at Techwood belonged to Kitty, did it not?"

Juice seemed to understand her resolve. "That's all'a them girls'. She charge it out. Tryin' to pimp 'em space. I put a stop to that."

Amanda couldn't imagine another woman charging rent to whores, but in the last few days, her worldview had expanded considerably. "Tell me about Hank Bennett."

"What he tell you?"

"You tell me about him."

"Fool came onto *my* corner trying to order *me* around." His fist was clenched when he banged it on the table. "Man need to step back."

"When was this?"

"I don't know, bitch. I ain't keep a calendar."

Amanda made a slash mark on the paper. If she had a dollar for every time a man had called her "bitch" lately, she could retire. "Did Hank Bennett see you before or after Lucy disappeared?"

His tongue darted out as he thought it over. "Before. Yeah, before. Bitch up and gone a week, two week later. I figure he took her. Lucy talk about him all the time."

Amanda's dictation was rusty, but it came back to her as she scribbled notes across the page. "So, Hank Bennett approached you before

Lucy disappeared?" Another lie they'd caught the lawyer in. "What did he want?"

"Wanted to tell me my bidness. Brother better be glad I didn't beat down his skinny white ass."

"What business?"

"Told me cut Kitty loose. Said he'd pass me some bills if I stop givin' her the Boy."

Amanda was sure she'd heard wrong. "Kitty? You mean Lucy."

"Naw, bitch. It was Kitty he wanted to talk about. Dude had a hard-on for her."

"Why would Hank Bennett care about Kitty?"

He shrugged his shoulders, but still answered, "Her daddy some big-time lawyer. Disowned the bitch when he found out she was sip-pin' some Juice." He gave her a lurid grin, making sure she got his meaning. "She got another sister somewhere. She the good one. Kitty always been bad."

"Kitty's father is Andrew Treadwell."

He nodded. "You finally gettin' it, bitch. Ain't the mayor tell you this already?"

Amanda flipped back through her notes. "Hank Bennett offered you money to stop giving Kitty heroin."

"Why you keep repeatin' everything I say?"

"Because it doesn't make sense," Amanda admitted. "Hank Ben-nett comes to you about Kitty. He doesn't ask about his sister? Ask to see her?" Juice shook his head. "He's not worried about Lucy?" Again, Juice shook his head. "And, a week later, Lucy disappeared?"

"Yeah, an' about a week after—" He snapped his fingers. "Kitty gone."

Amanda remembered Jane's words. "Just disappeared."

"Thass right."

"What about Mary?"

He snorted. "Bitch gone, too. 'Bout two, three months later. Ain't been a while since I lose that many girls at a go. Usually some other pimp tryin' to poach me off."

"You had three girls disappear in as many months." Amanda

wasn't asking him a question. She was trying to get her head around what had happened. "Did you ever see Lucy with a letter from her brother?"

He gave a curt nod. "Had it in her purse."

"Can you read?"

"Bitch, I ain't ignert."

Amanda waited.

"Some bullshit 'bout how he missed her when I knowed that ain't the truth. Said he wanted to meet with her." Juice thumped the table with his fingers. "Shee-it, brother wanna see her, he coulda spent five mo' minutes on my corner. I tole him she be right there."

Amanda scribbled down his words as she tried to think through her next question. "Was there anyone hanging around who was . . ." "Scary" wasn't the right word for a man like Juice. "Who wasn't right? Someone who was dangerous or violent? Someone you wouldn't trust with your girls?"

"Bitch, I charge extry for that." He smiled. One of his front teeth was missing. The gum was raw. "They some weird motherfuckers out there." He cleared his throat. "'Scuse me."

Amanda nodded at the apology. "What weird people?"

"They's a dude likes to fist 'em." He pumped his fist in the air. Amanda guessed he meant punching the girls. "They's one use a knife, but he all right. He never stick nobody. Least not with the blade."

"Anyone else?"

"They's that tall dude runs the soup kitchen."

"I've heard about him."

"He real tight with the dude at the mission."

So, Trey Callahan had lied to them, too.

"Dude always comin' 'round at night, trying to preach to my gals."

"The man from the soup kitchen?" Juice nodded. "Were the girls ever afraid of him?"

"Shit. They ain't afraid'a nothin' when I'm around. That's my job, bitch."

She made yet another slash on the paper. "This man from the church came at night to your street corner and tried to preach to Lucy and Kitty and—"

"Nah, they gone by then. Mary, too." He sat up in his chair. "Lookit, that salvation shit okay during the day, but don't come shootin' off 'bout Jesus while I'm tryin' to do my bidness. You feel me?"

"I do." Amanda leaned forward. "Tell me who killed Jane Delray."

"You get me outta here?"

Amanda was getting good at this game, but she wasn't quite there yet. Juice obviously read her expression.

"Shit." He slumped back in his chair. "You cain't do nothin', bitch."

"If I could find someone from City Hall to talk to you, could you tell him who killed Jane?"

"Another slit?"

"No, a man. Someone in charge." Amanda didn't know anyone downtown except for a bunch of secretaries. Still, she kept her shoulders straight, put some threat into her tone. "But you have to tell him something meaningful. You have to give him a name that can be followed up on. Otherwise, that deal you made with Butch and Landry goes out the window. I promise you, the state *will* bring back the death penalty. By the time it goes to the Supreme Court, you'll be dead."

There was a tapping sound. His leg had started moving up and down. The heel of his patent leather shoe clicked against the concrete. "I gotta deal. Done made my confession."

"That doesn't matter anymore."

"Whatchu mean?"

"I mean, you confessed to killing Lucy Bennett, not Jane Delray. Once I tell them about the mistake—" She shrugged. "I hope they remember to shave your head before they strap that metal cap on."

He was nervous. His breath whistled through his broken nose. "Whatchu mean, bitch?"

"You hear about the last guy they executed? His hair caught on fire. The switch was too hot. They couldn't turn it off. He burned alive. Flames went as high as the ceiling. He screamed for two whole minutes before they found the junction box and shut it down."

Juice's throat worked. His leg was shaking so hard that his knee bumped the table.

"Give me a name, Juice. Tell me who killed Jane."

His fist clenched and unclenched. The table trembled.

"Give me a name."

He pounded his fist against the table. "I ain't gotta name!"

Amanda clicked her pen. She closed her notebook. She hadn't flinched. She kept perfectly calm, waiting.

"Got damn." He spoke through clenched teeth. "Got damn them bitches. Gettin' me on the hook for this shit."

"Who would want to kill Jane?"

"Ever'body," he said. "She mouth off all the time. Make enemies on the street."

"Anyone who would murder her?"

"Not without gettin' they throat slit. Bitch kept a knife in her purse. All them do. Girl knew how to use it. Cain't turn your back on her fo' a minute. Bitch mean as a snake."

"That's pretty rich coming from her pimp."

He didn't respond. His shoulders rounded. He gripped his hands in his lap. "What'd that other bitch say? 'Bout Kitty knowin' the mayor? You think he can give a brother a hand? Get me outta this mess?"

"I told you, if you tell me the truth, maybe I can help you."

He stared at her, eyes going back and forth as if he was reading a book.

"Shee-it," he mumbled. "You think they gone lissen to you?" He pushed himself up from the table. Amanda's body tensed, but she stayed seated as he loomed over her. "Look 'round you, bitch." He held out his hands. "They let a black man run this world 'fore they let a slit do."

*   ★   ★

Amanda stood at Evelyn's front door with a bottle of wine in her hand. It wasn't the cheap stuff, but she was uncertain whether or not price had anything to do with taste. As with many things, she was out of her element. Especially when Kenny Mitchell opened the door.

A smile spread across his mouth. His teeth were perfect. His face was perfect. There wasn't anything about him she would change. Not that Amanda would be given the chance.

He said, "Amanda. Great to see you again." He leaned toward her, and without thinking, Amanda pulled back.

"Oh," she said, then leaned back in, looking more like a pecking duck than a grown woman. The moment could've been made more awkward, but Kenny laughed as he put his hand to her face and kissed her cheek. She could feel the rough texture of his skin, the prickly hairs of his mustache. His other hand rested lightly on her arm. A rush of heat went straight through her.

"Come in." He held open the door. Amanda walked into the house, feeling instantly enveloped by the cool air. "It's nice, right?" Kenny took the bottle of wine from her. Every move he made had a certain kind of grace, like an athlete on the field. "Ev's in back putting down the kid. I'm afraid that odor you smell is from me and Bill trying to cook supper. May I bring you a glass of wine?" He looked at the bottle and gave a low whistle. "Classy stuff. Maybe I'll keep it for myself."

"That's fine," Amanda said, not sure which question she was answering. She looked down at the floor, surprised to see that her feet were still there, that she wasn't melting into a bubbling pool of adolescent giddiness. "Whatever you like."

Kenny seemed not to notice, or maybe he was used to women acting so foolishly around him. He pointed down the hallway. "First door on the right."

Amanda felt his eyes on her as she walked down the hallway. Oddly, she thought about Juice, the things he'd said about her bottom. Amanda bit her lip. Why, of all the things the pimp had said, had that particular one stuck in her head? Surely, Kenny wasn't like that. He wasn't craven or crude. Neither was Amanda, which didn't explain the obscene images that were flashing in her mind as she gently knocked on the bedroom door.

Evelyn whispered, "Come in."

Amanda pushed open the door. Evelyn was sitting in a rocking chair. Zeke was in her arms. His head was flopped back. His arm hung down to the side. He was towheaded with pink cheeks and a button nose. It wasn't surprising that Evelyn had such a beautiful baby. Or that his nursery was so playfully decorated. Fluffy white sheep were painted on the light blue walls. His crib was a glossy white. The yellow in the sheets matched the carpet, which in turn matched the glowing nightlight that provided the only illumination in the room.

"You look nice," Evelyn whispered.

"Thank you." Amanda self-consciously patted her hair. She'd washed it four times in an attempt to remove the odors from the jail, then dabbed some Charlie on her wrists and neck for other reasons. "Do you want me to help in the kitchen?"

"No, it's Bill's night." Evelyn groaned as she leveraged herself out of the chair. She cradled Zeke as she carried him to the crib. He flopped onto the mattress like a rag doll. Evelyn pulled up the sheet and tucked it around his narrow shoulders. Her fingers brushed back his hair. She leaned down and kissed his cheek before indicating they should leave.

Instead of heading toward the kitchen, Evelyn took Amanda into the next room. Her dress was a short blue crinoline that rustled as she walked. She turned on the overhead light, revealing an office. Two desks were on opposite walls. Both were very tidy. Amanda guessed the black metal desk belonged to Bill Mitchell. She doubted he was using the elegantly curved white rococo desk with pink glass knobs. Evelyn's spiral notebook was neatly lined up to the edge. A grocery list was beside it. Most remarkably, their earlier project was displayed on the wall. Evelyn had used thumbtacks to pin up the various pieces of construction paper.

"I thought it would be easier this way." Evelyn rolled Bill's chair over for Amanda. She sat down at her desk and opened the top drawer. "I found these at the Five."

Amanda took the licenses. Lucy Anne Bennett. Kathryn Elizabeth Treadwell. Mary Louise Eitel. Donna Mary Halston. Mary Abigail Ellis.

She studied the photos carefully and set aside two of the Marys, leaving Donna Mary Halston. "This one looks like Kitty and Lucy."

"That's what I thought."

"He has a type." Amanda had never considered such a thing, but of course it made sense. Men always had certain types they were attracted to. Why would murder be any different?

Evelyn said, "They all look so normal. You'd never guess what they were doing."

Amanda stared at the girls' photographs. They did look normal. There was nothing to suggest that they were prostitutes, nothing to indicate they had sunk to the lowest levels of depravity in order to feed an addiction.

Most striking was their similarity. Long blonde hair. Blue eyes. Tall and slim. Lush lips. Expressive eyes. They were not just pretty, but beautiful. "They all list the same address," Amanda noted. "Techwood Homes. I can call back Pam Canale and see if she can trace the apartment to a roll number. I have a feeling it belongs to Kitty, but it wouldn't kill us to be certain." An idea occurred to her. "We could take these license photos to Techwood tomorrow. Like you said, it's ninety percent black there. Three white girls would stick out."

"That's good. You hold on to them." Evelyn grabbed her notebook off the desk, but didn't open it. "I checked all the missing persons files at the rest of the precinct. There was nothing for Lucy or Jane, but I found one for Mary Halston. She has a sister who lives in Virginia who's been looking for her for almost a year."

"We could call her." Amanda tucked the licenses into her purse. "I'm sure she'd talk to us."

"We'll have to do it from here. If we call long-distance from the station, they'll have our hides."

Their hides were already in enough jeopardy. "Did anything else stick out?"

"I checked the DNF." She looked down at the notebook. "None of them seemed to match our case. But all those missing girls, Amanda. At least twenty of them, and no one thought to do anything but shove them in a file at the back of the cabinet." She slowly shook her head. Amanda felt ashamed for having told her about it in the first place.

Evelyn continued, "They're dead, or they've been abducted, or hurt, and no one cares. Or at least no one knows to care. They must have families who are looking for them. But there are hardly any missing persons reports on black women. I guess their families know it doesn't matter. At least not . . ." Her voice trailed off as she opened her notebook. "I wrote down their names. I don't know why. I just thought that somebody should. Somebody has to acknowledge that they're gone."

Amanda looked at the long list of women's names. All dead. All tossed into files that no one ever looked at.

Evelyn let out a long sigh. She put the notebook back on her desk. "How was the jail?"

"Disgusting." Amanda dug around in her purse, though she hardly needed to refer to her notes. "Juice confessed to killing Lucy Bennett, but only to avoid the death penalty."

"Did no one explain to him that we're no longer allowed to execute people?"

"They said they'd bring it back for him."

Evelyn nodded. "I suppose that's a smart move on Juice's part, then."

"If you want to spend the rest of your life in prison." Amanda opened her notebook. "He confirmed Kitty is Andrew Treadwell's daughter."

"Well." She smiled smugly. "Our black sheep theory was correct."

"I wouldn't hold my breath for a commendation," Amanda advised. "Here's the best part: Juice said that Hank Bennett came to see him a week or so before Lucy disappeared."

Evelyn grunted. "God, that man would rather climb a tree and lie than stand on the ground and tell the truth." She took the pen off her desk and stood up to write on the puzzle wall. "Saw sister one week prior to disappearance," she called out, writing down the words under Hank Bennett's name. "What else did Juice say?"

"Hank Bennett told him to cut Kitty off heroin."

"You mean Lucy?"

"No, I mean Kitty."

Evelyn turned around. "Why would Hank Bennett want Juice to cut Kitty off heroin?"

Amanda pulled a Sergeant Hodge. "That's an interesting question."

Evelyn groaned as she looked back at the puzzle. "Maybe Andrew Treadwell sent Hank Bennett to get Kitty cleaned up."

"Maybe."

Amanda could tell she wasn't convinced. "Okay, try this: Trey Callahan at the Union Mission said that Kitty stuck out from the other girls. She was obviously from an upper class. It wouldn't take much poking around to find out who her people were. Maybe Juice tried to blackmail Treadwell, and Treadwell sent Hank Bennett to do his dirty work." She scanned her notes. "Juice said it himself, that Bennett offered him money to get Kitty off the Boy."

Evelyn breathed a heavy sigh. "Bennett went to bribe Juice about Kitty, but then he saw that his sister was there?"

"Juice said that Bennett didn't see Lucy that time, but who knows? They all lie."

"Yes, they do." Evelyn bent down and studied the yellow page with the timeline drawn out. "We need to update this. Call it out to me."

"Thanks for taking the hard part." Amanda flipped through her notes as Evelyn waited. "Okay. The letter for Lucy Bennett comes to the Union Mission. We have both Trey Callahan and Juice confirming that."

Evelyn took out a new piece of blue construction paper, stuck it on the wall, and wrote THE LETTER across the center. "Did Juice know what it said?"

"That he wanted to see his sister. That he missed her. Juice took it for a load of bull."

"Look at me, agreeing with a pimp."

Amanda continued, "Hank Bennett shows up at the mission a few days later and talks to Trey Callahan. Then, presumably soon after, he goes to Juice on his street corner. He sees Kitty instead. He tells Juice to cut Kitty loose. He doesn't ask about his sister." She squinted at her scribbles. "Juice made a point of telling me that he told Bennett to wait around for a few minutes, that Lucy would be right along, but Bennett didn't wait."

Evelyn guessed, "So, seeing Kitty put finding Lucy on the back burner for our boy lawyer."

"Evidently," Amanda concurred. "Then, two weeks later, Lucy is gone. A week or so after that, Kitty is gone. And then Mary disappeared after that." Amanda looked up from the notebook. "Three girls gone. But why?"

"Tell me so I can stop writing." Evelyn shook a cramp out of her hand before she finished the updating. Finally, she stood back and stared at the timeline. They both did. The puzzle was sprawling now, different bits of information floating around without a seeming connection. "I feel like we're missing something."

"Okay—" Amanda stood up. Pacing sometimes helped her think. "Let's think about it this way: Bennett was trying to get in touch with his sister. His father was dead. His mother wanted to see her daughter, to let her know what had happened. So Hank goes to the streets looking for Lucy, only he finds Kitty Treadwell."

"All right."

"Bennett said that he sent Lucy the letter in August. He remembered it because he'd just graduated law school and his father was recently deceased. Later, he told us that he was a first-year associate at Treadwell-Price."

"Oh-h-h." Evelyn drew out the word. She picked up her pen and wrote down the approximate dates. "Bennett sees Kitty whored out on the street and parlays that into a job with Treadwell-Price?" She smiled. "That's a top firm. A job there sets you up for life. I can totally see that weasel trying to work his sister's tragedy to his own benefit."

"Right."

Evelyn sat back down in the chair. "But what does this have to do with Jane Delray? And why would Bennett lie about the ID? What does he gain from Lucy being dead? Oh!" She excitedly jabbed the pen in the air. "Insurance. I was looking at it from the wrong angle. Of course there's no policy on Lucy. Bennett told us himself—his father's dead, the mother's just as good as, which leaves the estate and whatever policies the parents have to the children." She sat up in the chair. "Maybe Bennett wanted to see Lucy in order to get her to sign away her claim to the estate. That happened with one of Bill's clients last year. The old man was batty as a fruitcake. His children got him to sign away every last dime."

"Hank Bennett certainly strikes me as an opportunist."

"And besides, what would be the alternative?" Evelyn asked. "That Bennett killed Jane Delray? We saw him two days ago. His hands were perfectly clean. No cuts or bruises, which is exactly what you'd get if you attacked somebody."

Amanda remembered the skin under Jane Delray's fingernails. "She scratched her assailant. You would think he'd have a mark on the back of his hands or his neck or face."

"Unless she scratched his arm. His chest. He was wearing a three-piece suit. Who knows what was under there?" Evelyn blew out a puff of air. "I don't see Hank Bennett strangling a prostitute to death, then throwing her off the roof of Techwood Homes. Do you?"

Amanda didn't know what the man was capable of. "I just get a bad feeling about him."

"Me, too."

They both stared at the wall. Amanda let her gaze wander, pick-

ing up different names out of order. She said, "Juice told me that
Kitty was renting out her apartment to the other girls."

"I guess she gets that entrepreneurial spirit from her father."

"The next logical step would be to interrogate Andrew Treadwell
and Hank Bennett."

"Or, we could flap our hands and fly to the moon."

"We should go back to Trey Callahan at the Union Mission. Juice
said that he's friends with the guy who runs the soup kitchen."

Evelyn's mouth dropped open in surprise. "Is it just me, or does
everyone lie to us?"

"They lie to the men, too. No one tells you the truth if you have
a badge."

"Well, I suppose we should tell Betty Friedan we've finally
achieved some parity."

Amanda smiled.

"We should talk to the soup kitchen guy, too."

"We still don't know who Butch's CI is. Someone at Techwood
identified Jane Delray as Lucy Bennett."

Evelyn took a clean sheet of paper out of her desk drawer. "Okay,
first thing tomorrow: Union Mission, then the soup kitchen, then
Techwood to show around the photographs of the girls. Do you
think we could sneak a picture of Hank Bennett?" She tapped her
pen on the desk. "I know a gal over at the driver's license bureau. I bet
we can get his photograph that way."

Amanda looked at her friend. She was showing the same mixture
of excitement and purpose that Amanda had felt all week. Something
about working this case made them forget the danger involved. She
said, "Two people warned me off this today."

"Landry?"

"Three, then. Holly Scott and Deena Coolidge. They both told
me that I was crazy to be doing this."

Evelyn chewed her lip. She didn't have to say that the women
were right.

Amanda asked, "Are we really going to keep doing this?"

Evelyn stared back at her rather than respond. They both knew that they should stop. They both knew what was on the line. Not just their jobs. Their lives. Their futures. If they were fired from the police force, no one else would hire them. They would be pariahs.

"Girls!" Bill Mitchell called. "Supper's on."

Evelyn stood up. She squeezed Amanda's hand. "Pretend it's wonderful, whatever it is."

Amanda didn't know whether Evelyn was referring to Bill's supper or the mess they were getting themselves into. Either way, she couldn't help but feel admiration as she followed the other woman into the hallway. Evelyn was either the most upbeat person the world had ever offered or the most delusional.

"Ladies." Kenny was standing beside the hi-fi with a record in his hands. "What's your pleasure?"

Evelyn smiled back at Amanda as she headed toward the kitchen, leaving her to answer the question.

Kenny suggested, "Skynyrd? Allman Brothers? Clapton?"

Amanda figured she might as well get this out of the way. "I'm sorry to say I'm more Sinatra."

"Do you know that I saw him at Madison Square Garden last year?" Kenny smiled at her surprise. "I flew up to New York just to see the show. I was three rows back. He came into the ring like a champ and belted on for hours." Kenny thumbed through the record collection. "Here you go. I let Bill borrow this six months ago. I doubt he's even looked at it." Kenny showed her the record sleeve. *The Main Event—Live.*

Bill called, "Dinner's getting cold."

Amanda waited for Kenny to put on the record. The overture played softly through the speakers. Kenny held out his arm and escorted her to the dining room. Evelyn was sitting in her husband's lap. He patted her bottom. She kissed him before getting up. "Amanda, the wine is lovely." She took a hefty sip from her glass. "You shouldn't have."

"I'm glad it's palatable. I had a feeling the man at the store was misleading me."

"I'm sure you're an excellent sommelier." Kenny pulled out a chair. Amanda sat down, letting her purse slide to the floor. Kenny's hand brushed across her shoulder before he sat down opposite his brother.

Amanda held her wineglass to her mouth as she exhaled a breath of air between her lips.

Bill asked, "What were you two gals up to? Should I be worried you're going to wallpaper the house with construction paper?"

"Maybe." Evelyn raised an eyebrow as she took another sip of wine. "We've got this case that's probably going to get us both fired."

"More time with my gal," Bill exclaimed. He hardly seemed worried as he stabbed a dry-looking piece of roast and put it on her plate. "Have you been mouthing off or making trouble?" He forked another piece of roast for Amanda. "Or both?"

Evelyn said, "We're likely going to get a black man out of jail."

Kenny laughed. "Making friends wherever you go."

"No kidding." Evelyn finished her glass of wine. "This particular fella is called Juice."

"Like the football player?" Bill topped off Amanda's glass, then refilled Evelyn's. "Rushed for seventeen hundred yards in '68."

"Seventeen hundred *nine*," Kenny corrected. "Ran 171 against Ohio State in the Rose Bowl."

"To football." Bill raised his glass.

"Hear, hear." Kenny followed suit. They clinked their glasses in a toast. Amanda felt a warmth spread through her body. She hadn't realized how tense she was until the wine made her relax.

Evelyn said, "The non-football Juice seems to have a crush on Amanda." She winked across the table. "Says she's a fine-lookin' woman."

"A very astute man." Kenny winked at Amanda, too. She took a large drink of wine to cover her embarrassment.

"He's a pimp," Evelyn said. "We met him at Techwood Homes last week."

Amanda felt her heart lurch in her chest, but Evelyn kept talking. "He runs white women."

"My favorite kind." Bill refilled Amanda's glass. She hadn't realized she'd finished the first one already. Amanda looked down at the food on her plate. The vegetables had obviously been frozen. The meat was overcooked. Even the roll was burned around the edges.

"This prostitute, Jane—" Evelyn rolled her eyes. "Her apartment was not what you'd call tidy. What was it you said, Amanda? 'I'll look for back copies of *Good Housekeeping*'?"

The men laughed, and Evelyn continued the story. "She was an absolute terror to deal with."

Amanda sipped from her wineglass, which she kept pressed to her chest as she listened to Evelyn talk about the Techwood apartment, the mouthy whore. They all laughed when she mimicked Jane Delray's trashy accent. There was something about the way Evelyn told the story that made it sound funny instead of frightening. She could be relaying the plot of a television sitcom where two plucky gals stick their noses where they don't belong and end up escaping through wit and humor.

"Exit, stage left," Amanda said.

They all laughed, though Evelyn's smile wasn't quite as genuine. She tugged at the back of her hair.

Bill reached out and affectionately slapped away her hand. "You're going to snatch yourself bald."

Amanda asked, "Was it hard getting your hair cut?"

Evelyn shrugged. Obviously, it had been, but she said, "After Zeke, I didn't have time for it."

The wine had made Amanda brazen. She asked Bill, "Did you mind?"

He took Evelyn's hand. "Anything that makes my girl happy."

"I cried for at least an hour." Evelyn laughed, though her heart wasn't into it.

"I think it was closer to six," Bill said. "But I like it."

"It's very stylish," Kenny offered. "But long is nice, too."

Amanda patted the back of her hair. She was worse than Evelyn.

"Why don't you let it down?" The request came from Kenny.

Amanda was both surprised and deeply embarrassed. She was also dangerously close to complete inebriation, which was probably why she complied with the request.

Amanda silently counted out the bobby pins as she pulled them from her hair. Five, six, seven. There were eight total, plus the hair spray, which made her fingers sticky as she ran them through her hair. It draped to the middle of her back. Amanda cut the ends once a year. She only kept it down in the winter, and then only at night when she was alone.

Evelyn sighed. "You're so pretty."

Amanda finished her wine. She was already dizzy. She should at least eat a dinner roll to absorb some of the alcohol, but she didn't want to hear the sound of her own chewing. The room was quiet except for the record playing. Sinatra singing "Autumn in New York."

Bill picked up the bottle and topped them off again. Amanda thought to cover the glass with her hand, but she couldn't make herself move.

The phone rang in the kitchen. Evelyn startled. "Gosh, who could be calling this late?"

Amanda couldn't be alone in the room like this. She followed Evelyn into the kitchen.

"Mitchell residence."

Amanda pulled back her hair, twisting it around the crown. She stuck the bobby pins back in. Her movements were clumsy. Too much wine. Too much attention.

"Where?" Evelyn asked. She pulled the long telephone cord across the room and got a pen and paper out of the drawer. "Say that again." She scribbled as she spoke. "And when was this?" She made some noises, encouraging the caller to continue. Finally, she said, "We'll be right there," and hung up.

"Right where?" Amanda asked. She kept her hand on the kitchen counter. The wine had pickled her brain. "Who was that?"

"Deena Coolidge." Evelyn folded the piece of paper in half. "They've just found another body."

Amanda felt her focus snap back. "Who?"

"They don't know yet. Blonde, thin, pretty."

"That sounds familiar."

"They found her at Techwood Homes." Evelyn pushed open the door to the dining room. "Sorry, boys, we need to step out."

Bill smiled. "You're just trying to get out of doing dishes."

"I'll do them in the morning."

They exchanged a look. Amanda realized that Bill Mitchell wasn't as naïve as she had first imagined. He saw through his wife's funny stories the same as Amanda.

He raised his glass in a toast. "I'll wait up for you, my love."

Evelyn grabbed Amanda's purse before letting the door swing closed. "I'm drunk as a lord," she muttered. "I hope I don't end up driving us into the creek."

"I'll drive." Amanda followed her out the kitchen door.

Instead of heading to the car, Evelyn went to the shed. The men had finished the job except for the painting. Evelyn ran her hand along the top of the door trim and found the key. She tugged on the chain to turn on the light. There was a safe bolted to the floor. Evelyn had to try the combination three times before she finally got it open. "I think we drank that whole bottle between us."

"Why did Deena call you?"

"I asked her to let me know if anything else came up." Evelyn pulled out her revolver. She checked there was ammunition in the cylinder, then snapped it back into place. She took out the speed-loader, then shut the safe door. "Let's go."

"Do you think you'll need that?"

Evelyn tucked the revolver into her purse. "I'm never going anywhere without it again." She grabbed the shelf as she stood up. Her eyes closed as she oriented herself. "They're probably going to give us both DUIs."

"That'll hardly make us stand out."

Evelyn pulled off the light and locked the door. Amanda took deep breaths of air as she walked to her car, trying to clear her head.

Evelyn said, "You know this means Juice didn't do it."

"Did we ever really think he did?"

"No, but now they'll know, too."

Amanda climbed into the car. She threw her purse into the back seat as she waited for Evelyn to get in. The drive to Techwood wasn't a long one, especially at eight o'clock in the evening. There was no traffic on the road. The only people who stayed in Atlanta after dark were the ones who had no business being there. Which was a good thing considering Amanda's state of intoxication. If she accidentally hit a pedestrian, no one was likely to care.

The traffic lights were flashing yellow as she traveled up Piedmont Road. Amanda took the steep curve that turned into Fourteenth Street, then slowed for the blinking light before turning left on Peachtree. Another right on North and she was following the same pattern they'd worn last week: past the Varsity, over the interstate, left on Techwood Drive, and straight into the hell of the projects.

Several police cruisers were blocking the path to their usual berm. Amanda parked behind a familiar Plymouth Fury. She glanced inside the car as she passed. Wadded-up packs of cigarettes. A half-empty bottle of Johnnie Walker. Crushed cans of beer. She followed Evelyn toward the buildings. Again, Rick Landry was standing in the middle of the courtyard. His hands were on his hips. His face twisted with anger when he saw Amanda and Evelyn.

"Whatta I gotta do, beat it into you broads?" He looked ready to do just that, but Deena Coolidge stopped him.

"Y'all ready?"

Landry glared at her. "Ain't nobody called for a pickaninny, Sapphire."

She puffed out her chest. "You need to get your cracker ass out my face before I pimp you up to Reggie."

Landry tried to stare her down, but Deena, who was at least a foot shorter than him, stood her ground. Landry finally relented, but not without mumbling "Cunts" as he stomped away.

Deena asked, "Y'all wondering what him and Butch are doing here when they're both on day shift? Because I sure am."

Amanda looked at Evelyn, who nodded. It did seem strange.

Deena said, "Pete's around back with the body, but I've got somebody for you to talk to first."

Neither of them spoke as they followed Deena into the building. The hall was packed with women and children dressed in housecoats and pajamas. Their faces were guarded and frightened. They had probably been settled down for the night when the police cars showed up. They'd all left their front doors open. The lights from the cruisers filled the apartments. Amanda was very conscious that hers and Evelyn's were the only white faces as Deena took them deeper into the building.

Only one apartment door on the floor was closed. Deena knocked on it. They waited for a chain to slide back, deadbolts to turn. The old woman who opened the door was dressed in a black skirt and jacket. Her white blouse was crisply starched. She was wearing a fine black hat with a short veil that hung to the top of her eyebrows.

"Whatchu doin' dressed up for church, Miss Lula?" Deena asked. "I told you these gals just want to talk. They ain't gonna drag you down to the jail."

The old woman stared at the floor. She was cowed by their presence, that much was evident. Even when she stepped back so that they could enter, it was obvious that she was doing so under great duress. Amanda felt deeply ashamed as she walked into the apartment.

Deena suggested, "Why don't you get us some tea, dear?"

Miss Lula nodded as she headed into the other room. Deena indicated the couch, which was a pale yellow and absolutely spotless. In fact, the living room was remarkably tidy. The one chair that faced the small television had a ruffled skirt and a doily. Magazines were neatly stacked on the table. The rug on the floor was clean. Pictures of Martin Luther King, Jr., and Jack Kennedy faced each other on the wall. There were no cobwebs in the corners. Even the stench of the building had not managed to permeate the space.

Still, neither Evelyn nor Amanda sat down. They were too mind-

ful of the setting. As spotless as this woman's apartment seemed, it
was still surrounded by filth. You might as well drag a clean blanket
through a mud puddle and expect it to remain unscathed.

They heard a kettle start to boil in the kitchen.

Deena's tone was firm. "Y'all best both be sitting your white asses
down by the time she comes back in here."

Deena took the chair by the television. Reluctantly, Evelyn sat on
the couch. Amanda joined her, keeping her purse clutched in her lap.
Both of them sat on the edge of the cushions—not from fear of con-
tamination, but because they were on duty. Years of wearing utility
belts around their waists had made it impossible for them to sit back
in their seats.

Amanda asked, "Who called in the body?"

Deena nodded toward the kitchen. "Miss Lula did. She's been
here since they integrated the place. They moved her over from Buttermilk."

"Why does she think we're going to arrest her?"

"Because you're white and you have a badge."

Evelyn mumbled, "That's never impressed anybody before."

Miss Lula was back. She had taken off her hat, revealing a shock
of white hair. The china cups and saucers on her silver tray rattled as
she brought the set into the living room. Instinctively, Amanda stood
to help. The tray was heavy. She lowered it to the coffee table. Deena
relinquished her chair to the old woman. It was a neat trick. Deena
carefully smoothed down the back of her pants, probably checking
for insects. A roach traveled across the wall behind her. Deena shuddered.

"Would you ladies like some cookies?" Miss Lula offered. Her
voice was unexpectedly refined. There was almost the tinge of an
English accent to it, like Lena Horne's.

Evelyn answered, "Thank you, no. We've just had supper." She
reached toward the teapot. "May I?"

Miss Lula nodded. Amanda watched Evelyn pour four cups of
tea. It was the strangest thing she'd ever been a part of. Amanda had

never been a guest in a black person's home. Usually, the point of her visit was to get in and get out as quickly as possible. She felt as if she was in one of those Carol Burnett sketches that was trying for social commentary rather than humor.

Deena said, "Miss Lula used to be a teacher at the Negro school off Benson."

Amanda offered, "My mother was a teacher. Elementary school."

"That was my field as well," Miss Lula answered. She took the cup and saucer Evelyn offered. Her hands were old, the knuckles swollen. There was a slight ash tone. She pursed her lips and blew on the tea to cool it.

Evelyn served Deena next, then Amanda.

"Thank you." Amanda could feel the heat through the china, but she drank the scalding tea anyway, hoping the caffeine would help chase away the wine.

She looked up at the photos of Kennedy facing King, again taking in the orderly apartment that Miss Lula called home.

When Amanda had worked patrol, some of the men made a game of terrorizing these old people. They'd roll their cruisers up behind them in the street and purposefully backfire the car. Grocery bags were dropped. Hands flew into the air. Most of them would fall to the ground. The backfire sounded like a gunshot.

"Now." Deena had waited until they'd all had some tea. "Miss Lula, if you could tell these women what you told me?"

The old woman cast down her eyes again. She was obviously troubled. "I heard a commotion in the back."

Amanda realized the woman's apartment faced the rear of the complex. It was the same area where Jane Delray had been found three days ago.

Miss Lula continued, "I peered out the window and saw the girl just lying there. She had obviously passed." She shook her head. "Terrible sight. No matter their sins, no one deserves that."

Evelyn asked, "Was there anyone else back there?"

"Not as far as I could tell."

"Do you know what the noise was? The one that made you look out the window?"

"Perhaps it was the rear door banging open?" She didn't seem sure, though she nodded as if that was the only explanation that made sense.

Amanda asked, "Have you noticed anyone strange hanging around?"

"No more so than usual. Most of these girls had evening visitors. They generally came in through the back door."

That would make sense. None of the men probably wanted to be seen. Amanda asked, "Did you recognize the girl you saw out back?"

"She's from the top floor. I don't know her name. But I said from the beginning that they should not have been allowed to live here."

Deena supplied, "Because they're prostitutes, not because they're white."

Miss Lula said, "They were operating their business out of the apartment. That is contrary to the housing laws."

Evelyn put down her cup of tea. "Did you see any of their customers?"

"Occasionally. As I said, they mostly used the back door. Especially the white men."

"They saw both white and black men?"

"Frequently one after the other."

They were all silent as they considered the statement.

Evelyn asked, "How many women were living up there?"

"At first it was the young one. She said her name was Kitty. She seemed nice enough. She gave candy to some of the children, which was allowed until we realized what she was doing up there."

"And then?" Amanda asked.

"And then another woman moved in. This was at least a year and a half ago, mind you. The second girl was white, too. Looked very similar to Kitty. I never got her name. Her visitors were not as discreet."

"Is that the woman you saw through your window tonight? Kitty?"

"No, a third one. I've not seen Kitty in a while. Nor have I seen the second one in some time. These girls are very transitory." She paused, then added, "Lord help them. It's a difficult path they've chosen."

Amanda remembered the licenses she'd tucked into her purse. She unzipped her bag and pulled them out. "Do you recognize any of these girls?"

The old woman took the licenses. Her reading glasses were neatly folded on the side table, resting atop a well-read Bible. They all watched as she unfolded the glasses, slid them onto her face. Carefully, Miss Lula studied each license, giving each girl her undivided attention. "This one," she said, holding out the license for Kathryn Treadwell. "This is Kitty, but I assume you know that by her name."

Amanda said, "We've been led to believe that Kitty was renting out the space to other girls."

"Yes, that would make sense."

"Did you ever talk to her?"

"Once. She seemed to think very highly of herself. Apparently, her father is very politically connected."

"She said that to you?" Evelyn asked. "Kitty told you who her father was?"

"Not in so many words, but yes. She made it clear she didn't really belong here. But then, do any of us?"

Amanda couldn't answer the question. "Do the other girls look familiar?"

The woman scanned the license again. She held up Jane Delray's. "The quality of men changed quite a bit for this one. She was not as discriminating as—" She held up Mary Halston's photo. "This one had a lot of repeat customers, though I would not call them gentlemen. She's the girl out back." She read the name. "Donna Mary Halston. Such a pretty name considering the things she did."

Amanda heard Evelyn suck in her breath. They were both thinking of the same question. Amanda asked, "You said Mary had repeat business?"

"Yes, that's correct."

"Did you ever see a white man who was about six feet tall, sandy blond hair, long sideburns, wearing a sharply tailored suit, probably in some shade of blue?"

Miss Lula glanced at Deena. When she handed back the licenses to Amanda, her expression was blank. "I'll have to think on that. Let me get back to you tomorrow."

Amanda felt her brow furrow. Either the wine was wearing off or the tea was kicking in. Miss Lula's apartment was at the end of the hallway. It was at least ten yards from the stairwell, even farther from the back door. Unless the old woman spent her days sitting behind the building, there was no way she could note the comings and goings of the girls or their visitors.

Amanda opened her mouth to speak, but Deena interrupted her.

"Miss Lula," she said. "We appreciate your time. You've got my number. Get back to me on that question." She put her saucer down on the tray. When Evelyn and Amanda didn't move, she grabbed their teacups and placed them beside hers. "We can let ourselves out." She did everything but clap her hands to get them moving.

Amanda led the way, clutching her purse to her chest. She was going to turn to say goodbye, but Deena pushed them out the door.

The hallway had emptied. Still Amanda kept her voice low. "How could she—"

"Give her until tomorrow," Deena said. "She'll find out whether or not your mystery man was here."

"But how could she—"

"She's the queen bee," Deena told her, leading them up the hallway. She didn't stop until she reached the exit door. They stood in the same spot where Rick Landry had threatened Evelyn. "What Miss Lula told you isn't what she's seen. It's what she's heard."

"But she didn't—"

"Rule number one of the ghetto: find the oldest biddy been around the longest. She's the one running the place."

"Well," Evelyn said, "I did wonder why she had a shotgun under the couch."

Amanda asked, "What?"

"That thing was loaded, too." Deena pushed open the door.

The crime scene was cordoned off with yellow tape. There were no lights back here, or at least no lights that were functioning. The bulbs on the light poles had all been broken, probably with rocks. Six patrolmen took care of the problem. They stood in a ring around the body, the butts of their Kel-Lites resting on their shoulders to illuminate the area.

The grounds behind the building were as desolate as the front. Red Georgia clay was packed hard by the constant pounding of bare feet. There were no flowers back here. No grass. One lone tree stood with its tired branches hanging down. Just below the tree was the body. Pete Hanson blocked the view with his wide frame. Beside him was a young man of about the same height and stature. Like Pete, he was wearing a white lab coat. He tapped Pete on the shoulder and nodded toward the women.

Pete stood up. He had a grim look on his face. "Detectives. I'm glad you're here, though I say that with reservations given the circumstances." He indicated the young man. "This is one of my pupils, Dr. Ned Taylor."

Taylor gave them a stern nod. Even in the low illumination, Amanda could see the green tint to his skin. He looked as if he might be ill. Evelyn wasn't much better.

Deena suggested, "Pete, why don't you run Amanda through this?"

Amanda supposed she should feel proud of her lack of squeamishness, but it was starting to feel like one more secret she would have to keep about herself.

Evelyn volunteered, "I'll go check the apartment. Maybe Butch and Landry missed something."

Deena harrumphed. "I'd bet my next paycheck on it."

"This way, my dear." Pete cupped his hand beneath Amanda's elbow as he led her toward the dead woman. The six officers holding flashlights seemed puzzled that Amanda was there, though none of them asked questions, probably in deference to Pete.

"If you would?" Pete got down on one knee, then helped Amanda kneel beside him. She smoothed down her skirt so that her knees would not grind against the dirt. Her heels were going to get scuffed. She hadn't exactly dressed for this.

Pete said, "Tell me what you see."

The victim was face down. Her long blonde hair draped down her shoulders and back. She was wearing a black miniskirt and red T-shirt. Her hand rested on the ground a few inches from her face. The nails were polished bright red.

Amanda said, "Same as the other victim. All ten fingernails expertly manicured."

"Correct." Pete pulled back the woman's stringy blonde hair. "Neck's bruised, though I'm going to guess the hyoid wasn't broken."

"She wasn't strangled to death?"

"I believe there's something else going on." He pulled up the red T-shirt. There was a line of injuries down the woman's side, almost like a dress seam had been ripped open. "These lacerations run the length of her body."

Amanda saw the pattern duplicated on the girl's leg. She had mistaken the damage for the seam in a pair of stockings. Likewise, the outside of the victim's arms showed the marks. It was like a McCall's pattern, where someone had tried to tear apart the stitches joining the front to the back of her body.

Amanda asked, "What—who—would do that?"

"Two very good questions. Unfortunately, my answer to both is that I have no idea."

Amanda didn't so much ask as wonder aloud, "You told Deena to call us, to get us here."

"Yes. The manicured fingernails were similar. The setting. I thought there was more, but upon further examination . . ." He started to pull up the miniskirt, then changed his mind. "I must warn you, even I was startled. I haven't seen this in a few years."

Amanda shook her head. "What do you mean?"

He pulled up the skirt. There was a knitting needle between the girl's legs.

Amanda didn't need to be coached this time. Automatically, she found herself taking deep breaths, filling her lungs, then slowly pushing out all the air.

Pete shook his head. "There's absolutely no reason for a girl to have to do this anymore."

Amanda noticed, "There's no blood."

Pete sat back on his heels. "No, there's not."

"You would expect to see blood, wouldn't you? From the knitting needle?"

"Yes." Pete pushed open the legs. One of the officers moved back a step. He nearly tripped over a broken tree limb. There were a couple of nervous laughs, but the man righted himself without incident. He trained the beam of his flashlight on the victim's legs.

Pasty white thighs. No blood.

Amanda asked, "Are her fingerprints on the knitting needle?"

Despite the circumstances, Pete smiled at her. "None. It was wiped clean."

"She didn't do this to herself."

"Not likely. She's been cleaned up. Someone brought her here."

"The same place our other victim was found."

"Not exactly, but close." He pointed to a spot several feet away. "Lucy Bennett was found over there."

Amanda looked back up at the building. Miss Lula's apartment was on the far end. She couldn't see the tree from her window. She certainly couldn't see where Jane Delray was found. Deena was right. There was someone else—or a series of someone elses—who'd seen everything but were too afraid to tell.

"Ned," Pete called. "Take her feet, I'll get her shoulders."

The young doctor did as he was instructed. Carefully, they rolled the victim over onto her back.

Amanda looked at the girl's face. The damage was incomprehensible. Her eyelids were shredded. Her mouth was torn to pieces. Still, there was enough left to recognize her. Amanda unzipped her purse and found the license, which she handed to Pete.

"Donna Mary Halston," he read. "Lives here?" He looked up at the building. "Top floor, I'm assuming. Same as Lucy Bennett."

Amanda shuffled through the licenses and found Lucy Bennett's. She handed this to Pete and waited.

"Hm." He studied the photo carefully. He was obviously mindful of the six patrolmen when he told Amanda, "This girl is unfamiliar to me."

Amanda handed him Jane Delray's license.

Again, he studied the photo. A deep sigh came out like a groan. "Yes, this one I recognize." He handed both licenses back to Amanda. "Now what?"

She shook her head. It felt good to have Pete weigh in on the identities, but his validation wasn't going to change much.

The back door opened. Evelyn shook her head. "Nothing in the apartment. It's still a mess, but I don't think anyone's—" She stopped. Amanda followed her gaze to the knitting needle. Evelyn put her hand to her mouth. Instead of turning away, she looked up at the tree. Then she looked down at the girl again.

"What is it?" Amanda asked. Something was obviously wrong. She stood up and joined Evelyn. It was the same as the construction paper puzzle. Sometimes a change in perspective was all it took.

The tree limb was broken. The girl lay on the ground. Her child had been aborted.

"Oh, my God." Amanda realized, "Ophelia."

nineteen

Present Day

SUZANNA FORD

The darkness. The cold. The noise.

Air sucking in and out, like a car zooming through a tunnel.

She couldn't take it anymore. Her body ached. Her mouth was dry. Her stomach was so empty that she felt as if the acids were eating a hole in her belly.

Meth.

That was what had brought her here. Brought her low. She had fallen too far. She had put herself in the gutter. She had brought herself to this place.

Dear Jesus, she prayed. *If you get me out of here, I will worship You every day. I will exalt Your name.*

The claustrophobia. The absolute darkness. The unknowing. The fear of suffocation.

Way back when they were still a family, her father had taken them all on a trip to Wales. There was a mine there, something from thousands of years ago. You had to wear a hard hat to go into the tunnels. They were small because people weren't as tall back then. They were narrow because most of the workers were children.

Suzanna had gone in twenty feet before she started freaking out. She could still see sunlight from the opening, but she'd nearly pissed herself running back toward the entrance.

That was what it felt like now. Trapped. Hopeless.

I will praise You. I will spread Your word. I will humble myself before You.

Arms couldn't move. Legs couldn't move. Eyes couldn't open. Mouth couldn't open.

Meth will never touch my lips, my nose, my lungs, ever again, so help me God.

The tremble started slow, coursing through her body, straining her muscles. Her fingers flexed into a fist. She clenched her shoulders, her teeth, her ass. The threads pulled. The pain was excruciating. Hot needles touching raw nerves. Her heart was going to explode in her chest. She could rip herself away. She was stronger than this. She could rip herself away.

Suzanna tried. She tried so hard. But each time, the pain won.

She couldn't make the skin tear. She couldn't make the thread break.

She could only lie there.

Praying for salvation.

Dear Jesus—

twenty

Present Day

TUESDAY

Will awoke with a start. His neck cracked as he stretched it side to side. He was at home, sitting on his couch. Betty was beside him. The little dog was on her back. Legs up. Nose pointed toward the front door. Will glanced around, looking for Faith. She'd driven him home from the morgue. She'd gone to get him a glass of water and now, judging by the clock on the TiVo, it was almost two hours later.

He listened to the house. It was quiet. Faith had left. Will didn't know how he felt about that. Should he be relieved? Should he wonder where she had gone? There was no guidebook for this part of his life. No instructions he could follow to put it all back together.

He tried to close his eyes again, to go back to sleep. He wanted to wake up a year from now. He wanted to wake up and have all of this over.

Only, he couldn't get his eyes to stay closed. Every time he tried, he found himself staring back up at the ceiling. Was that what it had been like for his mother? According to the autopsy report, her eyes had not always been sewn closed. Sometimes, they had been sewn open. The medical examiner posited in the report that Will's father would have to stay close by during these periods. He would have to use a dropper to keep her eyes from drying out.

Dr. Edward Taylor. That was the name of the medical examiner. The man had died in a car accident fifteen years ago. He'd been the first investigator Will had tried to track down. The first dead end. The first time Will had felt relief that there was no one around to explain to him exactly what had happened to his mother.

"Hey." Faith came out of his spare bedroom. He could see that the light was still on. His books were in there. All his CDs. Car magazines he'd collected over the years. Albums from way back. It had probably taken Faith less than ten seconds to figure out which items were most out of place. She held the books in her hand. *The New Feminist Hegemony. Applied Statistical Models: Theory and Application. A Vindication of the Rights of Women.*

He said, "You can go home now."

"I'm not leaving you alone." She put his mother's textbooks on the table as she sat in the recliner. The file was on the table, too. Will had left it there this morning. Faith had probably paged through everything while he was sleeping. He should've felt angry that she'd been prying, but there was nothing left inside of him. Will was utterly devoid of any emotion. He'd felt it happen when he first saw Sara at the morgue. His initial impulse was to weep at her feet. To tell her everything. To beg her to understand.

And then—nothing.

It was like a stopper being pulled. All of the feeling had just drained out of him.

The rest flashed in his mind like a movie preview that gave away every plot twist: The battered girl. The painted fingernails. The ripped skin. The sound of Sara's breath catching when Will told her—told everyone—that his father was to blame.

Sara was a verbal woman, outspoken at times, and not usually one to hold back her opinion. But in the end, she'd said nothing. After nearly two weeks of living with that inquisitive look in her eyes, there were no questions she wanted to ask. Nothing she wanted to know. It was all laid out in front of her. Amanda was right about the autopsy. Will shouldn't have been there. It had been like watching his mother being examined, processed, catalogued.

And Angie was right about Sara. It was too much for her to handle.

Why had he thought for even a second that Angie was wrong? Why had he thought Sara would be different?

Will had just stood there in the morgue, frozen in time and place. Staring at Sara. Waiting for her to speak. Waiting for her to scream or yell or throw something. He would probably still be there but for Amanda ordering Faith to take him home. Even then, Faith had to grab Will's arm and physically pull him from the room.

Close-up on Sara. Her face pale. Her head shaking. Fade to black. The end.

"Will?" Faith asked.

He looked up at her.

"How did you get into the GBI?"

He weighed the question, trying to spot her end game. "I was recruited."

"How?"

"Amanda came to my college."

Faith gave a tight nod, and he could tell she was chasing a train of thought he couldn't pin down. "What about the application?"

Will rubbed his eyes. There was still white grit in the corners from tearing apart the basement.

Faith pressed, "The background screening. All the paperwork."

She knew about his dyslexia. She also knew he could pull his own weight. "It was mostly oral interviews. They let me take the rest home. Same as you, right?"

Faith's chin tilted up. Finally, she said, "Right."

Will rested his hand on Betty's chest. He could feel her heart beat against his palm. She sighed. Her tongue licked out.

Will asked, "Why did the reporter from *The Atlanta Journal* call Amanda?"

Faith shrugged. "Don't worry about it. I told you I shut down the story."

Will had been so blind. Amanda had fed him the information this morning but he'd been too exhausted to process it. "My records are sealed. There's no way a reporter—or anybody—could know who my father is. At least not legally." He studied Faith. "And even if someone found out, why call Amanda? Why not call me directly? My number is listed. So's my address."

Faith chewed her bottom lip. It was her tell. She knew something that Will did not, and she wasn't going to share it.

Will leaned toward her. "I want you to go to the hotel. He's on parole. He doesn't have a legal expectation of privacy."

Faith didn't need to ask whose hotel room. "And do what?"

Will clenched his fist. The cuts opened up again. "I want you to toss his room. I want you to interrogate him and sit on him until he can't take it anymore."

Faith stared at him. "You know I can't do that."

"Why not?"

"Because we have to build a case, not a harassment suit."

"I don't care about a case. Make him so miserable he leaves the hotel just to get away from you."

"And then what?"

She knew what would happen next. Will would shoot him down in the street like a rabid dog.

She said, "I'm not going to do that."

"I can look up the layout of the hotel. I can go to the courthouse. I can find a way in there and—"

"That sounds like a great way to leave a paper trail."

Will didn't care about a paper trail. "How many men are on the hotel?"

"Five times as many as are sitting outside your house right now."

Will went to the front window. He pushed open the blinds. There was an Atlanta cop car blocking his driveway. A G-ride was in the street. Will slammed his hand against the blinds. Betty barked, jumping up from the couch.

He went to the back of the house. He opened the kitchen door. A man was sitting in the gazebo Will had built last summer. Tan and blue GBI regs. Glock on his hip. He had his feet propped up on the railing. He waved as Will slammed the door.

"She can't do this," Will said. "She can't sit on my house like I'm some kind of criminal."

Faith asked, "Why didn't you ever tell me about him?"

Will paced across the room. His body was suddenly filled with adrenaline. "So I can be another notch in your serial killer collection?"

"Do you really think I'd turn your life into a game?"

"Where's my gun?" His keys were on his desk. His phone. The Glock was missing. "Did you take my gun?"

Faith didn't answer, but he noticed that her thigh holster was gone. She'd locked her gun in the car. She didn't trust him not to take it.

Several thoughts came into Will's head. Punching a hole in the wall. Kicking over his desk. Breaking the windows in Faith's car. Taking a bat to that asshole sitting in his gazebo. In the end, Will could only stand there. It was the same thing that had happened at the morgue. He was too exhausted. Too overwhelmed. Too handled. "Just leave, Faith. I don't need you babysitting me. I don't want you here."

"Too bad."

"Go home. Go home to your stupid kid and get the hell out of my business."

"If you think being a dick is going to chase me away, you don't know me very well." She sat back in the chair, arms crossed over her chest. "Sara found semen in the girl's hair."

Will waited for her to continue.

"There's enough for a DNA profile. Once it's in the system, we can match it against his."

"That'll take weeks."

"Four days," she told him. "Dr. Coolidge put a rush on it."

"Then arrest him. You can hold him for twenty-four hours."

"Which means he'll bail out and disappear before we can pick him up again." Her voice had the annoying tone of someone trying to be reasonable. "APD put six guys on the hotel. Amanda probably has ten more. He won't be able to take a shit without us knowing."

"I want to be there when you arrest him."

"You know Amanda won't allow that."

"When you interrogate him." Will couldn't help himself. He started begging. "Please let me see him. Please. I have to see him. I have to look him in the eye. I want to see his face when he realizes that I got away. That he didn't win."

Faith put her hand over her heart. "I swear to God, Will. I swear to you on the lives of my children that I will do everything in my power to make sure that happens."

"It's not enough," Will said. He didn't just want to look his father in the eye. He wanted to beat him. He wanted to kick out his teeth. To slice off his cock. To sew shut his mouth and eyes and nose and beat him until he drowned in his own vomit. "It's not enough."

"I know it's not," Faith said. "It'll never be enough, but it'll have to do."

There was a knock on the door. Will didn't know who he was expecting when Faith opened the door. Amanda. Angie. Some cop telling him that Will's father had killed again.

Anyone but the person who was actually there.

Sara asked Faith, "Everything okay?"

Faith nodded, picking up her purse by the door. She told Will, "I'll call you the minute I know anything. I promise."

Sara shut the door behind her. Her hair fell in soft curls around her shoulders. She was wearing a tight black dress that wrapped around her body. Will had seen her dressed up before, but never like this. She was wearing extremely high heels with a black leopard print. They did something to her calf that sent a tightness into his groin.

She said, "Hi."

Will swallowed. He could still taste plaster in his throat.

Sara walked around the couch and sat down. She slid off her heels and tucked her legs underneath her. "Come here."

Will sat down on the couch. Betty was between them. She jumped down. Her toenails clicked across the floor as she headed into the kitchen.

Sara took his hand. She must've noticed the cuts and blisters, but she didn't say anything. Will couldn't look at her. She was so beautiful that it was almost painful. Instead, he stared at the coffee table. His mother's file. Her books.

He said, "I guess Amanda told you everything."

"No, she didn't."

Will wasn't surprised. Amanda loved torturing him. He pointed to his mother's things. "If you want to—" Will stopped, trying to keep his voice from cracking. "It's all there. Just go ahead and read it."

Sara glanced down at the file, but said, "I don't want to read it."

Will shook his head. He didn't understand.

"You tell me about her when you're ready."

"It would be easier if—"

She reached out to touch his face. Her fingers stroked his cheek. She moved closer. He felt the heat of her body as she pressed against him. Will put his hand on her leg, felt the firm muscle of her thigh. The tightness came back. He kissed her. Sara's hands went to his face as she kissed him back. She straddled him. Her hair draped across his face. He could feel her breath on his neck.

Unfortunately, that was the extent of his feelings.

She asked, "Do you want me to—"

"No." He pulled her back up. "I'm sorry. I'm—"

She put her fingers to his lips. "You know what I really want to do?" She climbed off him, but stayed close. "I want to watch a movie where robots hit each other. Or things blow up. Preferably from robots hitting each other." She picked up the remote and turned on the set. She tuned in the Speed channel. "Oh, look. This is even better."

Will could not think of a time in his life when he'd felt more miserable. If Faith had not taken his Glock, he would've shot himself in the head. "Sara, it's not—"

"Shh." Sara took his arm and wrapped it around her shoulder. She rested her head on his chest, her hand on his leg. Betty came back. She jumped into Will's lap and settled in.

He stared at the television. The Ferrari Enzo was being profiled. An Italian man was using a lathe to hollow out a piece of aluminum. Nothing the announcer said would stay in Will's head. He felt his eyelids getting heavy. He let out a slow breath.

Finally, his eyes stayed closed.

This time, when Will woke up, he wasn't alone. Sara was lying on the couch in front of him. Her back curved into his body. Her hair tickled his face. The room was dark except for the glow of the television set. The sound was muted. Speed was showing a monster-truck rally. The TiVo read twelve past midnight.

Another day passed. Another night come. Another page turned in the calendar of his father's life.

Will couldn't stop the thoughts that came into his head. He wondered if Faith still had his Glock. He wondered whether the patrol car was still blocking his driveway or the asshole was still in his gazebo.

He had a Sig Sauer in the gun safe that was bolted inside his closet. His Colt AR-15 rifle was disassembled beside it. Ammunition for both was stacked in a plastic box. Will worked the rifle in his mind— magazine, bolt catch, trigger guard. Winchester 55-grain full metal jacket.

No. The Sig would be better. Closer. Muzzle to the head. Finger on the trigger. Will would see the terror in his father's eyes, then the glassy, vacant stare of a dead man.

Sara stirred. Her hand snaked back and stroked the side of his face. Her fingernails lightly scratched the skin. She breathed a contented sigh.

Just like that, Will felt the anger start to drain away. Again, it was similar to what had happened at the morgue, but instead of feeling empty, he felt full. A calmness took over. The clamp around his chest started to loosen.

Sara leaned back into him. Her hand pulled him closer. Will's body was much more responsive this time. He pressed his mouth to her neck. The fine hairs stood at attention. He could feel her flesh prickle under his tongue.

Sara turned her head to look at him. She gave a sleepy smile. "Hey."

"Hey."

"I was hoping that was you."

He kissed her mouth. She turned to face him. She was still smiling. Will could feel the curve of her lips against his mouth. Her hair was tangled underneath her. He shifted and felt a sharp pain in his leg. It wasn't a pulled muscle. It was Angie's ring. He still had it in his pocket.

Sara mistook his reaction for a recurrence of his earlier problem. She said, "Let's play a game."

Will didn't need a game. He needed to get Angie out of his head, but that wasn't exactly news he could share.

She held out her hand. "I'm Sara."

"I know."

"No." She still had her hand out. "I'm Sara Linton."

And apparently, Will was a moron. He shook her hand. "Will Trent."

"What do you do for a living, Will Trent?"

"I'm a . . ." He glanced around for an idea. "I'm a monster-truck driver."

She looked at the TV and laughed. "That's creative."

"What are you?"

"A stripper." She laughed again, as if she'd shocked herself. "I'm only doing it to pay my way through college."

If Will's stupid wedding ring wasn't in his front pocket, he could've invited Sara to slip her hand inside to get some money for a lap dance. Instead, he had to settle on telling her, "That's commendable." He shifted onto his side, freeing up his hand. "What are you studying?"

"Umm . . ." She grinned. "Monster-truck repair."

He trailed his finger between her breasts. The dress was low-cut, designed in such a way that it opened with little effort. Will realized she had worn it for him. Just like she'd let her hair down. Just like she'd squeezed her feet into a pair of high-heel shoes that could probably break her toes.

Just like she'd been at the autopsy. Just like she was here now.

He said, "I'm actually not a monster-truck driver."

"No?" Her breath caught as he tickled his fingers down her bare stomach. "What are you?"

"I'm an ex-con."

"Oh, I like that," she said. "Jewel thief or bank robber?"

"Petty theft. Destruction of private property. Four-year suspended sentence."

Her laughter stopped. She could tell he wasn't playing anymore.

Will took in a deep breath and slowly let it go. He was doing this now. There was no going back. "I was arrested for stealing food." He had to clear his throat so the words could get out. "It happened when I was eighteen."

She put her hand over his.

"I aged out of the system." Mrs. Flannigan had died the summer Will's eighteenth birthday rolled around. The new guy who ran the home had given Will a hundred dollars and a map to the homeless shelter. "I ended up at the downtown mission. Some of the guys there were all right. Most of them were older and—" He didn't finish the sentence. Sara could easily guess why a teenager didn't feel safe there. "I lived on the streets . . ." Again, he let his voice trail off. "I hung out at the hardware store on Highland. Contractors used to go there in the mornings to pick up day workers."

She used her thumb to stroke the back of his hand. "Is that where you learned how to fix things?"

"Yeah." He'd never really thought about it, but it was true. "I made good money, but I didn't know how to spend it. I should've saved up for an apartment. Or a car. Or something. But I spent it on candy and a Walkman and tapes." Will had never had money in his pocket before. There was no such thing as an allowance when he was growing up. "I was sleeping on Peachtree where the library used to be. This group of older guys rolled me. They beat me down. Broke my nose, some of my fingers. Took everything I had. I guess I'm lucky that's all they did."

Sara's grip tightened around his hand.

"I couldn't work. My clothes were filthy. I didn't have anywhere to bathe. I tried to beg for money but people were scared of me. I guess I looked like a junkie." He told Sara, "I wasn't, though. I never did drugs. I never did any of those things."

She nodded.

"But I was so hungry. My stomach hurt all the time. I was dizzy from it. Sick. Afraid to go to sleep. Afraid I'd get rolled again. I went into this all-night pharmacy that used to be on Ponce de Leon. Plaza Drugs, right beside the movie theater?" Sara nodded. "I walked straight in and started taking food off the shelves. Little Debbies. Moon Pies. Anything with a wrapper. I tore it open with my teeth and shoved it into my mouth." He swallowed, his throat feeling raw. "They called the cops."

"They arrested you?"

"They tried." He felt shame welling up in his throat. "I started swinging my fists, trying to hit anything. They stopped me real fast."

Sara stroked back his hair with her fingers.

"They handcuffed me. Took me to jail. And then—" He shook his head. "My caseworker came in. I hadn't seen her in six, maybe seven months. She said she'd been looking for me."

"Why?"

"Because Mrs. Flannigan left me some money." Will still remembered his shock when he heard the news. "I was only allowed to use it for college. So—" He shrugged. "I went to the first college that would take me. Lived in the dorm. Ate in the cafeteria. Worked a part-time job on the grounds. And then I got recruited into the GBI, and that was it."

Sara was quiet, probably trying to absorb it all. "How did you pass the background check?"

"The judge said she would expunge my record if I graduated from college." Fortunately, the woman hadn't specified anything about his grades. "So I did and she did."

Sara was quiet again.

"I know it's bad." He laughed at the irony. "I guess in the scheme of things, it's not the worst thing you've heard about me today."

"You were lucky you got arrested."

"I guess."

"And I'm lucky that you got into the GBI, because I never would've met you otherwise."

"I'm sorry, Sara. I'm sorry I brought all this down on you. I don't—" He felt the words getting jumbled up in his mouth. "I don't want you to be scared of me. I don't want you to think that I'm anything like him."

"Of course you're not." She wrapped her hand around his. "Don't you know that I'm in awe of you?"

Will could only look at her.

"What you've been through. What you've endured. The man you've become." She placed his hand over her heart. "You chose to be a good person. You chose to help other people. It would've been so easy to go down the wrong path, but at every step, you chose to do the right thing."

"Not always."

"Often enough," she said. "Often enough so that when I look at you, all I can think about is how good you are. How much I want you—need you—in my life."

Her eyes were a clear green in the glow of the television. Will couldn't believe that she was still there beside him. Still wanted to be with him. Angie had been so wrong. There was no guile inside of Sara. No meanness. No spite.

If he were truly a good man, he would've told Sara about Angie. He would've confessed and gotten it over with. Instead, Will kissed her. He kissed her eyelids and her nose and her mouth. Their tongues touched. Will moved on top of her. Sara's leg wrapped around his. She deepened the kiss. Will felt the guilt slip away easily—too easily. All that he could think about was his desire, his need to be inside of her. He felt almost frantic as he started to undress her.

Sara helped him with her clothes. He ended up tearing the dress. She was wearing a lacy black bra that easily unclasped. Will kissed her breasts, used his tongue and teeth until she let out a deep moan. He traced his tongue down, biting and kissing the smooth skin. Sara gasped when he pulled down her underwear and pushed apart her legs. She tasted like honey and copper pennies. Her thigh rubbed against his face. Her fingernails dug into his scalp. She pulled him back up and started kissing him again. Sucking his tongue. Doing things with her mouth that made him start to shake. Will pushed himself inside of her. She moaned again. She gripped his back. Will forced himself to go slow. Sara took him in deeper with each thrust.

Her lips brushed his ear. "My love," she breathed. "My love."

twenty-one

July 15, 1975

LUCY BENNETT

The contractions started with the sunrise. He'd cut open her eyes, but not her mouth. Lucy could feel the thread tugging her lips as she groaned from the pain.

Her arms and legs were spread open, her body aligned straight down the center of the mattress. She had already ripped away her right shoulder. Just a few inches, but it was enough. The shock of being able to move had at first dulled the pain. Now, the flesh throbbed. Blood trickled down her arm and chest, pooled beneath her shoulder blade.

Another contraction started to build. Slow, slow, slow and then it erupted and Lucy felt her lips start to tear apart as she screamed in agony.

"Shut up," someone hissed.

The girl in the room next door.

She had spoken.

The floor creaked beneath her feet as she walked to the closed door.

"Shut up," she repeated.

The other girl had learned. She was compliant. She was welcoming. She talked to the man. Prayed with him. Screamed and thrashed and grunted with him. In a child's voice, she suggested he do things that Lucy had not even considered.

And for that, he let her off her leash sometimes.

Like now.

She was talking. Walking. Moving around.

She could leave at any time. Run to get help. Run to the police or her family or anywhere but here.

But she didn't. The other girl was a regular Patty Hearst.

Lucy's replacement.

twenty-two

July 15, 1975

Amanda sat in a back booth at the Majestic Diner on Ponce de Leon. She stifled a yawn. After leaving Techwood last night, she was too wired to asleep. Even Mary Wollstonecraft couldn't send her off. She'd tossed and turned, images of the construction paper puzzle seemingly burned into her retinas. She'd added the new details in her mind: Hank Bennett—liar. Trey Callahan—liar.

And Ophelia. What to make of Ophelia?

The waitress refilled Amanda's cup. She looked at her watch. Evelyn was fifteen minutes late, which was troubling. Amanda had never known her to be tardy. She'd used the pay phone in the back to call the Model City precinct, but no one had answered the phone. Amanda's own roll call had ended almost half an hour ago. She was assigned to Vanessa today, which suited them both. The other woman had decided to treat herself to a day of shopping. That new credit card was burning a hole in her pocketbook.

The door opened and Evelyn rushed in. "Sorry," she apologized. "I had the strangest call from Hodge."

"My Hodge?"

Evelyn waved away the waitress who came to take her order. "He had dispatch send me to Zone One."

"Did anyone see you?"

"No, the station was empty. It was just me and Hodge and his open door." She sat back against the booth. She was obviously flustered. "He wanted me to tell him everything we've been doing."

Amanda felt panic start to build.

"It's okay. He wasn't mad. At least, I don't think he was mad. Who knows with that man? You're absolutely right about his inscrutability. It's unnerving."

"Did he say anything?"

"Nothing. No criticisms. No comments. He just nodded and then told me to go do my job."

"That's the same thing he told me yesterday. To do my job." Amanda asked, "Do you think he was comparing our stories?"

"Could be."

"You didn't hold anything back?"

"Well, I kept Deena's name out of it. And Miss Lula's. I didn't want either of them getting into trouble."

"You told him about Ophelia?"

"No," she admitted. "I told him we were going to circle back on Trey Callahan, but I didn't tell him why. Luther Hodge doesn't strike me as a devotee of William Shakespeare."

"I don't know about that myself, Evelyn. Maybe we're leaping to conclusions. Trey Callahan quotes a line from Hamlet and then you and I see the victim last night and fill in the blanks. It smacks of too much coincidence."

"Is there really such a thing as coincidence in police work?"

Amanda couldn't answer her. "Do you think Hodge will make trouble for us?"

"Who the hell knows?" She threw her hands into the air. "We should get to the mission. Going over it with Hodge again made me think of some things."

Amanda slid out of the booth. She left two quarters on the table for the coffee and a generous tip. "Like what?"

"Like, everything." Evelyn waited until they were outside to speak. "This Hank Bennett situation. I think you're right. I think he's a snake in the grass, and he used the information he had about Kitty Treadwell to get a job with her father."

They got into Amanda's car. She asked, "How would Bennett know there was a relation?"

"Her name was on the apartment door," Evelyn reminded her. "Even without that, Kitty had a big mouth about her father. Miss Lula knew she was politically connected. Juice knew, too—he even mentioned another sister who was the golden child. It was an open secret on the street."

"But not higher up the social ladder," Amanda assumed. "Andrew Treadwell's a Georgia graduate. I remember reading that in the newspaper."

Evelyn smiled. "Hank Bennett was wearing a UGA class ring."

"Georgia Bulldogs, class of 1974." Once again, Amanda pulled out onto Ponce de Leon Avenue. "They could've met at a mixer or a social. All those frat boys are thick as thieves." She'd interviewed her share for the sex crimes unit. They lied like carpets.

"What's going on there?" Evelyn pointed at the Union Mission. An APD squad car blocked the entrance.

"I have no idea." Amanda pulled onto the sidewalk and got out of the car. She recognized the patrolman walking out of the building, though she didn't know his name. He obviously knew both Amanda and Evelyn. His pace quickened as he headed toward his car.

"Excuse me—" Amanda tried, but it was too late. The man got into his cruiser. Rubber squealed against asphalt as he peeled off.

"And the beat goes on," Evelyn said. She didn't seem too daunted as she headed toward the mission entrance. Instead of finding Trey Callahan, they saw a pudgy older man wearing a priest's collar. He was sweeping broken glass off the floor. The front window had been broken. A brick was among the shards.

"Yes?" he asked.

Evelyn took the lead. "We're with the Atlanta Police Department. We're looking for Trey Callahan."

The man seemed confused. "So am I."

Amanda gathered they'd missed something. "Callahan isn't here?"

"Who do you think caused this mess?" He indicated the broken glass. "Trey was supposed to open the shelter last night. He didn't show up, so one of the girls threw a brick through the window." He leaned against the broom. "I'm sorry, I've never dealt with the police before. Are you gals secretaries? The officer who just left said he would need a typed statement."

Amanda suppressed a groan. The officer had been giving him the runaround. "We're not secretaries. We're plainclothes—"

"Detectives," Evelyn interrupted, sounding very sure of herself. "And we don't type statements. What's your name, sir?"

"Father Bailey. I work at the soup kitchen down the street."

He didn't match the descriptions they'd been given. The priest was only a few inches taller than Amanda. "Are you the only one who works at the kitchen?"

"No, my associate does the cooking. Sometimes, I help with the cleaning, but my main duties are to provide spiritual support." He glanced at the clock on the wall. "I'm actually late, so if you girls—"

Evelyn interrupted, "If you work at the soup kitchen, why are you here?"

"I was supposed to meet with Trey this morning. We coordinate once a month, talk about the girls, who might be in trouble, who to look out for."

"And you pulled in and saw the broken window?"

"And a room full of girls sleeping away the morning when they should've been locked out of the building." He indicated the back of the room. "Trey's office has been rifled. Probably one of the girls."

"Did any of them see anything?"

"I hate to be uncharitable, but none of them are particularly helpful unless it directly benefits themselves."

Amanda remembered, "What about Callahan's girlfriend? She's training to be a nurse at Georgia Baptist."

He studied her for a moment. "Yes, I called over there looking for her. Eileen Sapperson. They say she missed her shift last night, too."

"Did the hospital have a home number for her?"

"She doesn't have a home line."

"Do you mind if we—" Amanda indicated Callahan's office. The priest shrugged. He resumed sweeping as they walked to the back of the room.

The office had clearly been tossed, but Amanda wasn't sure whether the perpetrator was a junkie looking for money or a man trying to quickly leave town. Callahan's desk was cleared of all his personal items. No framed photo of his dog and girlfriend. No Slinky. No funk posters. No transistor radio. There were a few joints smoked down to the last centimeter in the ashtray. The drawers hung open. Most important, the stack of typewriter pages was gone.

Evelyn noticed it, too. "Where's his manuscript?"

"I can't imagine a whore using it for anything but toilet paper."

"Callahan got out of here fast. He must've taken the girlfriend."

"On the same night Mary Halston was left dead at Techwood."

"Coincidence?"

Amanda didn't know anymore.

"Let's go talk to the guy at the soup kitchen."

"We can at least ask the priest his name." They walked back into the main room. The priest was gone.

"Hello?" Evelyn called, though they could see every corner of the room. Amanda followed her outside. The sidewalk was empty. No one was in the parking lot. They even checked behind the building. "Well, at least he didn't lie to us."

"That we know of." Amanda walked back toward the Plymouth. The inside of the car was already baking. She turned the key in the ignition. "I'm so sick and tired of being in this car."

"You never really see Columbo driving anywhere."

"I guess Ironside doesn't count."

"I'd like to see what Techwood Homes would make of a cripple in a bread truck."

Amanda pulled out onto the street. "Pepper Anderson just magically appears wherever she needs to be."

"One week, she's a nurse at the hospital. Next week, she's racing on a speedboat. Then she's a go-go dancer, then a flight attendant flirting with some dreamy pilot. Hey—"

"Shut up."

Evelyn chuckled as she leaned her arm on the door. They were both quiet as Amanda drove the few blocks up to Juniper Street.

She asked, "Left? Right?"

"Pick one."

Amanda turned left. She slowed the car, checking each building on the left as Evelyn scanned the right.

They were almost to Pine Street when Evelyn said, "That must be it."

The building was derelict, nothing to indicate it was a church except the large wooden cross stuck in the small patch of yard. It was painted black. Someone had thought to put nails where Jesus's hands and feet would've been. Little red dots of paint indicated His suffering.

"What a dump," Evelyn said.

She was right. The brick façade was crumbling. There were large vertical cracks in the mortar. Graffiti riddled the stoop, which was constructed of dry-stacked cinder blocks. Two of the four downstairs windows were boarded over, but the corresponding windows up top seemed intact.

They both got out of the car and headed toward the building. Amanda felt a breeze from a car passing in the street. It was an Atlanta

Police cruiser. The blue light flashed once in greeting, but the driver didn't stop.

The front door to the soup kitchen was open. Amanda smelled herbs and spices as soon as she crossed the threshold. Picnic tables filled the room. Plates and bowls were laid out. Napkins and spoons.

"No sharp objects," Evelyn noted.

"Probably wise." Amanda raised her voice. "Hello?"

"Just a minute," a gruff voice called from the back. They heard pots clattering. Heavy footsteps across the floor. The man came out of the kitchen. Amanda felt gripped by an unexpected fear. They'd learned at the academy that the average door was six feet eight inches high and thirty inches wide. It was a good gauge to estimate a person's height and weight. The man filled the kitchen doorway. His shoulders were almost as wide as the space between the jambs. His head nearly touched the top of the opening.

He smiled. His bottom tooth was crooked. His lips were full. "May I help you, Officers?"

Both of them stood frozen for a second. Amanda reached into her purse, found her badge. She showed it to the man, though he already knew they were cops. Amanda just wanted to say the words. "I'm Detective Wagner. This is Detective Mitchell."

"Please." He gestured to the table. "Have a seat."

He waited politely for them to sit, then took the bench across from them. Again, Amanda couldn't help but make comparisons. The man was almost as wide as both of them put together. Just the sight of his hands gripped together on the table was menacing. He could probably easily wrap his fingers around their necks.

Evelyn took out her notebook. She asked, "What's your name, sir?"

"James Ulster."

"Do you know Trey Callahan?"

He sighed. His voice was so deep that it came out as more of a growl. "Is this about the money he stole?"

"He stole money?" Amanda asked, though it was obvious he had.

"Father Bailey is more mindful of public relations than I am," Ulster explained. "One of the donors on the board noticed that some funds were missing. Trey was to be called to task first thing this morning. I gather he had other plans."

Amanda remembered the phone call Callahan had gotten yesterday when they were in his office. The man had said a donor was on the line. She asked, "They're certain it was Trey who was embezzling money?"

"I'm afraid so." Ulster rested his hands on either side of the bench. He was slumped down, probably out of habit. Such a large man would be accustomed to people feeling intimidated. Though, considering he ran a soup kitchen for Atlanta's huddled masses, his size was probably more of an advantage than not.

Amanda asked, "Do you have any idea where Callahan might have gone?"

Ulster shook his head. "I believe he has a fiancée."

They would have to go to Georgia Baptist next, though Amanda was fairly certain that was a dead end. "You're friends with Mr. Callahan?"

"Did he say that?"

Amanda lied. "He said that you were. Is that wrong?"

"We had theological discussions. We talked about many different things."

"Shakespeare?" Amanda asked. It was a stab in the dark, but it worked.

"Sometimes," Ulster admitted. "Many authors of the seventeenth century wrote in a coded language. It was not a time when subversives were rewarded."

"As in *Hamlet*?" Evelyn asked.

"That's not the best example, but—yes."

"What about Ophelia?"

Ulster's tone took a sharp edge. "She was a liar and a whore."

Amanda felt Evelyn stiffen beside her. She said, "You seem sure of that."

"I'm sorry, but I find the subject matter tiresome. Trey was obsessed with the story. You couldn't often have a conversation without him quoting some obscure line."

That seemed true enough. "Do you know why?"

"It's no secret that he was particularly interested in fallen women. Redemption. Salvation. I'm sure you were treated to one of his lectures on how all of these girls can be saved. He was quite adamant about it, and took it very personally when they failed." Ulster shook his head. "And of course, they do fail. They continually fail. It's in their nature."

Evelyn asked, "Did you ever see Trey acting inappropriately with the girls?"

"I wasn't often at the mission. My work is here. It wouldn't surprise me to learn that he availed himself. He stole money from a charitable organization. Why would he stop at exploiting fallen women?"

"Did you ever see him angry?"

"Not with my own eyes, but I heard that he had quite a temper. Some of the girls mentioned that he could be violent."

Amanda glanced down at Evelyn's notebook. She wasn't writing down any of this. Maybe she was thinking the same thing as Amanda. Trey Callahan was probably stoned out of his mind most of his waking hours. It was hard to imagine him experiencing anger, let alone acting on it. Of course, they hadn't pegged him for a thief, either.

Evelyn said, "Trey Callahan was writing a book."

"Yes." Ulster drew out the sibilant. "His opus. It wasn't very good."

"You read it?"

"A few pages. Callahan was more suited for the job he had than the job he wanted." He smiled at them. "So many people would better know peace if they just accepted the plans the Lord has for them."

Amanda got the feeling that Ulster was talking to them directly.

Evelyn must've felt the same. Her tone was curt when she asked, "What exactly do you do here, Mr. Ulster?"

"Well, we feed people, obviously. Breakfast is at six in the morning. The lunch hour begins at noon. You'll find the tables start to fill up well before then."

"Those are your only meals?"

"No, we provide dinner as well. That begins at five and is over promptly at seven."

"And then they leave?"

"Most do. Some of them stay the evening. There are twenty beds upstairs. A shower, though the hot water is not reliable. Women only, of course." He made to stand. "Shall I show you?"

"That's not necessary." Amanda didn't want to be trapped upstairs with the man. She asked, "Do you stay here at night?"

"No, there's no need for that. Father Bailey's parish is down the street. He comes by at eleven every evening to lock them in, then he lets them out at six every morning."

Amanda asked, "How long have you worked here?"

He thought it over. "It will be two years come fall."

"What did you do before that?"

"I was a foreman at the railroad yard."

Evelyn indicated the building. "You'll forgive me for saying, but I can't imagine the pay here is on par."

"No, it is not, and what little I make I try to give back."

"You don't get paid for working here—" Evelyn did the math quickly. "Thirteen hours a day?"

"As I said, I take what I need. But it's closer to sixteen hours a day. Seven days a week." He gave an open-handed shrug. "Why would I need earthly riches when my rewards will be in heaven?"

Evelyn shifted on the bench. She seemed as uncomfortable as Amanda felt. "Did you ever meet a working girl named Kitty Treadwell?"

"No." He stared at them blankly. "Not that I can recall, but we have many prostitutes here."

Amanda unzipped her purse and found the license. She showed him Kitty's photograph.

Ulster reached out for the paper. He was careful not to touch her hand. He studied the photograph, then his eyes shifted to the name and address. His lips moved silently, as if he was sounding out the words.

He finally said, "She looks markedly healthier in this photo. I suppose it was taken before she succumbed to the devil of her addiction."

Evelyn clarified, "So you knew Kitty?"

"Yes, if not by name."

"When's the last time you saw her?"

"A month ago? Maybe more."

That didn't make sense. Amanda laid out Lucy Bennett's license, then Mary Halston's. "How about these girls?"

He leaned over the table and studied them one by one. He took his time. Again, his lips moved as he read the names. Amanda listened to his breathing, the steady inhale and exhale. She could see the top of his head. Dandruff dotted his light brown hair.

"Yes." He looked up. "This girl. She was here a few times, but she favored the mission. I expect because she had a thing with Trey." He was pointing to Mary Halston, the murder victim from last night. "This girl." He pointed to Lucy. "I'm not sure about her. They both look very similar. They are both obviously drug addicts. It is the scourge of our generation."

Evelyn verified, "You recognize Lucy Bennett and Mary Halston as girls who've used this soup kitchen?"

"I believe so."

Evelyn was writing now. "And Mary was a favorite of Trey Callahan's?"

"That's correct."

"When's the last time you saw either Lucy or Mary?"

"A few weeks ago? Maybe a month?" Again, he studied the photos. "They both look very healthy in these photographs." He looked back up, first at Evelyn, then Amanda. "You are both police officers, so I assume you are more accustomed to the ravages of drug abuse. These girls. These poor girls." He sadly shook his head. "Drugs are a poison, and I do not know why our Lord caused it to be, but there is a certain type who succumbs to this temptation. They tremble before the drug when they should be trembling before the Lord."

His voice resonated in the open room. Amanda could imagine him holding forth from the pulpit. Or the streets. "There's a pimp whose street name is Juice."

"I am familiar with that sinner."

"He says you sometimes preach to the girls when they're working?"

"I do the Lord's work, no matter the danger."

Amanda didn't imagine he felt much danger, considering no sane person would be happy to run into a man as large as James Ulster in a dark alley. "Have you ever been to Techwood Homes?"

"On many occasions," he answered. "I deliver soup to the shut-ins. Techwood is Mondays and Fridays. Grady Homes is Tuesdays and Thursdays. There is another kitchen that services Perry Homes, Washington Heights—"

"Thank you," Evelyn interrupted, "but we're just concerned with Techwood."

"I've heard that there have been some awful things happening there." He gripped his hands together. "It tries the soul to see how those people live. But I suppose we all shuffle off the same mortal coil."

Amanda felt her heart stop mid-beat. "Trey Callahan used that same phrase with us. It's from Shakespeare."

"Is it?" he asked. "Perhaps I picked up his manner of speaking. As I said, he was incessant on the topic."

"Do you remember a working girl named Jane Delray?"

"No. Is she in trouble?"

"How about Hank Bennett? Have you ever met him?" Evelyn waited, but Ulster shook his head. "He's got hair about your color. Around six feet tall. Very well dressed."

"No, sister, I'm afraid I do not."

The radio in Evelyn's purse clicked. There was a muffled call, followed by a series of clicks. Evelyn reached into the bag to turn down the sound, but then stopped when her name came through the speaker.

"Mitchell?" Amanda recognized Butch Bonnie's voice.

"Excuse me," she said, taking out the radio. "Mitchell, ten-four."

Butch ordered, "Twenty-five me your location. Now."

There were more clicks on the radio—a collective response of laughter. Butch was telling them both to meet him outside.

Evelyn told Ulster, "Thank you for speaking with us. I hope you won't mind if we call with any questions?"

"Of course not. Shall I give you my telephone number?"

Her pen nearly disappeared in Ulster's left hand. He gripped it in his fist, not between his thumb and index finger, as he wrote down the seven digits. Above this, he carefully wrote his name. It was more like a child's scrawl. The ballpoint tore through the paper on the last letter.

"Thank you," Evelyn said. She was visibly reluctant to take back the pen. She slid on the cap and closed her notebook. Ulster stood when they did. He offered his hand to each of them. They were all sweating in the heat, but there was something particularly clammy about Ulster's skin. He held their hands delicately, but for Amanda's part, it only served to remind her that he could crush the bones if he so chose.

Evelyn's breathing was shallow as they walked toward the door. "Jesus," she whispered. As relieved as they both were to be away from Ulster, the sight of Butch Bonnie almost sent Amanda back inside. He was obviously livid.

"What the fuck are you two doing?" He grabbed Evelyn by the arm and dragged her down the cinder-block stairs.

Amanda said, "Don't you—"

"Shut your face!" He pushed Amanda against the wall. His fist reared back, but stopped short of punching her. "How many times do you have to be told?" he demanded. "Both of you!" He stepped back. His feet scuffed across the sidewalk. "Jesus Christ."

Amanda pressed her hand to her chest. She could feel her heart punching against her rib cage. And then she saw that Evelyn had fallen. She ran to help her up.

"No." Evelyn stood up on her own. She slammed both hands into Butch's chest.

"What the—" He stumbled back.

She slammed him again. Then again, until he was up against the wall. "If you ever touch me like that again, I will shoot you in the face. Do you hear me?"

Butch looked dumbstruck. "What the hell's gotten into you?"

Evelyn paced back and forth. She was like a caged animal. "I am so sick of you assholes."

"Me?" Butch took out his cigarettes. "Whadabout you broads? How many times you gotta be told to leave this be?" He dug his finger into the pack. "I tried to be nice. I tried to warn you easy. And then I hear you're snooping around my CI. Making trouble. Mr. Nice Guy ain't workin'. What else am I supposed to do?"

"Who's your CI?"

"None of your goddamn business."

Evelyn slapped away the cigarettes. She was so gripped by anger she had trouble speaking. "You know that dead woman is Jane Delray."

His eyes cut to the side. "I don't know shit."

"Who told you to say it was Lucy Bennett?"

"Ain't nobody tellin' me to do nothin'."

Evelyn wouldn't give up. "Juice didn't kill Lucy Bennett."

"You best be careful pining after some nigger in jail." He gave her a condescending look as he picked up his Marlboros. "Jesus, Ev. Why you comin' off like some kind of bull dyke?" He looked to Amanda for help. "Come on, Wag. Talk some sense into Annie Oakley here."

Amanda tasted bile in her throat. She threw out the filthiest thing she could think of. "You motherfucker."

He barked a shocked laugh. "You're motherfuckerin' me?" He fished in his pocket for his lighter. "You wanna know who's mother-fucked?" He lit the cigarette. "You're fucked"—he nodded toward Amanda—"for going to the jail yesterday, and you"—he pointed to Evelyn—"are fucked for putting her up to all this."

"Putting me up to what?" Amanda demanded. "She's not my keeper."

He hissed out a stream of smoke. "You're both gonna be transferred tomorrow. I hope you still got your white gloves for crossing duty."

"I hope you're up for a sex discrimination lawsuit," Evelyn shot back. "You and Landry both."

Smoke snorted out from his nostrils. "You ditzy bitches throw that around all the time, but you know what? Ain't a one'a you done it yet. Keep cryin' wolf while you're directing traffic." He waved to them over his shoulder as he walked away.

Evelyn stood watching him, her fists clenching and unclenching. For just a moment, Amanda thought she might chase after Butch and jump on his back. Amanda wasn't sure what she would do if this happened. Her fingernails were short but strong. She could probably scratch his eyes. Failing that, she would bite off anything she could get between her teeth.

"I am so sick of this." Evelyn started pacing again. "I am sick of taking bullshit from them. I am sick of being lied to." She kicked the Plymouth's tire. "I'm sick of not getting a car. I'm sick of people thinking I'm some kind of fucking secretary." She gripped her purse. "Why didn't I shoot him? God, I wanted to shoot him."

"We can do it now." Amanda had never been so ready to do anything in her life. "We'll go find him and do it right now."

Evelyn hefted her purse over her shoulder. She crossed her arms. "I'm not going to prison for that—" She stopped. "What did you call him? Motherfucker?" She gave a surprised laugh. "I didn't know you even knew that word."

Amanda realized her hands were clenched, too. She stretched out her fingers one by one. "I suppose this is what happens when you hang around pimps and whores."

"Crossing guard duty." Evelyn disgustedly huffed out the words. "It's summer. We'll be stuck with all the stupid kids who couldn't hack it during the regular year."

Amanda opened the car door. "Let's go to Georgia Baptist and see if we can find Trey Callahan's fiancée."

"Are you kidding me? You heard what Butch said."

"That's tomorrow. Let's just worry about today."

Evelyn walked around to the other side of the car. "And then what, Scarlett O'Hara?"

"And then we go to Techwood and see if Miss Lula found someone who remembered seeing Hank Bennett." Amanda turned over the ignition. "And then ask her if she's ever seen a giant weird man delivering soup to shut-ins."

Evelyn clutched her purse in her lap. "Ulster admitted that he's in and out of Techwood Homes. Mondays and Fridays. The same days our victims showed up."

"He lied to us." Amanda pulled out onto the street. "How could he read Trey Callahan's manuscript if he can barely read the name on a license?"

"You noticed that, too?" Evelyn said, "He didn't sound retarded."

"Maybe he's just a slow reader."

"Butch said we were messing with his CI. Do you think that's Ulster? Father Bailey? I wonder where that weasel scurried off to. Locking those girls in at night. It's a regular Triangle Shirtwaist Factory. Have you ever?"

"Ulster seemed pretty eager to put Trey Callahan in the frame for all this. The Ophelia line. That bit about his temper."

"You clocked that, too?" Evelyn rested her elbow on the door. "I know we're all Christians here, but I don't like the way Ulster uses it. Like it makes him better than everyone else. Did you pick up on that?"

Amanda was only certain of one thing. "I think James Ulster is the scariest man I've ever met in my life. There's something evil about him."

"Exactly," Evelyn agreed. "Did you see how big his hands are?"

Amanda felt a shudder working its way up her spine.

Evelyn said, "Someone higher up is working against us."

"I know," Amanda mumbled.

"Butch is connected, but not enough to get us transferred. It has to be somebody who knew you were talking to Juice at the jail yesterday. Who knew we were talking to Ulster today. And Father Bailey. And Trey Callahan. Or, maybe I stirred up something checking the DNFs." She chewed her lip. "Whatever we did, it pissed off someone enough to get us yanked off the street and tied to crossing duty."

"I know," Amanda repeated. She waited for Evelyn to say more, but the woman had probably jumped to the same conclusion as Amanda. Duke Wagner wasn't officially back in uniform, but he was already pulling strings.

Amanda looked at her watch. Eight-fifteen in the evening. Nighttime brought no relief from the summer heat. If anything, it gave the humidity reason to come out and play. Amanda felt as if her sweat was sweating. Mosquitoes circled her head as she stood in front of the phone booth on the corner of Juniper and Pine. She left the door open so that the light would not come on. The dime felt greasy between her fingers. Amanda dropped the coin into the slot, then slowly dialed her father's number.

She'd left Duke's house fifteen minutes ago. Amanda had cooked his supper. She'd listened with half an ear as he'd relayed the day's news, delivered the latest updates on his case. It was just a matter of time before Duke was back at his old post. Just a matter of time before Amanda was back under his thumb. She had only nodded—nodded as she watched him eat, nodded as she washed the dishes. An overwhelming sadness had taken hold. Every time she opened her mouth to speak, she shut it for fear of crying.

Duke picked up the telephone on the first ring. His voice was gravelly, probably from too many after-dinner cigarettes. "Hello?"

"Daddy, it's me."

"You home?"

"No, Daddy."

He waited, then asked, "Car break down?"

"No, sir."

She heard his recliner squeak. "What is it? I know something's bothering you. You were sulking all night."

Amanda caught her reflection in the chrome of the pay phone. She was twenty-five years old. She had touched a dead person last weekend. She had stared down a pimp yesterday morning. Helped examine a dead girl last night. She had stood up to Butch Bonnie in the street. She should be able to have a frank conversation with her father.

She asked, "Why did you have me transferred to crossing guard duty?"

"What?" He seemed genuinely surprised. "I didn't transfer you. Who the hell transferred you?" She could hear papers rustling, a pen clicking. "Give me the jackass's name. I'll talk to him about a transfer."

"You didn't do it?"

"Why would I transfer you out when I'm gonna be back at my old squad in less than a month?"

He was right. What's more, if Duke was displeased with someone, he generally told them to their face. "I'm on crossing duty, starting tomorrow." She'd already called dispatch to verify it was true. "Along with Evelyn Mitchell."

"Mitchell?" His tone changed. "What're you doing with that pushy broad? I told you to stay away from her."

"I know you did, but we're working a case together."

He grunted. "What kind of case?"

"Two girls have been murdered." She added, "White girls. They lived at Techwood Homes."

"Whores, I guess?"

"Yes, they were."

He was silent, obviously thinking. "This have something to do with that nigger got charged for killing a white girl?"

"Yes, sir."

She heard the flick of his lighter, a huff of air as he exhaled. "That why you were at the jail yesterday morning?"

Amanda couldn't swallow past the lump in her throat. She saw her life starting to disappear before her eyes. Her apartment. Her job. Her freedom.

Duke said, "Heard you stared that coon down. Locked yourself in a room with him."

Amanda didn't answer. Hearing Duke say the words made her realize how crazy she had been. How stupid. She was lucky she'd escaped with her life.

Duke asked, "Were you scared?"

She knew he would see through a lie. "I was terrified."

"But you didn't let him see it."

"No, sir."

She heard him take another long drag on his cigarette. "I guess you think you're going to be out late tonight?"

"I—" Amanda didn't know what to say. She glanced down the street. The moon was almost full in the sky. The black wooden cross cast a shadow across the sidewalk in front of the soup kitchen. "We're staking out a possible suspect."

"We?"

She let the question go unanswered.

"What evidence do you got?"

"Nothing," she admitted. "Just—" She searched for a better explanation, but could only come up with, "Women's intuition."

"Don't call it that," he ordered. "Call it a hunch. You feel it in your gut, not between your legs."

Amanda didn't know what to say other than, "All right."

He coughed a few times. "That's Rick Landry's case you're poking around, right?"

"Yes, sir."

"I wouldn't trust that idiot to find his asshole in a snowstorm." His chuckle turned into a sharp cough. "If you're out late, you'll need your sleep. I'll get myself breakfast tomorrow morning."

The phone clicked in her ear. Amanda stared at the receiver as if the plastic mouthpiece could explain to her what had just happened. She didn't look up until a pair of headlights flashed for her attention.

Evelyn's Falcon station wagon smelled of candy and cheap wine. She smiled as Amanda settled into the passenger's seat. "You okay?"

"Just puzzled." She told Evelyn about the phone call with her father.

"Well." Evelyn sounded circumspect. "Do you think he's telling the truth?"

"Yes." Duke was a lot of things, but he was not a liar.

"Then he must be telling the truth."

Amanda knew that Evelyn would never trust Duke. She could understand why. As far as the other woman was concerned, he was cut from the same cloth as Rick Landry and Butch Bonnie. And maybe he was, but he was still Amanda's father.

Evelyn stared down the street at the soup kitchen. "Is Ulster even in there?"

"He's cleaning up." Amanda had walked by earlier and seen James Ulster lifting a large soup pot off the table. His back was to her, but she'd still quickened her step. "There's a green van parked behind the building. I called in the license plate—it's registered to the church. There were some religious tracts in the front seat, a Bible on the dash. It has wooden crates in the back, a bunch of ropes. I guess he uses them to keep the food from spilling."

"Delivering food to the needy. That sounds like a serial killer to me."

"Surely you can think of one?"

Evelyn wasn't up for teasing. "Driving over here, part of me felt like I was going to my own funeral." She crossed her arms low on her waist. "Our last day on the job, or at least our real job. The job we want to do. I don't think I can fit into my crossing guard uniform anymore. I thought that thing was retired."

Amanda didn't want to talk about it. "Did you call Georgia Baptist?"

"Callahan's fiancée is named Eileen Sapperson so at least we were told the truth about that. She didn't show up for work this morning. No home phone number. No address. Another Doug Henning magical disappearance."

"Another dead end," Amanda noted. Miss Lula hadn't been able to find anyone at Techwood who remembered seeing a man fitting Hank Bennett's description, and while plenty of people knew the hulking Mr. Ulster, none of them had ever seen him cause trouble. It was hard to make enemies of people to whom you were bringing a hot meal.

Evelyn said, "James Ulster is at Techwood every Monday and Friday, the same days the victims were found."

"He's in and out so much that no one would notice him," Amanda added. "He knew Kitty, at least. He knew enough about Mary Halston to say that Trey had a thing for her. He probably knew Lucy Bennett, too."

"He's the only one who puts the girls as alive recently. Jane Delray, Hank Bennett, Trey Callahan, Juice—they all say the three girls have been gone at least a year."

"Maybe Ulster is Butch's CI. He could've said Lucy Bennett was dead so her brother would stop looking for her."

"Was he really looking for her?" Evelyn asked. "As far as we know, he stopped when he found Kitty. And none of this explains why Hodge sent us out in the first place. Or who transferred us if it wasn't your father. Any of it."

Amanda couldn't bear the thought of spinning it all around again. No matter how many times they talked it through, the construction paper puzzle would likely never be solved. Evelyn had her family to go home to. Amanda had her schoolwork, a major paper to write. They had never really been assigned this case, and tomorrow, their authority would be no greater than that conferred upon them by screaming school-aged adolescents.

Evelyn said, "I was thinking—what would happen if I really did file a sexual discrimination suit?" She rested her hand on the steering wheel. "What would they do? The law is on my side. Butch is right.

We can't keep threatening it without following through. It's lost its teeth."

"You'd never get promoted again. They'd stick you at the airport, which is only marginally more humiliating than crossing duty." Amanda felt the need to tell her, "But I would testify for you. I saw what Rick did. And Butch. They had no right to do that."

"Oh, Mandy, you're such a good friend." She reached out and grabbed Amanda's hand. "You've made this stupid job almost bearable."

Amanda looked down at their hands. Evelyn's were so much more elegant than her own. "You've never called me Mandy before."

"You don't really seem like one."

Amanda didn't feel like one anymore. Did a Mandy go into a jailhouse and rattle a pimp? Did a Mandy stand up to bullies and call them nasty names?

Evelyn said, "You know, I was so scared of you when Hodge first sent us on that call."

Amanda didn't have to ask why. If this week had taught her anything, it was that the Wagner name was not the asset she once believed.

Evelyn said, "But you turned out to be so swell. If there's anything good that came out of this, it's our friendship."

Amanda had been fighting weepiness all night. She could only nod.

Evelyn squeezed her hand before letting go. "I don't have many friends. Any friends, really."

"I find that hard to believe."

"Oh, I used to have lots of them." She twisted her fingers into her hair. "Bill and I would go to parties every weekend. Two or three. Sometimes four." She let out a long sigh. "Everyone thought it was a gas when I joined the force, but then they saw I wasn't going to quit and suddenly there was nothing we could talk about. I didn't want to swap recipes or plan bake sales. They couldn't understand why I would want to do a man's job. You should hear my mother-in-law on the subject." She laughed ruefully. "This job changes you. It changes how you think, how you see the world. I don't care what the boys say. We *are* cops. We live it and breathe it as much as they do."

"You don't see Butch and Landry out here right now."

"No, they're probably home with their families."

Amanda doubted that. "Their mistresses, more likely."

"Hey, that's him." They saw Ulster locking the front door of the building. The darkness did him no favors. He was a hulking man. Amanda could not imagine anyone putting up much of a struggle against such raw power.

He glanced up the street. Both Amanda and Evelyn ducked, but Ulster didn't seem to notice the red station wagon, or if he did, he didn't think much of it. In retrospect, the car—with its children's toys in the back and crayons melted into the carpet—was the perfect cover.

Amanda held her breath as she waited for Ulster to reappear. It felt like hours but was only minutes before Evelyn finally said, "Here he comes."

The green van turned onto Juniper. They stayed hunched down as it passed. Evelyn cranked the key. The engine sputtered, then caught. She pushed the knob to make sure the headlights were off, then swung the nose out into the street and smoothly entered the opposite lane.

"You're getting better at this," Amanda said.

"Last hurrah," she muttered.

There were no streetlights on Juniper. The moon was enough to drive by, and where she couldn't see, Evelyn coasted her way through.

Ulster took a left onto Piedmont Avenue. He drove deep into Bedford Pine. The stench of Buttermilk Bottom filled the car, but they kept the windows down.

"Where is he going?" Evelyn asked.

Amanda shook her head. She had no idea.

The van braked at the last minute, taking a sharp turn onto Ralph McGill. Amanda directed, "Cut over to Courtland."

Evelyn had to reverse to make the turn. "Do you think he spotted us?"

"I don't know." Their headlights were still off. The car's interior was dark. "Maybe he's just being careful."

"Why would he be careful?" Evelyn sucked in her breath. The green van was up ahead. "There he is."

They followed the van up Courtland. The road was a straight shot. Evelyn hung back at least a hundred yards. When the van turned onto Pine, the lights from Crawford Long Hospital illuminated the interior. They saw Ulster's unmistakable frame. Evelyn slowed, peering down the street before making the turn to follow him. The lights from the expressway made the going more difficult. He turned onto Spring Street.

"Evelyn," Amanda said.

"I know." She followed him up North Avenue. Past the Varsity. Over the expressway. He was going to Techwood. "Get my radio."

Amanda found Evelyn's purse on the back seat. The revolver was cold in her hands. She passed this to Evelyn, who kept one hand on the wheel as she slid the gun underneath her leg.

Amanda clicked the radio. "Dispatch?"

There was no answer.

"Dispatch, this is unit sixteen. Over?"

The radio clicked. "Unit twenty-three to unit sixteen," a man's voice said. "You gals need some help?"

Amanda gripped the radio in her hand. She had called for dispatch, not some hillbilly out on patrol.

"Copy sixteen?" the man asked. "What's your locale?"

Amanda spoke through gritted teeth. "Techwood Homes."

"Repeat, please."

Amanda enunciated the words. "Tech. Wood. Homes."

"Copy that. Perry Homes."

"Jesus," Evelyn hissed. "He thinks this is a joke."

Amanda clutched the radio as hard as she could, wanting to break it over the man's head. She put her finger to the button, but couldn't bring herself to press it.

"Amanda," Evelyn mumbled. Her voice had a tone of warning.

Up ahead, the green van didn't slow to turn on Techwood Drive. Instead, it continued straight, going into the heart of the ghetto.

"This isn't good," Evelyn said. "There's no reason for him to be here."

Amanda didn't bother to vocalize her agreement. They were in a part of town that no one—black, white, cop, or criminal—willingly entered after dark.

The van turned again. Evelyn slowed, nosing into the turn, making sure they weren't sitting ducks. Just ahead, they saw the van's taillights glowing softly. Ulster obviously knew where he was going. His pace was slow and deliberate.

Amanda tried the radio again. "Dispatch, sixteen going north on Cherry."

The man in unit twenty-three answered. "What's that, sixteen? You wanna gimme your cherry?"

There was more clicking as the radio was jammed.

Dispatch cut through the chatter. "Ten-thirty-four, all units. Sixteen, repeat your ten-twenty."

Evelyn said, "That's Rachel Foster." The women in dispatch were the only ones who could override the nonsense. Evelyn grabbed the radio. "Sixteen heading north on Cherry. Possible thirty-four on a green Dodge van. Georgia license plate—" She squinted at the van. "Charlie, Victor, William, eight-eight-eight."

Rachel said, "Verify ten-twenty, unit sixteen?"

Amanda took the radio so Evelyn could return both hands to the wheel. "Verify Cherry Street, Dispatch. Heading north."

"Are you kidding me?" Rachel's tone was terse. She knew the streets better than most cops on the road. "Sixteen?"

The car was silent. They both stared at the green van heading deep into the ghetto. Was Ulster leading them into a trap?

"Sixteen?" Rachel repeated.

Amanda said, "Verify heading North on Cherry."

Static filled the seconds. Rachel said, "Give me five minutes. Hold your location. Repeat, hold."

Amanda put the radio in her lap. Evelyn kept driving.

Amanda asked, "Why did you report the van as possibly stolen?"

"All we need is whoever that cowboy is on unit twenty-three rushing in here with lights and sirens."

"Maybe that wouldn't be such a bad thing." Amanda had never been in this part of town. She doubted any white woman ever had. There were no street signs. No lights on inside the houses that dotted either side of the street. Even the moon seemed to glow less brightly here.

The van took another left. The air felt too thick. Amanda had to breathe through her mouth. The street was lined with junker cars on both sides. If Evelyn followed Ulster, there would be no way to hide the station wagon from him. In the end, they didn't need to. The van's brake lights flashed as he slowed down and turned into the driveway of a clapboard house. As with the others, there were no lights on inside. Electricity was a luxury in this part of town.

"Are they abandoned?" Evelyn asked, meaning the houses. Some of them were boarded up. Others were so dilapidated that the roofs had caved in.

"I can't tell."

They both sat in the car. Ulster got out of the van and entered the house. Neither woman knew what to do. They couldn't very well kick down the door and go in guns blazing.

Amanda said, "Rachel should've radioed back by now."

Evelyn kept her hands gripped around the steering wheel. They both stared at Ulster's house. A light came on in one of the back rooms. It cut a sliver of white across the front of the green van parked in the driveway.

Evelyn's voice was little more than a whisper. "Would you think I was a coward if I said we should call in unit twenty-three?"

Amanda had been wondering how to ask the same question. "He could tell Ulster the van was reported stolen."

"And ask to look around inside the house."

And get shot in the face. Or chest. Or punched. Or stabbed. Or beaten.

"Do it," Evelyn said.

Amanda pressed the button on the radio. "Twenty-three?" There was only static. Even the clicks were gone. "Dispatch?"

"Shit," Evelyn cursed. "We're probably in a pocket." There were dead spots all over the city. Evelyn put the car in reverse. "It was working the last block over. We can—"

A scream pierced the air. It was feral, terror inducing. Something inside of Amanda recoiled. Her body broke out in a cold sweat. Every muscle tensed. The sound triggered a primitive urge to flee.

"My God," Evelyn gasped. "Was that an animal?"

Amanda could still hear the sound echoing in her ears. She'd never heard anything so terrifying in her life.

Suddenly, the radio came to life. "Sixteen? Twenty-three here. You foxes reconsider my offer?"

"Thank God," Evelyn whispered. She pressed the button, but didn't have time to speak.

The second scream was like a knife cutting straight through Amanda's heart. It wasn't an animal. It was the desperate cry of a woman begging for help.

The radio crackled. "Sixteen, what the hell was that?"

Amanda's purse was on the floorboard. She reached inside and pulled out her revolver. She grabbed the door handle.

Evelyn's foot slipped off the brake. "What are you doing?"

"Stop the car." It was rolling back. "Stop the car."

"Amanda, you can't—"

The woman screamed again.

Amanda pushed open the door. She stumbled as she got out of the car. Her knee dug into the asphalt. Her hose ripped. She couldn't stop herself. Wouldn't stop herself. "Get twenty-three. Get everybody you can." Evelyn yelled for her to wait, but Amanda kicked off her shoes and started running.

The woman screamed again. She was in the house. Ulster's house.

Amanda tightened her grip on the revolver as she ran down the street. Her arms pumped. Her vision tunneled. She slipped as she rounded into Ulster's driveway. Her hose bunched up at the balls of her feet. She slowed. The front door was shut. The only light was toward the back of the house.

Amanda tried to quiet her breathing, keeping her mouth open, taking in gulps of air. She squeezed past the van. She crouched down low, though no one could see her. The house blocked the moonlight, painting everything in shadow. She pointed her revolver straight ahead, finger on the trigger, not on the side like they had taught her, because she was going to shoot anybody who walked into her path.

The scream came again. It wasn't as loud this time, but it was more desperate. More frightened.

Amanda steeled herself as she approached the open window. The light was coming through a pair of heavy black curtains. She could hear the woman moaning with each breath. Almost mewing. Carefully, Amanda peered through the part in the curtains. She saw an old washstand. A sink. A bed. The woman was there. Sitting up. Blonde hair streaked red. Emaciated but for her distended belly. The skin on her arms and shoulders was a bloody pulp. Her lips and eyelids were torn where she'd ripped them open. Blood coated every inch of her skin—her face, her throat, her chest.

The girl screamed again, but not before Amanda heard something behind her.

A shoe scuffing on concrete.

Amanda started to turn, but a large hand grabbed her from behind.

twenty-three

July 15, 1975

LUCY BENNETT

Her shoulders were free, but she did not care.

Her arms were free, but she did not care.

Her waist, her hips—free for the first time in over a year.

But she did not care.

Could not care.

There was only the baby delivered from her body. The beautiful little boy. Ten fingers. Ten toes. Perfect blond hair. Perfect little mouth.

Lucy ran her finger along his lips. The first woman to touch him. The first woman to open her heart and feel the absolute joy that was this creature.

She wiped the slime from his nose and mouth. She lightly rested her palm on his chest and felt his beating heart. Flutter, flutter, like a butterfly. He was so beautiful. So tiny. How had something so perfect grown inside of her? How had something so sweet come out of something so utterly spoiled?

"You're dying."

Lucy felt her senses sharpen.

Patty Hearst.

The second girl. The other woman from the other room.

She stood in the doorway, afraid to come in. She was dressed. He let her wear clothes. He let her walk around. He let her do anything but come into Lucy's room. Even now, both of them alone, her toes would not cross the threshold.

"You're dying," the woman repeated.

They both heard the noises outside the window. Yelling. Gunfire. He would win. He would always win.

The baby cooed, legs kicking up.

Lucy looked down at her child. Her perfect baby. Her redemption. Her salvation. Her one good thing.

She tried to concentrate on his beautiful face, the light flowing back and forth between their bodies.

Nothing else mattered. Not the pain. Not the smell. Not the wheezing breaths coming from her own mouth.

Not the sucking of wind around the large knife sticking out of her chest.

twenty-four

Present Day

WEDNESDAY

Sara woke to the smell of Betty's hot breath. The dog was curled on the couch in front of her, body twisted, snout inches from Sara's face. Sara rolled the little thing over like a baker making bread. Betty's collar tinkled. She yawned.

Will's clothes were on the floor, but he wasn't in the room. Sara put her hand to her face. Touched her lips where Will had touched them. Stroked her throat. Her mouth felt bruised from his kisses. Her skin tingled at the thought of him.

She was in it now. Maybe it had happened back when Will was washing dishes in her mother's kitchen. Or that day at work when Sara had felt completely inconsolable until he gently caressed her hand. Or last night when he had stared at her so intently that she felt as if everything inside her was opening up to him.

No matter when it had happened, the possibility had been rendered fact. Sara was deeply and profoundly in love with Will Trent. There was no walking back from it. No denying it. Her heart had made the decision while her brain was making excuses. She knew it the minute she saw him last night. Sara would do anything to keep him. Accept his secrets. Tolerate his silences. Put up with his awful wife.

Help send his father to death row.

Pete Hanson would be dead by the time the case went to trial. Sara would be called to testify. It would be a capital case. The girl had been kidnapped and murdered, the combination of which met Georgia's legal requirement for seeking the death penalty.

Will's father had meticulously cleaned Ashleigh Snyder, but the man had been behind bars for the last three decades. Television and prison science would've educated him on the forensic progress happening outside his cellblock, but it was highly unlikely that he'd ever heard of hair extensions. Which was ironic, considering the killer's predilection for needle and thread.

The process of weaving hair took hours. A thin cornrow, or "track," was braided in a tight half circle around the back of the head. Then a needle and thread were used to sew in patches of new, longer, fuller hair. Several more rows were added one at a time, depending on how much money and time the woman was willing to spend. It wasn't cheap. The natural hair eventually grew out. The weave had to be tightened every two weeks. More stitches were added each time. Simple shampooing couldn't clean out all the nooks and crevices between the old hair and new.

This was where Sara had recovered traces of semen—tiny dried specks trapped between thin strings of thread. She would eventually have to walk the jury through her discovery, describe the weaving technique and explain why the proteins in seminal fluid fluoresce under black light.

And then the judge would likely hand down a sentence of death by lethal injection.

Sara let out a heavy sigh. She looked at the clock. Six-thirty in the morning. She was supposed to be at work by eight. She found Will's shirt and put it on, buttoning it as she walked into the kitchen.

He was standing at the stove making pancakes. He smiled at her. "Hungry?"

"Very." Sara kissed the back of his neck. His skin was warm. She resisted the urge to wrap her arms around him and declare her love. Will's life was complicated enough right now without Sara putting him on the spot. Telling someone you loved them was tantamount to asking them to repeat the words back.

Will said, "Sorry I don't have any coffee."

Sara sat down at the table. Will didn't drink coffee. He drank hot chocolate every morning, and because that wasn't enough sugar, he usually complemented his beverage with a Pop-Tart. "I'll get some later."

He offered, "I can make eggs if you want."

"No, thank you." Sara rubbed her face with her hands. Her brain wasn't awake yet, but she could tell that there was something wrong. Will was already dressed for work in a navy suit and tie. His jacket was draped over the kitchen chair. His hair was combed. His face was freshly shaven. He seemed happy, which wasn't that unusual, but he was too happy. Too bouncy. He couldn't stand still. His foot tapped as he stood at the stove. When he slid the pancakes onto a plate, his fingers drummed on the counter.

Sara had seen this kind of attitude before. It usually came when someone had made up their mind. The pressure was off. The decision was made. They were all in. Ready to get it over with.

"Madam." He put the plate in front of her.

She smelled it then—oil and cordite. On his hands. On the table.

"Thanks." Sara stood from the chair. She washed her hands at the sink. The smell was stronger now that she was awake and thinking. Will had cleaned up after himself, but not well enough. She wiped her hands with a paper towel. When she opened the cabinet for the trash, she saw the dirty cleaning patches.

Sara closed the cabinet door. She'd grown up around guns. She knew the smell of cleaning oil. She knew Will kept a backup weapon in his safe. She knew the look of a man who'd made up his mind.

She turned around.

Will was sitting at the table, fork in his hand. His plate was dripping with syrup. He talked around a mouthful of pancakes. "I got your gym bag out of the car." He used the fork to point to the bag on the floor. "Sorry about tearing your dress."

She leaned against the sink. "You're working at the airport today?"

He nodded. "Mind if I borrow your car? Mine's acting up."

"Sure." They would be looking for Will's car around the hotel. Sara's BMW was practically nondescript in that part of town.

"Thanks." He shoved another forkful of pancakes into his mouth.

She said, "Let's call in sick today."

His chewing slowed. He met her gaze.

"I want us to go away together," she said. "My cousin has a house on the Gulf we can use. Let's just get out of here. Leave town."

He swallowed. "That sounds nice."

"We can take the dogs and run on the beach every morning." She wrapped her arms around her waist. "And then we can go back to bed. And then we can eat lunch. And then we can go back to bed."

He gave her a forced grin. "That sounds really nice."

"Then let's do it. Right now."

"Okay," he agreed. "I'll drop you off at your place, then go run some errands."

Sara stopped pretending. "I'm not going to let you do it."

Will sat back in his chair. The nervous energy was gone. She watched it slowly leave his body. Now there was only the grief and sorrow that had broken her heart the day before.

"Will—"

He cleared his throat. The sound turned into a cough. His throat worked as he fought back tears. "She was just a student."

Sara bit her lip.

"She was walking to class one night, and he saw her, and he took her, and that was it. Her life was over." He put down his fork. "You know what was done to her. You saw the girl yesterday. He did the same thing to both of them."

Will's cell rang. He grabbed the phone out of his pocket. "Did you arrest him?" The devastation on his face told Sara the answer. "Where?" He listened a few seconds longer, then hung up. "Faith's waiting in the driveway."

"What happened?" Even as she said the words, Sara knew they were pointless. Another body had been found. Another life destroyed. Will's father had killed again.

Will stood. He grabbed his jacket off the back of the chair. He wouldn't look at her. She could practically hear his thoughts: He should've gone through with it. He should've taken his gun and gone to the hotel the minute he heard that his father was free.

He said, "Amanda wants you to come, too."

Sara didn't want to be a burden. Amanda had dragged her into this once before. "Do you want me there?"

"Amanda does."

"I don't care about Amanda. I only want to do what's best for you. Easiest for you."

Will stood in the doorway. He seemed about to say something profound, but then he reached down and retrieved her gym bag. "Try to hurry. I'll be outside."

twenty-five

July 15, 1975

James Ulster grabbed Amanda by the back of the neck. She felt like a kitten snatched by its scruff. Her arms went slack. Her toes lifted from the ground.

And then she remembered the revolver in her hand.

She snaked the gun around her side and pulled the trigger. Once. Twice. Three times. His body jerked as he was hit, but his grip only tightened. She pulled the trigger again. The muzzle flash singed Amanda's side. The gun was ripped from her hand. Ulster grunted. The muzzle was hot enough to burn his flesh. The gun clattered to the ground.

Amanda dropped to her knees, feeling blindly for the weapon. Ulster jerked her up by her arm. She felt like the bone was cracking. Her feet left the ground again. Her back slammed against the house.

The breath was knocked out of her. She kicked and clawed as Ulster's hand wrapped around her neck. She dug her fingernails into his skin. His face contorted in rage. Amanda felt dizzy. There wasn't enough breath to fill her lungs.

"Let her go!" Evelyn screamed. She had her Kel-Lite crossed under her revolver. "Now!"

Ulster didn't believe her. He tightened his grip on Amanda.

Evelyn pulled the trigger. Ulster's grip loosened around Amanda's neck. Evelyn fired again. The bullet hit his leg. He dropped Amanda. His arm was bleeding. His side was bleeding. Still, he didn't go down.

"Don't move," Evelyn ordered. But Ulster didn't listen. He walked straight toward Evelyn. She pulled the trigger, but the shot went wild. He slapped the gun out of her hand. His fist swung. Evelyn stepped back, but not fast enough. His knuckles grazed her chin. Evelyn collapsed to the driveway.

"No!" Amanda screamed. She jumped on his back. Her fingernails scratched into his eyes. Instead of spinning around blindly, Ulster fell to his knees, rolled onto his back. His weight crushed Amanda. Breath huffed out of her chest. Still, she wrapped her arm around his neck, locked it tight with the other one. Choke hold. She'd seen it done before. It looked so easy, but no one was really fighting back. No one had over two hundred fifty pounds of muscle to leverage out of the hold. Ulster pulled Amanda's arms apart as easily as a child untying a bow. She fell back hard, her head smashing into the concrete drive.

She kicked and punched. Her blows were useless. He easily pinned her to the ground, trapping her arms at her sides, the weight of his body grinding her tailbone into the concrete. Blood soaked the front of Ulster's shirt, dripped from his mouth. "You must repent, sister." He pressed harder. He was pushing the air out of her body. "Repent to me your sins."

"No," Amanda whispered. "Please."

"Our Father."

She struggled, gulping for air.

"Our Father," he repeated, pressing harder.

Her ribs flexed back into her stomach. Something was tearing inside. She couldn't fight anymore. She could only look up at his cold, soulless eyes.

"Our Father," he said a third time, the beginning of the Lord's Prayer.

Amanda huffed out, "Father."

"Who art in Heaven."

"Who art . . ." She couldn't get enough air to speak.

"Who art in Heaven."

"Who—" She pushed up against him, but his weight was like a mountain. "Please," she panted. "Please."

Ulster lifted up just enough so her chest could draw breath.

"Who art—"

"Who . . . ," she tried. "Who art . . ."

She felt her arms moving of their own volition. Ulster stopped her at first, pressing down his weight again, but then he understood. Carefully, he shifted back a fraction of an inch. Amanda slid out her arm, feeling her flesh scrape against the inseam of his pants. She pulled out the other arm, then clasped her hands together. Fingers laced one into the other. Palms tight. Thumbs outside.

Ulster stared at her intently. There was a smile on his lips. He rocked slowly, his pelvis grinding into hers. She felt as if her hipbone might crack in two. He leaned over more. He wanted to see her, wanted to enjoy the pain on her face.

She whispered, "Our Father . . ."

"That's right." His voice slow, as if he was teaching a child. "Who art in Heaven."

"Who art in Heaven." She stopped, gasping for breath.

"Hallowed be—"

The words rushed out. "Hallowed be thy name."

"Thy kingdom come." He leaned over farther, staring down at her face. "Thy kingdom come?"

"Thy—"

Amanda didn't finish the prayer.

Instead, she drove her clenched hands as hard as she could straight up into his neck. Her knuckles smashed into cartilage and bone. His throat flexed. Something snapped. It sounded like a stick breaking.

Hyoid. Just like Pete had shown her.

Ulster dropped on top of her like a pile driver. Amanda tried to push him off. He groaned, but wouldn't budge. He was too heavy to shift. She had to crawl out from under him. His weight was suffocating her. She forced herself to not pass out. To not throw up. To not give in.

Amanda's palms scraped for purchase. She pressed her toes into the concrete. The going was slow, painstaking. Her heart was in her throat. Bile was in her mouth. And then, with one final push, she finally managed to wrench herself free.

Evelyn was still out cold. Her revolver lay in her open hand. The Kel-Lite had rolled to the side.

Amanda reached for the gun, but Ulster grabbed her ankle, jerking her back. Amanda kicked as hard as she could. She felt his nose break under her heel. He let go. Amanda scrambled, pulling herself to her knees, but he grabbed her again. His arms went around her waist. Amanda slammed back her head, going for his broken nose. He faltered, which gave her time to twist around, take aim, and drive her elbow straight into the soft meat of his throat.

The loud crack sounded like a shotgun blast.

Ulster's hands went to his neck. Air whistled into his mouth. Amanda slammed her elbow a second time. Another crack. She did it again. Ulster fell onto his side. He rolled onto his back, wheezing for air. Amanda pushed herself up again. Her arms ached. Her head was pounding. Her chest hurt. Her throat hurt. Everything hurt.

She managed to stand, clutching at the van so that she would not fall back down.

Ulster made a gurgling sound. Blood dribbled from his mouth and nose.

Amanda pressed her bare foot into his neck. The sensation was just as Pete had described, bubbles crackling against the arch of her foot. She leveraged her weight back and forth, watching Ulster's eyes widen in terror, wondering if hers had done the same when he was pressing the life out of her.

"'Manda," Evelyn murmured. She was sitting up. Her lip was split. She had her hand to her face. Her jaw was so swollen that the lump showed through her fingers.

"Hey!" A patrolman ran around the van. He screeched to a stop when he took in the scene. "Jesus fucking Christ." His gun was drawn, though it hung limply out in front of him. "What the fuck did you broads do?"

"Amanda." Evelyn's voice was stilted, as if it hurt to talk. She said, "The girl."

twenty-six

Present Day

WEDNESDAY

News vans and reporters scurried like ants on the outer motor court of the Four Seasons. This wasn't just a hotel. High-priced lawyers and money managers filled the office spaces on the upper levels. The residence floors were packed with the rich and famous. Rap singers. TV reality stars. Fame-seeking socialites.

Crime scene tape had been strung along the marble fountain fronting Fourteenth Street. Someone noticed that Faith's turn signal was on. The reporters thronged forward. Will could hear their questions shouted through the closed window. What happened? Why are you here? Can you tell us who the victim is?

They would get the story soon enough. A woman murdered in a high-class hotel room. A paroled killer on the loose. There was not one part of the city this crime didn't touch, from the mayor's office to the Convention and Visitors Bureau.

Will had seen these stories spin out of control before. Every salacious detail would be discussed and analyzed. Rumors would be fed into the machine and regurgitated as fact. The obvious questions would be asked: Who did he kill? Why was he released? The Sunshine Law would be invoked. Files would be photocopied and couriered and Sam Lawson, Faith's ex who worked at the newspaper, would probably be on CNN before night fell.

"Crap," Faith mumbled, nosing her Mini up to the police barricade. The car shook as reporters jockeyed for position. She flashed her badge at the cop on duty.

"The BMW, too," Faith told him, pointing to Sara's car behind them.

The cop made a note on his clipboard, then pushed his way through the crowd to lift the barricade.

A reporter knocked on Faith's window. She mumbled, "Asshole," as she rolled the car forward. She hadn't said much on the ride over. Will didn't know if that was because she didn't know what to say or because Amanda was playing her usual game of hide the details.

Another body. Same M.O. His father nowhere to be found. The new victim was a prostitute. Will knew this with absolute certainty. It was his father's pattern. First a student, then a working girl. He didn't get rid of one unless he had another to take her place.

Will turned around to check for Sara. The BMW followed them inside the barricade. His Sig Sauer was still under her front seat. She wasn't going to stop him this time. Amanda could put fifty guards on Will and he'd still grab the gun and find his father and shoot him in the head.

Exactly as he should've done last night. This morning. Last week.

So many opportunities missed. His father had lived in this hotel for two months, and he'd somehow managed to come and go with no one being the wiser. He'd managed to abduct two girls. He'd managed to dump one at Techwood and murder another one in his hotel room. All while the police, hotel security, and undercover agents were supposedly watching his every move.

If that bastard could give them the slip, then so could Will. He was nothing if not his father's son.

Faith jerked up the handbrake as she parked behind Amanda's G-ride. Will got out of the car. Sara's BMW stopped in front of two Atlanta police cruisers. There were just as many cops on scene as reporters. He had to push past two uniformed patrolmen to open Sara's door for her. The cameras flashed as she got out of the car. She crossed her arms self-consciously. She was dressed in her yoga pants and his shirt. Hardly work attire. Will took the opportunity to reach in behind her and retrieve his gun from under the seat.

Except the gun wasn't there.

When he looked up, Sara was staring at him.

"Dr. Linton," Amanda said. "Thank you for coming."

Sara shut the car door. She locked it with the key fob, which she put in her shirt pocket. "Is Pete on the way?"

"No. He's testifying in court this morning." Amanda motioned for them to follow her inside. "I appreciate your coming on such short notice. It would behoove us all to get this body quickly removed."

A patrolman opened the side door. There was a whoosh as the air pressure changed. Will had never been inside the hotel before. The lobby was opulent in its excesses. Every surface was a different color of marble. A large staircase dominated the center of the room, splitting into two opposite sides as it reached the second floor. The treads were carpeted. The handrails were polished brass. The chandelier overhead looked as if a crystal factory had exploded.

The setting would've been impressive but for the fact that every shade and variety of police officer filled the lobby. Plainclothes division. Uniformed patrol. Special agents from the GBI. Even a couple of women from vice were there, their gold detective's shields looking incongruous against their skimpy attire.

Amanda told Faith, "Security is pulling footage from the last twenty-four hours. I need you to expedite that."

Faith nodded, heading toward the front desk.

Sara asked, "Have you identified the victim?"

"Yes." Amanda motioned over Jamal Hodge. "Detective, if you could please clear out all but the bare minimum of your people?"

"Yes, ma'am." He walked over to the crowd and raised his arms for attention. Will tuned out the man. He watched Amanda instead. She adjusted the sling on her shoulder as she gave orders to one of the hotel rent-a-cops.

Sara asked, "What is it?"

Will didn't answer. He scanned the lobby, trying to find a senior Atlanta Police officer. No Leo Donnelly. No Mike Geary, the captain in charge of this zone.

Amanda took over the case, Will realized. It didn't make sense. As far as the Atlanta Police Department knew, a dead prostitute had nothing to do with a kidnapped student. He asked Amanda, "What happened?"

Amanda indicated the rent-a-cop. He was in an expensive-looking charcoal suit, but the radio in his hand gave him away. "This is Bob McGuire, head of hotel security. He called it in."

Will shook the man's hand. McGuire was too young to be a retired cop, but he seemed fairly collected considering what had fallen into his lap. He led them toward the elevator, saying, "I got the call from the kitchen this morning. The room service girl said that he wasn't responding to her knock."

Amanda explained, "He's been adhering to a regular schedule."

The elevator doors opened. Will stood back to let Sara and Amanda on first.

McGuire said, "He's been staying here for two months." He waved a keycard over the panel, then pressed the button for the nineteenth floor. "We can track his movements in and out of the room through the software on the door lock. His schedule's been roughly the same since he got here. Room service at six in the morning, then the gym, then he goes back to his room, then he orders room service at noon." He tucked his hands into his pockets. "Once or twice a week, he uses our restaurant for dinner, or eats at the bar. Most nights, he orders room service at six o'clock. Then we don't hear from him until six the next morning."

Amanda noted, "He's keeping to his prison schedule."

Will glanced around the elevator car. The security camera was tucked into the corner. "How long have you been watching him?"

"Officially?" McGuire asked. "Just a few days." He told Amanda, "Your people have been doing most of the heavy lifting, but my folks have supplemented."

"Unofficially?" Will asked.

"Since he checked in. He's a strange man. Very off-putting physically. He never did anything overt, but he made people uncomfortable. And, frankly, the Presidential Suite is four thousand dollars a night. We normally try to find out who our higher-end clients are. I did a little poking around and realized that we needed to keep a closer eye on him."

Amanda asked, "Did anyone talk to him? Socialize with him?"

"As I said, he was off-putting. The hotel staff avoided him whenever possible. We never let the maids go up alone."

"What about other guests?"

"No one mentioned anything."

Will asked, "How did he pay for the room?" The man had been in prison. He wouldn't have a credit card.

McGuire explained, "His bank arranged everything. We're holding a hundred-thousand-dollar deposit against the room."

A bell dinged. The doors opened.

Will stepped aside, then followed them out of the elevator. Sara held his gaze for a few seconds. He nodded for her to go ahead of him.

McGuire said, "There are five other suites on his floor. The Presidential is in the corner. It's around twenty-two hundred square feet."

Three uniformed Atlanta Police officers stood at the end of the hallway. They were at least fifty feet away. The red exit sign glowed over their heads. The suite was directly across from the stairs.

McGuire led them down the hall. "Three of the suites were occupied. Entertainers. There's a concert in town. We arranged for them to be moved to our sister property. I can give you their information but—"

Amanda said, "I'd rather not waste time talking with lawyers."

Will felt a pain in his jaw, running down his neck. His teeth were clamped together. His shoulders tensed. He could hear his own breathing over the Muzak. The thick carpet was soft under his shoes. The walls were painted a deep brown that made the long hallway feel like a tunnel. Chandeliers hung at even intervals. There was a room service cart beside a closed door. No number on the room. The suites were probably the equivalent of three or four rooms. In movies, they always had Jacuzzi tubs and bathrooms the size of Will's house.

She wouldn't be in the tub. She wouldn't be in the bathroom. She would be on the mattress. She would be pinned down like a specimen in a science project.

Another victim. Another woman whose life was over because of a man whose DNA roiled inside of Will.

He had never stayed in a hotel suite before. He had never run on a beach. He had never flown in an airplane. He had never brought home a school report and watched his mother smile. The clay ashtray he'd made in kindergarten had been one of sixteen Mrs. Flannigan received on Mother's Day. All the Christmas gifts under the tree were labeled "for a girl" or "for a boy." The evening Will graduated high school, he'd looked out at the crowd of cheering families and seen only strangers.

Amanda stopped a few feet from the uniformed officers. "Dr. Linton, perhaps you should stay out in the hall for a moment?"

Sara nodded her acquiescence, but Will asked, "Why?"

Amanda stared up at him. She looked worse than she had the day before. Dark circles rimmed her eyes. Her lipstick was smeared.

"All right." For once, Amanda didn't argue. She continued down the hallway.

The cops looked bored with their assignment. Their thumbs were looped through their heavy utility belts. They stood with their legs wide apart to keep their backs from breaking under the weight of their equipment.

"Mimi," Amanda said to the female officer. "How's your aunt Pam?"

"Hating retirement." She indicated the room. "No one's been in or out."

Amanda waited for McGuire to open the door with his keycard. The green light flashed. There was a clicking sound. He held open the door. Sara and Amanda walked in, then Will.

McGuire said, "I'll be in the hall if you need me." There was a metal latch on the doorjamb. He swung it out to catch the door and keep it from locking.

"Well," Amanda said.

They stood in the foyer, looking into a room that was larger than Will's entire house. The curtains were open. Sunlight streamed in. The corner unit offered a panoramic view of Midtown. The Equitable building. Georgia Power. The Westin Peachtree Plaza.

And, in the distance, Techwood.

Two couches and four chairs were arranged around a fifty-two-inch flat-screen television. DVD player. VCR. CD player. There was a galley kitchen. A wet bar. Dining room seating for ten. A large desk with an Aeron chair. A half bath with a telephone mounted on the wall. The toilet paper was folded into a rose. The faucet was a gold-plated swan, its mouth opened to release a stream of water as soon as its wings were turned.

"This way," Amanda said. The door to the bedroom was half-closed. She used her foot to push it the rest of the way open.

Will breathed through his mouth. He expected to smell the familiar, metallic scent of blood. He expected to find a thin, blonde girl with vacant eyes and perfect fingernails.

What he found instead was his father.

Will's knees buckled. Sara tried to hold him up, but she wasn't strong enough. He slumped against the door. There was no sound in the room. Amanda's mouth was moving. Sara was trying to tell him something, but his ears wouldn't work. His lungs wouldn't work. His vision skewed. Everything took on a red tone, as if he was looking at the world through a veil of blood.

The carpet was red. The curtains. The sun coming through the windows—it was all red.

Except for his father.

He was on the bed. Lying on his back. Hands clasped together on his chest.

He had died in his sleep.

Will screamed in rage. He kicked the door, crushing the handle into the wall. He grabbed the floor lamp and threw it across the room. Someone tried to stop him. McGuire. Will punched him in the face. And then he collapsed to the floor as a baton pounded against the back of his knees. Two cops were on top of him. Three. Will's face was pushed into the carpet. A strong hand kept it there as his arm was wrenched around. A handcuff clamped around his wrist.

"Don't you dare!" Sara yelled. "Stop!"

Her words were like a slap. Will felt his senses come back. He realized what he was doing. That he had been completely and totally out of control.

And that Sara had seen it all.

"Officers." Amanda's tone held a steely warning. "Let him go. Immediately."

Will stopped struggling. He felt some of the pressure lessen. The female cop leaned down so that Will could see her face. Mimi. She asked, "Are we gonna be okay?"

Will nodded.

The key clicked into the handcuffs. His arm was freed. Slowly, they all climbed off him. Will didn't stand immediately. He turned his head to the carpet. He pressed his palms flat to the floor. He sat back on his heels. He was breathless. The sound of his blood pounded in his ears.

"Asshole." Bob McGuire's hand covered his nose. Blood seeped between his fingers.

Amanda said, "Mr. McGuire, I hope you'll excuse us?"

The man looked like he would prefer to kick Will in the teeth.

Mimi offered, "I'll get you some ice." She put her hand to McGuire's elbow and escorted him from the room. The two other cops followed.

"Well." Amanda let out a long sigh. "Dr. Linton, can you estimate time of death?"

Sara didn't move. She was looking at Will. She wasn't mad. She wasn't disgusted. There was a slight tremor to her body. He could tell she wanted to help him. Longed to help him. That she did not made him love her with a piercing clarity.

Will pushed his hands to the floor. He stood up. He straightened his jacket.

Amanda said, "The last time anyone saw him was approximately seven last night. He called room service to remove his tray. He put the breakfast card on the door."

Room service. Penthouse suites. Dying peacefully in his sleep.

"Dr. Linton?" Amanda said. "Time of death would be very helpful."

Sara was shaking her head even before Amanda finished her request. "I don't have the proper tools. I can't move the body until it's photographed. I don't even have gloves."

Amanda unzipped her purse. "The thermostat was set on seventy when the first unit arrived." She offered Sara a pair of surgical gloves. "I'm sure you can give us something."

Sara looked at Will again. He realized that she was waiting for his permission. He nodded, and she took the gloves. Her face changed as she walked over to the bed. He'd seen this happen many times before. She was good at her job. Good at separating who she was from what she had to do.

Will had witnessed enough preliminary exams to know what Sara was thinking. She noted the position of the body—he was lying prone on the mattress. She noted that the sheet and bedspread were neatly folded down at the foot of the bed. She noted that the victim was dressed in a white, short-sleeved T-shirt and white boxer shorts.

And that beside him on the table was a black velvet manicure kit.

The tools were neatly laid out: nail clippers, a tiny pair of scissors, a nail buffer, three types of metal files, an emery board, tweezers, a clear glass vial that held the white, crescent-shaped clippings of his father's fingernails.

Will had never seen the man in the flesh. His mugshot photo showed swollen features marred by dark bruises. Months after his arrest, a newspaper photographer had managed to snap a blurred image of him leaving the courthouse in shackles. Those were the only two photos Will knew of. There was no background information in his file. No one knew where he was from. No friends came forward. No parents. No neighbors claimed that he had always seemed so normal.

The *AJC* had been two newspapers back then—*The Atlanta Journal* and *The Atlanta Constitution*. Both editions covered the court proceedings, but there was no trial. His father had pleaded guilty to kidnapping, torture, rape, and murder. With the death penalty rendered illegal by the Supreme Court, the only enticement the prosecutor could offer in exchange for not having to prove his case at trial was life with the possibility of parole. That everyone assumed that possibility would never roll around was understood.

So, in the scheme of things, Will supposed his father was lucky. Lucky to miss the ultimate punishment. Lucky the parole board finally released him. Lucky to die on his own terms.

Lucky to kill one last time.

Sara began the examination with his face. That was where rigor always started. She tested the laxity of the jaw, pressed against the closed eyelids and mouth. Next, she checked the fingers, flexed the wrist. The nails glinted in the sunlight. They were trimmed down to the quick. The cuticle on his thumb had bled before he died.

Sara said, "My best guess—and it's only a guess—is that he died sometime within the last six hours."

Amanda didn't let her off that easily. "Care to hazard a cause of death?"

"Not really. Could be a heart attack. Could be cyanide. I won't know until I get him on the table."

"Surely, there's something else you can tell me about him?"

Sara was visibly annoyed by the question. Still, she answered, "He's in his mid-to-late sixties. He's well nourished, in good shape. His muscle tone is appreciative, even in rigor. His teeth are false, obviously penal-system quality. He has what looks like a scar on his chest. You can see it in the V-neck of his undershirt. It looks surgical."

"He had a heart attack a few years ago." Amanda frowned. "Unfortunately, they managed to save him."

"That might explain the trach scar on his neck." She indicated the metal bracelet on his wrist. "He's diabetic. I'm not going to move his clothes until after he's photographed, but I imagine we'll find injection sites on his abdomen and legs." She took off the gloves. "Is there anything else?"

Faith stood in the doorway. "I have something." She had a computer disc in her hand. She wouldn't look at Will, which told him that the victim's identity came as no surprise. She was a better liar than he'd thought. Or maybe not. At least he understood why she'd been so quiet on the drive over.

Amanda said, "We can watch it in the other room."

The three of them stood in a half circle as they waited for Faith to load the DVD player. Amanda was between Will and Sara. She took her BlackBerry out of her purse. Will thought at first that she was reading her emails, but it was easy to look over her shoulder. The screen was shattered like a spiderweb. He recognized the news site.

Amanda read the headline, " 'Recently paroled con dies in Midtown hotel room.' "

"They were hoping for somebody famous." Faith picked up the remote control. "Idiots."

"The story isn't dead yet." Amanda kept scrolling. "Apparently, a hotel employee tipped them off to a heavy police presence over the last few days." She told Will, "This is why we try to make friends."

"Here we go." Faith pointed the remote at the player. The security camera showed an empty hotel elevator. The recording was in color. Will recognized the gold-inlaid tile on the floor of the car. Faith fast-forwarded through the video, saying, "Sorry, it's not cued."

The lights on the elevator panel flashed, indicating the car was moving down to the lobby. Faith slowed the recording when the doors opened. A woman got onto the elevator. She was thin and tall with long blonde hair and a floppy white hat. She kept her head down as she entered the car. The hat brim covered most of her face. Just her chin showed before she turned around. "Working girl," Faith provided. "Hotel security doesn't know her name, but she's been here before. They recognize the hat."

Will checked the time stamp. 22:14:12. He'd been sleeping on the couch with Sara.

"She has a keycard," Amanda said, just as the woman swiped the card across the pad, the same as Bob McGuire had done. She pressed the button for the nineteenth floor. The doors closed. The woman faced the front of the car, showing the security camera the top of her hat, the back of her slinky, matching white dress. The elevator doors were solid wood. There was no mirrored reflection.

Amanda asked, "Did the lobby cameras pick up her face?"

"No," Faith said. "She's a pro. She knew where the cameras were." The woman got off the elevator. The doors closed. The car was empty again. "She stayed up here for half an hour before coming down again. I checked with APD vice. They say that's about the right amount of time."

Amanda said, "She's lucky she got away with her life."

Faith fast-forwarded the video again, then slowed it when the elevator doors opened. The woman entered the same as before, head tilted down, hat covering her face. She didn't need the keycard to go to the lobby. Her finger pressed the button. Again, she faced the doors, but this time, she reached up and adjusted her hat.

Will said, "Her fingernails weren't painted before."

"Exactly," Faith agreed. "I checked it four times before I came up here."

Will stared at the woman's hands. The nails were painted red, undoubtedly in Bombshell Max Factor Ultra Lucent. According to the crime scene report, it was his father's preferred color. Will said, "There's no nail polish by the bed. Just manicure stuff."

Faith suggested, "Maybe she brought her own?"

"That doesn't seem likely," Amanda told them. "He liked to control things."

Sara offered, "I'll check the other room."

Amanda told Faith, "Security says the girl's been in the hotel before. I want you to comb every second of video they have. Her face has to be on camera somewhere."

Faith left the room.

Amanda pulled a latex glove out of her purse. She didn't put it on, but used it as a barrier between her fingers as she opened the drawers on the desk. Pens. Paper. No Max Factor nail polish with the distinctive pointy white cap.

Amanda said, "This doesn't take two people."

Will checked the galley kitchen. Two keycards were on the counter. One was solid black, the other had a picture of a treadmill on it, probably for the gym. There was a stack of crisp bills. Will didn't touch the money, which he guessed to be around five hundred dollars, all in twenties.

"Anything?" Amanda asked.

Will went behind the wet bar. Swizzle sticks. Napkins. A martini shaker. A Bible with an envelope stuck between the pages. The book was old. The leather cover was worn off the corners, showing the cardboard underneath.

He told Amanda, "I need your glove."

"What is it?" She didn't hand him the glove. Instead, she wiped her palm on her skirt, then forced her hand into the latex. She opened the Bible.

The envelope lay flat against the page. It had obviously been in there for a while. The paper was old. The ink had worn off the round logo in the corner. The typewritten address had grayed with time.

Amanda started to close the Bible, but Will stopped her.

He leaned down, squinting hard to make out the address. Will had seen his father's name enough times to recognize the words. "Atlanta Jail" came just as easily. He'd used one or both in almost every report he'd ever written. The postmark was faded, but the date was clear. August 15, 1975.

He said, "This was mailed a month after I was born."

"So it appears."

"It's from a law firm." He recognized the scales of justice.

"Herman Centrello," she supplied.

His father's defense attorney. The man was a gun for hire. He was also the reason they were here. It was the threat of Centrello's superior courtroom performance that persuaded the Atlanta city prosecutor to offer the plea bargain of life with the possibility of parole.

Will said, "Open it."

In fifteen years, Will had only once seen Amanda's composure crack, and even then, it was more like a fissure. For a split second, she showed something akin to dread. And then just as quickly, the emotion was gone.

The envelope was glued into the spine. She had to turn it over like a page. The glue along the flap had dried long ago. She used her thumb and forefinger to press open the envelope. Will looked inside.

No letter. No note. Just faded ink where some of the words had rubbed off.

Amanda said, "Apparently, it's nothing more than a bookmark."

"Then why did he keep it all these years?"

"No luck." Sara was back. She told them, "No nail polish in the bathroom or the bedroom. I found his diabetic kit. His syringes are in a plastic disposal box. We'll have to have the lab cut it open, but from what I could tell, there's nothing in there that doesn't belong."

"Thank you, Dr. Linton." Amanda closed the Bible. She took out her BlackBerry again. "Will?"

He didn't know what else to do but continue searching the bar. He used the edge of his shoe to open the bottom cabinets. More glasses. Two ice buckets. The minibar was unlocked. Will used the toe of his shoe again. The fridge was full of vials of insulin, but nothing else. He let the door close.

There were at least two dozen liquor bottles on the shelves behind the bar. The mirror backing showed Will's reflection. He didn't look at himself, didn't want to fall down that rabbit hole of comparing himself to his father. He studied the colored labels instead, the shape of the bottles, the amber and gold liquids.

Which was why he noticed that one of the bottles listed at a slight angle. There was something underneath, shimming it to the side.

He told Amanda, "Pick up this bottle." For once, she didn't ask him why. She took the bottle off the shelf. "It's a key."

Sara asked, "Is it for the minibar?"

Will checked the lock on the refrigerator. "No. It's too big."

Carefully, Amanda picked up the key by the edges. The head was stepped instead of round or angled. There was a number stamped into the metal.

Will said, "That's for a Schlage factory lock."

Amanda sounded perturbed. "I have no idea what that means."

"It's a heavy-duty deadbolt." Will went out into the hallway. The cops were gone, but McGuire was still there. He held a bag of ice to his nose.

Will said, "I'm sorry about before."

McGuire's curt nod did not indicate forgiveness.

Will asked, "What door in this hotel opens with an actual metal key?"

He took his time lowering the bag of ice, sniffing back blood. "The keycards—"

Amanda interrupted him, holding up the key. "It's to a Schlage deadbolt. Heavy duty. What door in your hotel does this open?"

McGuire wasn't stupid. He got over himself fast. "The only locks like that are in the sub-basement."

Amanda asked, "What's down there?"

"The generators. The mechanicals. The elevator shafts."

Amanda headed toward the elevators. She told McGuire, "Radio your security team. Tell them to meet us down there."

McGuire jogged to keep up. "The main elevators stop in the lobby. You have to go to the second floor in the service elevator, then use the emergency exit stairs behind the spa."

Amanda jabbed the button. "What else is on that floor?"

"Treatment rooms, a nail suite, the pool." The doors opened. He let Amanda on first. "The stairs to the sub-basement are behind the gym."

twenty-seven

July 15, 1975

"Amanda," Evelyn repeated.

Amanda stared down at Ulster. Her foot was still jammed into his neck. With the slightest pressure, she could crush his windpipe.

"Amanda," Evelyn said. "The girl."

The girl.

Amanda stepped back. She told the patrolman, "Take him." The man took out his cuffs. He called dispatch on his shoulder mic, sounding as scared as Amanda had felt ten minutes ago.

She wasn't afraid now. The steeliness was back. The fury. The anger. She headed toward the house.

"Wait." Evelyn put her hand on Amanda's arm. The lower half of her face was swollen. It obviously hurt to talk, but she whispered, "There could be someone else."

Not another girl. Another killer.

Amanda found her revolver on the ground. The wooden grip was cracked. She opened the cylinder. One bullet. She looked at Evelyn, who checked her own revolver and held up four fingers. Five bullets between them. That was all they had.

That was all they needed.

The front door was unlocked. Amanda reached in with her hand and turned on the switch. A single bulb hung from an old fixture in the ceiling. The house was shotgun style, one story with a front door that lined up to the back. There were two chairs in the front room. A Bible was open on one of them. A silver bowl of water was on the floor. She was reminded of Easter church services. The women would bring bowls of water and wash the men's feet. She'd washed Duke's every year since her mother died.

The distant wail of a siren broke the silence. Not just one siren. Two. Three. More than she could decipher.

Evelyn joined Amanda as she walked down the hall. The kitchen was straight ahead. Two doors were on their right. One on the left. All closed.

Evelyn indicated the first door. She gripped her revolver in her hand. She nodded that she was ready.

They stood on either side of the closed door. Amanda reached down and turned the knob. She pushed open the door. Quickly, she reached in and flipped up the light switch. A floor lamp came on. There was a metal bed in the middle of the room. The mattress was soiled. Threads jutted up. Broken threads. A washstand. A sink. A chair. A bed table.

On the table was a pair of nail clippers. Cuticle nips. Buffer. Three types of metal files. An emery board. Tweezers. Red Max Factor nail polish with a pointy white cap. A glass vial filled with the crescent-shaped clippings of women's fingernails.

Jane Delray.

Mary Halston.

Kitty Treadwell.

Lucy Bennett.

Filthy rooms. Cracked plaster walls. Bare bulbs in the ceiling. Animal droppings on the floor. The stench of blood and terror.

This house was where he'd kept them.

Evelyn gave a low hiss for her attention. She nodded toward the next door. Amanda saw the patrolman enter the front room. She didn't wait for him. They did not need his help.

She stood to the side of the closed door and turned the knob. The light was already on in the room. Washstand. Sink. Manicure kit. Red polish. Another glass vial of nail clippings.

The girl was slumped against the headboard. Blood spilled in a steady stream down her abdomen. Pink foam bubbled from her mouth. Her hand was wrapped around the large knife in her chest.

"Don't!" Amanda lurched forward, dropping to her knees beside the bed. She covered the girl's hand with her own. "Don't take it out."

Evelyn yelled to the patrolman, "Call an ambulance! She's still alive!"

The girl's throat made a sucking sound. Air whistled around Amanda's hand. The blade was angled to the left, piercing the lung, possibly the heart. The knife was huge, the kind of weapon hunters used to skin their kill.

"Ha . . . ," the girl breathed. Her body was shaking. Torn threads hung from holes around her tattered lips. "Ha . . ."

"It's okay," Amanda soothed, trying to keep the knife steady as she peeled away the girl's fingers.

Evelyn asked, "Is she having a seizure?"

"I don't know."

The girl's hand dropped. The fingers twitched against the mattress. Her breath was stale, almost sour. Amanda's muscles burned as she gripped the handle of the knife, trying desperately to hold it in place. No matter what she did, blood poured steadily from the wound.

"It's all right," Amanda mumbled. "Just hold on a little bit longer."

The girl tried to blink. Pieces of eyelid stuck to her brow. Her arm reached out, fingers flexing as she tried to point to the open door.

"That's right." Amanda felt tears streaming down her face. "We're going to take you out of here. He's not going to hurt you anymore."

She made a noise, a sound between a breath and a word.

"We'll get you out of here."

Again, she made the sound.

"What is it?" Amanda asked.

"Laa . . ." The girl breathed. "Vah . . ."

Amanda shook her head. She didn't understand.

Evelyn got down beside her. "What is it, sweetheart?"

"Laa," she repeated. "Laa . . . vah . . ."

"Lover?" Amanda asked. "Love?"

Her head shook in a trembling nod. "Him . . ."

Her breath stopped. Her body went limp as the life drained out of her. Amanda couldn't hold her up anymore. Gently, she let the girl fall back onto the bed. Her eyes took on a blank stare. Amanda had never seen another person die before. The room got cold. A breeze chilled her to the bone. It felt as if a shadow hovered above them, then just as quickly, it was gone.

Evelyn sat back on her knees. She spoke quietly. "Lucy Bennett."

"Lucy Bennett," Amanda repeated.

They stared at the poor creature. Her face. Her torso. Her arms and legs. The horrors of the last year were writ large across her body.

"How could she love him?" Amanda asked. "How could she . . ."

Evelyn used the back of her hand to wipe away tears. "I don't know."

Amanda stared into the dead girl's eyes. She had seen her through the window just moments ago. The image flashed into Amanda's mind like a scene from a horror movie. The girl on the bed. Her hand at her chest. It was a knife she had been holding. Amanda realized that now.

The sound of the sirens got louder.

"House is clear." The patrolman came up behind them. "What

did you—" He saw the body. His hand slapped to his mouth as he ran from the room, retching.

Evelyn said, "At least we were here for her."

Tires screeched in the street. Blue lights flashed.

"Maybe we brought her . . . I don't know. Comfort?"

Amanda said, "We were too late to save her."

"We found her," Evelyn said. "At least we found her. At least the last few minutes of her life, she was free."

"It's not enough."

"No," Evelyn said. "It'll never be enough."

The sirens wound down as the cruisers pulled up. They heard talking outside; gruff voices barking orders, the usual palaver of men taking charge.

And something else.

Evelyn obviously heard it, too.

Still, Amanda asked, "What's that noise?"

twenty-eight

Present Day

SUZANNA FORD

She knew what the noise was now. The elevators rushing up and down. She heard the wind whistling like a train—up and down, down and up—as the doctor cut the threads with a pair of office scissors.

"You're going to be okay," the woman said. She was obviously in charge. She'd been the first to come to Suzanna's side. The only one who wasn't afraid of what she had seen. The other guys hung back. She could hear their breathing like steam pushing out of an iron. And then the doctor told one to call an ambulance. Another to get a bottle of water. Another to get a blanket. Another to find some scissors. They jumped to obey, running off so fast that Suzanna could feel the ghosts of their presence long after she could no longer hear their sneakers pounding against the floor.

"You're safe," the doctor said. She put her hand to Suzanna's head. She was pretty. Her green eyes were the first thing Suzanna saw. They looked at her down the blade of the scissors as she carefully snipped apart the threads. She'd covered Suzanna's eyes with her hand so that the light would not blind her. Her touch was so light when she cut apart Suzanna's lips that she'd barely felt the metal grazing her skin.

"Look at me. You're going to be okay," the woman said. Her voice was steady. She was so damn certain that Suzanna believed her.

And then she saw the man. Hulking. Lurking. He looked different. Younger. But it was still the same guy. Still the same monster.

Suzanna started screaming. Her mouth opened. Her throat scratched. Her lungs shook. She screamed as loud as she could. The noise wouldn't stop. She screamed even when the man left. She screamed over the doctor's soothing voice. She screamed when the paramedics came. She didn't stop screaming until the doctor stuck the needle in.

The drug rushed through her body.

Immediate relief.

Her brain calmed. Her heart slowed. She could breathe again. Taste again. See again. There was no part of her that did not feel it. Her hands, her fingers, her toes, all tingled from the rush.

Release. Salvation. Oblivion.

And Zanna was in love all over again.

twenty-nine

Present Day

WEDNESDAY

Sinatra crooned softly through the speakers in Amanda's Lexus, but Will could only hear Suzanna Ford's screams. He had been so relieved to find the girl alive. He'd wanted to weep as Sara freed the girl. His father had hurt her. He'd tried to destroy her. But Will had stopped him. He'd won. He'd finally beaten the old man.

And then Suzanna had taken one look at Will and seen James Ulster come back to life.

He leaned his head into his hand as he stared at the passing cars. They were on Peachtree Road, stuck in the patch of traffic near one of the many strip malls.

Amanda turned down the volume on the radio. Sinatra's voice mellowed even more. She put her hand back on the wheel. The other rested in the sling that was strapped around her shoulder and waist.

She said, "It's supposed to get cold this weekend."

Her throat sounded raw, probably from talking nonstop on her BlackBerry for the last twenty minutes. Hotel security. The Atlanta Police Department. Her own agents at the GBI. No one was going to skate on missing the fact that Ulster's morning trips to the gym were simply an excuse for him to gain access to the stairs that led to the sub-basement. How many times had he gone down there to hurt her? How many opportunities to stop him had been missed?

The girl had been held at least a week. She was dehydrated. Starved. Mutilated. God knows what else.

Amanda said, "Of course, you can't trust the weatherman. Never could."

Will still didn't answer.

The car accelerated as they drove past Amanda's condo. The Regal Park complex was nice, but paled in comparison to its neighbors. They were in the Buckhead fingerbowl. Habersham Road, Andrews Drive, Peachtree Battle—residences on these streets started at two million dollars and jumped sharply north. The area contained the most expensive real estate in the city. The zip code was listed among the top ten wealthiest in the country.

"We could use some rain."

Will looked at the side-view mirror as they approached the heart of Buckhead. An Atlanta PD cruiser was following them. Amanda hadn't told him why and Will couldn't bring himself to ask her. His breathing was shallow. His palms were clammy. There was no explanation for his feelings, just that he knew deep in his soul that something bad was about to happen.

Amanda slowed the car. Horns blared as she took an illegal turn onto West Paces Ferry Road. Her lips parted, but only to take a breath.

He waited for her to say something more about the weather, but her mouth remained closed, her eyes on the road ahead of them.

Will stared out the window again. The dread was making him feel sick. She'd already surprised him once today. It was a cruel thing to do. The shock had almost killed him. What else did she have planned?

Amanda pointed to a sixties-style house with fake Tara columns. The Governor's Mansion. "A tornado cut straight through here a few months before you were born. Took the roof off, cut through Perry Homes."

Will wasn't going to take the bait. "What will happen to his body?"

She didn't ask whom he meant. "No one will claim him. He'll be buried in a pauper's grave."

"He has money."

"Do you want it?"

"No." He didn't want anything from his father. Will would live on the streets again before he took a dime of the man's blood money.

Amanda slowed down for another turn. Will finally asked the question. "Where are we going?"

She signaled for the turn. "Don't you know?"

He studied the street sign. The X in the middle gave it away. Tuxedo Road. They were in the wealthiest part of the wealthiest section. Two million dollars would probably be just enough to cover property taxes for one estate.

"No?" she asked.

Will shook his head.

She made the turn. The car traveled several more yards before she said, "Your juvenile records are sealed."

"I know."

"You don't have your father's name."

"Or my mother's." Will loosened the knot in his tie. He couldn't get enough air. "That reporter with the *AJC*. Faith's ex-boyfriend. He called you—"

"Because I worked on the original case." Amanda glanced at him. "I'm the one who put your father in jail the first time."

"No, you didn't. Butch Bonnie and—"

"Rick Landry." She braked for a steep curve. "They were the homicide detectives. I was in what was euphemistically called Vagina Crimes. If it went into a vagina or came out of one, that was my case." She glanced over again, but only so she could enjoy his reaction. "Evelyn and I did all the work. Butch and Landry took all the credit. Don't be so shocked. It was a common occurrence. I hazard to say it's still going on."

Will couldn't answer even if he wanted to. It was too much to take on board. Too much information. Instead, he stared at the mansions rolling by. Castles. Mausoleums. Finally, he managed, "Why didn't you tell me?"

"Because it didn't matter. It was just another case. I've worked on lots of cases over the years. I don't know if you've noticed, but I've been doing this job an awfully long time."

He unbuttoned his collar. "You should've told me."

She was honest for once. "I probably should've told you a lot of things."

The car slowed again. She turned on her blinker and pulled into a long driveway. A Tudor-style house stretched out the length of half a football field, the front entrance peering down a rolling green lawn twice as long as the house was wide. The turf was crisscrossed in a checkered pattern. Azaleas and hosta spilled in rings around the tall oaks.

Will asked, "Who lives here?"

Amanda ignored the question as she pulled up to the closed gate. The scrollwork was painted a gloss black that matched the brick and wrought-iron fence ringing the property. She pressed the intercom button on the security panel.

A full minute passed before a woman's voice said, "Yes?"

"It's Amanda Wagner."

Static came through the intercom, then the sound of a long buzz. The gate started to swing open.

Amanda mumbled, "Swell digs," as she drove up the curving driveway.

"Who lives here?" Will repeated.

"You really don't recognize the place?"

Will shook his head, but there was something familiar about the house. The rolling green hill—tumbling down headfirst, grass stains streaking his pants.

The driveway laced across the front of the house in a gentle arc. Amanda pulled into the circular drive. A large fountain was in the center. Water slapped against a concrete urn. Amanda parked the Lexus parallel to the heavy wooden front doors. They were oversized—at least twelve feet tall—but fit with the scale of the building.

Will checked over his shoulder. The APD cruiser was thirty yards down, hanging back at the end of the driveway. Exhaust trailed from its tailpipe.

Amanda adjusted the sling on her arm. "Button your collar and fix your tie." She waited until he complied, then got out of the car.

Will's shoes crunched on the pea gravel driveway. Water splashed from the fountain. He looked down the vista of the front yard. Had he rolled down that hill? His mind could only recall fragments. None of them felt happy.

"Let's go." Amanda held her purse by the straps as she walked up the front steps. The door opened before she could ring the bell.

An older woman stood in the shadow of the door. She was the prototypical Buckhead Betty—extremely thin in the way of all wealthy women, with a tight face that had obviously been stretched back onto her skull. Her makeup was thick. Her hair was stiff with hair spray. She wore a red skirt with hose and high heels. Her white silk blouse had tiny pearl buttons at the wrist. A red cardigan was draped around her narrow shoulders.

She didn't bother with formalities. "He's waiting for you in his office."

The foyer was almost as large as the lobby of the Four Seasons. Another wide staircase. Another two-story entrance. Dark wooden beams arched into the white plaster ceiling. The chandelier was wrought iron. The furniture was sturdy-looking. The Oriental carpets showed a mixture of dark blues and burgundies.

"This way," the woman said, leading them down a long corridor that ran the width of the house. Their footsteps echoed on the slate tiles. Will couldn't help but look into each room they passed. He felt like a lightbulb kept flashing on in his head. The dining room with its large mahogany table. The delicate china hanging on the walls in the front parlor. The game room with its billiard table that Will had never been allowed to touch.

They finally stopped at a closed door. She turned the knob, opening it as she knocked. "They're here."

"They?" Henry Bennett stood from his desk. He was impeccably dressed, his blue suit tailored to his body. His mouth opened, then closed. He shook his head, as if to clear his vision.

Will almost did the same. He hadn't seen his uncle in almost thirty years. Henry was just out of law school when Lucy was murdered. He'd tried to keep a connection with his sister's only child, but by law an unmarried man could not adopt an infant. Henry had lost interest by the time Will turned six, which put Will right at the age when no one wanted him. Even Henry. Will had never laid eyes on his uncle again.

Until now.

And he had no idea what he was supposed to say.

Apparently, neither did Henry. "What the—" He was visibly angry. His mouth twisted in disgust as he asked Amanda, "What game are you playing?"

Yet again, Will felt a cold sweat come on. He looked down at the floor, wishing he could disappear. If Amanda thought this was going to be a happy homecoming, she was dead wrong.

"Wilbur?" Henry prodded.

Amanda took over. "Hank, I need to ask you some questions."

"It's Henry," he corrected. He obviously didn't like surprises, just as he obviously did not like Amanda. He couldn't even look at her.

Will cleared his throat. He told his uncle, "I'm sorry that we showed up like this."

Henry stared at him. Will felt an odd sense of déjà vu. Even after all these years, Henry shared similar features with his dead sister. Same mouth. Same high cheekbones. He had all of her secrets, too. All the stories about her childhood, her parents, her life.

And Will had a thin file that told him nothing more than that Lucy Bennett had been brutally murdered.

"Well," the Buckhead Betty said. "This is awkward." She extended her hand to Will. "I'm Elizabeth Bennett. Like in Austen, only older." Her smile was as practiced as the joke. "I suppose I'm your aunt."

Will didn't know what else to do but shake her hand. Her grip was firmer than he expected. "Will Trent."

She raised an eyebrow, as if the name surprised her.

Amanda asked, "How long have you been married?"

"To Henry?" She laughed. "Too long." She turned to her husband, saying, "Let's not be rude, sweetheart. These people are our guests."

Something passed between them, the sort of muted, private exchange that old married couples hone over the years.

"You're right." Henry pointed to the two chairs in front of his desk. "Sit down, boy. Would you like a drink? I need a drink."

"I'm fine," Amanda said. Instead of sitting in front of the desk, she sat on the couch. As usual, she stayed on the edge of the cushion, not leaning back. The leather was old. It creaked under her slight weight.

"Wilbur?" Henry asked. He was standing beside a cart with a full bar.

"No, thank you." Will sat beside Amanda on the couch. The frame was so low that he could easily rest his elbows on his knees. His leg wanted to shake. He felt nervous, like he'd done something wrong.

Henry dropped a piece of ice into a glass. He picked up a bottle of scotch and unscrewed the cap.

Elizabeth sat down in the matching leather chair. Like Amanda, she sat on the edge of the seat, back straight. She opened a silver box on the side table. She took out a cigarette and lighter. Will couldn't remember the last time he'd been around a smoker. The house was large enough to absorb the smell, but the pungent odor of burning tobacco filled his nostrils as the woman lit the cigarette.

"Now." Henry pulled over one of the chairs from his desk. "I assume you came here for a reason. Is it money? I have to warn you, all my cash is tied up right now. The market's been volatile."

Will would've preferred a knife in his groin. "No. I don't want your money."

Amanda said, "James Ulster is dead."

Henry's lips pursed. He got very still. "I'd heard he got out."

"Two months ago," Amanda confirmed.

Henry leaned back in his chair. He crossed his leg over his knee. His glass rested lightly on his palm. He smoothed out the arm of his suit jacket. He said, "Wilbur, I know that despite Ulster's terrible actions, he was still your father. Are you holding up?"

"Yes, sir." Will had to loosen his tie again. The air was stifling. He wanted to leave, especially when the room turned silent. No one seemed to know what to say.

Elizabeth took a deep drag off her cigarette. There was an amused smile on her lips, as if she was enjoying their discomfort.

"Well," Henry said. "As I said, your father was a very bad man. I think we're all relieved to learn of his demise."

Will nodded. "Yes, sir."

Elizabeth tapped the cigarette against the ashtray. "And how is your life, young man? Are you married? Do you have children?"

Will felt a tingling in his arm. He wondered if he was having a heart attack. "I'm doing well."

"What about you, Hank?" Amanda asked. "I saw when you made partner. Three years out of law school and you rocketed to the top of the firm. Old Treadwell certainly took care of you."

Henry finished his scotch. He put the glass on the table. "I'm retired now."

Amanda spoke to Elizabeth. "It must be lovely having him home."

She held the cigarette to her lips. "I cherish every moment."

Another muted exchange, this time between Amanda and Elizabeth Bennett.

Will reached up to unbutton his shirt collar. Amanda touched his elbow to stop him. Elizabeth took another drag off her cigarette. A clock ticked somewhere in the house. The water from the driveway fountain continued its rhythmic sound.

"So." Henry's fingers tapped against his knee. "Wilbur." His fingers stopped tapping. He looked down at his hand. "Was there anything else? I was about to head off to the club."

Amanda asked, "How old would Lucy be now?"

Henry kept staring at his hand. "Fifty-three?"

"Fifty-six," Will said.

Henry straightened his leg. He reached into his pants pocket and pulled out a pair of fingernail clippers. "Wilbur, I was thinking about your mother the other day." He swiveled the handle. "I suppose news of Ulster's parole put her in my mind."

Will felt that familiar clamp start to tighten around his chest.

"Lucy had this friend. Not a pretty girl, but very demure." Henry lined up the clipper to his thumbnail and pressed the handles together. "I'll hazard Lucy was a bad example for her. That's neither here nor there." He placed the cut fingernail on the table beside the ashtray and started on the next nail. "At any rate, the summer I was home from school, I would hear them giggling in Lucy's room, listening to records. One day I went in to see what all the racket was, and caught them dancing in front of a mirror, singing into their hairbrushes." He put the second nail by the first. "Isn't that silly?"

Will watched him clip the nail of his middle finger. Henry flinched as he cut too close. Still, he managed to remove the tip in one piece. He put the crescent-shaped nail beside the others. When he looked up from his work, he seemed surprised that they were watching him. "I suppose that's not an interesting anecdote. I just assumed you'd want to know something about your mother."

Amanda asked, "Do you remember Evelyn Mitchell?"

He grunted at the name. "Vaguely."

"You know, Evelyn was determined to track Ulster's money." She told Will, "This was before the Miami cocaine heyday when the government started requiring banks to report large deposits."

Henry tucked the clippers back into his pocket. "Is there a point to this?"

Amanda picked up her purse from the floor. The bag was huge.

She carried the world on her shoulder. "Ulster lived in a slum, but he had enough money to hire the top defense attorney in the Southeast. It raised some questions. At least among some of us."

Henry's tone was arrogant. "Again, I don't know what this has to do with me."

"Ulster had a savings account at C&S bank. We knew a gal there. She told us he had less than twenty dollars. He didn't use a dime of it to pay his lawyer."

Henry said, "He owned property."

"Yes, a house in Techwood that he sold in 1995 for four million dollars." She unzipped her purse. "He was the last holdout. I'm sure the city was pleased when he finally accepted."

Henry sounded annoyed. "A lot of people made money off the Olympics."

"Ulster certainly did." Amanda took a latex glove out of her purse. As usual, she wiped her palm on her skirt. With her arm in a sling, it was more difficult to push her fingers into the latex, but she managed to pull on the glove. And then she reached into her purse again and pulled out his father's Bible.

Henry laughed when she placed the book on the coffee table. "Are we going to pray for Ulster's soul?"

Amanda opened the Bible. "Here's your mistake, Hank."

He studied the envelope. One shoulder went up in a shrug. "So?"

"This is addressed to James Ulster at the Atlanta Jail." She pointed to the name. "And this logo says Treadwell-Price. Your law firm."

Will was past the point where he could be surprised by Amanda's lies. Less than an hour ago, she'd told him that the letter was from his father's defense attorney.

"So?" Henry shrugged his shoulder again. "There's nothing inside."

Amanda asked, "Isn't there?"

"No, there's not." He seemed very sure of himself. "Obviously, I wrote him a letter giving him a piece of my mind. The man murdered my sister. You can't prove otherwise."

"I can prove what a lazy pig you are."

He gave her a sharp look. "Where do you—"

"You gave this envelope to your girl to type."

He glanced at his wife, but Elizabeth was staring at Amanda. She was smiling again, but there was no warmth in her expression.

Amanda asked, "Do you see your name typed above the Treadwell-Price logo?" She turned the Bible so Henry could see it. "That's what you're supposed to do when you send out a business correspondence. They teach you that in secretarial school."

"My secretary passed away years ago."

"I'm sorry for your loss." She turned the Bible back around. "The thing about those old typewriters—and you wouldn't know this—is the rollers were heavy. If you weren't careful, you could pinch your fingers between them."

Henry straightened the nail clippings on the table. He used the tips of his fingers to move them around. "Again, I ask for your point."

"The point is, you had to line up the envelope just right so the address wouldn't come out crooked. Sometimes you had to twist the envelope back and forth between the rollers to get it straight. It's almost like an old printing press, where you turn the screw to press the ink onto the sheet of paper. Do you still use a fountain pen?"

Henry froze. He finally seemed to get it.

"The ink wasn't dry when you put the check inside." Amanda carefully pinched open the paper. "So, when your girl pressed the envelope between those two heavy rollers, the ink on the check transferred to the inside of the envelope. This envelope." She smiled. "Your name. Your signature. Your money paid to the order of Herman Centrello, the defense attorney working for the man who murdered your sister."

Henry took out his nail clippers again. "That's hardly a smoking gun."

"He kept it all these years," Amanda said. "But Ulster was like that, wasn't he?"

"How should I know what—"

"He didn't care about the money. It was a means to an end. He lived to control people. I bet every time he opened this Bible, all he could think about was how easily one word to the right snitch, one phone call to the right lawyer, could turn your world upside down."

"You have no proof that—"

"You licked the envelope flap to seal the letter, didn't you, Hank? I don't imagine you'd let your girl do that for you. She might wonder why you're sending such a sizable check to another law firm, care of the man looking to be sent away for murdering your sister." She smiled. "It must've galled you to have to lick your own envelope. How many times has that happened over the years?"

Henry looked frightened, then angry. "You don't have my DNA to compare."

"Don't I?" Amanda leaned forward. "Were you ever scratched, Hank? Did Jane scratch you on the arm or chest while you were strangling her?"

He stood up so fast the chair fell over. "I'd like for you to leave now. Wilbur, I'm sorry you've entangled yourself with this—" He cast about for a word. "Lunacy."

Will unbuttoned his collar. The room was suffocating.

Amanda took off the glove. "You worked out a deal with Ulster, didn't you, Hank? He got what he wanted. You got what you wanted."

"I'm calling the police." He walked to his desk. His hand rested on the phone. "Out of deference to Wilbur, I'm giving you one last opportunity to leave."

"All right." Amanda took her time standing. She straightened her sling. She lugged her purse onto her shoulder. But she didn't head directly for the door. First, she stopped by Henry's overturned chair. She took the fingernail clippings off the side table.

Henry demanded, "What are you doing?"

"I always wondered about Jane. She wasn't killed like the other girls. She didn't have the marks on her body. She was strangled and beaten. You tried to make it look like a suicide, but you were too stupid to know that we could tell the difference."

Henry didn't speak. He eyed the fingernails in Amanda's hand.

"Jane was telling anyone who would listen about the missing girls. So you used Treadwell's name to pull some strings down at the station house. You thought Jane would be afraid of the police."

"I have no idea what you're talking about."

"You've never understood women, have you, Hank? All you did was piss Jane off and make her talk more." Amanda opened her hand. The fingernails fell to the carpet.

Henry nearly jumped across the desk. He caught himself at the last minute, telling his wife, "Pick those up. Immediately."

Elizabeth seemed to debate her answer. "Oh, I don't think so, Henry. Not today."

"We'll talk about this later." He angrily punched the numbers on the phone. "I'm calling the police."

"They're right outside," Amanda told him. "The envelope is enough to arrest you. I know a gal at the lab who's just dying to get her hands on your DNA."

"I told you to leave." Henry hung up the receiver and picked it back up again. Instead of dialing three digits, he dialed ten. He was calling his lawyer.

Elizabeth said, "You're nothing like him, you know?"

She wasn't talking to Amanda or Henry. She was talking to Will.

"There's a kindness about you," she said. "James was terrifying. He didn't have to speak, or move, or even breathe. Just being in his presence was like staring into the pit of hell."

Will stared at the ugly shape of her mouth.

"He said he wanted to save them. Funny how none of them actually lived up to his promise." Elizabeth inhaled deeply from the cigarette. "He gave Lucy a chance, at least. A chance to do something good, to bring something pure into the world."

Will asked, "What are you saying?"

"Girls don't matter. They never matter." Her red lipstick had wicked into the deep lines around her mouth. "But you, handsome boy. You were saved from James. Saved from his brutality. His madness. You were our salvation. I hope you've earned it."

Will watched her round off the ash of her cigarette in the ashtray. Her nails were long, painted in a flame red that matched her skirt and sweater.

Amanda said, "They were working together, weren't they?"

"Not like you're thinking," she answered. "Yes, Hank had some fun, but I'm sure you've noticed that he doesn't like to get his hands dirty."

Henry ordered, "Shut up. Right now."

She ignored him, telling Will, "He didn't really want you, but he didn't want anyone else to have you, either." She paused. "I'm sorry about that. I really am."

"I'm warning you, Elizabeth." Henry's voice was terse. Sweat rolled down the side of his face.

She continued to ignore her husband, staring at Will with what could only be described as a sinister smile. "He'd get you from the children's home and bring you here for a day, two days at a time. I would hear you downstairs playing—inasmuch as a child can play without touching anything. Sometimes, I would hear you laugh. You loved rolling down that hill. You'd do it for hours. Down and up again, laughing the whole time. I would start to feel attached to you, and then Henry would take you away, and I was alone again."

"I don't—" Will had to stop to catch his breath. "I don't remember you."

She held the cigarette to her mouth. Her lipstick ringed the filter. "You wouldn't. I only saw you once." She gave a soft laugh. "The other times I was tied up."

The tinny sound of a woman's voice came through the telephone receiver in Henry's hand. He stood holding it from his ear, staring at his wife.

Elizabeth told Will, "It could've just as easily been me, you know. I could've been your mother. I could've—"

Amanda hissed, "Shut up, Kitty."

She blew out a stream of smoke. The tendrils swirled up into her thin blonde hair. "Bitch, was I talking to you?"

thirty

July 15, 1975

There was definitely a noise. A banging sound. Tapping. Amanda wasn't sure. The house was full of men tromping around in heavy shoes, yelling across the rooms. The attic stairs were pulled down. Someone was checking the crawl space. They could see the beam of a Kel-Lite through the planks in the hardwood floor.

Amanda stood in the hallway. "Shut up!" she yelled. "Everyone just shut up."

The men stared at her, not quite knowing what to do.

Amanda heard the noise again. It was coming from the kitchen.

Evelyn pushed past the crowd, fighting to get to the back of the house.

"Hey!" one of them complained.

Amanda followed her into the kitchen. The cabinets were metal.

The white laminate countertop had a gold swirl pattern. The appliances dated back to the thirties. The overhead light was a single bulb, the same as in the other rooms.

"Do you hear it?" Evelyn kept her jaw tight. The lump was dark red now, taking up the lower half of her face.

Amanda closed her eyes and listened. There was no banging. No tapping. Nothing. Finally, she shook her head. Evelyn let out a long sigh.

The men in the house had lost their patience. They started talking in low voices that got louder as more of their compatriots arrived on the scene. The front door was wide open. Amanda could see into the street. An ambulance had arrived. The medic jumped out of the back and headed toward the house. A patrolman stopped him and pointed toward the driveway.

James Ulster was still alive. She could hear him moaning through the open window.

"Crawl space is clear," a voice called. "Somebody get me the hell out of here."

Evelyn asked, "You heard it, right?"

"Yes." Amanda leaned against the counter. They both stood there, ears straining for the noise. And then they heard it again. Papers rustling. A thumping. It was coming from under the sink.

Evelyn still had her gun. She held it in front of her. Amanda wrapped her hand around the cabinet knob. She silently mouthed the countdown, "One . . . two . . . three . . . ," and opened the door.

No one jumped out. No bullets were fired.

Evelyn shook her head. "Nothing."

Amanda looked into the cabinet. It was much like her own. On one side were the usual cleaning supplies: bleach, a few rags, furniture polish. On the other side was a large kitchen trashcan. It was wedged under the sink, almost too big for the space.

Amanda was about to close the door, but the trashcan moved.

"Jesus," Evelyn whispered. Her hand went to her chest. "It's probably a rat."

They both looked down the hallway. There were at least thirty men on scene.

Evelyn whispered, "I'm terrified of rats."

Amanda wasn't crazy about them, either, but she wasn't about to erase everything they'd done tonight by asking some big strong man to help them.

The trashcan moved again. She heard a noise that sounded like a cough.

"Oh, my God." Evelyn dropped her gun on the counter. She got to her knees and tried to pull out the trashcan. "Help me!"

Amanda grabbed the top of the plastic can. She yanked as hard as she could. The edge came free and she saw two eyes staring up at her.

Almond shaped. Blue. Eyelids as thin as tissue paper.

The baby blinked. His upper lip formed a perfect triangle as he smiled up at Amanda. She felt an ache in her heart, as if he was pulling on an invisible string between them. His tiny hands. The fat little dots of his curled toes.

"Oh, God," Evelyn whispered. She wedged her fingers between the trashcan and cabinet, trying to bend back the plastic. "Oh, God."

Amanda reached down to the baby. She cupped her hand to his face. His cheek was warm. He turned his head, leaning into her palm. His hand brushed against hers. His feet came up. They curved as if he was pressing against an invisible ball. He was so impossibly small. And so perfect. So beautiful.

"I've got it." With one last pull, Evelyn finally freed the trashcan. She picked up the boy, holding him close to her chest. "Little lamb," she murmured, pressing her lips to his head. "Poor little lamb."

From nowhere, Amanda felt a flash of jealousy. Tears sprang into her eyes, blurring her vision. Blinding her.

And then came the rage.

Of all the horrors Amanda had seen in the last week, this was the worst. How had this happened? Who had thrown away this child?

"Amanda?" It was Deena Coolidge. The scarf around her neck

was blue. She had a white lab coat on. "Ev? What happened? Are you two okay?"

Amanda's bare feet slapped against the floor as she stalked out of the kitchen. She was running by the time she reached the front door. They were loading Ulster into the ambulance. She bolted into the street and pushed the medic out of her way.

Ulster was strapped down to the gurney. His wrists were handcuffed to the metal stiles. His clothes had been cut open. A bloody bandage was taped to his side, another to his leg. Gauze was wrapped around his arm. His throat was as red as Evelyn's jaw.

The EMT said, "We need to trach him. He's not getting enough air."

"We found him," Amanda told Ulster. "We beat you. I beat you."

Ulster's wet lips curved into a self-satisfied smile. He could barely breathe, but he was still laughing at her.

"Amanda Wagner. Evelyn Mitchell. Deena Coolidge. Cindy Murray. Pam Canale. Holly Scott. You remember those names. You remember the names of the women who brought you down."

Air wheezed from Ulster's mouth, but he was shaking with laughter, not fear. She had seen the look in his eyes a million times before—from her father, from Butch and Landry, from Bubba Keller. He was amused. He was humoring her.

All right, doll. Run along now.

Amanda stood on the bottom rung of the gurney so she could loom over Ulster the same way he had loomed over her.

"You're never going to see him." He blinked as her spit flew into his eye. "He'll never know you. I swear before God he'll never know what you did."

Ulster's smile would not fade. He took a deep breath, then another. His voice was a strangled gasp. "We'll see."

thirty-one

July 23, 1975

ONE WEEK LATER

Amanda smiled as she pulled into the parking lot of the Zone 1 station house. A month ago, she would've laughed if someone suggested that she'd be happy to be back here. A week of crossing guard duty had taught her a hard lesson.

She took one of the far spaces in the back of the lot. The engine knocked when she turned the key. Amanda checked the time. Evelyn was running late. Amanda should go inside the squad and wait for her, but she was thinking of this as their triumphant return. Having to spend five days in the grueling heat dressed in a wool uniform while lazy children tromped in and out of traffic had not negated the fact that they had caught a killer.

Amanda unzipped her purse. She took out the last report she was ever going to type for Butch Bonnie. She hadn't done it out of kindness. She'd done it because she needed to make sure it was right.

Wilbur Trent. Amanda had named the baby because no one else would. Hank Bennett did not want to sully his family's name. Or perhaps he didn't want the legal entanglement of Lucy having an heir. Evelyn had been right about the insurance policies. With Hank Bennett's parents dead and his sister murdered, he was now the sole beneficiary to their estate. He'd let the city bury his sister in a pauper's grave while he walked away from probate court a millionaire.

So, it fell to Amanda to buy Wilbur his first blanket, his first tiny T-shirt. Leaving him at the children's home had been the most difficult thing Amanda had ever done in her life. More difficult than facing down James Ulster. More difficult than finding her mother hanging dead from a tree.

She would keep her promise to Ulster. The child would never know his father. He would never know that his mother was a junkie and a whore.

Amanda had never written fiction before. She was nervous about the details she'd put into Butch's report, the blatant lies she'd told about Lucy Bennett's life before her abduction.

The boy could never know. Something good had to come out of all this misery.

"What's the skinny?" Evelyn stood outside the car. She was dressed in brown slacks and a checkered orange shirt that buttoned up the front. The bruise on her jaw had started to yellow, but it still blackened the bottom half of her face.

Amanda asked, "Why are you dressed like a man?"

"If we're going to be running around the city, I'm not going to ruin another pair of perfectly good pantyhose."

"I don't plan on doing much running anymore." Amanda tucked the report back into her purse. She zipped the bag closed quickly. She didn't want Evelyn to see the application she'd requested from the Georgia Bureau of Investigation. Her father had gotten his old job back. Captain Wilbur Wagner would be running Zone 1 again by the end of the month.

Evelyn frowned sympathetically as Amanda got out of the car. "Did you go by the children's home again this morning?"

Amanda didn't answer. "I need to wash my hands."

Evelyn followed her to the back of the Plaza Theater.

Amanda gave a heavy sigh. "I only said that so you would leave me alone."

Evelyn held open the exit door, releasing the pornographic grunts of *Vixen Volleyball*. The two men standing in the lobby looked very startled to see them.

"Your wives send their regards," Evelyn told them, heading toward the bathroom.

Amanda shook her head as she followed. "You're going to get us shot one of these days."

Evelyn picked up their earlier conversation. "Sweetie, you can't keep looking in on him every day. Babies need to bond with people. You don't want him getting attached to you."

Amanda turned on the faucet. She looked down at her hands as she washed them. That was exactly what she wanted with Wilbur, but she couldn't quite bring herself to say the words. It was hopeless. She was twenty-five and single. There was no way the state would let her adopt. And they were probably right not to.

Evelyn asked, "Did you get that slide with the skin on it from Pete?"

She patted her face with cold water. She had the sealed evidence envelope in her purse. "I still don't know why it matters."

"Pete's right about the science. They can't use it now, but maybe one day." She added, "You don't want it getting lost in lockup. They'll throw it out in five years."

Amanda turned off the sink. "If we had the death penalty, none of this would matter."

"Amen." Evelyn took her compact out of her purse. "Where are you going to put the envelope?"

"I have no idea." She couldn't very well walk into the bank and ask for a safe deposit box without Duke's signature. "How about your gun safe?"

"It should stay with the baby. Get Edna to hide it somewhere." She smiled. "Make sure she doesn't lock it in the pantry."

Amanda laughed. Edna Flannigan had a reputation around child services, but she was a good woman who cared about the kids. She had taken a shine to Wilbur. Amanda could tell. He was an easy baby to love.

"Can I have one of your textbooks?"

Evelyn stopped powdering her nose. "Why?"

"Edna said we could leave some stuff for the baby to have when he grows up. I thought we could . . ."

Evelyn knew about the story of Lucy Bennett, star student. She'd helped craft it, giving some inside details about Georgia Tech so the lies seemed more plausible. "If I give you one of my statistics books, will you promise to stop moping?"

"I'm not moping."

Evelyn snapped her compact closed. "We need to talk about our next case."

"What's that?"

"The DNF. We can look into those murders."

"Are you forgetting Landry's the one who got us busted to crossing guards?" Duke had found him out in two phone calls. Landry was drinking buddies with the commander who'd signed off on the transfer. It wasn't a conspiracy so much as a male chauvinist pig who couldn't take two women trying to do his job. "That's all we need to do is put ourselves in his crosshairs again."

"I'm not afraid of that blowhard." She fluffed her hair in the mirror. "We saved a life, Amanda."

"We lost three, maybe four." God knew where Kitty Treadwell was. Probably buried in the city dump. Not that her father cared. Andrew Treadwell refused to return their phone calls, let alone admit that he had a second daughter. "And neither one of us came out unscathed."

"But we know people now. We have sources. We have a network. We can work cases just like the boys—even better."

Amanda could only stare at her. The grunting sounds from the porn movie only added to the ridiculousness of her statement. "Is there anything you can't put a positive spin on?"

"Hitler. World hunger. Redheads—I just don't trust them." Evelyn checked her makeup again. Amanda did the same, frowning at what she saw. Evelyn wasn't the only one who was bruised. Amanda's neck was still ringed dark from Ulster's hands. Her ribs were tender to the touch. The cuts on her palms and the soles of her feet were just starting to scab.

Evelyn caught her eye in the mirror.

War wounds.

They were both smiling as they left the bathroom.

Evelyn asked, "Did I tell you about that Green Beret in North Carolina who murdered his entire family?"

"Yes." Amanda held up her hand to stop her. "Twice. I would rather talk about the case again than hear the details, thank you very much."

The lobby was empty. Evelyn stopped. She put her hands on her hips. "You know the insurance policies still bother me."

Hank Bennett. She couldn't let it go.

Evelyn pressed, "Bennett went to the mission looking for Lucy. It follows that he'd end up at the soup kitchen and meet James Ulster."

"Maybe they met, but to say they were working together . . ." Amanda shook her head. "Why? What would be the point?"

"Bennett gets his sister out of the picture so she can't inherit his parents' money. He keeps Kitty Treadwell for himself—and her money, because you know there has to be some."

"You think Hank Bennett's hiding Kitty somewhere." It wasn't a question. She'd been beating that dead horse all week. "To what end?"

"To blackmail Andrew Treadwell." She had a smile on her face. "Mark my word, Hank Bennett's going to be running that firm one day."

Amanda sighed. She wondered if Evelyn's magazines were to blame for these crazy conspiracies. "Kitty Treadwell is buried somewhere in a shallow grave. Ulster took them to kill them, not rehabilitate them."

"Someone put that baby in the trashcan."

Amanda didn't have an answer for her. Part of Lucy's body was still sewn to the mattress when they found her. Pete Hanson couldn't give them an exact window for the time between Wilbur's birth and Lucy's death. They could only assume the girl had been free at some point and hidden the baby.

And then Ulster had come home and sewn her back down?

Evelyn said, "I just feel like we're missing something."

Amanda didn't want to feed the flame, but she had the same bad feeling. "Who else could've helped him?" she asked. "Trey Callahan was caught in Biloxi with his fiancée." The man claimed that he'd only stolen the money from the mission in order to self-publish his book. "Obviously, Ulster was trying to frame Callahan with all that Ophelia stuff. Don't you think if there was a second killer, then Ulster would've framed that person instead?"

"How about this: where's the money coming from?"

Herman Centrello. Evelyn was determined to find out how James Ulster was paying for the best criminal defense lawyer in the Southeast.

Amanda shook her head. "Why does it matter? No lawyer in the world can get him out of this. Ulster was caught red-handed. His bloody fingerprints are on the knife."

"He'll skate on the other girls. We don't have anything to tie him to Jane or Mary. We don't have Kitty's body—if it's out there. Ulster could eventually get paroled. That's why you need to hold on to that slide. Maybe the science will be ready for it by then."

"He'll be in his sixties. He'll be too old to walk, let alone hurt anybody."

Evelyn pushed open the exit door. "And we'll be retired little grannies, living with our husbands in Florida, wondering why our children never call."

Amanda wanted to hold on to that image. She wanted to think about it tonight when she tried to go to sleep and all she could see was that condescending look in Ulster's eyes. He'd been laughing at her. He was holding something back, and he knew that it gave him power over everyone else.

Evelyn asked, "Did Kenny call you?"

Amanda let her blush be her answer. She adjusted her purse over her shoulder as they walked toward the station. There was a commotion going on by the front door. Two cops were wrangling with a wino. He already had a resisting-arrest turban. His hands waved wildly as he was jerked back by his collar.

Amanda said, "We actually wanted to come back to this."

Evelyn looked at her watch. "Crap, we're late for roll call."

So much for their triumphant return. Luther Hodge would probably put them on desk duty all week. Amanda hated filing, but at least she'd have Evelyn to commiserate with. Maybe they could look at some of the cases on the missing black girls. There was no harm in putting together another construction paper puzzle.

"Hey!" The wino was still struggling as they walked to the entrance of the station. One of the patrolmen smacked him on the ear. The man's head jerked like a sling.

The squad was as smoke-filled and dingy as usual. The room looked the same: crooked rows of tables crossing the room, white on one side, black on the other. Men in front, women in back. Hodge was at the podium. Everyone was seated for roll call.

But for some reason, they started to stand.

First, it was some of the white detectives, then slowly the blacks stood from their tables. It went around the room in a slow wave, ending with Vanessa Livingston, who, as usual, was sitting in the last row. She gave them both a thumbs-up. Her teeth showed in a proud grin.

Evelyn seemed momentarily stunned, but she kept her head high as she walked into the room. Amanda tried to do the same as she followed. The men cleared a path for them. No one spoke. They didn't whistle. They didn't make catcalls. Some of them nodded. Rick Landry was the only one who remained seated, but standing beside him was Butch Bonnie, who seemed to have some grudging respect in his eyes.

Then the moment was ruined as the wino was thrown into the squad room. He jumped up from the floor, screaming, "I'll sue you motherfuckers!"

The room tensed. The drunk's eyes widened as he realized he was facing down a room full of cops. He nervously glanced at Amanda, then Evelyn. "Uh . . . s'cuse the language, ladies."

"Shee-it." Butch took the toothpick out of his mouth. "They ain't no ladies, fella. They're the po-lice."

The room heaved a collective sigh. Jokes were passed around. The drunk was wrangled out the door. Hodge banged the podium for silence.

Amanda fought the smile on her lips as she walked to the back of the room. She could feel Evelyn behind her, knew she was thinking the same thing.

Finally—acceptance.

thirty-two

Present Day

WEDNESDAY

Will sat on the wooden bench at the top of the rolling hill. He rested his elbows on his knees. He looked down at the street as the police cruiser pulled out of the driveway. His father a murderer. His uncle a murderer. Will had it on both sides.

Footsteps crunched across the gravel driveway. Amanda put her hand on his shoulder, but only to help herself sit.

They both stared into the empty street. Seconds turned into minutes. Will could hear a white noise in his ears. A humming that made it impossible for his brain to hold on to any one thought.

Amanda gave a heavy sigh. "Evelyn's never going to let me live this down. She always thought there was someone else."

"Is she going to testify against him?"

"Kitty?" Amanda shrugged with her good shoulder. "I doubt it.

If she was going to talk, she would've done so years ago. I have a feeling she's still too much under Henry's control." She gave a rueful laugh. "You've come a long way, baby."

Will couldn't pretend he was all right with all this. He couldn't brush off tragedy with a wry comment the way Amanda did. "Tell me what happened. The truth."

Amanda stared at the front lawn, the vast green space that was larger and better tended than most public parks. She obviously needed time to collect her thoughts. Honesty wasn't a natural act for Amanda Wagner. Will could tell it took effort.

Finally, she said, "You know that there were two victims. Your mother and Jane Delray."

"Right." Will had found the reference in his father's file. There wasn't enough evidence to tie James Ulster to the murder of Jane Delray, but it was assumed that he was guilty of the act. "It was his pattern. He takes two and decides which one to keep."

"There were two other girls. Mary Halston and Kitty Treadwell."

Will gripped together his hands.

She said, "Your mother and Mary Halston showed the same damage. The sewing. The needle marks. But Jane was different. She wasn't abducted. Her murder was spur-of-the-moment. She was strangled, then thrown from the roof so that her death would look like a suicide."

"Henry?"

"I wasn't sure until I saw that check. What I said was the absolute truth. It bothered Evelyn that Ulster had a high-priced lawyer. Frankly, it bothered me. Ulster was never interested in material things. He wanted control, and I guess making Hank mail him that check at the jail exerted some control."

"Henry's going to skate on the envelope. You know the check isn't enough."

"Henry's DNA is going to match evidence from Jane Delray's case. I called the gal who's in charge of archival evidence the minute I heard your father was out. It's a miracle the chain of custody was still intact, or we'd never be able to use it."

"What's the evidence?"

"It's what I said in there. Jane scratched her attacker. It's going to match Henry's DNA from the envelope."

"Are you sure of that?"

"Aren't you?"

Will had seen his uncle's face. He was sure.

"What about Kitty?"

"I can only give an educated guess. Ulster got her off heroin. Hank kept her to leverage money out of Treadwell." She nodded back toward the house. "Not a bad plan, as you can see."

Will looked at the house. *Mansion* wasn't even the right word for it. *Museum,* maybe. *Prison.*

Amanda asked, "Is there anything else you want to know?"

There was a lifetime of questions. "Why are you making me pull teeth?"

"Because this is difficult for me, too, Will."

He hadn't considered that. For all her bluster, Will knew that Amanda was close to this. Her first case. Her first homicide. She tried to act like it was nothing, but the fact that they were both sitting here right now belied that assertion.

Eventually, she said, "Hank always hated women. I imagine he hated Lucy for her independence. Her free spirit. That she made choices for herself. She was going to school. Living in Atlanta. Hank thought women should stay in their place. Most men did back then. Not all of them, but—" She shrugged her shoulder again. "All you need to know is that your mother was a good person. She was smart and independent, and she loved you."

A cable truck drove down the street. Will could hear the hum of the wheels on the road. He wondered what it felt like to live in a mansion, to watch the rest of the world pass you by.

Amanda said, "Everyone I interviewed at the school loved her."

Will shook his head. He'd heard enough.

"She was funny and kind. She was very popular. All of her professors were devastated when they heard what happened. She had great promise."

He tried to swallow the glass in his throat.

"I was there when she died." Amanda paused again. "Her last words were for you, Will. She said that she loved you. She wouldn't let go until she was certain we heard her, until she knew that we understood that with every breath in her body, she loved you."

Will pressed his fingers into his eyes. He wasn't going to cry in front of her. There would be no going back from that.

"She hid you in the trashcan to save you from your father." Amanda paused. "Evelyn was there. We found you together. I don't think I've ever been so angry in my life. Not before or since."

Will swallowed again. He had to clear his throat to speak. "Edna Flannigan. You knew her."

"A lot of my cases took me to the children's home." Amanda adjusted the strap on her sling. "No one told me she'd passed away. When I found out—" She looked Will straight in the eye. "Trust me, her replacement was duly punished for his actions."

Will couldn't help but take some pleasure in the thought of Amanda annihilating the man who'd kicked him out into the street. "What was in the basement? What were you looking for?"

She stared back at the lawn, letting out a long sigh. "I wonder if we'll ever know."

Will remembered the scratches in the coal chute. He'd assumed they had been made by an animal, but now he knew it was probably one of Amanda's old broads. "Someone went back there while we were at the hospital."

"Really?" Amanda pretended to be surprised.

Will tried to let her know he wasn't a complete idiot. There was no way a slide had been in police custody for thirty-seven years. "Archival evidence."

"Archival evidence?" She had an infuriating smile on her lips, and he knew she was back in full dissembling mode before she even opened her mouth. "Never heard of it."

"Cindy Murray," he continued. Will's caseworker, the woman who'd helped him get off the streets and into college.

"Murray?" Amanda drew out the name, finally shaking her head. "Doesn't ring a bell."

"Captain Scott at the jail—"

She chuckled. "Remind me to tell you stories about the old jail sometime. It was awful before Holly cleaned it up."

"Rachel Foster." Amanda still called on the federal judge to sign off on her warrants. "I know you're friends with her."

"Rachel and I came up together. She worked dispatch, the night shift, so she could go to law school during the day."

"She expunged my record when I graduated from college."

Amanda would only say, "Rachel's a good gal."

Will couldn't help himself. He had to find at least one crack. "I've never known you to go on another GBI recruiting trip. Not once in fifteen years. Just the one where you got me to sign up."

"Well." She adjusted the sling again. "No one really enjoys those trips. You talk to fifty people and half of them are illiterate." She smiled at him. "Not that that's a bad thing."

"Did I get it from him?" He couldn't look at her. Amanda knew about his dyslexia. "My problem?"

"No." She spoke with certainty. "You saw his Bible. He was constantly reading."

"That girl—Suzanna Ford. She saw—"

"She saw a tall man. That's all. You're nothing like him, Will. I knew James Ulster. I talked to him. I looked him in the eye. There's not a drop of your father inside of you. It's all Lucy. Everything about you comes straight from your mother. You have to believe me on that, at least. I wouldn't waste my time on you otherwise."

Will clasped his hands in front of him. The grass was lush beneath his feet. His mother would be fifty-six years old now. Maybe she would've been an academic. Her textbooks were well read. Words were underlined. Asterisks were scribbled in the margins. She might have been an engineer or mathematician or a feminist scholar.

He had spent so many hours with Angie talking about the what-ifs. What if Lucy had lived? What if Angie's mom hadn't taken that overdose? What if they hadn't grown up in the home? What if they'd never met each other?

But his mother had died. So had Angie's, though it'd taken longer. They'd both grown up in the home. They'd been connected to each other for nearly three decades. Their anger was like a magnet between them. Sometimes it pulled them together. Most times it pushed them apart.

Will had seen what it took to hold on to resentment that long. He read it in Kitty Treadwell's emaciated body. He saw it in the arrogant tilt of his uncle Henry's chin. And sometimes, when she didn't think anyone was looking, he saw it flash in Amanda's eyes.

Will couldn't live like that. He couldn't let the first eighteen years of his life ruin the next sixty.

He reached into his pocket. The metal of the wedding ring was cold against his fingers. He held it out to Amanda. "I want you to take this."

"Well." She pretended to be embarrassed as she took the ring. "This is rather sudden. Our age difference is—"

Will tried to take it back, but she wrapped her hand around his.

Amanda Wagner was not an affectionate woman. She rarely touched Will in kindness. She punched his arm. She smacked his shoulder. She'd even once pulled back the safety plate on a nail gun and feigned surprise when the nail shot through the webbing between his thumb and index finger.

But now, she held on to his hand. Her fingers were small, her wrist impossibly tiny. There was clear polish on her fingernails. Age spots dotted the back of her hand. Her shoulder leaned into his. Will gently returned the pressure. Her grip tightened for just a second before she let go.

She said, "You're a good boy, Wilbur."

Will didn't trust himself to respond without his voice cracking. Normally, he would've made a joke about crying like a girl, but the phrase was a contradiction to the woman sitting beside him.

Amanda said, "We should go before Kitty turns the hose on us." She dropped the ring into her purse as she stood from the bench.

Instead of hefting the bag onto her shoulder, she gripped it in one hand.

Will offered, "Do you want me to carry that?"

"For God's sakes, I'm not an invalid." She pulled the bag onto her shoulder, as if to prove a point. "Button your collar. You weren't raised in a barn. And don't think we've had our last conversation on the subject of your hair."

Will buttoned his collar as he walked with her to her car.

Kitty Treadwell stood at the open front door, watching them carefully. A cigarette hung from her lips. Smoke curled up into her eye.

She said, "I paid the property taxes."

Amanda was reaching for the car door. She stopped.

"On the Techwood house." Kitty walked down the stairs. She stopped a few feet from the car. "I paid the taxes. Worth every penny. It chapped Henry's ass when James sold it."

"Mine, too," Amanda admitted. "Four million dollars is quite a profit."

"Money's the only thing Henry understands." Kitty took the cigarette out of her mouth. "I thought it would go to Wilbur."

"He doesn't want it," Amanda said.

"No." Kitty smiled at Will. It gave him a cold feeling inside. "You turned out better than all of us. How on earth did that happen?"

Will couldn't answer her. He couldn't even bear to look at her.

Amanda asked, "Hank met Ulster at the soup kitchen?"

Kitty reluctantly turned back to Amanda. "He was looking for Lucy. He wanted to make sure she wouldn't lay claim to their parents' estate. It must've seemed like a match made in heaven." She held the cigarette to her lips. "They struck a grand bargain. Hank gave him Lucy, no strings attached. In return, Ulster got me off the dope. Though I don't recommend his methods." She smiled as if this was all a joke. "I suppose James thought Lucy was a good trade. A fallen angel with no parents or family to make a stink." She huffed out some smoke. "And besides, Mary wasn't really doing it for him anymore."

"Why did he kill her?"

"Mary?" Kitty shrugged. "She couldn't be broken. Something about being pregnant changes you. At least it seems that way from the outside. Commendable, but look where it got her."

"And Jane Delray?"

"Oh, they fought constantly about Jane. Henry wanted her out of the way. She wouldn't shut up. She kept telling anyone who would listen about Lucy, about Mary, about me. I suppose I was lucky I didn't meet the same end. I was constantly throwing around my father's name." She stuttered a laugh. "As if anyone in the ghetto gave a rat's ass who my father was."

"They fought about it?" Amanda echoed.

"James didn't care who that little slut talked to. He got quite high and mighty about it, unsurprisingly. He was doing the Lord's work, after all. He wasn't a hired killer. God was going to protect him."

Amanda made the obvious connection. "You were kept in the house with Lucy."

"Yes. I was there the whole time." She seemed to be waiting for Amanda to ask another question. "The entire time."

Amanda said nothing.

"Anyway." Kitty tapped some ash onto the driveway. "I reconciled with my father at the end." She huffed a bitter laugh. "More money for Henry's coffers. What's the saying? God doesn't close a door without first nailing shut all the windows?"

Amanda offered, "If you testify, I can—"

"You can't really do anything. We both know that."

"You can leave him. You can leave him right now."

"Why would I do that?" She seemed genuinely perplexed. "He's my husband. I love him."

Her matter-of-fact tone was as shocking as anything Will had heard today. She really seemed to want an answer.

Amanda asked, "How could you? After all he did?"

Kitty snarled out a long stream of smoke. "You know how it is with men." She flicked the cigarette into the yard. "Sometimes it's criminal what a woman has to do."

thirty-three

Present Day

ONE WEEK LATER

Sara's greyhounds had been spoiled rotten. Will had started giving them cheese, which Sara had discovered the hard way. Apparently, it was an ongoing thing. The dogs were obsessed. The minute they recognized Will's street, they started pulling on their leashes like huskies running the Klondike. By the time she got to his driveway, Sara's arms felt as if they'd been ripped out of the sockets.

She gripped the leashes in one hand as she dug around in her pocket for the key to Will's house. Thankfully, his Porsche pulled up behind her. He waved as he pulled past. The dogs pounced.

"Look at you," Will cooed. He rubbed the dogs up and down. "Aren't you good boys?"

"They're nasty," Sara said. "No more cheese."

Will was laughing when he stood up. "Dogs need cheese. They can't find it in the wild."

Sara opened her mouth to counter his argument, but he kissed her so long and so well that she didn't care anymore.

Will smiled down at her. "Did you hear back from your cousin?"

"We can have his beach house the whole week."

His smile turned into a grin. He took the leashes. The dogs were considerably better behaved as they led Will up the walkway. Sara couldn't help but think how much better Will looked. He was back at his real job. He was sleeping through the night. He wasn't so shell-shocked anymore.

Will waited until Sara had closed the front door to let the dogs off their leashes. They bolted to the kitchen, but Will didn't follow them. He told Sara, "Henry's arraignment is next week."

"We can postpone the beach if—"

"No."

She watched him empty his pockets, putting his keys and money on the desk. "How's the case going?"

"Henry's fighting it, but you can't argue with DNA." He slid his paddle holster off his belt. "What about you? How was your day?"

"I need to tell you something."

He looked wary. Sara couldn't blame him. He'd had enough bad news lately.

"Your father's tox screen came back."

Will straightened the pen on his desk. "What did they find?"

"He had Demerol in his bloodstream. Not a lot."

He gave her a careful look. "Pills?"

"Medical grade, injectable."

He asked, "How much is not a lot?"

"He was a big guy, so it's hard to be sure. I'd guess enough to make him relax but not knock him out completely." She said, "They found the vial in the refrigerator under the bar. There was a syringe in the disposal box with residue. His fingerprints were on both."

Will rubbed the side of his face with his fingers. "He never used drugs before. That was his thing. He was against them."

"You know how bad prisons are. A lot of people change their minds about drugs when they get inside."

"Where would he get liquid Demerol?"

Sara cast about for an explanation. "The prostitute who visited him the night before could've brought it. Did the police ever find her?"

"No," Will answered. "They never found the nail polish, either."

Sara knew Will hated loose ends. "Maybe she stole it. Most of those girls are addicts. They're not having sex with twenty to thirty men a day because it's fun."

"What was the cause of death?" He seemed wary of saying the word. "Overdose?"

"His heart wasn't in great shape. You know these things aren't always conclusive. The medical examiner listed natural causes, but he could've had other drugs on board—inhaled something, swallowed something, had a bad reaction. It's impossible to test for everything."

"Did Pete handle the case?"

"No, he's taken medical leave. It was one of his assistants. He's a smart guy. I trust him."

Will kept working his jaw. "Did he suffer?"

"I don't know," she admitted. "I wish I could tell you."

Betty barked. She pranced around Will's feet. "I'd better feed them."

He headed toward the kitchen. Sara followed him. Instead of picking up the bowls and getting out the cans from the cabinet, Will stood in the middle of the room.

There was a padded envelope on his kitchen table. A bright red lipstick print kissed the center. Sara instantly recognized Angie Trent's handiwork. She'd found a note with the same lipstick kiss on her car every morning this week. She doubted very seriously that Angie had written "Whore" inside, but she asked Will anyway, "What does she want?"

"I have no idea." Will sounded angry, then defensive, as if he could control his wife. "I changed the locks. I don't know how she got in."

Sara didn't bother to respond. Angie was an ex-cop. She knew how to pick a lock. Working vice, she'd learned how to skate back and forth across the lines with impunity.

Will said, "I'll throw it away."

Sara tried to quell her irritation. "It's all right."

"No, it's not." Will picked up the envelope. It wasn't sealed. The flap opened.

Sara jumped back, though what clattered onto the table was hardly dangerous. At least not anymore.

The prostitute at the Four Seasons had been the last person to see Will's father alive. She knew the regular girls. She knew how they dressed, where they picked up their johns. More important, she knew that adjusting her hat in full view of the elevator security camera would draw attention to her recently manicured fingernails.

And that still wasn't enough.

Like a cat leaving a dead animal on its owner's doorstep, Angie Trent had taken a souvenir from the crime scene so that Will would know exactly what she'd done for him.

Glass bottle. Pointy white cap.

Bombshell red.

It was the missing bottle of Max Factor nail polish.

ACKNOWLEDGMENTS

Ben Hecht said, "Trying to determine what is going on in the world by reading newspapers is like trying to tell time by watching the second hand of a clock." With that in mind, I perused many 1970s editions of both the *Atlanta Journal* and *Atlanta Constitution,* whose archives offered a fascinating glimpse into the daily lives of Atlantans. The *Atlanta Daily World* offered a sometimes countervailing and often more in-depth take on the same events. *Atlanta* magazine provided a great source for historical context, including their "best of" issues as well as a shockingly hilarious profile of the swingin' Riverbend apartment complex. Back issues of *Cosmopolitan* magazine gave tips on hairstyles, celebrities, and achieving sexual satisfaction—so different from what they focus on today. *Newsweek, Time, Ladies' Home Journal,* and the Sears catalogue were also great guides for apparel and decorating. AtlantaTimeMachine.com showcases myriad before and after photos of city hotspots. There are an alarming number of 1970s TV commercials on YouTube that sucked away hours of my life that I will never get back. My only consolation is that the posters spent more time uploading them than I did watching them.

I enlisted Daniel Starer at Research for Writers to help pull material I needed for this story. I thought this was a brilliant cheat on my part until the volumes of research arrived on my doorstep and I realized that I would then have to read everything. (A full list can be found on my website.) Dan also located a man named Robert Barnes, who filmed a documentary on the Atlanta Police Force in 1975. Robert, an Atlanta native, was kind enough to send me a copy of the film, which shows much of the Atlanta skyline and features lots of helicopter shots of Techwood Homes and downtown. He also shared his memories of growing up in Atlanta, for which I am very grateful.

I spent many hours either online or in person at the Atlanta History Center, the Auburn Avenue Research Library, the Georgia Tech Library, the Georgia State University Pullman Library, and the Library of Congress. (Hey, didja notice all these places have "library" in their names? Maybe we really do need libraries after all.)

To say I hit paydirt at the Atlanta History Center is an understatement. It was there that I first found mention of Patricia W. Remmington's *Policing: The Occupation and the Introduction of Female Police Officers* (University Press of America, 1981). This dissertation is based on Remmington's year-long field study of the Atlanta Police Force in 1975. She rode along on beats. She often watched interrogations. They even trusted her with a revolver. From Ms. Remmington's work, I was able to cull staff rotations, statistical data, organizational structure, and socioeconomic details of the Atlanta force. As the focus of the study was on women officers, there were several transcripts of interviews performed with both male and female police officers regarding women on the force. Many of the ten-codes, slang ("hummy," "trim," and "crack"), and often horrendous practical jokes officers played came from Remmington's observations.

Though I used the dissertation as a starting point, I also spoke with several women police officers who came up in the 1970s. Marla Lawson at the GBI is as entertaining a storyteller as I've ever heard. I would also like to thank law enforcement officers Dona Robertson, Barbara Lynch, and Vickye Prattes for driving all the way into Atlanta to talk with me. SL, EC, and BB gave me insider knowledge on how things still work (or don't) in various Georgia forces. And, though men don't exactly get the star treatment in this book, I would like to thank, as always, Director Vernon Keenan and John Bankhead at the GBI. Actually, I would like to thank all the officers out there who take care of the rest of us. Y'all are doing the Lord's work.

I feel I should mention Reginald Eaves, who features prominently in this story. Eaves has long been a controversial figure in Atlanta politics. A 1978 test-rigging scandal forced him out of the police force. In 1980, he was elected to the Fulton County Commission. By 1984, he was under investigation for extortion and eventually imprisoned in 1988. And, yet . . . there's no denying that under Commissioner Eaves, Atlanta saw its crime rate drop significantly. He increased recruit training, instigated a formal path to promotion, and made all officers take "crisis intervention" classes to learn how to better deal with domestic cases. He focused most of his resources on black-on-black crime, saying, "No matter how poor you are, there is no excuse for knocking a lady in the head or stealing her purse." To me, this makes Eaves a quintessential Atlanta politician.

Though some still think of the 1970s as a decade of love and freedom, women of that time were generally still facing an uphill battle. Opening a checking account, getting a car loan or mortgage—even signing a lease—were out of reach for many American women unless their fathers or husbands co-signed. (Don't get ahead of yourself, New York City. It wasn't until 1974 that gender discrimination in housing was legally barred.) In 1972, it finally became legal for unmarried women to use the Pill, though some still had a difficult time finding a doctor who would write the prescription and a pharmacist to fill it. The Sex Discrimination Act of 1975, meant to put a finer point on the Equal Pay Act of 1963, highlighted the fact that women were earning only 62 percent of men's salaries. The APD, as all police forces, had to follow the law, so policing was one of the few jobs for women that gave them both economic and social power.

That was the extent of the progressive side of policing. Most men—and many women—felt that women should not be police officers. The stories about people laughing when a female officer came on scene are true. Women were routinely set up to fail, and punished when they did not. There were many areas of law enforcement where women were strictly verboten. This is not to say that men were entirely the problem. A 1974 article in the *Atlanta Constitution* talks about phone calls coming into the station—all from women—saying they'd seen a woman stealing a police car. They could not fathom that the "thief" was actually a female police officer who was driving the car on her beat. (Another quote, this one from H. L. Mencken: "Misogynist: a man who hates women as much as women hate one another.")

Thank you, Valerie Jackson, for giving me a glimpse into Mayor Maynard Jackson's thinking during his first term. The statements he made on behalf of women and minorities are commonplace among politicians these days, though seldom followed through in the way Mayor Jackson managed. I think I speak for many Atlantans when I say that his legacy lives on in so many positive ways.

Vernon Jordan was extremely helpful in giving context to the story. I thank you, sir, for your insightful suggestion, which gave me the key to unlocking the narrative. You kept saying you couldn't tell me much, but you pretty much told me everything. I'm certain I'm not the only person on whom you've had this effect.

Linda Fairstein is not just one of my favorite authors, but a woman who served on the front lines of New York City's first sex crimes unit. Her groundbreaking work was made possible by the same LEAA grants that benefited many women in policing. Linda, I applaud your efforts to pay it forward for women all over the country.

Special thanks goes to Jeanene English for showing me how hair weaves work. Kate White, you constantly remind me of the great things women can accomplish when we support each other. I would especially like to thank Monica Pearson (nee Kaufman) for one of the more pleasant afternoons of my life. Emily Saliers, thank you for telling me about your Atlanta. Though I've never had the honor of meeting Tyne Daly or Sharon Gless, any woman my age knows this story holds a special debt of gratitude to both.

As usual, Dr. David Harper helped make Sara and Pete look like they know what they are doing. I feel I should say something about Grady Hospital, the largest public hospital in the country. This H-shaped behemoth is a testament to the best and worst of us. The ER Sara works in is nothing like the real Grady ER, mostly because it would take thousands of pages to do justice to the wash of humanity packed into the halls on a daily basis. My hat is off to the Grady doctors and nurses for running toward the problems instead of away from them.

Henrik Enemark, my Danish translator, sent me some groovy photos of his high school trip to Atlanta. Ineke Lenting, my Dutch translator, was also a tremendous help. Marty, curator of the Pram Museum, answered a strange question quickly and unblinkingly. Kitty Stockett lent her name to a prostitute (maybe this will finally get her work the attention it deserves). Pam Canale was the big winner of the "Have Your Name Appear in Karin Slaughter's Next Book" auction to benefit the Dekalb County Public Library system. Diane Palmer put a wicked idea into my head. Debbie T., thank you for your continuing help with capturing Will's world. Beth Tindall at Cincinnati Media has long been my webmaster and BFF. Victoria Sanders, Angela Cheng Caplan, and Diane Golden are the best team a gal could ask for. Thanks, too, to Kate Elton, my good friend and longtime editor, for making my job so easy. Susan Sandon and Richard Cable—thanks for the driving tips and drinking all my daddy's liquor. Georgina Hawtrey-Woore, I appreciate your help and input over the years. Further thanks go to Claire Round, Rob Waddington and the rest of the Cornerstone gang for keeping the wheels turning. Adam Humphrey, I think this will be the last time I kill you.

My father regaled me one night with tales from the underbelly of 1970s Atlanta. He put me onto Mills Lane and the kidnapping case (as well as Mike Thevis, who will certainly show up in other stories, though I am hesitant to ask my father about his connection to the man who changed the face of American porn). I am grateful to my sister, Jatha Slaughter, for talking to me so openly about her life. And to D.A.—as always, you are my heart.

History is a dangerous thing, especially in the hands of a novice. In researching this novel, I came to understand that no one sees the past in the same way. For Atlanta, there is the white perspective, there is the black perspective, and then, there are the (at times, polar opposite) perspectives of the men and women within these categories. Extrapolate this to the melting pot of our current population and you can begin to understand why, as a writer, I chose to settle on one point of view.

That being said, I'm a novelist, not a historian. I don't claim to be an expert on Atlanta in the 1970s—or present day, for that matter. I have certainly taken liberties with some details. (There were no five-story buildings at Techwood Homes. Monica Kaufman, like Spike, Snoopy's brother, did not show up in Atlanta until August of 1975. You will probably get arrested if you hang out in front of the Four Seasons too long looking for that marble fountain.) My main focus in writing this book was to tell a good story. I understood from the beginning that there were several traps inherent in being a southern woman writing about race and gender issues. Please know I worked very hard to make sure everyone—no matter race, religion, creed, gender, or national origin—was equally maligned.

Karin Slaughter

Atlanta, Georgia

www.karinslaughter.com

ABOUT THE AUTHOR

KARIN SLAUGHTER was born and raised in a small Georgia town in the American South.

The author of eleven bestselling novels, Slaughter, a passionate supporter of libraries, has spearheaded the Save the Libraries campaign in America (www.savethelibraries. com) and advocates that everyone 'should fight for libraries as we do for our freedom'. She has donated all income from her short story *Thorn in My Side* to both the American and British library systems.

For her twelfth novel, *Criminal*, Slaughter exhaustively researched both the racial and gender politics of the Atlanta police department and American society in the 1970s resulting in a deeply personal exploration of her hometown and her country during a period of enormous social change.

To find out more about Karin Slaughter, visit her website www.karinslaughter.com, or catch up with her on www.facebook.com/AuthorKarinSlaughter.

ABOUT THE TYPE

This book was set in Bembo, a typeface based on an old-style Roman face that was used for Cardinal Bembo's tract *De Aetna* in 1495. Bembo was cut by Francisco Griffo in the early sixteenth century. The Lanston Monotype Company of Philadelphia brought the well-proportioned letterforms of Bembo to the United States in the 1930s.

Available exclusively as a digital short story

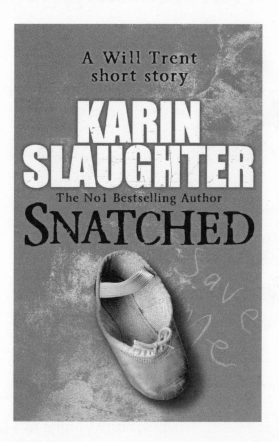

On assignment at Atlanta's busy airport Special Agent Will Trent is forced to make a split-second decision. But is it the right one?

For more information about
Karin and her books, visit:

www.karinslaughter.com

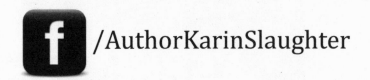 /AuthorKarinSlaughter